Issaura's Claws

Katharine E. Wibell

Phaesporia Press

This book is a work of fiction. Names, characters, places and incidents either are the product of the author's imagination or are used fictitiously. Any resemblance to actual persons, living or dead, events or locales is entirely coincidental.

Issaura's Claws

Printed in the United States of America.

First edition November 2016

Visit us on the Web! KatharineWibellBooks.com

Phaesporia Press

ISBN-13: 978-0-9983779-0-2

DEDICATION

To Mama, without whom I would never have been able to succeed in this journey,
To Papa, who supports me unconditionally, and
To sister Sarah, the white tigress in my life.

CONTENTS

SPECIAL THANKS

To April Wells-Hayes, my primary editor, and Mike Naples; to Karen Wibell, Stephanie Smith, and Stephanie Vandegrift, who served as readers; to Bob, David, Marilyn, and the Madison Writers Group, who reviewed content; and to Calvin Williams and C. M. Soto for digital and artistic assistance.

And I tip my hat to all those who told the stories that became the myths and legends that I grew up reading...and still do!

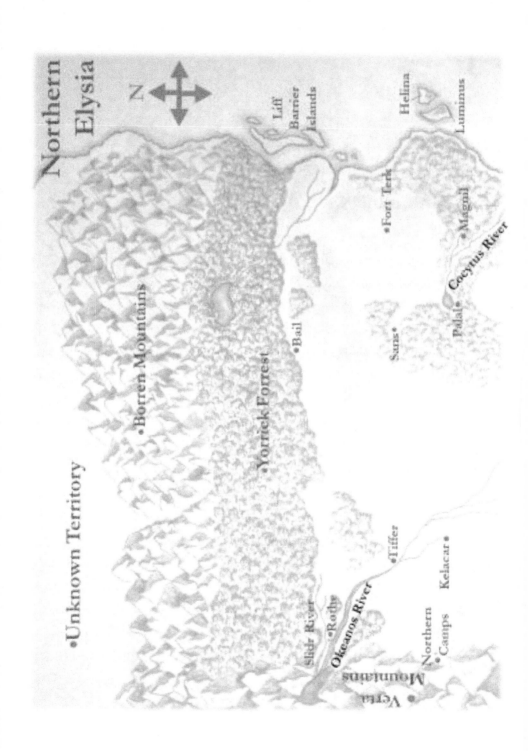

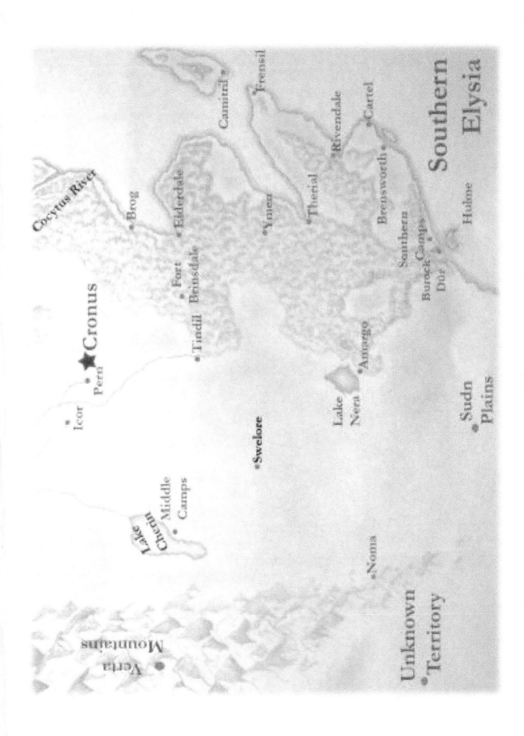

ISSAURA'S CLAWS

PART I

Prologue

Soft waves lap against the shore, altering the land that has endured so much over the centuries. Never judging what has happened or what will be, the silent moon watches. Emotionless, she observes, listens, and learns, never letting the secrets she knows slip past her silver tendrils. Glinting on the ocean surface, the moonbeams faintly illuminate the dark forms of snarling dragons that leer off the bows of the wooden ships. Quietly she watches as longboats bearing dark-faced crewmen are lowered into the ocean, landward bound.

Swiftly beaching rawhide boats on the fog-laden shore, burly men with horned helmets grab their gear and march toward the slumbering village. The only sounds from the mud-brick houses are the lullabies a young mother sweetly sings to her half-awake children and the creaking of a wooden rocker under an elderly man's feet. Waiting for morning's light, all but one lantern has long since been doused. The seaside village slumbers while fur-trimmed boots tread in unison along the cobblestone road. Swiftly and quietly the rugged seamen spread through the village. Each claims a house; each raises his weapon of choice: battle-ax, broadsword, or javelin.

A flaming arrow is shot into the air.

Like small parts of a single beast, they bellow as one and shoulder their way through the doors like human battering rams. Mayhem ensues. A cacophony of shattering furniture and breaking glass mingles with futile cries of helpless victims. A man tries to fight back in a hopeless attempt to protect his family; unskilled in the arts of war, he is quickly silenced.

Mixing with the sandy soil, crimson liquid oozes from cracks in the wooden floors. The nearby river slowly clouds, feeding an ever-growing red tide. The ruby sand is eroded away by the continuous pull of the waves. Land affected by sea; sea commanded by moon. An uncaring presence in the sky stares darkly at all that lies below.

Chapter 1
Lamb in a Yellow Dress

Trouble.

In the schoolyard, Lluava spotted a group of boys near a large oak. Definitely humans. Ranging in age from eight to fourteen, they had encircled a young lamb tangled up in a simple yellow dress. The small thing bleated and shook off the clothes. It tried to escape, but the jeering boys chased it back into the center of their circle while poking at it with sticks. One small, dark-haired boy snagged the lamb's neck with a shepherd's crook and yanked the frightened animal toward him.

At seventeen, Lluava was one of the few older students, and she instinctively watched over the younger children. She could not ignore the lamb's sounds of distress. A rising wind blew the girl's long platinum hair into her emerald eyes, and she shook her head to clear her vision. She recognized Thane, a red-headed, twelve-year-old bully, leading the boys in a human song altered for the occasion:

> *Mary was a little lamb, little lamb, little lamb;*
> *Mary was a little lamb with fleece as white as snow.*
> *Everywhere that Mary went, Mary went, Mary went,*
> *Everywhere that Mary went; she as a lamb would go.*

Lluava detested both Thane and his smug, oily-haired, older brother Malnus. Especially Malnus, who was her age. Both boys were troublemakers, but their father was Mayor of Rivendale so they got away with it. Disgusted at the lot of them, Lluava ran over and stepped between the bleating lamb and the boys. "All of you go home now!" she snarled. "Leave her alone! I said, leave her *alone!*"

Most of the boys slouched off, but Thane remained. Malnus sauntered up behind him. "Boys will be boys," he smirked. "Let them have their fun."

4

"How dare you! Just letting them torture her!" Lluava was enraged as she pointed at the shaking animal between her legs. "If I ever see you, your brother, or any of his twisted friends near her again—" She cut herself short before she said something that she would regret.

"You'll what?" he goaded, looking at the girl as if she were a rabid beast. Lluava was strong and fit; she knew she could take him in a fight. As Malnus sized her up, Lluava could hold in her anger no longer. A low growl rumbled from her throat. She locked eyes with Malnus, her green reflected in his brown. Lluava's pupils narrowed like a cat's preparing for a kill. Her growl grew louder.

Malnus took a step back and turned to his brother. "Come on!" he ordered. Both of them ran off across the yard.

Thane, looking over his shoulder, yelled back, "You're monsters! Freaks! Both of you!" Not paying attention, Thane tripped over a root and fell. He jumped up at once but grimaced when he saw his soiled pants. Lluava knew his mother would switch him for ruining his clothes.

"Theriomorphs are not monsters," Lluava retorted. "Humans, on the other hand …"

"Malnus. Thane," Miss Blakely called from the doorway of the one-room schoolhouse, "I need to talk with you." The new teacher nervously pushed thin-rimmed glasses up her long beak-like nose then smoothed her plain brown hair in its tight bun. Had she seen what had happened?

Thane dusted himself off. As he followed Malnus, he turned to Lluava and made one of the most vulgar hand signs she had ever seen before slipping through the school room's door.

Lluava took several deep breaths, then looked down at the small lamb. Its big brown eyes stared up at her.

"Are you okay?" she asked. It bleated and flicked its tail twice.

Lluava bent down and carefully picked up the shaking animal with one hand and the dress with the other. She carried both to the edge of the woods where some tall elderberry bushes grew. "Here," Lluava said, placing the lamb behind the bush. "Put on your clothes."

As she stood guard to make sure no one would disturb them, Lluava scanned the playground. The schoolyard was split down the middle: human children on one side, Theriomorphs on the other. No surprise there, thought Lluava sourly.

When humans first landed on the shores of Elysia, they had discovered an unknown native race called Theriomorphs— a race that appeared human but had the ability to change into an animal form. Theriomorphs were denounced as monstrous savages and their lands, encampments, and livelihood were seized. When the Theriomorphs fought back, raiding human settlements and attacking the invaders, King Landon raised an army to defeat them. The Landon Wars spanned the better part of two centuries, but it was not until his descendent, King Hammond, conquered the Theriomorphs fifty years ago that the land was unified under one rule. Royal edicts proclaimed humans and Theriomorphs to be equal but could neither nullify centuries of bloodshed nor eradicate the unspoken prejudice and distrust between the two races.

Worse, while Theriomorphs had considered females equal to males, humans regarded females as the weaker sex. Theriomorph clothes did not indicate gender; girls and boys dressed alike. However, humans judged females attired in clothes associated with the male gender to be slovenly. Instead, they accentuated their feminine figure with cinched waists; long, flowing skirts covered their legs. The more skin they hid from view, the more alluring they became. From birth, human girls were raised to be as delicate and pretty as dolls. Now Theriomorph females were pressured to follow suit. It was a far cry from the rough-and-tumble memories of Lluava's early years.

After a few moments, a small girl wearing a yellow dress emerged from behind the leafy shrub, interrupting Lluava's thoughts. The girl was about five years old. Her lips were red, her eyes were big and brown, and her hair was cut short at her ears. The young girl's skin had the same deep olive tint as Lluava's, although several ugly bruises were deepening on her arms.

"Are you sure you're all right, Lamb?" Lluava knelt down to inspect the bruises.

"I'm fine," the girl replied meekly.

"I'm sorry I wasn't there to protect you," Lluava said sadly.

"It's okay."

"No, it's not. I'm your sister, Lamb. I'm supposed to protect you," Lluava replied, sorrow creeping into her voice.

The little girl hugged her. Lluava stood up and fondly looked down at Lamb, her pet name for her sister. Although Lluava had been blessed with a rare platinum-blonde color that appeared every fifth generation on her mother's side, or so her mother, Maessa, claimed, her little sister's hair was the same golden-blonde shade as their mother Maessa's. Examining the rip in Lamb's clothes, Lluava felt a raw heat grow as she remembered the day her mother had told them they must dress like human girls. That was also the day her mother had given them human-sounding nicknames. Her sister became Mary rather than Maruny; her younger brother became Tom instead of Tomius.

That day Lluava's anger was so great that she lost control. She lashed out at everything and everyone around her. It was the only time Lluava had ever reacted violently. Although she was sorry to have frightened her mother, Lluava refused to change—not her name, not her clothing. Although Maessa never openly confronted her daughter again, she still found subtle ways to encourage Lluava to conform. Why couldn't her mother be happy with their culture? Was she scared? Did she think their family would be treated as equals if they changed?

"I'm going to tell Miss Blakely what happened. She can decide what to do to Thane and Malnus. Stay here, okay?"

"Okay," Lamb replied.

As Lluava approached the schoolroom, she heard Miss Blakely's voice. Poking her head inside the doorway, she spied Thane and Malnus standing in front of the teacher.

"I hate them more than you do," Miss Blakely confided to her two students. Her hands smoothed her hair in its bun once again. "Theriomorphs are a disgrace to the educational system. I would not have them in my school, but it is the law, so I must endure their presence here. They're monstrosities, all of them. It doesn't surprise me that Lluava pushed you down and threatened you. Don't worry about your clothes; Lluava is responsible. And don't worry about your mother, either. I'll explain everything. Tomorrow, I'll have Lluava pay for her misconduct. It's about time her race found out they are not above the law."

Did Miss Blakely really say that? She was even worse than the last teacher! At least he had tried to get to know each of his students as individuals. Lluava's rage returned. Perhaps good humans did not exist.

Lluava ran back to her sister. "Let's go home," she said harshly. They picked up their books and headed down the road. Lluava was angry, and when she noticed her sister lagging behind, she grabbed the girl's wrist and pulled her along. She heard Lamb sniffle and saw that she was crying. Lluava knew she should apologize. She stopped, turned, and squatted down at eye level with her sister.

"Listen to me, Lamb. No matter what anybody says, we are *not* monsters. What makes a monster is not *what* someone is but *who* someone is. What counts is on the inside, not the outside. There are many bad people out there, both human and Theriomorph, and I'm sorry that you had to cross paths with some." Lluava looked down the road leading away from the small village. "Somewhere out there are good humans, but not here. I have yet to meet a nice human, but that does not mean that there aren't any. Do you understand what I'm telling you, Lamb?"

Lamb nodded meekly. Lluava wondered if the little girl's large brown eyes saw through Lluava's lie.

"I love you so much, and I hate when you get hurt."

Slipping her small hand into Lluava's, Maruny said, "I love you, too."

Lluava stood up and, with her sister at her side, began to walk home at a pace set by the smaller girl.

"I drew this in class today." Maruny held up a picture with her free hand. On it was a small house surrounded by five animals: a lamb, a small brown mouse held by a mother duck, an old owl, and a white tiger. "It's the family. See, there's me." She pointed to the lamb. "There's Mommy holding Tom."

She pointed to the duck and the mouse. "Grampy." She indicated the owl. "And you." Grinning, she pointed to the white tiger.

"It's beautiful," Lluava agreed.

They walked home quietly. The air was warm and smelled of salt. Usually, a gentle breeze caressed everything it touched, but today the wind blew with a purpose as it wound through the small village. They passed Walden's Hardware where old men in rockers told tales of their youth. Next came Galdwin's Grocers where their mother traded eggs for produce. After that was the Sea Dragon, Rivendale's only pub and the most popular place in town unless the church across the road held a service and was packed with humans and "good" Theriomorph converts. To the left of the church was the smithy, owned by the Drycin brothers, a pair of proud Theriomorphs and the only members of their race who owned a business. No human could match a Theriomorph blacksmith. A few other stores were scattered among several homesteads. The rest of the small community consisted of farmers or the fishermen who lived down by the docks.

Maruny spotted a toad hopping ahead of them in the road. She let go of Lluava's hand and ran over to try and catch it. The poor thing kept sliding out of the girl's light grip in a bid for freedom.

Lluava heard the galloping horse before she saw it. Stampeding into view over the ridge, it headed straight for the church. "Move aside!" the rider shouted. Lluava had only seconds to think before she leaped and shoved Maruny from harm's way. The dark beast flew past only inches from where the small girl had crouched.

Lluava was relieved that she had rescued her sister. The toad had not been so lucky. After confirming that her sister was all right, she looked for the heedless rider. The horse, breathing heavily, was tethered outside the church. "What was that man thinking! I could have lost..."

Her words disappeared in the rapid tolling of the church bell. From all directions, people came running to the churchyard. The entire town seemed to migrate into the small, fenced-in yard that enclosed their holy place. Lluava and Maruny did the same.

On the top step stood the bedraggled young man whose horse had nearly trampled Maruny. He yelled at the people to quiet down and listen.

"They are coming!" the man shouted and paused to catch his breath.

"Who's coming?" asked a bearded man near the front of the mob.

"The king's soldiers! A half dozen at least! I saw them riding this way from the top of my hill as I was plowing."

"The king's soldiers? What do they want? Why are they coming?" These and many other questions were shouted by the townspeople, but before they could finish questioning the young man, a teenage girl squealed, "Look!"

All heads turned in the direction the girl was pointing. Seven horses appeared over the ridge in a wedge formation. The lead rider blew his shiny trumpet; two riders followed, with the remaining four in the final row. The two outside riders in the back row each held triangular pennants emblazoned with the king's emblem: a crowned raven holding an olive branch in its bill with a prostrate lion at the raven's feet. The emblems and borders were mossy green on a field of gold, and the riders' colors matched their pennants. As they galloped forth, dirt and dust coated the horses' shiny coats and braided manes and tails.

As one, the riders halted in front of the church. One rider leapt from his mount and walked briskly and assuredly through the crowd which backed away to create a path for him. Climbing the steps of the church, he turned to the waiting people and pulled a scroll from the pouch that hung over his left shoulder.

Lluava knew that this was the most important rider; he was the only one with crimson woven into his cape, and he wore a tricolored beret cocked to one side. He scratched his groomed beard with a gloved hand, then cleared his throat. Unrolling the scroll, he read aloud in a deep voice:

"Your Majesty, Thor, has decreed that there will be a draft to raise an army. One person from each household will be conscripted. If that household contains Theriomorph blood, the person they send must be Theriomorph. All household members over one year of age were recorded in last year's census; therefore, no household can escape the draft. Any attempt to evade the draft will be considered a treasonable action. All members of the household will be judged traitors to His Majesty and to this great kingdom of Elysia and will be punished accordingly."

The man rolled up his scroll and replaced it carefully in his pouch. The town was in an uproar; everyone began to talk at once.

Lluava could not stop herself from shouting above the others: "What war? Both Theriomorph and human have been living quietly side by side for just over fifty years. Whom are we fighting? Why are we fighting? We need to know why!"

Waiting for the answers, the people quieted. The king's messenger looked at the crowd. "Who is asking these questions?" he rapped out. "Step forward!"

Lluava made her way to the front of the villagers.

"I asked," Lluava responded fearlessly.

The man glowered at her for a moment. "What is your name?"

"I am Lluava Kargen, daughter of Haliden Kargen. I am Theriomorph," she stated in the proper introductory fashion.

After another long pause, the man finished the formal introduction. "I am Marren Sihia, son of Thadius Sihia. I am His Majesty's dispatcher. I trained with your father in our youth. He was as repugnant as you are. I will answer your questions although those with young children should probably leave now," he said with a grimace.

Several women took their children by their arms and pulled them away.

Marren continued, "About three months ago, the seaside village, Camitril, was attacked by men from across the sea. No villagers survived."

There was an audible gasp from his audience.

"Since then, three more villages have been raided, with the same results. King Thor has ordered his soldiers to protect all major seaside villages and towns. Two weeks ago, Frensil was attacked, but the Elysian military successfully fought off the marauders. One person was captured and forced to tell their plans."

More likely tortured, Lluava thought.

"This person confessed that the raids were to test our strength and our weaponry. He said that the people across the sea will invade us soon. We suspect that their king wants to either expand his empire or conduct slave raids. This is why we are preparing for war. King Thor wants to defend our kingdom."

The people were silent.

"In four days, another band of soldiers will pass this way. Those chosen among you must be ready to accompany them to the training facility. You may send more than one person from each household, but the minimum is one. Go home. Pack only what you can easily carry. Say your goodbyes. Then be ready to fight."

Refusing further questions, Marren strode back through the crowd and remounted his steed. The trumpeter gave the signal, and they were off to the next village to spread the news.

After a pause, voices rose in a hubbub. "They can't do this!" "It's not right!" "What if we are attacked? Will soldiers be sent here to protect us?" "I'm too young to be killed!" Their questions went unanswered, but many accused the king of unjustness. Eventually, people drifted away. All seemed to wear a veil of darkness about them. The darkness shadowed the village and the surrounding countryside as news of the impending attack spread from the town to the docks and across the farmlands.

The late spring air was so warm that sweat trickled down the sisters' backs as they trudged home. The cicadas' steady drone was almost hypnotic, and the twenty minutes it took to reach the gate to their house seemed to shrink to only a few. The fence was old; most of the white paint had worn off, and the gate creaked as they opened and closed it. The yard had not been cut in a while, and a variety of weeds had taken root. The yellow of dandelions was interspersed with the purples and pale blues of other wildflowers whose names Lluava did not know. Her mother's tiny garden in front of the small porch was also weed infested. Lluava looked up at the unpainted home that held so many fond memories. She knew she needed to re-thatch the roof. She found it in her heart to pity her mother. Since her father's death a year ago, they hadn't been able to keep up with needed repairs.

As the sisters neared home, Maruny ran ahead shouting that they had seen the king's soldiers and their beautiful horses. Giam, Lluava's grandfather, a thin, frail man who walked with a cane, appeared at the door of the barn. Maessa scooped up baby Tomius and ran into the yard to hear the news. They listened in shock to Lluava's tale. Tomius began to cry. Almost two, the baby had been born shortly before their father died. Like his father, he had dark brown hair and deep brown eyes. Maessa carried him inside, her head bent low, almost touching his.

The sun still shone through gaps in the ever-darkening clouds. Lluava walked through knee-high grass that tickled her legs. The barn was in worse shape than the house. Holes in the roof filtered golden columns of sunlight, and several large rats scurried away at her approach.

Lluava walked through the barn to the corral behind it and gave one short, loud whistle. As it had for the past twenty years, Gogen, a graying mule, trudged up to her and walked into its stall. Lluava latched the stall door and patted the tired beast on its side. She could feel every rib for the skin was stretched tightly over them. Climbing a rickety ladder to the loft, she threw down a bale of hay. Some she fed to the mule; the rest she spread as bedding for the animal.

By the time Lluava had completed her chores, Maessa was placing a steaming pot of stew on the table where a blue crystal vase held freshly picked flowers. The vase was an heirloom and the most valuable possession Maessa owned. No one knew how it had come into the family, but for generations it had been passed down through her mother's line to each firstborn daughter. Soon it would be Lluava's, but, for now, it rested in its place of honor in the middle of the table.

The family sat down. Maruny licked her lips as Giam served the stew then stood to say a blessing. Lluava saw her mother fiddle under the table with the hem of her dress. Trying to hide her discomfort, Maessa bowed her head; her golden hair, having escaped her bun, fell into her eyes. She had lost belief in the old ways long ago and converted to the humans' belief in one solitary god. Although Maessa often took Mary and Tom to church, her oldest and most stubborn child refused to join them. Lluava sighed. She knew her mother considered this a failure, but Lluava would not change. She was as adamant about the old ways as her father had been and her grandfather continued to be.

"O Giahem," invoked Giam, " Great Master of the Universe, bless this house and all who dwell in it. Hendran, Valcum, and all the great gods who reside in the heavens, guard us, our land, and our progeny. Lady Issaura, help the food before us nourish our bodies and our souls. Keep us faithful to the old ways and keep our family strong. We give all of you our thanks."

"We give you thanks," they replied. Lluava noticed her mother merely mouthed the words.

The day's events had exhausted everyone. When Maruny hugged her grandfather, mother, and elder sister before climbing the ladder to the loft the sisters shared, Lluava kissed the bristly cheek of the old man, wished her mother a good sleep, and followed her. The loft was dark and cool with walls so thin she could hear the wind whistling outside. The room was too small to be a comfortable living space for the pair, yet they had learned to make do. Lluava lit a candle stump. Its flickering light barely illuminated her surroundings.

Thankfully, she knew the room so well that she no longer needed the light. She looked at the far side of the straw mattress; Maruny had pulled the quilted cover above her head.

"Sleep well, my little Lamb," Lluava whispered.

Lluava changed into her nightshirt, blew out the light, and crawled into bed. As she closed her eyes, the first of the summer rains began to pour. She hoped the old, thatched roof would keep them dry. Soon she drifted into a restless sleep.

Unsettling images flew before her. Lluava dreamt of rivers of blood and screams of faceless people. She tried to focus on the faces, but they would not become clear. Looking around, she saw the bare remains of houses that had been torched. The air was thick with smoke. There was a sound, one she had never heard before but immediately understood: the beating of numerous war drums. She began to search for survivors but there were none.

Walking toward the closest house, Lluava tripped. Catching herself, she looked down and saw the body of one of the faceless people. Around the still figure, a pool of blood was forming. Gasping in shock, Lluava backed away and stumbled through the debris of the destroyed village. Her stomach heaved as she made her way to the edge of the river that bordered one side of the town. She caught a glimpse of her reflection in the water, but it wasn't her face she saw. She peered closer. A fearsome white tiger glared back at her. Stunned, she could not move. The beast in the water came closer. Suddenly it opened its gaping maw and roared.

Lluava awoke with a jerk. Breathing heavily, she recognized the loft. It's just a bad dream, she thought. Sweat trickled down her back, yet she shivered. She could not know that this was just the beginning of many horrid nightmares to come.

Chapter 2
Theri's Gift

Lluava woke early after her restless sleep. She peered through the tiny circular window overlooking her mother's garden and saw the sun's rays peeking over the forest. Outside, puddles filled every low spot in the yard, and all greenery was clothed in a dewy sheen that reflected the faint morning light. She dressed quickly and silently crept out of the house. A pair of swallows had made a nest in the rafters under the porch roof. Lluava smiled at the featherless babies who gaped wildly when their mother swooped in bringing a wriggling treat.

Giam waited by the barn. His smile revealed yellow, smokeweed-stained teeth. He was dressed for a journey: loose gray shirt, dusty brown pants with a rope belt, and a long, lightweight coat awkwardly draped over his small frame. His eyes sparkled behind thick brown spectacles. "I'm going to visit Markley. Help me hitch, Gogen."

Orphaned in the Landon Wars, Markley had been adopted by a human couple as a sign of peace when the war ended. Both Markley and her grandfather had become good friends in childhood. Despite his human upbringing and name, Markley became one of the best historians of Theriomorph culture in Rivendale, second only to her grandfather.

As the two trudged through muddy puddles into the barn, Giam said, "A fox found its way into the hencoop and killed many of the chicks. You will need to patch the hole. It isn't big, but it must be taken care of."

The old mule flicked his ears rapidly at their approach. Giam opened the right side of the split door to the barn while Lluava harnessed the animal to the wagon. The mule snorted when Lluava led him outside and tethered him to the hitching post in the yard. As Lluava helped her grandfather into the wagon, he clasped her hand. His smile had faded. She looked into his careworn face. Without words, they both understood what she must do.

When Giam left, Lluava finished her morning chores then went to feed the hens and collect firewood for the stove. Re-entering the house, she found her mother cooking breakfast. Maruny, still in her nightgown, rubbed her eyes with one hand and held her ragdoll with the other. Afterward Lluava inspected the chicken coop. She found the corner where the wire screen was torn. A small tuft of reddish fur was snagged on one of the jagged ends. Lluava grimaced when she spied the red specks scattered over the ground. The danger now past, the hens and both roosters were scratching at the damp, bare earth, hoping to find an unlucky insect. The handful of surviving chicks huddled under their mothers. Returning to the barn, she found a spare plank of wood and blocked the opening.

Finally, she made her way to the woodpile. It was hard to find three good-sized logs that were dry enough to burn. As she left, she heard the peeping of a baby bird. Putting down the wood, she searched for the lost chick. The frightened ball of yellow fluff was hopping around the woodpile. Scooping it up, she inspected it for wounds; finding none, she put it back with the other babies. Chirping, the chick ran up to its mother who clucked and cooed at the sight of it. Lluava wondered if the mother hen felt relief that it had found her lost child.

"Lluava? Where are you?"

Hearing her own mother's call, Lluava remembered what she was supposed to be doing. Grabbing the firewood, she hurried back. Throwing open the door, she stopped when she saw her mother's exasperated expression.

"Well, what took you so long? The fire is almost out."

"Sorry," Lluava replied as she spied one of the chick's downy feathers floating in the air.

Realizing she was still holding the logs, she placed them into the stove one at a time, giving the fire a chance to catch.

School had been cancelled until the draftees had departed, so Lluava climbed up to the loft and opened a small cupboard tucked away in a dark corner. Her father had been a carpenter by trade, and many pieces of furniture in their home had been crafted by him. Slowly and meticulously, she removed one piece of her clothing at a time and folded it. She placed her clothes in the shoulder bag which normally carried schoolbooks and then turned to her bed. Shoving the mattress aside, she pulled up the loose plank that hid the small space in which the sisters kept their most prized possessions.

When Lluava was little, her father had spent several months of the year in military service even though the country was at peace. He had written her a letter every week. Lluava chose two of those letters from the stack that she had saved.

She pulled out the necklace her mother had given her when she turned sixteen: a diamond-shaped emerald suspended from a very thin silver chain. When she held it up to the window, the stone, matching the brilliant color of her eyes, glittered and shone. Like the vase, it was an heirloom, one that each mother passed down to her firstborn daughter when she came of age. Finally, she removed her father's copy of the *Karmasana*, the religious book of the Theriomorphs. She had hidden it in this place after his death. She slid the letters between the pages of the book and carefully packed all the items in the bag.

Grabbing the pouch, she climbed down the ladder. Halfway down, she heard her mother demand, "Lluava, what in god's name do you think you are doing?"

Once on the ground, Lluava turned to Maessa and replied, "Preparing for war, Mother. Just as King Thor ordered."

"The hell you are! Unpack your bag this instant!"

"I have to go. You know that."

"No, you do not!" Maessa screamed as tears streamed down her face. "I curse the king's name for forcing innocent families apart for a campaign we are not part of!"

Unusually calm, Lluava put down her bag and went to her mother. "This *is* our war. The people who were killed were just like us. They didn't have a chance to defend themselves. The king wants to make sure that all his subjects, including us, are protected from these raiders."

Hoping to make her mother understand, Lluava continued to speak but very slowly. "I am going to war. I am going to protect our family. You know I am the only choice. Grampy can barely walk. You must stay here with Mouse and Lamb. You provide the money for our family, and you keep us together. They need you. We both know that I am the only one of age who is capable of going to war. We will be punished as traitors if we do not send someone from our household. If that happens, our lives will be worse than they are now. Mother, Maessa, this is what I must do. This is my calling." Mother and daughter locked eyes. Maessa turned away, walked into her room, and shut the door.

The next two days were filled with chores and packing. No one talked much; even Maruny was quiet. Each morning, Lluava awoke to find Maruny sleeping next to her in bed. Little Tomius seemed to know something was wrong; he cried every time Lluava tried to pick him up.

On their last night together, Maruny insisted on story time. Until this recent development, their grandfather had always settled into his rocker after dinner – he called it his dream chair –and regaled the children with tales both old and new.

"Come, Grampy! Story time! Story time!" Maruny chanted as she pulled him to his dream chair. He sat down as fast as his achy joints would allow.

She plopped down onto the rug; Lluava sat next to her. Story time was a family ritual, a time to bond. For as long as Lluava could remember, she had loved to curl up on the floor and listen to their grandfather. The old ways were preserved through stories of heroes and epic battles passed down from their ancestors. Lluava had learned her greatest lessons sitting by the old, battered boots of this wise man.

"Which story should I tell tonight?" Giam muttered to himself as he pondered which was the most important one to share with his waiting granddaughters. "Ah, I know. Maruny, do you know the creation story of our race?"

Maruny shook her head. Her mouth was slightly open in anticipation. As Lluava looked at the young girl's wide-open eyes sparkling with excitement, Lluava remembered the time, years ago, when she was just as enthralled as Maruny was now. Smiling to herself, she turned to the old man and prompted, "Go on."

"Well, long ago, before you or I or anybody we know was born, there was a time when the world—new in its life—had never seen a Theriomorph. We had not been created. The gods looked at the world that was their pride and joy, but they were not content. They had created the earth, the trees, and all the animals that crawled upon, swam below, and flew above the earth. But still, the gods were not content. They longed to have beings with which they could communicate, beings who would give them the praise that they deserved. Giahem, king of the gods, decided to create a race of beings in his own likeness. He took clay from the earth, sculpted forms, and then breathed life into those bodies, thus creating the race of man. Content with what he had done, he placed the men upon the earth and commanded them to thrive.

"The rest of the gods and goddesses came down from the heavens one by one and admired the men. They each brought a gift for these new creations. Hendran the Wise taught them to speak and to learn. Valcum the Smith taught them to control fire and work metal. They were given weapons and taught to hunt by Ullr the Warrior, while fair Slypher taught them to sing and dance. But when the goddess Issaura came down and admired the race of man, she did not know what to give them.

"Issaura did not forget about her gift, but as the days passed, she did not bestow the first men with anything. She did have love for them and came every night to watch over them in her animal form. You do know about the gods and their animal forms, right, Maruny?" Grampy asked.

Maruny paused, then answered, "All gods have an animal form they take when they visit the earth, right? Just like we have an animal form, right? But humans don't. Why is that, Grampy? Why can't humans change like us? Why can't they?"

"Hold on, hold on. I will tell you that in due time," the old man promised. "So many questions! I will answer them soon enough. Now, where was I?"

"Issaura and her animal form," Lluava gently reminded her grandfather. She knew he was aging, and it was harder for him to remember things.

"Ah, yes. Thank you, Lluava. Issaura, in her animal form, would watch over the race of man every night.

"Now, Shennu, god of mischief and mayhem, had recently had an argument with Issaura. He thought it was unfair that all other gods and goddesses had given gifts to these men but Issaura had not. So he found a way to punish her. He created a net in which every fiber had magic cast within it. Once trapped inside, no being, animal, or god, could escape it. He set the trap in the woods where Issaura made her nightly visit.

"That evening, Issaura the Wise and Beautiful, in her animal form, was caught in the trap. The net swung up around her and lifted her into the air. She scratched and clawed but could not escape. The magic of the net prevented her from transforming into her goddess form. Exasperated, she gave a mighty roar that shook every tree in the forest.

"In their small village, the race of man heard the roar. At first, they trembled in fear, but soon they went to investigate the cause of the sound. Discovering the net trap, they encountered a beast they had never seen. The creature was a white tigress with piercing green eyes. When she saw the men, the beast purred.

"The men spoke among themselves. What should they do with the animal? Many believed that it was a gift from the gods, meant as food to sustain them. A smaller group argued that, because they had never seen a white tiger, it must be a beast of importance and should not be harmed. After a long debate, the men in the larger group said they would kill the creature in the morning after they had rested and gathered their weapons. As the race of man headed back to the village, the smaller group backed away and retraced their steps to the net. They had secretly decided to release the animal.

"Shennu had placed many spells on the net to keep what was in it captured, but he had not placed any spells that would prevent it from being untied from the outside. Several men lowered the net and untied its bindings. The tigress leapt out. After a few bounds, she turned and transformed into the goddess Issaura. The men, afraid, cowered in front of her radiant form.

"Issaura spoke. Her voice was comforting and reassured them. 'Do not fear me. I am Issaura, Goddess of Warcraft, Wisdom, and Womanhood. Because you have rescued me from that cursed net, I will bestow upon you my gift. Those who did not help to release me will not be so blessed.'

"Thereupon she rewarded these chosen men with the gift of the gods: the ability to take an animal form. Those who received this gift were known as Theriomorphs. As you know, Issaura's other name is Theri, and so we are 'the children of Theri.' The men who wanted to kill the tiger were known as humans.

"Before she returned to the heavens, Issaura made the Theriomorphs a promise: 'When, in the course of your history, you are at the point of destruction, I will come once more and fight for you. You will know me by my animal form.' As those final words slipped past her lips, she rose into the sky to resume her position in the heavens."

When he had finished his tale, Giam looked down at his two granddaughters. He could see his son in the faces smiling back at him.

"Time for bed," Maessa said. Rocking the sleeping Tomius, she nodded to Maruny.

Giam asked to speak to Lluava in private. He took her to his room—a space too small to be called one—and asked her to sit down. Lluava had an odd feeling knotting her stomach. Her grandfather had never done this before, and it made her nervous.

"Lluava," the old man said in an unusually quiet voice, "I know who you are." There was something unsettling in his words. Lluava fidgeted as Giam continued, "I know who you are, *Issaura*. I know you. You have come to protect us at our moment of destruction, as you have promised. I have always remained faithful to you and given you the praise you so justly deserve. You said that we would know you by your animal form. I should have realized long ago, but because of these recent events, my eyes are now opened."

"Grampy, I'm not…" She was cut off. Giam was not listening to her.

"You will save us," Giam stated with unfaltering belief. He knelt before her and kissed her hand. "You will save us all."

That night, Lluava barely slept for whenever she began to fall asleep, her mind filled once again with horrendous nightmares. When she awoke, her grandfather's words ran through her thoughts. By morning's first light, she was already downstairs gathering her belongings. Giam, Maessa, and the rest of the family were also awake; no one seemed to have slept well. They shared a final meal together.

Giam cleared his throat to pray before their breakfast: "O Giahem, Lord of All, protect this family, the king, and the kingdom. You great gods, whose unending love for us is so strong, help us be resilient in this time of war. Issaura, Blessed of the Blessed,"— Lluava saw Giam glance at her — "we are ready for your return and your protection. We give you all our thanks."

"We give you our thanks," they all replied, even Maessa.

Lluava washed the dishes with Maruny one last time and then said her farewells to her family. After hugging each of them and receiving a blessing from Giam, Lluava gathered her belongings and headed out the door.

As she closed the gate behind her, she heard her mother calling for her to wait. Maessa ran to the gate and placed a tiny leather pouch in Lluava's hand.

"Here, you may need this later on," her mother told her.

Lluava looked into the pouch and saw that it was filled with money, more money than her mother made selling eggs.

"Where did you get this?" asked Lluava.

"That does not matter. It is for you to use when you are in need."

"Where did you get this, Mother?" she asked again with more force.

Her mother was silent for a moment; then, with her voice cracking, she said, "I sold the vase yesterday. Don't worry, Lluava. You need the money more then we need the vase."

Lluava was shocked. She had not noticed the vase when she came in from her chores, and, thinking back, she did not remember whether it had been on the table last night. The heirloom had been in her family for generations; now it was gone for a small pouchful of coins, hardly its true worth.

"Oh, Mother," Lluava sighed.

Maessa stood straight and tall. "It was my choice, and I made it. I want you to be safe and well, but you are going to war. . ." She could not finish her sentence.

Lluava hugged her distraught mother and quickly turned to the road once more. The sky was crystal clear; only a few swifts flirted with each other overhead. Their melodious voices rang out. The sun shone brightly and warmed the earth around her while the sea breeze kept the air just the right temperature. Everything seemed so peaceful.

Lluava wondered how a world this serene and beautiful could be on the verge of catastrophe. Her thoughts suddenly shifted to her grandfather's unnerving words. Lluava had not been a believer of any one religion in a long time. This did not hinder her from accepting that something greater existed, though she did not know what. *Could* she be Issaura in human form? Was she the one who would save them? Lluava could not make herself believe that, but his words would remain etched upon her soul. All the girl knew was that she was heading off to find her destiny. A war was coming, and she would meet it head on.

Chapter 3
A Traveler's Way

When Lluava saw the large number of people already gathered in the town square, each one with a pouch or bag, her heart beat a little faster. They ranged in age from sixteen to the middle thirties with a few older men here and there. Although most were male, Lluava recognized several Theriomorph females.

No human women. Interesting, thought Lluava almost smugly. She joined the anxious throng. The atmosphere coursed with tension and anxiety, making the hairs on the back of her neck stand on end. The longer they waited, the stronger the sensation grew.

Lluava heard the voice she had come to loathe over the years. Malnus had crept up behind her and now asked in his sneering way, "You're going to play with the big boys now; are you sure you're ready for this?"

Locking eyes with her opponent, Lluava replied, "Are *you*? Once you leave this town, you can't hide behind your daddy anymore. The mayor's powers do not extend beyond this region. Can you protect yourself? *That* is the question." Leaving Malnus to mutter curses under his breath, she turned and made her way to the other side of the square.

As the morning slowly slipped by, more people joined the unsettled crowd. The sun climbed high into the sky, and the air grew heavy with humidity. At last the sound of hoofbeats was heard at the far end of town. A solitary rider galloped over the ridge followed by four of the King's Guard carrying flags that snapped in the breeze. The five long wagons they escorted were partially filled with strangers, all destined for the camps. The entourage halted in the square. The leader slid off his horse, climbed stiffly to the top of the church's stairs, and announced in a booming voice well trained in public discourse:

20

"All those who have come to answer the call of His Majesty Thor to serve this great kingdom of Elysia, step forward and sign this parchment when your surname is called. The Acrian family!"

A dark-haired man about twenty years old walked up the steps.

"Name, last then first, and race."

The young man signed the parchment held out by the soldier.

"The Assian family! Name, last then first, and race."

Another human of paler complexion who must have been about sixteen walked up the stairs.

Lluava waited patiently for her name to be called. Eventually the soldier's husky voice shouted out, "The Kargen family!" Taking a breath, Lluava walked up the church stairs—stairs she had never envisioned climbing—and wrote her full name and race on the scroll.

As the last signature was gathered, the escort's voice was again heard over the throng. "Humans ride in the first three wagons. Theriomorphs in the last two!"

There were as many Theriomorphs as there were humans. Lluava wondered why the group was segregated by race with Theriomorphs squeezed into fewer wagons, but she kept her suspicions to herself. Last-minute goodbyes were said, and, all around Lluava, families and friends hugged and kissed those about to depart as tears streamed down their faces. Brushing aside thoughts of her own family's farewells, Lluava savored the last few minutes in the only town she had ever known.

The other Theriomorph girls were already clustered in the fourth wagon, but when she tried to climb aboard, the driver yelled, "This one's full; try the one in back!" Lluava asked if she could squeeze in, but he refused. By this time, she was the only person not on board. Approaching the last wagon, she realized it had even less room than the previous one.

Suddenly a voice said, "You can sit next to me." Looking up, she saw the driver watching her. Had he realized what had happened and made the offer in pity?

"Thank you," Lluava replied as he bent to help her climb onto the seat. Never before had a man given her aid, whether boarding a wagon or mounting a horse. Her parents had always expected her to take care of herself. She looked at the young man in his soldier's uniform; he was only a few years older than she. Dusty blond hair pleasantly framed blue-green eyes. His face was not too bad to look at, though he did have several freckles.

"I'm Byron Larson," he said with a smile.

"I'm Lluava Kargen," was all she could say. Before they had a chance to start a conversation, the leader of the guards strode up to Byron and told him that this was the last village. They were headed to the camps.

The wagons turned around one by one and headed back down the road the way they had come. Lluava glanced back one last time as the town slipped into the distance; she saw the solemn faces of the townsfolk looking at the passing caravan through cracked doors and from behind curtained windows. When she could no longer see the village, she turned to face the road they traveled on and looked toward her future.

Slowly, conversations began among the riders in the wagon bed. All sought comfort from one another. The driver turned to Lluava and inquired if she had ever traveled before.

"Of course. I have been to Brensworth once and Cartel maybe three times, when my father was selling his furniture."

Byron smiled. "Your father builds furniture? I apprenticed in the trade several years ago. I wonder if I have seen his work."

"You would have been lucky to do so. You see, he died a year ago," Lluava said sorrowfully. She remembered her father showing her how to carve decorations on the leg of a chair when she was Lamb's age. She remembered how he laughed when she held the carving tool backward.

"I'm sorry. My father also died last year, in an accident scouting in the Borren Mountains. I miss him greatly." Byron's sympathetic voice brought her back to the present.

"Your father was a soldier, too? Mine trained but was inactive for the majority of the time."

"Yes. He's the reason I became one. He was a lieutenant and began training me as soon as I could hold a sword and bow."

"The only way I know how to fight is with my fists."

They both laughed and happily continued their conversation until well into the afternoon, when they stopped to eat. The wagon train pulled off the road into a field overgrown with knee-high grass. Several elm trees bordered a nearby pond. The sun's rays glinted off its dark surface while a small flock of geese paddled lazily in the water.

Lluava reached into her shoulder bag and grabbed the parcel of food that her mother had packed. Tucking it under her arm along with a small water pouch, she jumped off the wagon and followed Byron toward the pond. She intended to fill her pouch but, smelling the stagnant water, decided that she wasn't that thirsty. They sat in the shade of one of the trees. The late spring heat was intense, and everyone else followed suit.

Lluava unwrapped her parcel. There was a large wedge of her mother's homemade cheese, half a loaf of bread, and two plums—one ripe, the other almost ready to eat.

"Byron, how far is it to the camps?" Lluava wanted to plan rations for the rest of the trip.

"Five good days from your village." Byron pulled out three biscuits and a small jar of jam from one of his pockets and then took off his jacket and placed it over a low branch.

Lluava sighed as she looked hungrily at her measly rations. Byron seemed to read her thoughts. "The drivers have plenty of food for the trip. You are welcome to it," he said reassuringly.

"I couldn't do that. I would be taking it away from someone else." Lluava would never accept charity.

"You *will* have some, and that is that. We cannot have half-starved people arriving at the training camps. I won't allow it." He said it with a sense of purpose, or was it authority that had slipped through? Realizing how he sounded made him grin, which, in turn, made Lluava smile.

"Well, if you say it that way, how can I refuse?"

Lluava still ate a slightly smaller meal than she would have at home, but she was not as worried about her supplies running out. Byron shared his water, which was cleaner than the algae-filled pond. Nearby, young goslings chased after a frog. Every time the frog hopped, they followed, but when the frog stopped to bellow out a croak, they backed up warily. After several minutes of the game, the frog jumped into the water, and the goslings stared longingly after it. The adult geese, trying to catch their late lunch, bobbed up and down in the shallows. A small breeze attempted to blow through the trees, but the warm, muggy air was far from comforting.

When they had eaten, Lluava threw the crumbs of her bread and cheese toward the young birds. Their fussy grey bodies ran up to their new find. Peeping gratefully, they devoured their tidbits.

A whistle summoned everyone back to the caravan. As Lluava accepted Byron's help climbing into the wagon, she thought she could easily enjoy this kind of treatment.

They continued on their journey until well after dark, finally stopping in another open field. The caravan looped itself into a semicircle, and they made camp. Completing the circle, the soldiers and drivers set up small tents in a curved line. Byron offered to teach Lluava how to pitch a tent since she had never used one before. He demonstrated how the flexible wooden rods, made of extremely tall river reeds, were crossed in the center and a thick, woven tarp thrown over them. Effortlessly, Byron tethered the corners of the tarp to stakes set in the ground.

"There. Now you know how to set up a standard field tent. It's a 'must know' for anyone in the army." He winked at her.

When they finished, both walked to the blazing bonfire in the middle of the circle. A group of Theriomorphs had laid it while Byron and Lluava had been setting up the tent.

Everyone had a job to do: pitching tents, tending the fire, gathering wood. One group brought water from a nearby stream. Two men staked the horses in the grass outside the ring of wagons so the animals could graze and rest.

It was growing late, and the recruits began to settle in for the night. Byron brought Lluava a small pouch filled with jerky, something she had never eaten before. They conversed quietly by the fire's flames; the warm light flickered on the faces of those gathered nearby. People were beginning to become acquainted, gradually becoming more comfortable with their fellow travelers.

Byron told Lluava of his experience training in the camps and answered her questions about what to expect. Suddenly he stood up and told her to wait. When he returned, she saw that he was wearing a scabbard with sword.

Pulling the sword from its sheath, Byron said, "This is Phin, the sword I was given when I finished my training. Hold it if you want."

"Really?" inquired Lluava.

"Be careful. It's sharp," warned Byron. He offered the sword, handle first, to Lluava. "Take note of its weight. A true warrior does not feel whole without the weight of his weapon on his back or at hand."

Lluava gingerly took it from him and, with his nod of assurance, carefully swung it around in the air. "It is heavier than I expected." She handed it back. "I wish I knew how to fight with it already."

"Do you really?" He smiled knowingly. "You will learn all about that sort of thing soon enough, I expect. But…if you really cannot wait, I can show you a thing or two."

"Really?" Despite the shadows cast upon her face by the fire, Lluava's face lit up.

"Yeah, I could. And I will." Byron led Lluava outside the ring of wagons, grabbing two sticks from the pile for the fire as they passed by. In the flickering firelight, he showed her how to block, slowly at first, then moving faster. He moved so quickly that Lluava could not evade his stick, but, when he asked if she wanted to quit, she said no. They had practiced for a good while when Byron said they should rest.

Weaving back through the tents, she and Byron turned to the sound of a slow, solitary clapping. Malnus stepped from the shadows and said mockingly, "Well, I am impressed. You may actually live for more than a minute during the war. If you keep it up, you may actually live a whole five minutes." Smiling evilly, he backed into the shadows and disappeared.

"What an eerie fellow," Byron said, peering at the spot where Malnus had stood.

"Yeah," was all Lluava could say.

The stars shone brightly in the sky as Lluava lay down for the night. Byron gave her a small blanket so she would not have to sleep on the bare earth. She had picked a patch of ground with a thick layer of grass that acted as a poor cushion. Although sore and bruised, she still thanked him for the practice session. Watching the stars slowly rotate in the heavens, she drifted off to sleep.

Morning came too early. The sun had not even risen when Byron gently awakened her. She took a moment to gather a sense of her surroundings, and when she did, she saw that everyone seemed to be moving already. People were shaking out blankets, gathering supplies, and loading the wagons. She watched one of the drivers pour water on the smoldering fire, cover it with loose soil, and make sure that the fire would not relight.

To Lluava's dismay, there was no time to wash. She hurriedly shook out and folded her blanket and then climbed onto the wagon. Before she knew it, she and the rest of the caravan were on their way to the camps.

Byron told her there were four training facilities in the southern region of the kingdom, all fairly close to each other. Both humans and Theriomorphs had separate camps, as did both genders. The first stop would be Delphine for the female humans, followed by Calitron for human males. Theriomorph males would be taken to Durog, and the final stop would be Thowcelemine, the female Theriomorph camp.

Byron explained that Theriomorph training was different from human training because Theriomorphs had the ability to change shape. Toward the end of training, each recruit would be paired with a partner of the opposite race, and each pair would live and work together for the remainder of their service.

"So, who is your partner?" inquired Lluava.

Byron's jaw twitched. "I haven't been assigned one yet. The camps try to pair you up with someone whose skills and strengths are comparable to yours. When I completed my training, there was no one right for me. I hope that this season I will find my partner."

"Maybe you are looking at her," sassed Lluava.

"Wouldn't that be something?" Byron said, yet his tone let her know it was unlikely.

Lluava pushed the subject. "Why are the genders kept apart?"

"I'm not sure. I think that there is a difference in the methods used to train the men and the women. I do not understand the what or the why, but I do believe that there is a difference."

Lluava grunted, "Humph. Expected."

"Oh, come on, Lluava. Not every girl is as strong willed as you," Byron responded, joshing. They both smiled and then changed the subject to pleasanter topics.

Lluava admired the slow change in the scenery they passed. Flat ground gave way to small hills; the grasses became thicker and shorter, with a darker tint than the taller, almost yellow grass at home. Even the trees, though the same species as those at Rivendale, seemed different, although she did not know why. The piercing blue sky, clear and clean, dared clouds to challenge its perfection. Only the sun took up the gauntlet— a bright yellow stain on rich blue silk. As the sun rose, so did the temperature. By noon, the caravan halted to take shelter under a small grove of trees. The drivers had begun to fear the horses might die of heat exhaustion.

While Byron took care of the animals, Lluava wandered among the trees. Spotting a pleasant-looking red oak, she took it upon herself to climb it. The oak was quite old with large branches that swung low to the ground. Lluava effortlessly pulled herself up. The years of racing other children to the tops of trees had taught her how to shift her weight and where to find a good limb to grip. About twenty feet up, the trunk split into three branches and made a wonderful place to sit and observe her surroundings. Through a gap in the leaves, she had a panoramic view of the hilly landscape. Turning to the other side, she spied a nest with three pale green eggs. Lluava wondered where the mother was. She did not wonder long. A screeching arrow of brown feathers dove at her, snatched a clump of her hair, and tried to pull her away.

"Ouch!" she yelped, batting at the bird. As quickly as she could, Lluava backed down the tree. Another bird flew at her, pulling at her hair. She quickened her pace and, nearing the ground, jumped. Once soil was under her feet, she took off running. The two birds chased after her, then one at a time flew back to their precious nest. Lluava returned to the wagons.

"There you are," Byron called to her. "I've been wondering where you went. We are going to stay here for another hour to give both us and the horses a chance to cool off and get water. There is a farmer who will let us use his well. He and his wife live at the small farm down there." He pointed to a small mud-brick house in the distance.

"I'm fine right now. Thanks, though," she said courteously.

"Well, then, would you honor me with a walk through the grove?" he asked with a smile.

A different voice chimed into the conversation. "You can wait for that, Byron. Right now, you need to help me water the horses." The young driver of the second wagon strode up to them.

"You always find the perfect time to ask me to do something, don't you, Trent?" Byron pretended to complain.

"I try," Trent gave her a wink. "Aren't you going to introduce me to your *very* pretty friend, or are you going to keep her all to yourself?"

"Oh, how rude of me!" Byron made the introductions. "Trent, this is Lluava. Lluava, Trent."

"Nice to meet you," Trent said.

"Likewise."

"Trent," Byron explained, "is in my regiment. He's my closest friend and comrade." Turning to Lluava, Byron said, "We'll walk some other time." He shrugged, and both young men, shoving each other playfully as they went, walked off.

Lluava strolled back to the wagons. A group of boys flirted with several girls near the forest edge. Some of the men were napping in the grass; nearby, five girls were picking wildflowers. Everyone seemed to be chatting with one another. To Lluava, it seemed that everyone was trying to distract each other from thinking of the camps and the war to come.

Something caught her eye—a movement inside her wagon. Walking closer, she peered over the side. A small boy no older than ten was curled up in the far corner. His knees were pulled close to his face, and his arms were wrapped tightly around them. His head tilted downward, rusty brown hair covering his eyes. She wondered from where he had come and why he was in the wagon.

"Hey, are you okay?" Lluava asked.

The boy stirred. He slowly turned his head upward and looked sadly at her. He had been crying; from his swollen, reddened eyes, Lluava knew he had been doing so for a while. Tear tracks tinted his freckled cheeks, which were still round in that cute-little-kid way. He did not say anything, nor did he attempt to wipe his eyes.

Lluava climbed into the bed of the wagon to be closer to him, but he pressed his body as close as he could to the back of the wagon and gripped himself even tighter.

"It's okay. I'm not here to hurt you," Lluava said reassuringly. After a pause and a change of strategy, she asked, "Why are you here all alone?"

The boy stared at her with his large brown eyes but did not respond. It was not going to be easy to persuade him to talk. Then Lluava thought of something that made her stomach churn. They looked at each other, and Lluava instantly knew the answer to her own question. "You were drafted, weren't you?" He was another young soul recruited for war. There was something wrong with this. Lluava asked softly, "How can you be going off to train? You can only be nine, maybe ten?"

"I'm almost eleven," the boy said in a hoarse whisper.

"What?" The sound of his voice had startled her.

"I said, I am almost eleven," he repeated, louder this time.

"Oh. I'm sorry," Lluava said. "I'm Lluava from Rivendale."

"I'm Chattern. Chat for short," the boy replied.

"Well, Chat, I was starting to think you couldn't talk."

"Well," he responded huffily, "I can." Then he grinned, and his two large front teeth stuck out in a rather rodent-like way. She thought of Tomius and wondered if he would look like Chat when he was a little older.

"Want to take a walk under the trees?" asked Lluava. "I'd like some company." Chat paused for a moment, suspecting the girl's motives, and then nodded. As they strolled, Chat pointed out interesting birds or insects. Lluava was charmed and complimented him on his knowledge. As he grew more comfortable, he began to talk about many other things. Upon returning to the wagon, Chat seemed a creature metamorphosed. The seeds of comfort and trust had been sown between the boy and his new friend.

Byron caught up with Lluava as the caravan prepared to leave and asked where she had been. A bit too curious, Lluava thought; she decided to test the waters and told him she had found someone else to walk with her. Hearing this, Byron looked a little hurt, which somehow pleased her. Not wanting to be cruel, she introduced him to her escort, Chat. Byron chuckled.

"I'm going to sit next to Chat for now," Lluava told Byron. She turned to Chat. "That is, if it's okay?"

"Sure," the boy replied excitedly and smiled in his squirrelly way.

As if trying to make up for lost time, the caravan continued at a quick pace. When the sun was low on the horizon, they stopped and made camp. Chat stayed close to Lluava the entire time. As she watched over the pesky child, Lluava found herself becoming quite protective of him. Sensing that it wasn't the right time, she asked him no personal questions, yet she wondered why one so young was going to war.

Lluava shared some of her food with Chat at dinner. He thanked her and did the same. Later that night, Byron came by and asked if Lluava wanted to practice her swordplay. Chat watched as Byron and Lluava swatted at each other with sticks. Lluava never seemed to land a hit, while Byron landed blow after blow. After Lluava was thoroughly bruised, Byron worked with Chat. She knew Byron was being very easy on the small boy. Chat seemed to love the experience.

That night, Chat slept next to her. Lluava did not know when she fell asleep or how long she slept, but she was rudely awakened by Byron in the early morning hours.

"Wha...wha...what's happening?" she stammered, trying to regain her bearings.

"You were tossing and turning, yelling 'stop' constantly. Chat came and woke me. Are you okay?" he asked, looking worried.

"I...I guess I was having a bad dream." Lluava tried to remember what she had been dreaming about but could not. "I'm sorry for startling everyone."

After reassuring them that she was fine, Lluava tried to fall back asleep. Yet, the ever-growing sensation that something dark was building could not be pushed aside.

Chapter 4
Bird of Grace

When dawn's light arrived, it was a blessing to Lluava, for she no longer had to lie quietly, staring blankly at the sky. She could rise and move around without fear of waking anyone else.

Sitting next to the young boy again, Lluava decided that Chat was the perfect name for a boy who never stopped talking. Even at lunch, he spoke without pausing to swallow. Comparing today's talkative boy to the solemn and silent child of the day before, Lluava was both happy and entertained. He chattered about random things like shoeing horses and watching tadpoles and then peppered her with such questions as why water was blue in lakes and streams yet clear in cups and glasses. Without waiting for an answer, he would move on to something entirely different. Without warning, he began to talk about his family. Lluava listened attentively.

"Don't believe what people say about orphanages. They are horrible. I was adopted when I was six, but I still remember the stink of unchanged babies, vomit-stained carpet, and that nasty sludge they call gruel. I didn't think I'd ever be adopted. Folks only want newborns. The older you are, the more likely you'll live the rest of your childhood in that filth." Chat sighed and then continued. "Yet, I was chosen. Not by ordinary parents, you know, the young kind. Their names are Mr. and Mrs. Ryalls, an elderly human couple. Don't misunderstand me; they are kind and generous, but they chose me, a Theriomorph child, because it would look good. You know, the merging-of-the-races thing. They needed help around the farm and didn't have children of their own, so they wanted an older boy."

Chat paused to scratch the tip of his nose and catch his breath. He spoke quickly, as if, by clearing everything off his chest, he could reduce the pain. "When they announced that war was coming and there was going to be a draft, I had to go."

Lluava did not have to ask why. It did not matter that he was too young or that the couple he lived with was too old. Someone had to go. And that someone was Chat.

"I'm a Theriomorph, so…" Chat continued, as if reading her mind.

"So you had to go," Lluava finished his statement. Although a human couple had adopted Chat, he was Theriomorph and the obvious choice for the draft. She felt sorry that Chat had to be punished because of a poorly thought-out rule.

Chat had turned his attention to something in the distance. "Are those more wagons?" he asked.

She turned and looked, and as she did so, another person in her wagon yelled, "Hey everyone, another wagon train is approaching!"

It was true. A second caravan, with seven wagons, was heading toward them. She could tell by their guide's gold and moss-green clothes that these were more recruits for the camps. Soon both caravans merged into one.

This was only the beginning. Throughout that day and the next, train after train of wagons came together. All were heading to the same destination, the camps. Lluava had never seen anything like it. There had to be a hundred wagons, filled to the point of bursting with young people her age. There were more people in the wagons than in all of Rivendale, maybe twice as many. Three columns of wagons traveled side by side, stretching far ahead and far behind Lluava's own.

During their lunch stop on the fourth day, Lluava slipped off into the forest bordering the road. She soon found a small river, about fifteen feet across, that wound its way through the ever-thirsty trees.

Lluava longed for a bath. Still wearing the clothes in which she had left home, she felt horrible that she had let her cleanliness deteriorate. She followed the river more deeply into the woods to make sure no one would stumble upon her as she was bathing. At a bend in the river, she stopped and began to remove her clothes.

Suddenly she heard voices. With belt in hand, she peered around a short holly bush. A group of three girls apparently had had the same idea and were already taking off their dresses. Lluava recognized them from the first train that had joined hers the other day.

Dratted humans, Lluava thought; they had beaten her to the water.

One was short, with dirty-blonde hair. A second girl, a tall strawberry blonde, was already wading into the water. The third girl was the prettiest. Shorter than Lluava, she had long, silky black hair tied back in a deep-blue bow that matched her dress. Her skin was as white as the porcelain china in the Lady's Shop in Rivendale. All three were smiling and conversing with one another. Lluava couldn't help but listen in.

"Rosalyn, come on in. I know we are traveling, but we do not have to smell like we are," the tall girl said to the dark-haired one as she dove into the water.

"Are you sure it is safe? We are so far from anyone else. What if we encounter trouble?" the pale-skinned girl responded in a melodious voice. She was hesitant and a little afraid.

"Come on, Rosy, the water feels great," the short one chimed in as she stepped gingerly into the stream.

"What if someone sees us? I don't know what I would do," contested Rosalyn. "I don't think I can, Selphy. You and Alison can wash. I will stay here and watch."

"No, Rosy, you are going to take a bath. We do not have to make ourselves *obvious* to others, you know," said the small girl with a sly smile. Lluava thought that must be Selphy.

The girl slipped under the water and emerged as a young doe. Lluava was caught by surprise. The girls' clothes, their names, the way they acted...they had seemed to be human.

The water dripped off the head and back of the doe as she gently shook herself. Lluava looked over at the girl called Alison, but she was no longer there, only a small orange butterfly flitting across the water. Next, her attention turned to the blue dress and ribbon on the riverbank. Something moved under it, and soon an elegant swan slipped out and gracefully slid into the water.

That figures, Lluava thought, with a note of dissent that surprised her. Beautiful girl, beautiful animal. Deciding that she was not meant to have a swim this afternoon, she started to leave when she heard a loud squawking. Quickly turning, she ran toward the sound. Two men were pulling in a net with a struggling swan. Rosalyn!

Ducking behind shrubbery, Lluava slipped toward the men. She was close enough to hear one say, "Finally, we can eat something other than stale bread!"

Lluava knew she had to do something and fast. She let her instincts take over. The muscles of her throat began to tremble, emitting a prehistoric sound. She let go; the roar grew louder and louder, ending in a high-pitched scream.

One man tugged the other's sleeve, "Come on! We have to go!"

"But, but, but...," his companion stammered as he dropped the net and ran after his friend.

Watching them run stirred something in Lluava that forced her to give chase. Bolting after them, she purposefully shook bushes and branches as she went. As though they thought some demonic beast was after them, the two men pushed themselves to run faster. Their very lives depended on it.

Lluava could have snared them, but, in a moment of clarity, she remembered why she was terrorizing them in the first place. She doubled back to make sure Rosalyn was safe. Sadly, she was not. Reaching the edge of the water, all Lluava saw was a netted wing being pulled under by the weight of the waterlogged rope. A butterfly flitted frantically to and fro above the sinking swan.

Lluava dove into the river, struggling to swim against the weight of her saturated clothes. Peering through the murky water, she spotted the bird entangled in the netting and reeds at the bottom of the river. Pushing downward, she grabbed the net and fought her way back to the surface. She reached the bank, crawled out, and carefully untangled the mass of sopping white feathers. The swan lay on the bank, motionless.

"Come on! Live! Live!" She willed the bird to breathe. Suddenly the swan spat up mouthfuls of water.

Knowing the girl would want to change form, Lluava retrieved Rosalyn's dress, the same deep blue as the swan's eyes. Looking up as she bent over the bird, she saw a trembling deer staring at her.

"Get away from her!" a sharp voice demanded from behind Lluava. Turning, she saw Alison in her human form and nothing else. As the strange girl bounded up to her, Lluava backed off, saying, "I think she'll be okay."

Selphy, who had also transformed, put on her dress and then handed Alison her clothes. As Lluava turned to leave, a meek voice said, "Wait."

Looking back, she saw Rosalyn's pale face peering at her. Though most of the girl's body was hidden behind her two squatting friends, Lluava could see that she had already changed back to human form.

"Thank you for saving me. I would have died without you," she said as she coughed up more water.

Lluava nodded and then walked quietly back to camp, pondering how close to death that sweet girl had come. Reaching the wagons, she climbed into hers and sat there till everyone started to pack up and move out. Chat and Byron came toward her, but she paid no attention to them.

"What happened?" Chat said, his mouth wide open. "You're all wet."

"Oh, I decided to take a swim," Lluava replied dismissively.

"With your clothes on?" Byron inquired.

Lluava thought fast. "I needed a bath, and my clothes needed a wash. I did two in one." Her obviously fake smile warned the boys not to pursue their questioning.

That night, the three friends sat by the blazing fire. All were unusually quiet; even Chat did not speak. This solemn silence was the result of Byron's news that tomorrow they would reach the camps. This would be their last night together. No one was ready to say goodbye.

When the need to break the silence became too great, Byron stood up and told them that they must not let their final memories of their journey together be sad ones. Making a pact to pretend that this was not their last few hours together, the three sparred with one another and then walked through the fields, looking at the stars and watching Chat try to catch enough fireflies to create a lantern. That night was the last time Lluava would sleep well.

The next morning was different from the others. Everyone was reorganized. Not only were Theriomorphs separated from humans, but women and men had to ride in separate wagons. Chat held back tears when he heard that he could not sit next to Lluava anymore. He was losing his only friends.

By midmorning, the caravan had reached Delphine, the human girls' training camp. Although they were far from the main road, Lluava could still make out a large, walled-in area. Beyond lay the great expanse of the ocean. Only a fifth of the wagons veered off, but that was enough to drastically shorten their wagon train.

Around midday, they passed Calitron. It lay closer to the road than Delphine, and Lluava could see that its walls were high, maybe thirty feet. Half of the caravan would remain here. She spotted Malnus as his wagon turned down the dirt road to the camp. He looked worried, perhaps even afraid. Watching his wagon disappear through the gateway, Lluava was surprised. She couldn't be feeling sorry for him, could she?

Soon they stopped for lunch and a midday stretch. The three friends met under a small dogwood. Byron brought dried pear slices and salted pork; both Lluava's and Chat's food supplies had been consumed days ago. They ate quietly before standing and separating for the last time.

"Take care of yourself, Chat. If you let those guys be mean to you, I'll hike over and beat them up myself," Lluava said with a smile.

He ran up and hugged her. "I won't. I don't want you to go."

"I know." Lluava squeezed him back.

"Just listen to your drill sergeant," Byron told him, "and you'll be fine." Byron and Chat shook hands, and the young boy joined the Theriomorph men. Byron was still the driver of Lluava's wagon, so they postponed their own farewells.

Around four that afternoon, Lluava watched Chat enter Durog. She could see two guardsmen outside the gate watching all who entered. She realized how quiet it would be without Chat around and felt a pang of loss for that smiling, freckled little face. Far beyond the gates of Durog, the lonely mountain, Burok Dûr, stood like a sentinel guarding its eternal post.

Thowcelemine was only two miles from Durog, so they reached it in less than an hour. A long road led to the fourth walled enclosure. The gates groaned as they slowly swung open in anticipation of the approaching wagons. As they passed through, all craned their necks to be the first to glimpse their new home. Above them, the wooden gateway formed an arch, with the name Thowcelemine carved into heavy oak planks. The thick walls were made of immense stones layered one on top of another.

The wagons lined up next to the massive wall. After she had gathered her possessions and climbed down, Lluava looked around at the place where she would live for the next few months. There were five rows of wooden barracks with ten identical long, thatched-roof structures in each row. Beyond them were several large buildings with similar roofs and faded wooden walls. The perimeter walls disappeared into the woods behind the larger buildings. What, she wondered, was hiding behind those trees?

A sharp whistle blew. All eyes turned to a man in a moss-green uniform. On his right breast were pinned a dozen badges and medals. Lluava recognized the silver Medal of Bravery attached to a gold and green ribbon; her father had received one. A thick black belt held a scabbard with sword. His salt-and-pepper hair was cropped short in typical army style.

Standing next to him was a very tall man with skin as dark as coal. Lluava had never seen dark-skinned people before this journey for none lived in Rivendale. There had been many dark-skinned individuals traveling to the camps but none as black as this man. She innocently wondered if he could actually blend in with his surroundings in the dark. He wore the same uniform as the first man but had fewer badges. Neither man smiled.

The first man whistled again and shouted out, "Attention! Attention! All of you line up in alphabetical order by last name as quickly as you can." Chaos erupted. Girls yelled out their last names and searched through the hundred or so people to find others with similar last names.

There must be a more efficient way of going about this, thought Lluava. She jumped up onto a wagon to gain everyone's attention, but this did not work. Somehow, she knew she had to convince them to listen, so she did the only thing she could think of: she roared. Silence fell as they all looked at her.

"Okay, now listen! All those with last names that start with an A, stand at the far wagon," she commanded, pointing to the wagon at the end of the row. "All those with B names, go to the wagon to the right of that one."

Girls started moving, and as others caught on, they began to alphabetize those with names that started with their letter. After Lluava sorted all of them into letter groups, she helped organize the K's. Everyone lined up quickly and with relative ease.

As soon as they were lined up, the older man who had given the order looked them over and said, "Let's see how you did." Pulling out a roster, he called out names as he walked by each girl. Amazingly, everyone was in the correct order.

"I applaud you, for this is the first time a group this large has organized itself perfectly and so quickly. This task was a test. It showed me those of you who rose above the others to become leaders. You see, leaders are not taught; they are born." He looked at Lluava and then continued, "I am General Kentril. I will be your superior drill sergeant. This is Major Ojewa." He pointed to his dark-skinned companion, who was at least six and a half feet tall. Until this moment, Ojewa had stood still, looking off into the distance.

Now, he focused his gaze on the new recruits as if he were just now noticing them. Kentril continued, "He is second in command and *will* be given the same respect you *will* give me."

"Whenever I announce attention, you will stand as Major Ojewa is standing now." Ojewa had his feet together and stood upright, shoulders rolled back and hands clasped behind him. "If I say 'At ease,' you will stand like this." Ojewa moved to stand with his feet apart and arms at his sides. "When I give an order, you will respond with 'Sir, yes sir.' Is that clear?"

Everyone said yes. Kentril barked, "I said, is that clear?"

Warily they replied, "Sir, yes, sir."

"I can't hear you!" Kentril yelled.

"Sir, yes, sir!" everyone yelled back.

"That's more like it. Now, your barrack assignments are on alphabetized lists nailed onto the wall behind you. Barracks are identified by letters and bunks by numbers. Use this to find your barracks and bunk. Unpack and then meet back here in a half hour. Dismissed" The girls tentatively clustered around their respective lists.

After Lluava read her assignment, she grabbed her bag and went in search of her barracks: CA-49. It only took a minute to find the building with a large CA burned into the wood. She opened the door and went inside. Two rows of bunk beds with a dark aisle between them stretched all the way to the back. Odd numbers were on the right, even on the left. The second-to-last bunk was hers. It had tan sheets and a blanket folded at the end of the bed and a pillow at the top. Two trunks were stowed under each bottom bunk. Next to each bunk bed was a small table with a candle. A curtain was attached at one end of the bed and rigged so that it could be pulled around bed and nightstand for privacy.

So this is home, Lluava thought. Placing her things in the trunk closest to the end of the bed, she carefully unpacked.

As other girls began to enter the barracks, she slipped out, wanting to say goodbye to Byron before he left. But when she arrived at the gate, she saw that she was too late; all the wagons had gone. She could see them in the distance through the crack of the closing gate.

Lluava stood lost in thought as Ojewa approached her. "Do you need help with anything?" His voice was kind, but his accent was strange.

"Where do the drivers go now that they have dropped us off?" She still wished she had had the chance to say goodbye to Byron.

"They will practice their fighting skills at the advanced training camp near Swelore before being sent on scouting missions." Ojewa paused and looked down at her, for he was at least eight inches taller.

"Thank you," she said. He nodded to her, and then walked away. He had more important things to do than comfort a heartbroken girl. This was the army. War was on the way. Emotions would have to be pushed aside, at least for a while.

Lluava decided to follow the road that led past the large buildings into the woods. She heard the whistle before she saw Kentril and Ojewa.

"Attention!" barked Kentril. Everyone lined up. "That was good, but, from now on, you will line up in alphabetical order. I hope you remember next to whom you stood before. Let's try this again. Attention!"

It took only a moment for the recruits to run to their places and stand as they had been shown. Ojewa walked down the line correcting the stance of those who needed it. He asked each person her clothing size for the uniforms they would receive. Lluava was instructed to hold her head up higher and look straight ahead. She followed his command.

Kentril continued to talk. "The first building to the right is the mess hall, where dinner will be served shortly. The building opposite is the Grand Barracks, where the officers live. The one to the left of the mess hall is the gym and weight room. All other buildings are different training arenas. The stable is located at the end of the road through the woods. Is this clear?"

"Sir, yes, sir!" replied the girls after a moment. This response would soon come as naturally as breathing, but, for now, they still had to think about it.

"At ease. Everyone to the mess hall. You have one hour to eat your dinner; then I expect you all to hit your bunks. Tomorrow will be a hard day. Welcome to Thowcelemine."

The girls walked quietly down the dry dirt road. The mess hall resembled a barracks with more windows. Rows and rows of long thin tables and benches stood inside, with a serving table at the far end.

Wordlessly the girls queued up, took thin wooden trays, and moved down the line. Lluava took utensils and a ceramic plate. There were several types of steamed vegetables, ground meat patties, and rolls. As she picked up one of the patties, she wondered why anyone would grind up meat to cook it. None of the food looked exceptionally good, but at least it wasn't horrible. At the end of the table, she picked up a cup filled with water and went to find a seat.

Most of the girls were sitting with friends they had made on the journey. Lluava's two companions were gone, and now she was alone again in unknown territory. Could she intrude on an already-formed group? No. Instead, Lluava sat at a vacant table and ate quickly, not slowing down even when others sat down beside her. She wanted to leave. As soon as she was done, she dumped the tray into a large tin wash bin by the door and left.

It was still light when she reached the barracks, but she was exhausted from the journey. As she reached her bunk, she saw a girl with raven-black hair in a pale blue dress sitting on the bottom bed, facing away from her. Lluava cleared her throat to announce herself. The girl turned around, and Lluava recognized the deep-blue eyes looking up at her. It was Rosalyn.

"Hi," was all Lluava could think to say.

"Hello. I am Rosalyn, and I was hoping that we would have the pleasure of meeting again. It seems that we will be bunkmates. It is very fortunate that you saved my life as you did. And I thank you for that," she said in her sweet voice.

"No problem. Oh, uh, I'm Lluava." Still shocked to discover that her roommate was the girl whose life she had saved, she stuttered out her reply.

"It is nice to formally meet you," Rosalyn said, raising a small, pale hand. Lluava shook it gently, as if she might break the delicate-looking girl. They smiled at each other.

A question popped into Lluava's head. "Why are you back so early?"

"I was not hungry after the trip. It is all the excitement; I am afraid it makes me lose my appetite." As she spoke, she discreetly slipped a letter into her trunk. "What about you? Why are you back early?"

"Oh, I'm not a people person," Lluava lied. Why let on that she had no friends here?

"Well, that can be changed," Rosalyn said, smiling.

"Maybe. I'm really tired. I'm turning in now." Lluava quickly climbed the built-in ladder at the end of the bed to the top bunk. The sheet was tightly tucked in, and it took her a second to pull it loose. The sheets were scratchy, and it was too hot to use the only somewhat softer blanket. Deciding to sleep without a cover, she soon fell into another restless slumber. Lluava was so tired that she did not hear the other girls come in and start chatting with one another. She slept right through the barked cry to "Quiet down!" from one of the corporals.

In her dreams, wars raged and people ran screaming to and fro, in and out of the darkness. Thatched huts were ablaze, and bodies were strewn all over the ground. A shrill screeching erupted from nowhere. One of the huts blew up before her and then another and another, each after the same piercing sound. Soon she heard another one. It grew louder and louder. She knew that whatever made the huts explode was connected with the earsplitting noise. This one sounded right above her. She knew there was nowhere to run. It was too late…

Wide awake and sweating, Lluava vaulted up in her bed. The sound did not go away. It was so strident, she had to cover her ears. Around her, girls jumped from their beds and ran toward the door.

Lluava's thoughts were going everywhere. Was this a dream? Was this real? Had her worst fear come true? Were they under attack? She did not understand, but she believed her last thought was true.

They were unprepared, and they were under attack.

Chapter 5
When a Black Cat Crosses Your Path...

The sound was deafening. Lluava could hardly think. Instinctively, she felt she had to move, to get far away from this noise. If they were under attack, she had to find somewhere safe, wherever that was. Rosalyn waved frantically to her to follow and then ran down the aisle to the door.

Jumping off her bunk, Lluava landed on all fours, ready to bound out of the barracks. Was that someone crying? Turning, Lluava saw a girl with bedraggled brown hair holding onto the edge of the very last bed in the opposite row. How Lluava heard the girl through all the ear-shattering sound was nothing less than a miracle. Without hesitation, Lluava ran up to the girl and tried to pull her from the bed, but the terrified recruit would neither budge nor release her death grip on the bedpost.

Lluava knew she needed to get the girl to come to her senses. Only one thing came to mind. She slapped the girl, hard, across the broad side of her right cheek. The blow jolted the girl back to reality, for she stopped staring into the distance and focused on Lluava. Tears still streamed down her face.

"Come on! We have to go!" Lluava shouted. She didn't know if the girl heard her over the noise or just sensed what she needed to do, but she rose and stumbled toward the door, Lluava at her heels.

Outside, they raced between the barracks toward a crowd of girls gathered near the entryway of the camp. But the gate was closed; there was no way out. Lluava's heart beat faster as she tried to think what to do next, but nothing came to her. She felt like a horse trapped in a burning barn.

Suddenly the screeching stopped. The abrupt silence was far worse and more unsettling than the sound. Lluava's senses were going haywire. Then, from out of the darkness Ojewa and Kentril emerged, in what seemed like an unusually cool manner. Something was wrong. The general and his second in command were too calm.

Kentril picked up the whistle around his neck and blew it. "Attention!" he yelled.

The girls, half in shock, half questioning, shuffled to their places in line. Kentril's mouth twitched into a smile.

"Morning, recruits. Isn't it a beautiful day?" Kentril spoke in a teasing manner as it was still too early for sunrise. Several uniformed women arrived and stood behind the two men. "It is five in the morning, your new wake-up time. The sound you heard is your signal to awaken. You will have fifteen minutes to dress, make your beds in standard military fashion, leave your area spotless, and then line up out here as you are doing now. The women you see behind me are officers of Thowcelemine and are in charge of your barracks. They will show you how to make your bed properly and clean your area. Pay attention to them. Only when your barracks are spotless, which they will judge, will you be allowed to line up. If you take longer than fifteen minutes, you will have to run extra laps. Is this clear?"

"Sir, yes, sir!" was the unanimous reply.

Lluava responded affirmatively, although the idea of waking this early was not to her liking. Yet she would rather wake up on time than run laps. Is that how they were to be disciplined?

General Kentril continued, "Now, since these officers will show you what we expect of you, you will have thirty minutes today. Tomorrow you will be expected to finish in the allotted time. Understood?"

"Sir, yes, sir!" the girls responded.

"Be back in line in thirty minutes, no later. Dismissed." He blew his whistle, and the girls scattered to their designated areas.

When Lluava entered her barracks, she heard a whistle behind her. One of the officers strode down the aisle and yelled a command: "Stand next to your beds and clear the aisle!"

The girl that Lluava had slapped was at her own bed but seemed unwilling to meet Lluava's eyes. Was she embarrassed? Well, she shouldn't be. It was amazing that no others froze up like that. Even Lluava was surprised at how quickly she had taken action herself.

The officer, a daunting woman, proceeded to demonstrate how to make a bed. This included tucking the sheets so tightly that the officer claimed one could bounce a small pebble off of them. She then instructed them in keeping the area by their bunks clean. Luckily for the girls, they had not had time to be sloppy or dirty. They quickly made their beds and straightened their areas; the commander pulled apart any bed not made up to standard, and that girl had to start over. It took everyone at least three attempts before all did it right.

After completing that task, they dressed and lined up in front of the mess hall. Only a couple of other barracks had begun to line up when their group arrived. Within a few minutes, the rest of the girls— with the exception of one group which had found this task particularly troublesome— stood at attention.

Kentril and Ojewa soon arrived and examined the recruits' stances. When the last group finally arrived, Kentril explained, "We are starting daily laps around the compound. We will begin with five and will add one lap each week. You are expected to complete this at a quick jog, nothing less. Major Ojewa will lead the way, and I will make sure there are no stragglers." Kentril glared at the late arrivals which embarrassed the girls. "Do not be late again or you will receive extra laps."

"Now," Kentril continued, "When I blow this whistle, you will all follow Major Ojewa. Do not push each other; there is plenty of room."

The whistle sounded, and they were off.

Ojewa led them up to the front gates then turned right. They followed the wall past several lines of barracks, turned right again, and passed behind several training buildings. Yelling at anyone who slowed down too much, Kentril followed. They ran to the edge of the woods, then turned to follow the tree line until they came to the wall again. Turning right once more, Ojewa led them behind the backs of more buildings and barracks. Reaching the front gates, Ojewa yelled back, "Lap one complete!"

As they ran, Lluava made it her goal to stay at the heels of Ojewa. That was much harder than she thought, for he maintained a fast pace. Shortly after completing the third lap, Lluava slowed down. A pain in her side worsened the longer she ran, and her legs began to ache. A third of the way through the fourth lap, Lluava dropped back, and a dozen other girls moved ahead of her. As the fifth lap neared its end, she struggled to keep her spot in the front group. She could see the gate grow larger as she neared it, yet it still seemed to take forever before they finally passed it.

The group turned and continued to run down the main road toward the mess hall. Upon reaching it, Ojewa stopped and ordered them to line up. Lluava guessed where her position would be in the line when the rest of the girls finished their laps and filled in the gaps. Trying to catch her breath, she bent over. She could not remember ever having run that far, that fast. Her side burned.

"Pace yourself next time." Lluava looked up into Major Ojewa's dark face. "You must learn to pace yourself until you are used to this amount of running. It means nothing to be first if you cannot be ready for what follows."

Unlike the girls who were lining up, Ojewa had neither broken a sweat nor breathed hard; he might just as well have completed a pleasant stroll instead of five brisk laps around the training camp. Lluava felt beads of sweat roll down her back and neck and longed to be in shape like him. Standing next to him, Lluava realized that he did not have a hair on his head. This was strange; baldness was rare for a man in his latter thirties. He must shave his head. Yet why would a man want to remove his hair?

Kentril barked at the stragglers to hurry and start moving as they headed toward the already forming line. When he shouted for attention, the girls stood waiting. All around Lluava, recruits struggled to catch their breath.

"You have twenty minutes to eat your breakfast and be back here in formation! Dismissed!" Kentril huffed as the girls quickly filed into the mess hall. Lluava filled her plate with scrambled eggs, blueberries, and two strips of bacon. She was not used to eating such a variety of food at a morning meal, and it felt strange for her to do so. Taking a glass of water from the end of the table, Lluava sat down at the same solitary spot she had found the day before.

As she took her first bite of food, she heard Rosalyn call her name. "Lluava, you simply cannot eat by yourself. Come join my friends and me. We are at the far table, over there." She pointed to where four other girls were sitting. Smiling in her sweet way, Rosalyn gracefully carried her tray to the table.

Grateful to have others to sit with, Lluava decided to try to acquaint herself with her new bunkmate and her friends. Lluava crossed the chaos of the mess hall and sat down next to Rosalyn. Looking around at the other girls, she recognized two of them as Alison and Selphy. The other two were identical twins, in matching outfits—tan, button-front blouses and pale blue skirts. They had the same wavy, bright orange hair, the same blue-green eyes: even their freckles seemed to be in the same places on their faces.

Rosalyn made introductions. "Everyone, this is Lluava, my bunkmate." The girls around the table nodded to her. "Lluava, this is Shenne and Sonty," she said, pointing to the twins. "Alison." She pointed to the brash tall girl Lluava remembered. "And my best and oldest friend, Selphy."

The girl with the dusty-blonde hair looked up from hazelnut eyes and smiled. "I remember you," she said.

The girls talked of their travels, of why they had been chosen, and of their past lives. They asked Lluava where she was from and what she thought of this place. Lluava told them about kind Chat and jovial Byron. As they talked, Lluava felt more at ease and found that she looked forward to making new friends.

A whistle blew, loudly and clearly.

Kentril appeared at the entryway. "Move out!" he barked.

There was a mad scramble to scrape half-eaten food off plates and dump everything else in the wash bins on the way to the door. For the fourth time that day, the recruits lined up. They were already tired of standing at attention.

As if he had read their thoughts, Ojewa walked down the line, making sure everyone was standing properly.

Kentril's voice rang out. "At ease!" It took a moment before the girls realized that they were supposed to switch stances.

"Each one of you has been assigned to a group based upon your barracks, and each group has a different schedule," continued Kentril. "Schedules are posted in your barracks and on the mess hall door. By tomorrow morning, you must have memorized your schedule to the minute.

"Also, it is your duty to develop a connection with each member of your group. This will help you function as one unit, not twenty individuals. At the end of every week, groups will compete against each other. This is a test to see what you have learned during the week and to discover whether you can work together as a unit. Since this is your first day, and you are adjusting to your new life here, your schedule has been pushed back an hour. Tomorrow you will be expected to follow it at the indicated times. Is that clear?"

"Sir, yes, sir!" replied the girls.

"Now, ten at a time will look at their schedules and then proceed to your designated areas, starting with the girls at this end." He pointed at those nearest the door, and the first ten girls left to look at their schedules.

Lluava walked up to the posted lists. Each one was different, so she looked for the one with the large letter CA printed at the top.

CA

5:00 Wake Up	
5:15 Laps	
6:00 Breakfast	Mess Hall
6:20 Mathematics	Strat Bldg., Rm. 3
7:00 Military Strategies	Strat Bldg., Rm. 1
8:00 Mechanical Engineering	Strat Bldg., Rm. 6
9:00 Weight Training	Gym 1
10:30 Wound Management	Health Bldg., Rm. 2
12:30 Lunch	Mess Hall
1:00 Botany	Health Bldg., Rm. 1
2:00 Dual-Form Training	Gym 4
5:00 Field Training	Left Quadrant
7:00 Meditation	Health Bldg., Rm. 2
7:30 Dinner	Mess Hall
8:00 Personal Time	
9:00 Laps	
9:30 Lights Out	

As Lluava studied her schedule, a feeling that something was missing nibbled at her, but concerned with finding her room, she ignored it. She spotted a large building with a sign saying, "Strategies and Military Analysis." Entering, she noted that there were six rooms, each marked by a number. She had never been inside a schoolhouse with more than one room. Room 3 had several rows of wooden tables and benches; in front was a desk and a large blackboard. A single window was centered on the wall opposite the door.

She took a seat in the front row and waited for the other girls to arrive. They filtered in, singly and in small groups. Everyone stood up respectfully when one of the female officers entered and faced the class.

"Be seated," said the woman and turned to write on the board. "I am Corporal Shenar. We will start with Level Six Basic Mathematics."

Lluava had studied this already and was not challenged. At first, she was surprised at how many girls struggled with the lesson. But how many of these recruits had actually taken any upper level courses? Probably very few.

Class over, Lluava walked up the hall to the next one. The room was identical to the one she had just left, except that worn books already lay on the tables. General Kentril was seated at the front desk and writing notes. When the girls had all found seats—Lluava again choosing a spot at the front— Kentril began to discuss the basics of the course.

"In this class, you will study the military strategies of the past and those we use at present. You will learn the benefits of preparation, how to plan an attack, and how to run a regiment of your own.

"Let us begin. The books will be your aids to the rich history of warfare, both human and Theriomorph. Open them to Chapter One, The Origin of Warfare." Kentril waited for all to open their text books and then asked a petite girl with large eyes to read.

In a squeaky voice, she started to read. "Warfare began as soon as culture developed. When men desired land to farm and raise animals, they laid claim to it. Certain warfare arises from greed, the greed of gaining another person's land, wealth, and property. When a people cannot get what they want through negotiations and bargaining, they sometimes choose the path of war to force others to give them what they want. This greed for more and more leads to the destruction of countless lives and has been the downfall of many wondrous cultures...."

Lluava tried to take in all the information as it was presented. Some of this she knew from history classes, but much of it was new. She realized that learning thrilled her; perhaps she would enjoy being here after all.

She did not want to stop hearing about past battles and skirmishes, even though it was time to change classes. Yet, when she found a seat in the next room, she was already looking forward to the new subject. Just as before, textbooks were in place. Lluava opened hers as soon as she sat down. Another woman, this one with very short hair, welcomed them. "This course is tied to your field training class. What you learn here will be applied later today. For this reason, you need to pay attention. We will learn how to build rope bridges that will allow travel through the canopy. These structures will help the army move quickly and allow us to attack from above as well as below. If you open your text to Chapter Ten, you will find several diagrams for these structures. Discussion today will cover how these structures work and what makes them efficient...."

Lluava found the discussion of the mechanics of bridge structures particularly tedious. She struggled to concentrate, but, when class ended, she was happy to head to the next event, weight training.

The girls crossed the road to a large, circular clay structure and passed the wooden sign with "Gym 1" burned into its wooden siding. Lluava smiled as she headed into the building.

Once inside, she admired its structure. A thatched roof was supported by wooden beams that angled upward and met in the center. Evenly spaced windows encircled the large, open space which held a variety of strange objects, including a chair with a wooden rod above it. The rod, in turn, was attached to a rope looped around a wooden arch. On the other end of the rope was a large wooden bucket filled with stones of uniform size. There were four more of the same contraptions. On the far side of those strange seats were placed several benches; next to them were wooden staves with what looked like weighted bags on both ends. In the center of the room, five knotted ropes hung from a horizontal beam that spanned the ceiling.

After a moment, Major Ojewa strode in. Turning to the mass of wide-eyed girls, he announced, "You will start with ten push-ups, follow with twenty crunches, and end with ten push-ups. Make four rows of five and then start."

Lluava fell to the ground and began. At first, it seemed fairly easy, but she was glad when it was over.

Ojewa then divided the girls into three smaller groups. One group went to the benches, another to the ropes in the center; Lluava's group went to the strange seat contraptions. While Ojewa surveyed the girls' progress, a female officer worked each of the stations.

Lluava sat on the chair and grasped the wooden bar. Pulling it down lifted the weighted basket on the other end of the rope. At first, the bucket was empty, but, with each repetition, Ojewa placed another stone in it. After the sixth stone, she began to have difficulty. Told to pull the bar twenty times, Lluava broke into a sweat halfway through and had to force herself to finish the set. How much did those stones weigh? With a feeling of growing embarrassment, she expected far less that she would have liked. She knew she was stronger than the average girl, but having trouble with such a small collection was unacceptable.

When a group completed their sets at one station, they rotated to the next. Lluava moved to the benches and once again was one of the first girls up. As demonstrated by the major, Lluava lay down on a bench and was handed one of the poles. She knew as soon as she picked it up that the bags on each end were indeed weighted. She completed her two sets of fifteen lifts and then slowly rose. Her arms ached, and she held them close to her body.

A final rotation; this time, the girls went to the center of the room and the rope ladders. They were shown how to climb the ladder and touch a red dot painted on the beam at the top. The girls, five at a time—one on each rope—struggled to climb. Although some succeeded with relative ease, most had trouble climbing up the swaying rope because their arms were sore. Lluava nearly slipped when the rope moved sideways; she hoisted herself up one knot at a time. What should have taken one or two minutes now took her nearly five. Ojewa noted down the difficulty, weight levels, and times of each girl.

When they were finally released, the girls trudged over to the Health Building where Kara, the petite nurse who ran the infirmary, waited to teach the girls basic first aid. She absentmindedly brushed off her red apron, straightened her nurse's hat over her tight bun, and surveyed the exhausted girls.

As Nurse Kara wiped off the board behind her, Lluava overheard her mutter quietly to herself, "I hope Kentril doesn't wear these girls out. He knows this is what they have come here to learn." The nurse sighed and turned back to the class. "Everyone, pay attention! We will be discussing a great deal of information; as soon as possible, you will learn how to treat sick and injured people. You cannot afford to make a mistake when others' lives are in your hands, so concentrate. You will be expected to use your training in the upcoming war...."

All ears turned to the minuscule gray-haired lady, who began with basics and explained in excruciating detail minor wound management. With wonderful images of festering wounds and maggot-infested cuts fresh in their minds, the girls were sent off to their midday meal. For some reason, Lluava had no appetite and barely nibbled at her fruit plate.

After lunch, the girls made their way back to the Health Building. Nurse Kara strode briskly into the room and laid on the table a basket filled with leafy branches.

"Hello again, everyone," she chirped. "We will work on identifying local trees and their herbal healing properties...."

Lluava could not pay attention. Her mind wandered to thoughts of her family. She was less than thrilled at wasting her time like this. Why was any of it important? The hour seemed to drag on forever, and she was happy to leave the leaves and grasses on the tables and head to Gym 4.

Kentril was waiting for the girls to line up. He blew his whistle sharply. "One at a time, starting from the right, you will each change into your animal form. I want to see your forms: your species, color, and size. We are going to take your measurements so uniforms can be made. Also, it is important that you recognize each other's animal forms. For instance, I am a gorilla."

When Kentril blew his whistle twice, an old man stepped forward. His long grey and white beard almost touched the ground; half-moon spectacles were perched on his thin nose. He wore a deep green traveler's cloak with a measuring tape tied around his tan pants like a belt.

The man hobbled up to the first girl and measured from fingertip to fingertip. Then he measured the circumference of her chest and waist. Finally, he noted the girl's height and length from waist to heel. Kentril then told the girl to step behind the wooden divider and shift into her dual form. When she reappeared, she had turned into a smoky kitten. The tailor marked on his piece of paper the kitten's color and size measurements. He turned to the next girl and repeated the entire process. When he was finished, the girls were allowed to transform and dress.

When Rosalyn changed into an elegant swan, the tailor cooed, "Very pretty. Yes, very pretty." She flew gracefully behind the wooden slats. All eyes watched as the beautiful girl emerged.

Lluava was next. She fidgeted when the tailor's old fingers quickly moved around her body, making notes of her size. Walking behind the inch-thick wooden wall before transforming, she wished it were thicker. She removed her clothes and concentrated on shape shifting. It was not as easy for her as for the other girls, for she had not changed as often as they had. Her father had warned her of the dangers of her animal form, so she had avoided changing shape. She had been eleven years old the last time, running from a stampeding herd of cattle in a neighbor's field.

Although the process would take only a few seconds, it always seemed to last much longer. Concentrating, she felt the heat build from inside her very soul, growing and growing until every part of her body burned. A sharp pain erupted from her spine; she heard cracking sounds, and her skin seemed to boil and bubble and ooze into a different shape. The sharp pains increased as her bones reformed and switched places; her gut twisted as her organs realigned in her new body. She tasted blood as sharp teeth erupted from her gums and the others dissolved. More cracking sounds occurred as her skull distorted and reformed. The pain was overwhelming, and she fell on all fours when her tail burst forth. Although pain blurred her vision, she could still make out the white and black fur sprouting from her skin. She lay still, panting, until the pain crept away.

Kentril heard the gasps of the girls and looked up as a large white tigress emerged from behind the divider. His jaw dropped. His eyes remained on Lluava as the tailor quickly scribbled notes. Rosalyn, too, caught her breath at the beast that slept above her bed.

Lluava saw the fear in the eyes of the girls and the men; she could taste the fear in the air. Her heart beat faster. An inner whispering encouraged her to run, but she did not understand and tried to ignore it. She approached the girls, but they backed away. Kentril was shouting at her. She tried to concentrate, tried to listen to what he was saying, but his words made no sense. She moved toward him, trying to figure out what he meant. She made out only a couple of words: *change, away, help*.

Was he in trouble? She wanted to help but did not know what was wrong. The tension in the air increased, which only agitated her further. She felt as if she were being smothered; she had to escape. A voice in her head began screaming, "Run, run!" She turned toward the door, but several officers ran in and closed the door behind them.

Lluava needed to flee, but her way out was blocked. Panic engulfed her; she *had* to be free. Leaping toward the drill sergeant, she tried to make him understand that she had to escape. The tall man grabbed the hilt of his sword, and she backed away, knowing, somehow, that he intended to hurt her. A roar emerged from her throat. Screams sounded throughout the room. Another pain erupted as small, sharp objects pierced her rump.

Lluava turned to defend herself. A sleek black panther faced her, one forepaw outstretched and claws extended. The dark beast snarled at her. She snarled back. Each tensed, waiting for the other to make a move. It was time to fight.

Chapter 6
...You Question Its Motives

The two large felines circled one another. Not daring to turn away, Lluava locked eyes with her opponent. She sensed the panther was not trying to hurt her. He hissed, and Lluava backed up. He was herding her to the corner behind the divider. She would be trapped, yet she did not resist. Crouching in the dark area between the wooden slats and the wall, Lluava felt her rear paw slip. She risked a quick, backward glance.

Her paw had landed upon a pile of clothes, her clothes. Then she remembered. And as she turned back toward the black panther, its fur suddenly regressed back into its skin, skin that loosened and melded like clay into the muscular body of Ojewa, dressed only in black shorts.

As Ojewa turned away, Lluava allowed her shape to shift, and then dressed her slim, human body. Embarrassed, she walked back to the girls. Several gave her dark looks; others seemed not to be able to look at her at all. Rosalyn leaned close and whispered, "It will be all right. You have done nothing wrong." General Kentril's look of disdain indicated otherwise.

"Back in line," he commanded. After telling the tailor to continue, he turned to the rest of the girls. "This is why we have this session. If you don't already know, the longer you stay in dual form, the more like that animal you become. You must not succumb to your inner beast. If you forget that you are Theriomorph, you will live the rest of your life in animal form. In this class, you will learn to transform quickly and to stay in your animal form for extended periods of time without yielding to any animal urges."

Lluava's face reddened, and she wished she could disappear. For the remainder of the class, the students were timed to see how fast they could transform. Lluava noted that both Kentril and Ojewa were on high alert when she shifted.

Afterward, the girls followed Ojewa down the trail that led through the woods to the field training grounds. As they walked, Lluava and Rosalyn pointed out to each other a variety of ropes, levies, ramps, and oddly shaped objects scattered among the trees. After a surprisingly long walk, the trail ended at a large wooden stable. In the back was a corral where three horses were tied up.

"Each of you must know how to ride a horse with ease," Ojewa stated. "By the end of today, you will know how to mount and dismount. In several weeks, your first exam will require you to trot. But first, one must be able to confidently remain on a moving steed." Lluava could stay on a horse but had never dared control the tempo of the animal.

In groups of three, the girls mounted the horses and attempted to ride them in a circle around the corral. Rosalyn, Lluava, and a third girl rode together. Lluava mounted her brown mare with ease and started her horse at a walk. As she gained confidence, she glanced at Rosalyn on a pretty dappled pony, who was effortlessly riding sidesaddle. All upper-class ladies were taught to ride in that fashion, but Lluava had never seen it done. This answered some of her questions about her new bunkmate. Rosalyn must be from a wealthy, upper-class family that had conformed to human culture. How else could she speak in such a refined manner, ride her horse with effortless grace, and afford lovely dresses and skirts? As much as she hated the idea of Theriomorphs emulating human culture, Lluava could not help her growing fondness for this sweet-natured girl.

Afterward, the girls rejoined other groups lining up in rows in the central yard. Ojewa demonstrated a variety of strange stretches. One of the hardest involved sitting on the ground with legs straight out in front and then grasping the feet and pulling the head down to rest on the knees. Lluava could not reach her toes. She grabbed her calves in frustration and pulled hard for a minute. For the "plow," the girls lay on their backs, then swung their legs over their heads and touched their toes to the ground. As if that wasn't bad enough, they had to hold the position for two minutes. Ojewa explained that they should be able to bring their knees down to rest on the ground by the side of their heads. They worked on a dozen more complicated stretches before heading to dinner.

Cramped, sore, and tired, the girls had to make themselves eat. Lluava took a piece of bread and put it in her pocket for later. After dinner, the girls had free time. Some relaxed in their barracks; others congregated in the gym, set with chairs and benches so the girls could become acquainted. This socialization was essential to building the bond between each girl and her group. In order to work as one unit, the girls had to trust each other. Time spent together would allow that strong trust to grow.

Lluava followed Rosalyn and her friends back to the barracks where they decided to play a card game. Lluava had never played cards; her mother had said the family could not afford to "waste money" on games. Lluava's toys had consisted of a small ball and a rag doll her mother made. Lluava had not minded the lack of material things; it had encouraged her to be creative and invent ways to entertain herself. Now she wished she had learned the town children's games instead of pretending that she did not want to play.

"How about Cat and Mouse?" Rosalyn asked, pulling out her playing cards. She dealt out six piles of seven cards.

Lluava watched as Selphy, Alison, and the twins each picked up a pile. Lluava followed suit and stared at the cards. "I…I don't know how to play."

"You must be kidding me!" Alison was wide-eyed. "This is the best-known game there is. It's played by everyone from the common street merchant all the way up to the king himself!"

Lluava blushed.

"Hush, Alison," Rosalyn reprimanded her friend. "It is really very simple, Lluava. I will help you."

It took several games, but with Rosalyn's help, Lluava began to grasp the idea. In the seventh round, she happily discovered that she held the winning hand. As she leaned over to display her cards, the siren sounded, startling the girls. Lluava dropped her cards, scattering them all over the floor.

"What now?" Selphy moaned as they hastily picked up the cards.

"Was there something else we were supposed to do?" Shenne asked.

"Yeah. We're running again," Sonty sighed.

"Let's go," said Lluava. "We don't want to be late."

The girls quickly made their way to the central yard along with the girls from the other barracks. Kentril blew his whistle.

"Time to run, chickadees," he said. "You will make the same loop you did this morning. Ojewa will not be leading you this time, but I will make sure none of you fall behind. Five laps. Go!"

As girls made their loops, Lluava tried to stay in the lead group. She knew she would not improve unless she pushed herself. The pain in her side returned halfway through, but she kept herself from falling behind. After the run, the girls were sent back to their barracks and told to get some sleep. They would be awakened at five on the dot.

That night, the nagging sense of something missing kept Lluava awake for a long time. She must have fallen asleep, for the blaring siren let her know that her second day had begun.

This day was a bit easier. She learned about the Code of Chivalry, the mechanics of making a longbow, the treatment of burns, and the benefits of maple trees in natural healing. In dual-form training, she practiced shifting again and again. Eventually she was able to stay in tiger form without feeling the need to run or protect herself. She rode a black stallion in field training and practiced new stretches.

Once again, the feeling that something was being held back kept sleep at bay. The following day, as she watched Rosalyn practice bandaging a girl's leg in wound management class, the answer came to her. If this was a training camp, why weren't they being trained to fight and defend? Where was the weaponry, the swords, bows, spears? How were they supposed to go into battle if they were taught everything *except* how to fight?

Lluava turned to Rosalyn, who was examining the leg of the "patient" and asked, "Do you have a feeling that something's missing here?"

Concentrating on pretending to clean the wound, Rosalyn replied, "I do not know what you mean."

Lluava followed her bunkmate as she went to the cabinet on the far side of the room to fetch bandages. "Don't you think it's strange that we are supposed to be training for an upcoming war, and we haven't even seen a weapon or been told what to do in a combat situation?"

Rosalyn began wrapping the leg, "It is odd, but I trust that the superiors are running this place as they should. Actually, I am glad that I do not have to wield a weapon. I would be terrified."

Lluava was about to respond when Nurse Kara walked by to view their group's progress. "Make the bandage tighter. You need a good amount of pressure to stop the bleeding," Kara trilled before moving to the next group.

Lluava whispered to Rosalyn, "Don't you want to know how to fight?"

There was a pause as Rosalyn started to rewrap the leg and then she said very quietly, "No, I do not want to fight. I would rather be in the background helping the injured. I could not take a life…even to defend my own."

Thinking about this statement, Lluava kept quiet. Could she take a life? That's what she would be doing when the war began. Maybe she shouldn't push the issue any further.

For the rest of the week, Lluava attended classes and tried to take in all the information. She did not pursue the subject of combat. All the other girls seemed carefree about their training. They did not seem worried, and, as the week came to a close, all looked forward to the seventh day, their day off.

That night, Lluava dreamt of home. In the dream she was walking up the dirt road to her house. The gate was not only unlocked, but it swung open as if to welcome her. Looking lovingly at her home, she realized that it seemed to have an orange glow, which made it stand out against the pitch black sky. The aura around the house grew brighter and brighter. Soon a reddening light shone from all the windows and the open door. It was a beautiful sight, and Lluava could not turn away from it.

A thick scent wafted through the air. As soon as she smelled it, her heart sank. She tried to run toward her house but could not make herself move. She could not lift her legs; when she tried to speak, no words came out. All she could do was stand and watch as flames engulfed her home. The fire not only burned through wood and a lifetime of memories but also into her very soul. Unable to contain herself any longer, she let out an ear-piercing scream—a scream that mingled with the shrill screech of the siren. She awoke to the wretched sound that announced the beginning of a new day.

While Lluava was relieved to awaken from her nightmare, she was not happy that on their day of rest they were not allowed to sleep. Grumpily, she lay on her bunk and recalled the events of her dream. As her mind cleared of sleep, she made a decision: she could not let it happen. She realized that the only way to protect her family would be to fight. Today she would find General Kentril and demand to know why the girls were not being trained for war. She resolved to talk to the general that afternoon.

Unwilling to fall back to sleep like the other girls, she decided to go for her daily run. She crept off her bunk quietly so as not to disturb Rosalyn.

Between the exercise and the cool morning air, any lingering sleepiness vanished. As she ran, she thought she saw a tall figure standing between the barracks. Without slowing down, Lluava glanced at the area again, but now no one was there. Was that Ojewa? Why would he watch her and not want her to know?

Finishing her jog easily, she headed to breakfast. It seemed that most girls had opted to sleep rather than eat, for only a fraction of the girls were in the mess hall. Lluava ate quietly and then wandered around the camp. Discovering a young maple growing next to Gym 1, she scrambled up and scooted along a branch until she was close to the roof. Hoisting herself up, she made her way to the peak of the roof and surveyed her surroundings.

She could see over the tall wall. To her right, the abysmally hot Sudn Plains stretched to the southern edge of the kingdom. The hilly landscape to the west became the Verta Mountains. The road leading back to Rivendale lay to the north, as did Durog. She wondered how Chat was doing? Towering over the camp like a sleeping sentinel, Burok Dûr, the lonely mountain, rose behind Durog. Though far away, the mountain still blocked part of the sky. She turned her attention eastward, where ocean met land somewhere beyond the dense forest.

Her visual map complete, Lluava climbed down and searched for Rosalyn. She found her in the barracks chatting with Selphy. They seemed to be having a serious talk, so Lluava decided not to intrude. Instead, she made her way to the gym and did her weight training exercises. Afterward she met her new friends, and they happily ate lunch together. When she finished, she stood to leave.

"Where are you heading?" Rosalyn inquired.

"I want to speak with General Kentril about something that has been bothering me."

"Is everything all right?" Rosalyn seemed genuinely concerned.

"Yeah, fine. I just want to have a word with him."

This seemed to satisfy Rosalyn.

"Well, after your meeting, you must play some more Cat and Mouse,"

Selphy said as Lluava turned to leave.

"Sure," she replied, at last making her exit.

Lluava found the general's barracks and entered after knocking. She admired the large hickory staircase that branched off from the right side of the entryway. The rest of the hall was lined with doors made from the same dark hickory as the stairs.

"Hello?" Lluava called out. Her voice echoed down the hall. When no one replied, she wandered inside. Portraits of men in military uniforms hung between each doorframe. She wondered if they were past drill sergeants of Thowcelemine. She was admiring a painting of one man with long whiskers—something Theriomorphs rarely grew—when she heard someone call her name.

Turning toward the voice, Lluava saw General Kentril leaning out the door she had just passed. "I thought that was you," he said. "Come in." He waved her through the door into his office, where a large wingback chair stood next to a wooden desk. Scattered papers, ink quills, and a partially unrolled map covered the top of the wooden desk. A mismatched pair of chairs faced each other like two opponents. The larger one was upholstered in the finest of leathers, while the other was wooden and plain.

"Take a seat," Kentril said, sitting down in his tall chair.

Lluava acquiesced, glancing around the room at the variety of landscape paintings.

"Do you like them? I paint in my spare time," said the general.

"They're yours? They're beautiful," Lluava said admiringly.

Kentril smiled. "For what is it you came?"

"I want to know why you aren't teaching us to fight. This program does everything but teach us to wield a weapon. If there is going to be a war, and we are the defenders, we need to know how to fight. Yet, you have not breathed even one word about hand-to-hand combat. It seems almost as if you were trying to shelter us."

The smile slipped from Kentril's face. "Lluava, you must trust the decisions we have made. There is more to a war than brute force." At her blank stare, Kentril continued. "In short, our plans are to merge Theriomorph camps with human camps after the recruits have reached a certain point in their training. When this happens, each Theriomorph will be paired with a human partner. The pairs will learn to use their combined strengths and abilities before the war begins. The military leaders agree that if we are going to defeat this oncoming threat, it is crucial that human and Theriomorph work together and have full trust in one another."

Lluava considered this but was not deterred by Kentril's response. "You still have not answered my question. Why are we not being trained for battle?"

Kentril sighed. "You are. You are learning to help the injured, to strategize, to think before you act. These are attributes needed in war. Not everyone can be a warrior. Thowcelemine is training those who will not be sent onto the field of battle. The young men at Durog will be the warriors. Not you. Not anyone here."

Lluava's jaw dropped. Struggling to keep her voice steady, she said quietly, "I may be a girl, but that doesn't mean that I cannot fight. I can do anything, *anything*, that a man does. Do you hear me? I came here to protect my family, to fight for what is right, not to watch others risk their lives for my freedom!"

"Hush, Lluava," Kentril said, trying to calm her. "It may be true that *you* have the potential to be as strong as a man, but they do not who train with you, who sleep next to you, who eat with you. I am not prejudiced, nor are the other Theriomorphs who made these decisions. It was the humans, not us, who decided to separate recruits by gender. Durog is the camp for those who will train to be solders on the front line. Thowcelemine is not meant for that. This camp was created to support those who fight.

"Lluava, you know Theriomorphs do not make the same distinctions between genders that humans do. Although you will not be trained to fight, you will be trained to lead. Your classes in military strategy, mathematics, and engineering are educating those of you who will make the plans and develop the strategies needed during the war. Our graduates will make advancements in our weaponry, and most important, they will save the lives of injured solders. We are training you for these purposes. Although these roles are not the same as those of warriors trained to kill, without the abilities, talents, and dedication of Thowcelemine's females, we will not have a chance of winning. As an overgeneralization, Durog will produce the muscle; we are creating the brain."

It was clear to Lluava that the old culture had not been entirely altered by human beliefs. The idea that the leader–female figure still held some power in this military social structure pleased her.

"I understand," continued Lluava, still determined, "but why do you separate us based on gender?"

"We did not separate based on gender; we separated based on physical strength, and it happens to split along those lines." Lluava scowled, yet Kentril went on. "Think of all the Theriomorphs you know. What are their dual forms? Do you notice any difference between the forms of males and those of females?"

Lluava thought about the Dryson brothers, who owned the smithy in Rivendale. The burly men's forms were an ox and a water buffalo. Ojewa was a black panther; her father had been a timber wolf. Then she thought of Rosalyn and her swan form, Selphy and Alison as doe and butterfly, and her mother's white duck form.

Kentril asked again, "Do you see any difference?"

After a long pause, Lluava answered. "Their animal forms. There is some sort of difference."

"Yes. Typically, female forms are weaker animals, prey animals, small and docile. Males are more aggressive, stronger, large herbivores or predators. Because we use the animal form to fight, that form must be a strong one. This is why it was decided to bring females here and males to Durog."

"Wait," Lluava responded. "My form is a tiger. That's a large predator. Where do I fit in?"

"It is true that you are different from the other girls," Kentril said coolly. "You happen to be one of the few exceptions to the rule."

This new truth made Lluava feel even more removed from those around her. Although she had never been accepted by humans, she had never cared to be. But now she had discovered that she was not exactly like other Theriomorphs, either. She listened reluctantly.

"What you must understand," Kentril added, "is that this system has worked perfectly for decades. I cannot change the rules for one individual. You must remain here."

Lluava's hopes dimmed.

"If it is any consolation, we will begin teaching the recruits defensive methods next week. Although we will not place you on the field of battle, we need all of you to know how to protect yourselves in the event that the battle comes to you."

He stood. "I must go now. You know the way out."

Lluava stood up quietly and left the room, though not before noticing Kentril shaking his head. As she walked down the hall, the faces on the canvases seemed to scowl darkly at her, as if she were some harbinger of doom.

She was almost at the entryway when a form quickly stepped from the shadows by the stairway and blocked the door. The sudden movement made her jump.

"You must develop quicker reflexes and a keener sense of what is around you," Ojewa advised.

"It wouldn't be worth anything if I did," Lluava muttered.

"You must not give up, either," replied the tall man smoothly.

Lluava realized that he must have overheard her conversation with Kentril. That he had observed her without her knowledge made her uneasy.

"Follow me," Ojewa stated in a commanding tone as he slipped out the door.

Lluava followed, unsure why she did so. Although he seemed to walk at a slow pace, she almost had to jog to keep up with him. She followed him to the southern wall, and then through the forest until they reached a clearing.

"We are here," he stated. "Stay."

As Ojewa walked to the edge of the woods, Lluava admired the semicircle of grass, hidden by the forest and marked by the wall. The grass is too short to be wild, she thought. Someone must have cut it. But for what purpose?

She turned back to the forest just as she felt the point of a sword at her neck, the cold steel ready to slice into her skin.

Ojewa's felid eyes stared down at her. In a barely audible voice, he purred, "Too slow."

Chapter 7
Point of No Return

Lluava's mouth went dry and her mind raced. Why would Ojewa want to harm her? Had she offended him? Did Kentril have something to do with this? Was he punishing her? Or was this because she was different from the other Theriomorphs?

Her body went rigid. She tried to swallow. Ojewa continued to stare at her. His top lip curled back, exposing his fanged teeth.

Again he hissed, "Too slow. Next time, pay attention to your surroundings. Every sight. Every sound. Every touch, smell, and taste. That is the only way you will survive."

Ojewa removed the sword from Lluava's neck. Backing away hastily, she touched her throat, expecting to feel blood.

"I did not cut you," he stated flatly.

"What in the pits of the seven hells possessed you to do that?" Lluava demanded, backing still farther away from him.

Ojewa smiled in an inhuman way, his two top canines protruding over his lower lip. "Technically, you may not be allowed to pursue your wish to be a great warrior, but there is another way. A secret way. I sense that you are meant to play a major role in the war. For this reason, I offer you an opportunity to learn the arts of war from me. This will be your training ground...if you wish to continue on this path."

Debating whether or not to trust him, Lluava slowly let her hand slip from her neck. He had had the chance to kill her, yet he had not.

"I would be...honored," she responded cautiously.

"That is good," said Ojewa. He came toward her quickly and placed his hand upon her shoulder. The suddenness of his action made her want to back away, but she stood her ground. She needed to trust him.

"This must be kept between us," Ojewa continued. "General Kentril, as you have discovered, would not approve and would demand an end to your training. Your day is already filled with assignments, so we will meet at night. During your hour of free time, you must slip away from the rest of the recruits and come here. This is where I will train you to fight. This is where you will learn to be a great warrior."

Lluava looked into the depths of Ojewa's black eyes, searching for the hint of truth.

"What do I have to do?" she asked.

"As I said, come tomorrow during your allotted free time. I will provide the rest." Both regarded each other once more before Ojewa said, "You may go now."

It was a command, not a suggestion, so she left. This time, she listened hard for any sound that might indicate Ojewa was on the attack.

For the remainder of the day, Lluava was in a daze. That night, as she stared at the thatched roof, she could not remember what had occurred after she had left Ojewa in the forest. She must have eaten, for she was full; she must have spent time with the other girls because she was with them when she climbed into her bunk. Everything else was a blur.

Lluava did not know when she fell asleep or when she awoke, but she was out of bed before the alarm sounded. She did not feel tired. Restlessness had taken control of her. She needed to move and was very happy when morning laps began.

At breakfast, although she was not hungry, she forced herself to eat; although she could not concentrate on them, she made herself go to classes. But when she met Ojewa for her field training class, her senses seemed to click into place. He explained the importance of defending oneself and one's surrounding allies, and he demonstrated several different ways to dodge a punch. Although most of the day's lesson involved listening, she paid close attention to every detail.

Lluava discovered that the talk of combat thrilled her, and she began to look forward to her rendezvous in the clearing. Her afternoon classes seemed to drag on forever. After gulping down dinner, she almost ran from the mess hall to make her way to the forest.

Silhouetted in the moonlight, Ojewa was waiting. The stars seemed to twinkle in expectation. He stood like a lithe animal waiting for unsuspecting prey to pass by close enough for the kill. As she approached, he appeared almost happy. Was it possible that he was pleased to have a personal pupil, someone to whom he could pass on his knowledge?

Expecting him to hand her a sword or some other weapon, Lluava stopped a few feet away, but he, watching her, just stood there.

After a few moments of silence, "Begin," was all he said.

"What about weapons? I thought you were going to teach me how to fight? Where is the sword? The knife?" Lluava did not understand.

"*You* are the best weapon. There is no need for an artificial aid. First, you must learn to let yourself become the weapon. When there is nothing but yourself with which to fight, you must know how to fight hand to hand." He waited for her to digest this information. Then he said once more, "Begin."

Lluava's muscles tensed. She waited for him to do something, but he just stood there watching her. After a minute, she guessed that he wanted her to attack, so she ran at the dark figure before her and tried to swing at his stomach.

She neither saw nor felt anything hit her, but she was instantly face down on the ground. Spitting dirt from her mouth and wiping off her face, she heard Ojewa say, "Never make the first move."

"What? I thought you wanted me to come at you." Lluava spat sand and dirt from between her teeth.

"I want you to learn. Never attack first because the other person can read your movements and will move aside just as I did. If I had had a weapon, you would be dead. Let's try again."

Lluava waited this time, yet still Ojewa did not move. Minutes passed. At last, he took a step toward her. She attacked, staying low and going for his side. Again, she hit the ground, making a complete somersault before stopping. This time, although he did not seem to have made a move, she had felt a slight push. Her head began to ring. Ojewa helped her up.

"What…what was that?" she stammered.

Ojewa's smile only aggravated her. Was he teasing her? Did he find this funny? She could feel herself becoming agitated.

"A good warrior uses the least amount of energy and force to fight his battles. When you came toward me, all I had to do was observe the direction in which you were moving and step aside. I turned your energy against you by moving to the side and then pulling you in the direction you were already headed. This extra energy caught you off guard, and I was able to flip you with ease. Try again."

Lluava waited until Ojewa stepped toward her before she took off. She ran to the right, then quickly dodged left. Ojewa must have anticipated her move, because he abruptly stuck out his leg and tripped her. She stumbled and tried to catch her balance, but Ojewa swiftly swung his arm and hit her in the chest, knocking her onto her back. After a moment of reflection, she winced and slowly rose.

"Good attempt. I am glad that you are trying not to make the same mistake twice. This time I will run at you; use my energy against me."

Lluava was happy not to be the one falling to the ground. When Ojewa came at her, she quickly sidestepped and pushed him. Of course, he had expected such a move, and as soon as he hit the ground, he sprang to his feet and drop-kicked her. She found herself becoming well acquainted with the ground.

"Up!" he exhorted and then went on to explain what she had done wrong this time. "You must pay attention to your opponent as a whole, not just his arms and legs." Sensing her annoyance, he switched tactics. "If someone grabs you," he said, taking hold of Lluava's shirt, "drop your body low in a crouch. This will help you keep your balance and will make it much harder for someone to manipulate you. Try it."

For the rest of the hour, Ojewa demonstrated different blocks and defenses along with an offensive move. By the session's end, Lluava was thoroughly sore in both her body and her pride. She thanked Ojewa for his time and tried not to limp as she left.

Lluava was eager to reach her barracks, but, as she placed her hand on the doorknob, the siren shrilled. She thought of ditching the night run but knew she could not let on that anything unusual had happened. Gathering her remaining strength, she walked with the other girls to the square. Choosing not to be in the front this time, she completed her laps, but she struggled to keep a steady pace.

After painfully completing her run, Lluava trudged back to the barracks and her bed. She intended to fall asleep in the soiled clothes she was wearing, too exhausted to care that she had not showered. As she climbed carefully onto her bunk and reached for her sheets, she spotted two small stacks of clothes neatly piled on her pillow. She wondered if she was so tired that she had entered the wrong barracks, but she knew this could not be true.

Picking up a solid white shirt with very short sleeves, she asked aloud, "What is this?"

"What is what, Lluava?" Rosalyn asked, sliding off her bed so she could take a look. "Oh, those," she giggled. "Those are our new uniforms. You left in such a hurry after dinner and did not come back with us. Everyone received a set, and we were told those are what we are supposed to wear while we are here."

Lluava admired the V-necked shirt in her hands. This material was thinner and lighter than what she was used to wearing. It had a more comfortable feel to it. She looked at the rest of the clothes. There was another short-sleeved shirt in white and one in black. Underneath these were one white and one black tank top. A long white jacket and a long-sleeved shirt were at the bottom of the stack. In the other pile were three pairs of shorts, two white and one black. There were also a pair of white pants, a small rimless hat that molded to her skull, and a bottom and a top of what looked like undergarments. She picked up the last two things and asked, "What are these?"

Rosalyn, who had been watching Lluava shuffle through her new clothes, explained, "They are supposedly swimwear. We all have a pair although I do not know if I could wear mine in public."

"We're supposed to swim in these? No. No. Definitely not! This barely covers anything. No way!" Lluava quickly put them at the bottom of the pile. She grabbed all the clothes, climbed down, and placed them carefully in her trunk. Next to it, she noticed a pair of shoes made out of the strange, light material. Too worn-out to think more about these new gifts, Lluava found just enough strength to swing the curtain around and change into her nightwear. She was so tired that she fell asleep almost instantly after slipping under her sheet.

The next day was a blur. The only memorable event was getting dressed in her new clothes. Looking around, Lluava noticed that all the girls seemed to have received different-colored wardrobes, and all the sets except hers were one color. Rosalyn's were all white, while the two girls across from her wore a light pink set and a bright blue one. She chose to wear the white short-sleeved shirt and black shorts.

When darkness fell, she slipped out of the dining hall to meet Ojewa, who was already waiting.

"How do you like your new garments?" he inquired.

"They're very comfortable," Lluava answered honestly, for the clothes were indeed lighter and softer than those she was used to. "Of what are they made? I don't recognize the material."

"The cloth is *endun*. Only a few weavers and tailors know how it is made. It was once thought to be magical, blessed by the gods, because when you change into your bestial form, it will stay on you and form as part of that animal."

"What?" Lluava could not understand what Ojewa meant.

"Let me show you." In seconds, he had shifted to his black panther form. His clothes seemed to become part of the animal until there was no sign that he had been wearing any. A minute later, Ojewa, his black shorts and tank still clinging to him, reverted to his humanoid form.

"That's amazing!" exclaimed Lluava.

"Theriomorphs have made this cloth for centuries. It was intended as a warrior's uniform, flexible and light so it does not constrict movement, yet very strong."

"Why have I not heard of it?" inquired Lluava.

"When the humans conquered our people, Theriomorph weavers were commissioned to make these for the Theriomorphs serving as Elysian soldiers and no one else. In time, the common folk forgot that once we wore clothes made from endun."

"It's a shame that our people are forgetting our past."

"In a way, it is."

"I have another question."

"Ask."

"Why is there no standard color for everyone's uniforms? I have seen a whole rainbow of colors today."

Ojewa almost smiled. "Have you not figured that out? The tailors try to provide colors as close as possible to the shade of the person's animal form."

The kaleidoscope of colors suddenly made sense. At lunch, she had seen Selphy in a tan suit, while Alison wore orange, and Rosalyn was dressed in pure white. It also explained why her clothes were white and black.

"One last question," she said.

"What is it?"

"Do I really have to wear the 'ran-out-of-material' swimwear? It'll look like I'm swimming in my undergarments!"

Her statement caught Ojewa off guard. He laughed. And then the night's training began.

The following day, Lluava slipped away after dinner, but just as she was heading to the forest, she heard someone call to her. She turned quickly and saw Rosalyn.

"I want to know what you have been doing the past couple of nights. You disappear after dinner only to reappear before our run, exhausted and filthy. Furthermore, someone should probably look at those bruises and cuts all over your arms and legs. I am worried about you. Tell me the truth. What are you up to?"

Lluava could see the concern marring Rosalyn's pretty face. There was something about her that made Lluava trust her and feel at ease around her. Before she knew it, Lluava was explaining everything to her friend.

"Okay. You know I went to talk to General Kentril?" Rosalyn nodded. "Well, I asked him why he wasn't teaching us fighting skills. He gave me his reasons, and, after I left, Major Ojewa stopped me. He told me that he would secretly teach me how to fight. That's what I have been doing at night and what I am about to do now. Please don't tell anyone. If word gets out, both Major Ojewa and I could be in a lot of trouble."

Lluava could see the disapproval in her friend's face. "I will keep your secret," Rosalyn promised, "because I do not want to see you hurt. Not because I approve of what you are doing."

"Thank you," Lluava replied honestly. Then, alone, she made her way to the clearing.

When she saw Ojewa, she felt as if she had somehow failed him. Did he know she had exposed their secret? But their sparring began, and she pushed the question to the back of her mind.

That night, Lluava slept easily. Her world seemed to be falling into place. The trust she had placed in Rosalyn was blooming into a strong friendship. She knew she was thriving and learning a great many new things. Even training to become a warrior felt strangely right. Although Lluava missed her family, the loss of her old life did not affect her as much as she had thought it would. They were safe and they would be so as long as Lluava kept true to this new path she was on.

Two days later, the entire camp stirred and buzzed like a giant beehive with news. That morning, everyone had lined up in a new format, each group forming an individual square, each square lined up next to another until they formed a large rectangle. Instead of the whistle to signal their morning run, Kentril stood in front of the entire regiment.

"Attention! The run has been canceled. What I am about to tell you is more important," he announced authoritatively.

Glad not to have to do their laps, several girls began to murmur in excitement.

"Silence!" shouted Kentril. Everyone quieted immediately.

"As you know, exams are held on the sixth day of the week. Tomorrow you will take your first exam. Unlike school exams, which measure individual accomplishments, this will challenge your strength as a group and your trust in each other. You will show that you can apply what you have learned in your first two weeks.

"Four barracks at a time will compete with each other in a relay race on an obstacle course. Each barracks will pick four contenders to represent them in the competition. Choose well. These contenders must be smart, physically strong, and able to think on their feet. Tomorrow morning, I will ask your teams to step to the front. Is this clear?"

"Sir, yes, sir!" was the unanimous response.

"Good." Kentril scanned the entire regiment, eyes briefly pausing on several particular recruits. "Classes will be dismissed early to allow you time to select your representatives. Now, eat and go to class."

As soon as they were released, the noise of hundreds of chattering girls erupted. Excitement and anticipation arose from every person in the camp. Lluava was also swept away in the moment and spoke excitedly with the other girls from her barracks.

"I bet it's going to be in the forest," Lluava declared.

"Why do you think that?" asked Allison, spooning porridge into her mouth.

"They already have all those contraptions spread out in there. It would be a good place to run around because it's not in the open. Plus, it's the only area far enough away from these buildings to have the feel of a combat mission."

"Combat mission?" repeated one of the twins.

The other one asked, "Why did you say that?"

Lluava still could not tell the two apart. "Well, we are being trained for war, and I believe this is testing us on those kinds of skills."

The others agreed. Many of the girls, including Lluava, found it hard to concentrate that day. Even the teachers were preoccupied with the next day's events.

After lunch, as they headed to botany class, Selphy pulled Lluava to the side.

"I know your secret," she whispered in Lluava's ear. "I know what you have been doing every night."

Lluava's heart raced. Rosalyn must have betrayed her! She knew that Selphy and Rosalyn were best friends and had grown up with each other, but she had trusted Rosalyn not to tell anyone what she and Ojewa were doing.

Seeing that Lluava was upset, Selphy tried to help. "It is all right. I won't tell. You can trust me."

Lluava was having doubts about trusting anyone at that moment.

Selphy continued, "I, too, used to have problems with my classes. There is nothing to be ashamed of when you get help. Academic problems can be overcome. You'll see. Don't worry."

This took Lluava by surprise. Rosalyn had not broken her promise after all. She almost laughed but sighed instead. She had worked hard for years to earn her reputation as one of the smarter students, and, in a single day, it had all been undone.

Oh, well, Lluava thought, cunning and a warrior's prowess were not usually thought of together. She turned to Selphy and said, "Thank you for understanding."

"Of course," responded Selphy. "And if you need any other help, I am here. I am really good with botany, by the way."

"I'll remember that," Lluava replied as they entered the classroom.

During meditation class, she barely heard Ojewa's whispered message as he passed: "Do not meet tonight." Lluava assumed he wanted her to be with her group when they picked the candidates to race. So, for the first time that week, she followed the girls to the barracks after dinner.

Everyone gathered to discuss who would race tomorrow. Two girls volunteered right away. One was a tall redhead named Raien, and the other was a petite brunette called Elean.

"We need two more candidates," Raien said. "Does anyone else want to volunteer? If not, we will have to vote on two more."

The girls grew quiet and looked at one another; each hoped someone else would volunteer. Lluava hesitated. She had no experience in pushing herself to the forefront. If anything, her school experience in Rivendale had made her cautious about drawing attention to herself.

"I will do it," announced Rosalyn.

Lluava was surprised. Rosalyn seemed too fragile to participate in anything very physical.

"Anyone else?" Raien asked.

When no one volunteered, she said, "Okay. We need to vote. Who would be a good candidate?"

"Lluava would," chimed in the quiet girl she had "saved" that first day.

Before Lluava could protest, several other girls agreed.

"Yes," Raien said. "Lluava should be our fourth candidate." She turned to Lluava. "You are obviously one of the strongest and most spirited girls at the camp."

It seemed that her weight training and running had been noticed. Expecting her to accept, everyone looked at her.

"Fine," sighed Lluava, "I'll do it."

Next morning, the entire camp stood in formation in the square. Kentril and Ojewa waited on either side of the flagpole in the middle of the yard.

When everyone had lined up, Kentril called out, "Barracks AA, send your candidates to the front!"

Four girls came forward. Kentril then called for the candidates of Barracks BA. When Lluava and the other three girls on her team were summoned, excitement began to grow in the pit of her stomach. Lluava thought she saw a slight smile flicker on Kentril's face when he saw her approach. Ignoring the chosen ones, Ojewa stared straight ahead. Lluava waited with the others as the teams from each barracks assembled behind the two corporals.

"All girls not involved in the race are to follow Corporal Fren," Kentril ordered, indicating an older woman. "She will show you where you can watch from a safe distance. The rest of you, follow me."

The candidates were ushered into the general's barracks and led down the hall of dark portrait faces to a cramped meeting room. Lluava and Rosalyn sat next to Selphy, who represented her barracks.

Kentril called for attention. "Four teams have been randomly chosen to compete at one time. The winning team will remain; the other three will be dismissed. The next four teams will then compete. The winners of each of the initial competitions in the first round will move to a different course, and the process will be repeated in the second round. At the end of the day, there will be a final elimination round to determine the winning team. The winning barracks will be acknowledged, and team members' names will be noted in our records. As an extra incentive, the winning team will receive two free passes exempting them from weight training class on a date of their choosing."

This caught the girls' attention. Lluava heard the excited murmurs around her and knew she was not the only girl who would love an opportunity to skip a difficult and grueling weight training session.

Kentril called the first four barracks' teams to approach. He spread out a detailed map of the course. "Who will be the initial runner on each team?" he asked.

Immediately four girls stepped forward.

"You will start here." He pointed to the map and reviewed the course, the obstacles they would encounter, and where they would meet the next group. When the girls had finished studying their route, Kentril motioned to the door where an officer waited. "Follow Corporal Bressil," he told them. "She will lead you there. Next four...."

Lluava was in the third leg of the race. She stared at the map, studying the clearing where she would wait and the winding route they would take through the woods. She mentally marked the spot where she was to climb to the rope bridges in the trees. She would swing from the aerial bridges by another rope to a sloping plain, run toward the bottomland, and climb over a small fence before tagging her partner.

Lluava, Selphy, and two other girls followed a waiting corporal to another station in one of the forest clearings. They were told to remain there until their partners tagged them.

"This is so exciting!" exclaimed Selphy, twirling around the clearing.

Both to save her strength and so as not to soil her pristine white outfit, Lluava squatted down. She laughed at Selphy's ridiculous enthusiasm. After several minutes of twirling, Selphy flopped down next to Lluava. "I wonder how we will know when the race has begun."

A moment later, the camp's siren erupted. "I think we know," Lluava stated, springing to her feet. Selphy quickly stood up and brushed herself off.

The four girls watched the far end of the clearing, waiting for their partners to emerge from the green foliage and send them off on their leg of the course. As the minutes passed, Lluava felt her heartbeat quicken. Her senses awakened, and she was alert to every rustle of leaves and crack of twigs in the surrounding forest.

"Lluava?" Selphy whispered. "I really want to win. I will not be easy on you just because you and Rosalyn are my friends; still, I want to wish you luck."

Lluava turned and looked into Selphy's brown eyes, "As I, to you."

"Here they come!" shouted the dark-haired girl.

Lluava searched the wood's edge and saw two girls running toward them. She felt a nudge of anxiety as the two forms came closer. Neither was Rosalyn. Tagging their partners, Selphy and another girl took off. At last, Lluava spotted Rosalyn bounding toward her. She was surprisingly fast. Lluava's respect for her bunkmate grew when she saw the determination on her friend's face.

Lluava turned in the opposite direction as Rosalyn tagged her. Then she was off. She regulated her breathing as Ojewa had taught her and bounded behind the leading girls. She was running faster than she had in a long while, and it felt strangely good.

Leaving a cloud of dust behind her, Lluava ran along the trail. The trees were a blur as she flew by them. Soon she saw the other girls, the green shirt leading the way, Selphy close behind. Lluava knew she could easily catch up, even pass them, but she held back. Instead, she followed the advice given to her by Ojewa that very first day: pace yourself so you will not wear out too quickly.

Several minutes later, they reached four knotted ropes leading to a platform in the canopy. Lluava pulled herself up at a steady pace close behind the other two. The ropes were forty feet long; she forced herself to look straight up, not down. Using a good bit of her strength, she hoisted herself onto the platform. Standing up, she chased after Selphy, who was already halfway across the first of the three rope bridges.

Lluava stayed in Selphy's shadow, certain she could pass her with ease at the end of the last bridge. But as the two bounded across the final platform, Lluava sensed something awry. When her foot hit the bridge, it shifted under her weight. Reaching the middle of the bridge, she knew what was about to happen. There was no preventing it or turning back. She had passed the point of no return.

Lluava did not need to hear the snapping of the ropes or the groaning of the bridge as it gave way under her. Clinging to the ropes, she hurtled toward the trunk of the tree. She risked a glance at the ground forty feet below.

Then she fell.

Chapter 8
Taking Counsel

Lluava was falling, falling fast, the air ripping at her clothes as she plummeted toward the ground. There was nothing she could do to save herself. Her instincts took over; she felt herself transform as her bestial side took control. In her felid form, she sank her claws into the wood planking as it swung toward the tree. When bridge and trunk met, gravity took hold; her claws were unable to get a firm grasp, and she slid ever toward the broken end of the bridge. Her sudden weight was too much for the ruined structure to bear. Planks shattered on her way down. Splinters sprayed into her nose and eyes and dug under her claws. Small beads of blood dripped from her brow where jagged wood sliced into skin, distorting her vision, tinting everything red.

With no way to stop, no friction to slow her down, the tigress plummeted to the ground twenty feet below. Instinctively, she contorted in mid-air, flipping herself around. A smaller cat would have arched its back before hitting the ground, but the tigress's weight and bulk prevented this maneuver. The best she could do was land feet first.

The impact was so great that she tumbled forward, rolling several times before coming to rest on her side. Pain shot up all four limbs. A large cloud of dust billowed around her and blocked her view of the screaming spectators watching in the distance.

Lluava tried to focus on the crowd of people running toward her, but her eyes had begun to swell from the flakes of wood in them. Suddenly, the crowd gave a collective gasp. Several people shouted for help; others pointed in the air at what remained of the bridge.

Turning her sore neck, she peered upward and saw Selphy desperately clinging to a swaying plank with one hand. Her other arm hung loosely at her side. She had to be a good thirty feet from the ground.

Lluava rapidly processed the options. With the bridge destroyed, there was no way to reach the injured girl by the course's route; the frayed ropes, out of reach, dangled high overhead. Although several people shouted for a ladder, Lluava was not sure the camp had one tall enough, nor did she know where it was kept. She knew only that she must act fast for, clearly, the injured girl could not hold on much longer.

Even as she watched, Selphy cried out as her grasp on the board began to slip. Lluava leapt to her feet and bowled through the swarm of spectators. Reaching the base of the tree, she leapt up and sank her claws into the thick bark.

An adult tiger is not built for climbing trees, especially their trunks; the animal's weight is an extreme disadvantage. All Lluava's weight was centered on her claws, and they burned as she hoisted herself up bit by bit. It was a painstakingly slow climb. Her claws felt as if they were ripping away from her paws. Blood dripped down the digits onto the bark.

Lluava wanted to scream out in pain, but huffing all the way up, she continued to climb. Just as she thought her claws could no longer hold, she reached the lowest bough. Carefully she leapt from limb to limb. Faster and faster she climbed until she landed on a branch above the top of the bridge.

Digging her back claws into the bark, she seized the first plank with her front limbs. She heaved with all her might and managed to pull the entire bridge upward. Reaching down, one paw grabbed a lower section and pulled it toward her. The bridge slowly inched upward, and with it, the frightened Selphy. The muscles of Lluava's overextended limbs and tensed back burned.

When Selphy reached the branch, the trembling girl carefully climbed onto it. Lluava released the plank. With a jerk, one side of the attached end snapped, leaving the remnants of the bridge hanging by only a small rope. Her friend climbed onto Lluava's back and grasped the tiger around the neck with her good arm. Slowly, limb by limb, Lluava backed down until she reached the lowest one and then began the treacherous climb backwards down the trunk.

Lluava willed Selphy to hold on. Her friend seemed to understand and pulled her arm tighter around Lluava's neck. Although this kept Selphy from plummeting to the ground, her grip was almost suffocating.

Lluava had scooted down only a few feet when she realized that her claws could not hold both of them. There was no time to climb back up and find another route; Selphy's grip was getting rapidly weaker. There was only one thing to do: she let go. Twisting in midair again so her feet would hit first, she hoped they were close enough to the ground to land without harm.

Selphy's weight in addition to the tigress's weight resulted in an impact that sent both of them flying. Her friend fell off in one direction, and Lluava tumbled in another. Dust engulfed everything.

A loud pop resounded as what was left of the bridge gave way and plunged to the ground. Lluava rolled away as shattered planks of wood and rope crashed close to where she had fallen. Every fiber of her body ached, and she felt herself slipping away. Barely aware that a group of people had surrounded Selphy, Lluava blacked out.

Time was nonexistent between the incident at the bridge and the point at which she fully awoke. It was hard to differentiate between sleep and waking; she could hear the constant movement of people around her. At one point, she felt someone rub salve over her swollen eyelids. Sometime later, she forced herself to open her eyes through the pain and glimpse her surroundings.

She lay wrapped in white sheets on a cot in Thowcelemine's emergency ward. With effort, she turned her head until she could see the group of people huddled around the cot to her right. Lluava gathered that that was where Selphy lay. Her eyes burned, and she closed them.

When she next opened her eyes, she found that the swelling had receded greatly. It still hurt, but the pain was only a fraction of what it had been. This time, she was alone in the room. The cot next to hers was vacant, and there was no sign of Nurse Kara. Outside the window, it was dark, and stars shone in the sky.

Lluava slowly pushed herself up until she rested on one elbow. After a pause, she struggled to a sitting position. Her stomach, either from hunger or from her bruised ribs, knotted. She tried to ignore her aching body as she rose unsteadily to her feet. As soon as she was vertical, she felt queasy. Painfully snatching up the small waste tin by her bed, she tried to vomit.

"Lluava! What in the names of the gods do you think you are doing?" The tiny woman in a red apron bustled toward her from the doorway.

"Why, I'm leaving, Nurse," she responded sarcastically. "I'm all better. Thank you for your concern." Lluava tried to step around the obviously upset woman.

"You lie down this instant! You need to stay here overnight at the very least." Though Kara was quite petite, in the dim light she appeared a daunting force of nature.

Lluava sat down. As she wriggled carefully under the covers, she asked the testy nurse, "Where's Selphy?"

The nurse paused and adjusted the sleeves of her brown shirt. "She is gone."

"What do you mean, *gone?*" persisted Lluava.

The nurse pursed her lips. "You will not be seeing her again." And with that, she disappeared through the door.

Lluava felt sick again, this time for other reasons. What had the nurse meant? Frightening thoughts slipped into her mind; perhaps she did not really want to know.

She waited a few minutes and then stood up with agonizing slowness. She might not want to know the answer, but she had to find out. She needed to talk to General Kentril. Carefully Lluava made her way to the main hall, quietly passing vacant rooms.

Outside, she moved stealthily through the camp to the general's barracks. The main door was unlocked. She went directly to Kentril's office. As she had expected, it was dark and no one was there. However, just as she was about to call his name, she heard voices from the conference room at the end of the hall.

The door of the conference room was ajar and Lluava peeked inside. General Kentril and Major Ojewa sat on the far side of a large, rectangular table. Lluava recognized other officers; the frazzled nurse was there, too, as well as others whom she did not know. One man, of average build, his head completely shaved, faced away from her. When he turned, she saw a small nose in a large face, and a scar that began at his left ear and traveled downward, disappearing into his shirt collar.

Deeply involved with the conversation, the man suddenly broke in. "Explain your reasoning!" he demanded. As he spoke, Lluava blinked several times to make sure what she saw was real. All his teeth were pointed, as if he had filed them. The sight of the sharp, serrated peaks grinding on each other gave her an unsettled feeling.

"That is preposterous!" trumpeted an enormous man who sat to the left of Razor-Tooth. The huge person's loud, booming voice echoed off the walls. More astonishingly, his voice barely began to convey the massive size of the man. Even seated, Lluava could tell he was close to seven feet tall, if not taller. His wide shoulders framed an overdeveloped, muscular body barely contained by his shirt. He had to wedge himself between the arms of the chair.

The mammoth man bellowed, "How can you think of such a thing? We have no reason to believe that! It was just a horrible accident!"

Major Ojewa's response was cool. "When we examined the bridge, we found that the ropes had been severed three-fourths of the way through. The cuts were clean, which indicates that they were caused not by natural wear but by some sharp object, like a knife or a sword."

"What of the girl? You said that she was extremely quick to react. Could she have had something to do with the collapse? It could explain how she seemed to hold back and then move so quickly afterward."

General Kentril spoke up at this remark. "Lluava is one of the best recruits we have. She is ambitious and curious to a fault, but I will defend her with all that I am. She had nothing to do with that incident. I called you here to discuss the possibility that the bridge was tampered with by a force outside this facility."

"What are you insinuating, Kentril?" the burly giant gruffly asked.

"Raiders." A powerful voice spoke from the other side of the door.

The room became deathly silent. All eyes locked on the speaker, who was hidden from Lluava's view. Should she push it open any wider?

Suddenly, the brightly lit room disappeared as the previously hidden man moved in front of the partially open door. Ready to run, Lluava swallowed her gasp of surprise and backed up.

The man was facing the table and the rest of the group; their attention was fixed on him. Although not as tall as Ojewa, his daunting presence sent an unsettling vibration through the room; it seemed to seep through the cracked door. Over the stranger's broad shoulders, Lluava observed the men across the table slip each other cautious glances. Everyone waited for him to continue. No one noticed the shadowy eavesdropper in the hall.

"I hope you have not graduated from your training institutions so long ago that you have forgotten what you were taught. There is a very old strategy in which the conquering party infiltrates a target group to discover their strengths and weaknesses. These infiltrators, unrecognized and unnoticed, may live among the opposing people for years, before they return and pass on the information they have acquired. I tell you, these invaders, these Raiders, have come to test our defenses. To see how we react and how we fight. I believe their spies follow a very intelligent leader, someone smart enough to have sent people to infiltrate our community. The idea of sabotage is not hard to entertain if you consider what I have just told you."

"Are you insinuating that someone among us is a traitor?" snorted the bulky giant.

"I am saying only that we should consider all possibilities and not be so quick to suggest that a trainee is a villainous mastermind."

Lluava saw some of the men shrink down in their chairs.

The nurse rose to her feet. "Please excuse me, sirs," she said. "You have reminded me that I must check up on the girl." She began to make her way to the door.

Lluava knew it was time to leave. She crept quickly down the dim hall and hurriedly left the barracks. Once outside, she made her way to the infirmary as fast as she was able.

Back in her bed, she tried to slow down her breathing. Within minutes, the nurse was at her side.

"You look a bit flushed. Are you feeling all right? Do you feel feverish?" she inquired.

"Oh, no. I'm fine. Just anxious to return to my training."

"Hmm. Well, tomorrow you can rejoin your group."

Lluava thanked her several times. Although she was able to hold back her cheer of elation, she could not prevent the smile that broke across her face.

The next day, Lluava envisioned skipping back to the barracks though she opted not to out of regard for her physical condition. She could not wait to see everyone again. She missed hearing the girls' gossip and wanted to know if anyone knew what had happened to Selphy. She hoped to see her friend's smiling face along with Rosalyn's and all the others'. Instead, she met the stern look of a waiting officer.

"You are wanted at General Kentril's office immediately. Go now."

Surprised, Lluava had no idea what to expect. Had someone spotted her eavesdropping last night? She wondered how angry Kentril would be and what he would say. She knocked on his door and waited until she was summoned.

"Sit down, Lluava." Kentril's tone and expression were unreadable. She quickly obeyed.

The general sat at his desk, jotting something on a pad. He did not look up at her but continued to write as he spoke.

"I know what you have been up to lately. And I am sure you know what I am talking about."

He must have seen me, Lluava thought. She was about to speak, but Kentril continued. "Ojewa informed me that he has been giving you private lessons in the woods at night. I am disappointed in you for not listening to me after I told you that that was not your place. Then I saw what you did at the tournament."

Lluava began to fear that he blamed her for the accident on the bridge. What had happened in the council after she left?

"After all that I have seen and heard, there is only one thing I can do." General Kentril finally looked up at her. "You are being transferred."

"What?" Lluava exclaimed aghast. She stood up so quickly that she knocked over her chair. "I saved Selphy. And, yes, I trained without your permission, but I was not harming anyone. Please don't send me away!"

"If you would give me a moment to finish," Kentril replied, sounding a little fatigued.

Lluava righted the chair and sat back down.

"You are going to finish your training in Durog."

"The boy's camp? How is that possible? You told me that..."

Kentril cut her off. "The two camps are divided according to the strength of the recruits. Most females are weaker than males, but you are an exception. Ojewa has told me how swiftly you are catching on to your...what shall we call it?...extra training. He said that you are quite skilled at learning new things. After your little show last week, Ojewa explained what he has been teaching you. Considering everything I have seen and heard, I think your skills are needed somewhere other than in the last row of a battle."

"But how...?" Lluava had so many questions.

"In only three cases in the past have exceptional females been sent to train at Durog. Each made her name stand out in our history. I believe that you are one of a few exceptional women who is both strong enough to endure the rigors of Durog's training and powerful enough to have some great purpose, which none of us can foresee, in the coming war." Kentril paused for a moment to let what he said sink in and then continued.

"You can choose to go or to stay. Because Durog is a predominantly male camp, you must sleep at Thowcelemine. You will rise and walk to Durog each day in time for morning assembly. The training will be very difficult. If at any point it becomes too tough for you, you can return to the women's camp. Will you go?"

Lluava had dreamt about an opportunity to prove herself worthy, to bring honor to her father's name. She would do all this and more. However, there was one thing she had to know before giving the general her decision.

"What happened to Selphy? Nobody will tell me. Is she...okay?" Llujava could not make herself say what she feared.

Kentril locked eyes with her and replied, "Selphy broke her arm during the incident. Although our infirmary can help one heal faster, that severe an injury requires significant time. She has been discharged from service and sent home. Nurse Kara thought it best not to tell you until you were better. She did not want to add more stress."

"She wanted to alleviate stress by not telling me?" Lluava almost laughed at the irony. Without hesitation, she said, "I will go to Durog."

"It is settled, then. You will have tomorrow to situate yourself before you head to Durog. That will give you time to prepare. You will need to be there by noon for orientation. Do not be late. Now, go and tell your friends the news." He smiled at her as she rose to leave.

Ojewa was quietly standing by the door, holding it open for her. She should have known that he would be listening.

"Thank you," Lluava whispered as she slipped past him.

Chapter 9
Through the Gates of Hell

That night, Lluava's friends were abuzz with her news. They had not seen her since the accident, and they bombarded her with questions. The girls were amazed at the thought that Lluava would be leaving them to train with the men.

Shenne and Sonty giggled in unison. They seemed to finish each other's sentences naturally…although, with their years of practice, who knew? Shenne quipped, "They probably sweat so much when they lift weights…" and Sonty finished the thought, "…that they have to take their shirts off." Both sighed with smiles on their faces.

"You'll probably return stinking like them," snorted Alison, feigning disgust.

"Jealous, are you?" questioned Sonty. Shenne shadowed a retort: "Wishing it were you?"

"That's not true!" The words tumbled out of Alison's mouth awkwardly. She blushed. With a laugh, the twins tried to calm her down as they continued to chatter about Lluava's new opportunity. Only Lluava noticed that Rosalyn was quiet.

In the morning, Lluava attended classes with the girls for the last time and then returned to her barracks to pull out her clothes for the next day. Rosalyn was sitting on her bed, waiting for her. She was holding a piece of paper. Lluava had seen her sneaking looks at it during the day.

"Are you alri…" began Lluava, but Rosalyn cut in.

"I want to thank you for saving Selphy's life." Rosalyn's voice was unusually loud, almost cracking. Her eyes began to brim with tears. "She is my best friend. We have known each other since we began school. If you had not…" She began to sob.

"She's going to be fine. It may even be for the best that she was sent away before the war."

"No." Rosalyn looked up once more. She did not wipe her tear-stained face. "I have left my family, my friends, and my home. My best friend was taken away from me, and my bunkmate, and…" She paused, clenching the paper tightly. "I am not good at being alone."

"I'm not leaving you. I'm just training elsewhere during the day. I'll be coming back at night. The times we hang out the most, I'll still be here. You have the other girls, too." Lluava sat down next to Roslyn and tried to comfort her friend. "All will be fine in the end."

"How can you be so sure?"

"I can't. But I have hope."

They sat together quietly, their hopes and prayers for the future mingling in undisturbed silence until the rest of the girls returned.

That night, Lluava was too restless to sleep. She waited eagerly for the first rays of light to shine through the windows. She decided to do the morning run and have breakfast with Rosalyn once more. Afterward, Lluava watched her friends head off to class. Unaccustomed to unstructured time, she headed out early for Durog.

Lluava left the confines of Thowcelemine for the first time in weeks. Outside the walls, the wind blew harder than in the calm campground. The grass, tall as her waist, danced in the wind, seeming to wave her on toward her destiny. She walked slowly down the dried-up road toward the dark fortress she had passed when she first arrived. Insects droned hypnotically, and in the brilliant blue air, swallows sang and flew past. She watched them chase each other until they flew from sight. Lluava watched the puffs of dust that her feet made as she walked. Each tiny cloud rose quickly, only to sink sluggishly back down to the hardened earth.

Lluava tried to take her time, but she arrived at Durog hours earlier than required. As she made her way toward the fort-like structure, a gloomy feeling grew inside her. Although Durog was built in the same fashion as Thowcelemine, it was four times the size. Approaching, she could begin to pick out differences in the details. The stone was a darker variety, fractured with veins of red-hued lichen, pulseless arteries coursing through an eyeless face. Wooden spikes surmounted the top of the wall like a row of snarling teeth. Something about the place made her uneasy.

Anticipating her entry, the gates parted as she neared. Ancient runes were carved into the wooden arch that formed the top of the gateway. The walls themselves were taller and thicker than Thowcelemine's. Why did this place need to be impenetrable? It was only a training camp.

Upon entering, she saw several regiments of men marching in formation. The clank of metal on metal resounded in the distance, and the odor of sweat hung heavily in the heat. One group of young men about her age was trooping.

Their drill sergeant screamed, "Halt!" As one, the rectangular mass stopped and turned toward Lluava, assuming attention stance. None of them looked directly at her. Instead, they seemed to focus on something in the distance.

Following their eyes, she recognized the sharp-toothed man from the meeting room. He approached, finally stopping so close to her that she could see her reflection in his eyes. His pupils were large and dark as the abyss. His minuscule nose flared as he caught her scent.

"Ah, so you're the new recruit. Early, I see. You must be anxious to begin, and I'm sure you want to see the camp. Talos, take her on a walk."

The man did not take his eyes off Lluava as a blond-haired recruit stepped from the line. "I'll let the grand master chief know you have arrived." He finally tore his eyes away from her and glared at the remaining men. "The rest of you, continue rounds. The clock has not stopped. Go!"

The recruits marched off in unison as one mass, like some great creature hunting its prey, before disappearing among the buildings that so resembled those of the other camp.

Lluava was alone with the one called Talos. For the first time, she gave him more than a quick glance. He was a rather handsome fellow. His hair, shining gold in the sunlight, swooped down in front of his face. Although he wore a short-sleeved shirt and matching shorts in a dull tan shade, the outfit did not disguise the toned body. His chestnut eyes regarded her for a moment, and then he said with a smile, "Let's walk."

Before the last word had slipped past his smooth lips, he had taken off in a full sprint. A moment later, Lluava was running behind him. He ran faster than she'd expected.

"These are the barracks," Talos pointed out as they flew by. "Over there's the infirmary, the mess hall, and the meeting hall." He pointed to every building and training facility as they ran. Lluava caught only a glimpse of what he called the coliseum. The roofless, circular building towered over everything around it. A smaller, identical structure was situated behind it. She wanted to ask what it was for but could barely catch her breath.

Running came naturally to Talos. His feet seemed to hover above the ground. As he gave his lightning-quick tour, he turned around to face Lluava and ran backward without slowing down. Lluava's lungs burned as they neared the end of their enormous loop. Durog truly *was* four times the size of Thowcelemine.

Lluava found her sweat refreshing when a subtle breeze caressed her burning limbs. As she leaned over, panting, a grim shadow enveloped her. She looked up at the dark mass blocking the sun. Rays of light, hindering her ability to make out details, shown around him and blinded her.

"If they don't teach you to run, what do you learn over there? How to sew?" Lluava recognized the gruff but unmistakably authoritative voice. It was the mystery man who had captivated the meeting the other night.

Lluava abruptly straightened and stood at attention. At this angle, the man's chiseled face and thick neck were all she could discern.

He stared coldly back at her and then snarled, "Do you have any respect? Get in line!"

She quickly turned around and saw that the same troop that had stopped earlier was now standing behind her. Quickly, she moved toward the only familiar face, but Talos, staring forward, snapped, "Other end." She immediately readjusted her course and took a place at the far end of the first row.

The monstrous man began to pace in front of the troops. "As you all have eyes and should know how to use them by now, you may have noticed that you have a new recruit joining your ranks today. Because you have worked hard...well, as hard as uncouth newborns can...the new recruit will start where you are today. She will have to catch up on her own time." He stopped in front of her. "Your name?"

"Lluava Kargen, daughter of Haliden Kargen, sir!"

"Hmm. I will give you a quick debriefing. Don't want you to fret. This is Durog. You're a recruit. Admiral Merrow is the aquatic instructor." He pointed to the chisel-toothed man. A second, smaller man with a thin, downward-curving nose had appeared next to Merrow. "That," the general continued, "is Colonel Skipe. His specialty is aerial combat. I am the grand master chief. You will always do as I say. Do you understand?" His words seemed to drip with insult like a starving dog salivating at rotting meat.

"Sir, yes, sir!" Lluava tried to stifle the rumbling in her throat and hoped it was not audible.

Somehow, excitement was brewing inside her. Staring at her new commanding officer, she knew that she was looking at an almost mythical character. Her father had taught her about military ranks. For career soldiers, the rank of general was a lofty and rarely attained goal. Yet there were three levels above that: chief general, master chief general, and grand master chief general. The last two were so revered that the word *general* was never used; everyone well knew what the title meant. A grand master chief stood before her. There were not more than three in all of Elysia, yet here, in Durog, a grand master chief was serving as drill sergeant for raw recruits.

"Do you have any training in fighting skills?" the grand master chief asked dubiously.

She smiled. "Sir, yes sir!"

He paused, then smiled back. "Let's try them out, shall we?"

Before Lluava had time to wonder what he meant, the grand master chief had removed his jacket and handed it to Merrow. His huge body seemed enchained by its heavy musculature; the gleaming bulges looked monstrous, casting dark shadows on the crevices that separated one mass from the next.

Turning his tree trunk of a neck to look at her, he commanded, "Begin!"

With a deafening roar, he stepped up to her and transformed. Long, thick, golden-brown fur sprouted from his scarred skin and blanketed him. Although the fur hid the bulging muscles, their main form could still be seen. Six-inch claws, all pearly black, sprouted from his hands. He grew several feet taller. His facial features distorted and realigned to form a hideous black muzzle. Again the beast roared.

A shiver ran down Lluava's spine as she stared at the great mountain bear in front of her. She had read descriptions and seen drawings of these animals in books. They had lived in a far northern area of the kingdom but were now thought to be extinct; she had never expected to see one alive.

The beast opened its maw as it raised one forearm. "Eat or be eaten!" it huffed.

It spoke! It spoke! He is in his dual form and spoke! Lluava's surprise was so great that she paused for a brief second. This was a mistake. The bear's claws hooked her left side and in the next moment tossed her in the air. She spiraled before crashing to the ground. Ignoring the pain of her bleeding side, Lluava rolled out of the way as the bear swiped at her again. She dodged the blow and sprang to her feet. The giant animal and the girl stared at each other for a split second. In that moment, Lluava could see the loathing it had for her. Was he actually trying to kill her? Suddenly the brute dropped to all fours and charged.

Transforming, Lluava loosed her own white-tiger war cry and attacked. The two beasts met head on. Lluava sprang into the air, just missing the burly bear's bite. Twisting, she landed on the blundering creature's back, digging in her claws to secure her position. The bear lurched up on its hind legs and fell backward. To avoid being crushed between the its massive body and the stony ground, Lluava retracted her claws. The bear moved unusually fast and spun around, knocking Lluava away with one massive forepaw. She skidded across the rough ground.

With the wind knocked out of her, Lluava gasped for air. The bear ran toward her and grabbed her with his forelegs. Standing upright, he held her above his head and then hurtled her to the ground. The world spun as she tried to focus.

As her vision cleared, she saw that the bear held something aloft. Squinting, she made out a large rock the size of the bear's immense head. The beast snarled and flung the stone toward her.

Her mind had time to form only a single thought: Why?

Chapter 10
A New Regiment of Order

Why was the only question. Lluava closed her eyes and waited for the impact. The air whipped angrily past her face as she heard a thud and the cracking sound of shattering stone.

Opening her eyes, she saw that the rock had landed a mere two inches from her face. She stared at the powerful man who stood over her. Although he was now in human form, his fierceness had not diminished. His eyes said that he wished he had finished the deed.

"Take her to the infirmary, Yamir, and then send her on her way," snarled the grand master chief. He sent the rest of the regiment to their next assignment and then left, presumably to oversee the other areas of his camp.

Lluava's head was ringing. For fear of causing more pain, she remained still. When she tried to stand up, the world began to spin. A pair of hands grabbed her left arm. The young man who helped her was startling in appearance. He had shredded all the edges of his uniform, and his dark hair, cut short, was spiked up in little clumps. Had it been allowed to grow longer, it might have covered the bruises around his right ear, which, like the left, had several metal rings in it. To Lluava, he seemed a likely candidate to belong to one of the traveling bands of thieves. But his dark eyes were kind.

"Don't worry. It's not you. He hates most everybody. That little scare you just went through is his welcoming gift. He does this sort of thing to everyone. I'm Yamir." Grinning, he stuck out his coppery hand for her to shake.

Making sure her grip was firm, she responded, "I'm Lluava."

"I know. We all know," Yamir said with a sweeping gesture toward the camp. Reading the surprise in her face, he added, "Didn't you think news of the first girl to come to Durog in who-knows-how-long would spread quickly? I mean, really! You must have known that as soon as you entered, all eyes would be on you."

Why had she not expected this? Lluava had envisioned being accepted by all the others at her skill level. Yet again, she must prove her right to remain in this place.

"The infirmary is this way," Yamir said, slipping his thin arm under hers to steady her. Though very lanky, he was able to keep her standing. "So, um, your form' a white tigress."

Lluava nodded .The throbbing in her head had increased. She was not in the best mood for small talk.

Yamir did not seem to notice. "That's sweet. I bet ya could have scared lots of little children. Not the nice ones, of course, just the brats." He chuckled. "Here we are." He helped Lluava hobble up the steps to the infirmary.

"Hey, Berk! Berkley!" Yamir called as they walked slowly down the aisle. "Got a patient for ya."

Somewhere in the back, a friendly voice answered, "If the patient is you again, Yamir, I will have to request a separate money pot."

A little old man hobbled into sight; at once Lluava recognized him as the tailor who had made the uniforms. The man pushed his half-moon spectacles up his nose with knobby fingers.

"I'm actually surprised that it's not you, Yamir," said Berkley.

Lluava looked at Yamir, who shrugged.

"I guess I'm a little clumsy at times." Yamir put his hand down on the bedside table behind him, knocking the metal pan that lay precariously on top. The pan overturned, spilling the instruments and small glass bottles it held. Every clattering and crashing sound that followed seemed to make Yamir twitch. He slowly turned his head to face the devastation of what once had been medical equipment.

A long sigh escaped Berkley. Yamir smiled meekly at Lluava. "See what I mean?" Bending over to clean up the mess, he slit his finger on a shard of glass.

"Leave that be, Yamir. I will clean it later." Berkley shooed Yamir away from the area and told him to sit on one of the cots. Yamir sucked his cut finger and waited quietly. The old man turned toward Lluava. "Now, let's have a look at you."

He sat her down on a bed and inspected her numerous cuts and bruises. As he looked at a particularly nasty gash in her leg, Lluava spoke up.

"Aren't you a tailor? Didn't I see you at Thowcelemine?"

Berkley smiled up at her from his kneeling position. "I have many talents, young one. Here I serve as the physician." The old man rotated her leg to get a better look at an abrasion. "Why are you in Durog?" he asked as he smoothed on salve from a green bottle tucked in his jacket pocket.

"I have been transferred here."

"Isn't that most unusual?" interjected Yamir. "No offense." He glanced at Lluava and, seeing that she was not offended, continued. "When was the last time you heard of such a thing? I mean, really...."

The old man paused in his ministrations, paying no attention to Yamir's banter. He seemed lost in thought as he rubbed ointment on a gash in Lluava's arm.

After a moment, Berkley stood up slowly. Muttering under his breath, he walked to the back of the room to pick up a vial. Upon returning, he handed Lluava the tiny bottle wrapped in deer hide. "Apply three drops of this ointment to your open wound before bed tonight and, if needed, two tomorrow. Keep the rest. I fear you will be needing more soon." He turned away, shuffled into a back room, and did not return.

As they headed back to camp, Yamir apologized for the old man's abrupt manner. The sun was still climbing to its zenith, but the heat was already scorching. Not a bird flew in the sky. The barking of drill sergeants and the clattering of weapons drowned out any soothing sound the wind might have blown to Lluava's ears.

In the bright light, she admired Yamir's face even more. His smooth features were unlike any she had seen before, and his eyes, incredibly dark and oval, seemed to suit his coppery skin.

Lluava followed Yamir into the smaller coliseum. She had never been in a structure like this one—the homes and buildings she knew were made of wood or wattle and daub. Like the perimeter walls, the coliseum's were built of large, rectangular stones. She noted the red lichen and blue-grey mosses that grew in the cracks and crevices of the stone. Once again, she was reminded of veins and arteries as she looked at the archaic structure. The building was centuries old. There was no door. She craned her neck to study how the stones were wedged against each other to create an arched entryway. Stepping into the shaded bowels, she saw an inner pathway circling through the stone chamber.

"That leads to the spectator seats," Yamir explained. Instead of following the dark path, Yamir headed toward another large arch at the far side of the chamber.

Following him, Lluava crossed back into the blazing sunlight. They had entered a large, open arena. Seven rows of seats were carved into the stone sides, each row rising a level. Thousands of people could fit in the coliseum.

She did not have long to marvel, for the recruits were marching in behind her. Suddenly she heard her name barked out by the grand master chief. She hurried to catch up with Yamir, who was already lining up in formation. Lluava ignored the glares from the recruits who stood next to her as she slid into her presumed place.

Without turning her head, she whispered, "What are we doing here?"

Nobody replied.

The grand master chief pulled two recruits from formation and told them to transform. One scarlet-headed boy, around fourteen years old and covered with freckles, melded into a red fox. The other recruit was Talos, who transformed into a magnificent stag. When the two had assumed their dual forms, the grand master chief asked each to answer a question. The fox screeched out barely recognizable words, while Talos spoke as fluently as a gentleman.

They could speak! They could *all* speak! At least, they were learning to speak in their dual forms. It was eerie to hear the words of her language emanate from the lips of animals. This concept amazed her. Realizing that she must be gaping, she quickly shut her mouth.

The grand master chief turned to the group and told them to pair up and shift to their dual forms, emphasizing the importance of being able to communicate with their human partners. At once, people began to move, calling out the names of those with whom they wanted to be partnered. Lluava started weaving around bodies, looking for Yamir. She glimpsed him on the far side, partnered with a boy wearing a woven military hat. Sighing, she turned back to find someone else.

Lluava approached recruits at random, but each one shrugged her off. Finally, she had to admit it was a lost cause. No male wanted to be partnered with an outsider…and a girl. She walked straight up to the general, who was talking to Colonel Skipe.

"Grand master chief," she interrupted. "I do not have a partner."

He turned and looked down at her. "What did you say, recruit?"

She cleared her throat and spoke louder. "I don't have a partner."

The general glanced up at all the pairs, then looked back at her. He snorted and called out, "Talos, partner up with Lluava." He sounded almost as if he were going to vomit at the sound of her name. "And do it now!"

Although he maintained a bored look on his face, Talos sprinted up to her.

"You ready?" The words had barely left his mouth before he started to change again.

Lluava let her body meld into its other form. Though the change was still painful, she didn't mind it as much. She looked at the buck pawing the ground before her. Glancing at his wide rack, she sniffed the air. The musk of whitetail deer was strong, at least to her felid senses. Her claws lightly scratched the surface of the ground, automatically testing it. The dry earth would allow her claws to catch easily, which meant that she would not slip if she charged. Her tongue slid over her sharp teeth, and she locked eyes with the stag. His eyes seemed to sparkle in the light. As she watched his flank twitch, she could almost taste fresh venison.

Lluava forced herself to clear the bestial thoughts from her mind. She struggled to concentrate, telling herself that it was Talos in front of her, not merely some prey animal.

The general walked up to them.

"Repeat this statement until I say stop." Looking at Lluava, he continued, "I am a worthless recruit who knows nothing." He seemed to smile without doing so and then moved to the next group.

She opened her mouth and tried to say the words. They came out as muffled growls and muted bellows. Undaunted, she tried again. She could hear herself think the words, but when she tried to say them out loud, they were only huffs and grunts.

Talos was repeating the statement over and over. He spoke loudly and clearly. Lluava could tell by the tone of his voice that he was annoyed, probably because he was partnered with her.

Desperately wanting to prove herself, Lluava tried again and again to no avail.

Talos finally looked over at her. "Try to visualize yourself forming the words with your mouth. It helps." Talos spoke in the same tone of voice as before, then effortlessly repeated the original statements. If Lluava had not paid attention, she would have missed it.

"What?" she wanted to ask, astonished that he had tried to help.

Talos did not reply; he just kept chanting.

Visualize myself forming the words, she thought. Closing her eyes, she envisioned herself mouthing the statement over and over again. Before long, she heard a voice. *Her* voice. It was distorted and hoarse, but she spoke. She almost roared with elation.

Talos gave her a congratulatory glance while continuing to repeat the statement.

The general approached them again. After listening to their progress, he backed up and shouted for everyone to stop.

"Attention!" he barked. An arena full of animals locked eyes on the massive man and waited for orders. "Group yourselves with similar types of animals. Large cats, up front with me...."

As the general continued to organize the other animals, Lluava moved to the forming group of wild cats. There were six, including herself. She looked at all of them carefully. A cheetah whispered something into the ear of a leopard. In front of them, a puma sat proudly between a brilliant orange tiger and a young lion whose mane was still growing in.

"Hello," she meant to say, but it was so garbled that it was almost incomprehensible. Lluava noted the tiger was a good head taller than she.

Embarrassed, she sat down apart from them. Although surrounded by animals, she felt alone. She missed the gossip of her friends back at Thowcelemine. She longed for Rosalyn's kind words and the games she played.

The voice of the grand master chief shook her out of her daydream.

"Pair up!" he snapped. "Give yourselves plenty of room to separate from the others around you. Then fight! Only through combat will you discover your strengths and weaknesses in this form. Continue until either Colonel Skipe or I tell you to stop." Lluava had forgotten Skipe was in the arena.

The grand master chief transformed as he spoke. "Blood is good. Pain is better. Pain proves you are still alive. Do not stop, even if it hurts. You will soon be able to fight through the pain. Begin!"

When Lluava turned back to her group, the young lion stood directly in front of her. So this was to be her partner, she thought. The lion opened his maw wide and roared. It was a magnificent sound. She could see his teeth shining white in the sun. She countered his roar with her own war cry.

The bellows of creatures resounded all around her. She heard the clattering of antlers and the scuffling of paws and hooves on dusty ground. The lion suddenly crouched and sprang at her. She, like his mirror image, did the same.

The impact was shocking. Though smaller, his body ended up on top of hers when they hit the ground. The air in her lungs exploded from her, and she gasped for breath. She tried to roll him off, but his claws dug into her shoulders. She twisted her body, trying to shake off those razor-sharp shards ripping into her hide.

Lluava raised her left paw, and her claws sprang from their pads. She slung this new weapon at her opponent. Her claws tore through his mane and then slashed at the side of his neck. It was just enough. The beast loosened his hold. She shoved him off with her rear legs and leapt to her feet.

The two felids circled, their eyes locked on one another. Lluava waited until she saw the lion's muscles twitch. It was the telltale predictor she needed to understand his next move.

Lurching toward each other, they reared up on hind legs, each grappling with fierce claws. Lluava seized the back of the lion's neck in her teeth, hard enough to keep her grip without tearing flesh. The lion's forearms reached around Lluava's body, claws hooking at the base of her ribcage. The beast pulled as if trying to tear off her skin. In retaliation, Lluava sank her teeth into the beast's flesh. Crimson liquid moistened the parched soil.

Lluava heard shouting and, distracted as she was by a mouthful of lion, had to concentrate to make out the words.

"Stop! I said stop!"

Claws pried her away. The mountain bear stood between her and the lion and bellowed, "Enough!"

The bear reared over Lluava and growled, "When I say stop, *stop*! Because you did not listen, you will stay after the others are released for the night and clean each spot of blood from this arena with a rake!" The general turned his massive head to the lion. "Back in line!"

As the other recruits began to transform, Lluava could not help but clench her jaw as she transformed and found her spot in line. There was no point arguing with the man in charge. The burden of punishment rested on her shoulders alone. There was no equality here.

The grand master chief spoke again. "Talos, take this group of measly wannabes to the lake. Do it now!"

"Let's go, recruits!" commanded Talos as the troop lined up four to a row. From the first row, he called, "Move out!"

Everyone around Lluava marched quickly and in unison. She stumbled several times, almost knocking down the male in front of her, before she figured out the correct pace.

The troop marched through the camp and into the forest. As in Thowcelemine, different obstacles were stationed throughout the area. She recognized several rope bridges (which she hoped she would not have to use any time soon), climbing walls, pits with thin beams…perhaps to walk across?

The trek had been under way a good quarter hour before Lluava heard the soft lapping of water on sand. The path they were on led straight to the water's edge. It was not a large lake, and the trees that encroached along its bank made it seem even smaller. Water reeds stretched toward the glowing orb in the sky, and patches of lily pads floated like little islands on the shimmering surface.

As soon as they arrived, the young men stripped off their shirts and dove into the murky water. Somewhere behind the growing number of soaked bodies, the water moved. The motion caught Lluava's attention. She scanned the lake's surface. Another series of ripples appeared a bit closer to the men. Then Lluava saw it; a triangular fin emerged and moved quickly toward the unaware recruits.

"Look out!" shouted Lluava.

The dark form must have been eight feet in length. In one fluid motion, it surged upward from the water. Shimmering droplets splashed down on those nearby. Everyone turned to see a large, dusky-gray shark soar into the air and then sink back into the depths.

Again the water stirred, now only several yards from the shore. Then an object slowly emerged. It was not the fin Lluava expected, but rather the head of Admiral Merrow. Water slid off his bald scalp as his body slowly emerged from the lake. His scar gleamed white in the light. Lluava tried not to stare, for the scar descended from his neck and wrapped around his torso to the edge of his navel.

"Everyone, get your dry asses into the water!" Merrow ordered, staring at Lluava, the sole person left standing on the bank. Then he turned to the others. "Line up! You have twenty laps to do."

Lluava took off her shoes and placed them next to the base of a willow.

She could feel the texture of the soil between her exposed toes. Though primarily sand, patches of damp clay stuck to her soles as she carefully waded into the cool water.

Without a word, Merrow dove back in and led the recruits to the far side of the lake. Lluava could handle herself well enough to keep from drowning, but she had never been taught correct and efficient ways to swim. Again, the nagging awareness of how much she had missed in those first few weeks came back to her as she saw that the troop was definitely using a certain stroke. Lluava tried to mimic it but found herself out of order. She tried to keep up, but her attempts could not prevent her from falling farther behind. She was the last to finish her first lap, and as she was about to start her second, she heard Merrow call out to her.

"Halt, recruit! Stay where you are."

"Sir, yes, sir!" Lluava responded once she'd caught her breath. Embarrassed, she waited for her orders.

"I know you are a late arrival," the admiral explained, "but you are expected to keep up with everyone else." Merrow paused. "This is why I am taking today and only today to give you a crash course in swimming techniques."

By the time the session had ended, Lluava's whole body ached. She would not have guessed how hard it was to learn to swim well. She felt a cramp in her left side as she slowly lowered her sopping wet body onto the sand. Closing her eyes, she wished the day were over.

"Get up, recruit!" Merrow shouted from above. "Time to move out!"

A moan slipped past her lips, and she forced herself up. The men were back, shaking off water as if they were dogs. Lluava grabbed her shoes and lined up with the others before marching back to the main part of the camp. This time, they headed to the large coliseum.

Entering the inner ring, Lluava's attention was drawn to the weapon racks lined up on the opposite side. The racks were mobile so that, depending on whatever weapon with which the recruits were to train, they could be easily exchanged. What these racks held made Lluava's heart leap. Swords! Dozens and dozens of shining, shimmering swords. Finally, here was something at which she might possibly excel.

The recruits paired up. An officer dispensed the swords and gave the signal to begin sparring.

As she was struck by her partner, a very plain-looking boy, Lluava was thankful that the edges of these weapons were encrusted with thick black tar to dull their blades. The boy was close to her age, but his body was bulky, making him strong but slow. That first blow jarred her so much that she almost clutched her arm in agony.

He swung again, but this time Lluava blocked him. From that moment on, she found it easy to quickly anticipate and dodge his attacks. As time passed, her swift sidesteps and speedy, low blows began to take their toll on her opponent. The youth started to huff and snort with each swing of his sword.

Ducking to miss one of his offensive thrusts, Lluava twisted her body with sword outstretched and disarmed her opponent. The youth stumbled backward and fell. Lluava shoved her weapon under his chin and declared, "Vanquished!"

The boy flushed.

Lluava, leaving the embarrassed young man to brush himself off, returned the gleaming object to the waiting racks. She knew he was angry that he had lost to the sole female in Durog.

When the final pairs had finished their task, the troop, led by their apparent leader, Talos, marched to the mess hall.

The grand master chief stood outside the entryway. "Troop, you have earned fifteen minutes of dining time because of yesterday's performance. Get in! Then get gone!"

For the first time at Durog, chaos erupted. Hungry men ran into the hall, grabbing anything they could fit on their plates before shoveling different-colored ground mash into their mouths. Lluava had not eaten all day. She, too, followed the crowd's behavior, grabbing anything she could get by muscling her way through the hungry throng that surrounded the food.

After garnering what she could, Lluava scanned the room but could not find Yamir. She decided to try to sit with the only other person who had spoken to her, Talos.

His table was filled with particularly strong-looking young men. Among them were the plain boy with whom she had sparred earlier and the striking young red-headed lad of fourteen years.

"May I sit down?" asked Lluava.

The plain boy glared at her. "This table is full."

"Surely there is room for one more," she responded sweetly. It had not been her intention to offend the boy. The others sat silently, glowering at Lluava—except Talos, who stared at his half-eaten food.

In a frigid manner, the large youth retorted, "I said, this table is full."

Lluava turned and quietly walked away. Lost in thought, she barely registered Talos's words: "That was cruel, Tartus." All around her, glares seemed to warn her not to approach. She ate alone at the vacant end of a table until the troop was ordered to leave.

Returning to the forest's edge, a tired-looking corporal instructed them on that day's group event—a timed run on one of the obstacle courses. Yamir approached Lluava and explained that group participation in daily tasks was intended to create a bond within each troop. Lluava could tell by the distaste in Yamir's voice that it was not working as planned.

The sun, low on the horizon, was barely visible through the thick tangle of trees. Talos, in the lead once again, led them down a shaded path. It soon narrowed, and they formed a single line in order to keep moving.

Lluava was near the back with several people she did not know. She was able to keep pace as she navigated the first obstacles, which included climbing a wall and traversing a deep pit by means of a ladder. She was caught off guard when she had to climb up to a ledge using a knotless rope. Lluava started up the rope but kept slipping. The remaining recruits shouted at her to clear the way. She dropped down, allowing the others to go ahead. They quickly hoisted themselves up and took off.

"Hey!" Lluava yelled as the last one disappeared over the edge. "Help me up!"

They were already gone.

It took four more attempts before Lluava pulled her body over the top of the ledge. Running in the twilight, she took off down the path. Within minutes, she had raced to the finish line of the course, where the rest of her troop waited impatiently.

Bracing her hands on her knees, Lluava tried to catch her breath.

"That," stated the surly voice of the lieutenant, "was the longest time your regiment has taken to complete a troop exercise. Disappointing. Time will be taken off your meals tomorrow. I do not know how much, but you will not like it."

As the recruits dispersed to their barracks for the night, their grumbling and griping about the loss of meal time was mixed with muttering about the stupidity of allowing a girl into Durog.

Sore, tired, and humiliated, Lluava trudged back to the small arena, where she knew the grand master chief was waiting for her. Yamir asked her where she was heading.

"If you didn't hear before, I'm supposed to—and I quote—'clean the blood out of the sand with a rake' back in the small arena." She mimicked the gruff tone of the grand master chief and then sighed.

"Don't be so downcast, my dear. Yamir is here!" he exclaimed, pretending to tip a hat.

"Okay" she said, smiling at him. "Okay…"

On the way, Lluava heard voices near a small elm tree.

A soft, pleading voice cried out, "Please, just leave me alone!"

The other one was familiar. "Hey, baby! Why does the baby still wear his bonnet?"

Both Yamir and Lluava moved closer to see what was happening. They beheld the unfriendly, plain-faced boy and, facing him, a smaller youth. Though they were still a good distance away, Lluava thought that the youngster was trembling.

At that moment, the older youth shoved his prey onto the ground and grabbed his brown woven hat, the hat assigned to all as part of their uniform.

Waving the hat in the air, the bully mocked him. "I asked you a question, baby. Why are you always wearing your baby bonnet? Huh? If you want to grow up like the rest of us, stop wearing it. Big boys do not wear baby bonnets."

The little boy stumbled to his feet. Lluava gasped. Even in the dusky light, she recognized the now gaunt face.

It was Chat.

Chapter 11
New Ties and Broken Trust

"Chat!" A single name, uttered in unison.

Lluava and Yamir turned toward each other. Before she could speak, Yamir asked, "You know him?"

"Yes. We met on the wagon train. How...?" That was a stupid question. Of course Yamir knew Chat; they had both been training together in this camp.

Yamir was no longer looking at her but at his small comrade. "We have to help him," he said.

Without a second thought, Lluava strode up to the two youths and slid between them, facing the larger one. The plain-faced bully hissed, "Move away!" At the same time, Lluava heard a gasp behind her.

"Tell me why, please, explain to me why those of strength always seem to find a thrill in oppressing those who cannot defend themselves. Does it make you feel important?" As Lluava spoke, she heard Chat pleading with her to just let it be, but she continued. "Does it make you feel good about yourself? Or is it a way of compensating for the courage you lack?"

Profanities came spitting from the young man's mouth.

"That's it, isn't it? You're tired of being pushed around by those in charge, so you take it out on those who are weaker than you. You spineless creature..."

She had plenty more to say, but the blur of the oncoming fist caught her short. Before she had time to react, Yamir stepped out of the dark, allowing his own face to intercept the blow. He stumbled back, his left hand tenderly touching his split lip. Instantly Chat was at his side, offering his own sleeve to wipe the blood.

"You...little...sneak!" The words emerged in short breaths as Lluava's rage spilled over. She grabbed the bully by his neck as if to strangle him. Shocked, he did not move. "I'm...going to..."

"LLUAVA!"

The roar of the grand master chief's voice caught everyone by surprise. Lluava stepped back, releasing the bully's pulsating neck.

"Tartus!" snapped the general. "Return to your barracks!"

Lluava couldn't help but notice the upturned corners of Tartus's mouth as he disappeared into the darkness.

After a moment of silence, the general spoke again. "Chattern, leave us now." Looking like a child afraid of his shadow, Chat turned and left.

When only three remained, the burly man glared at Lluava. "How dare you threaten another recruit and one from your own troop!" he bellowed.

"But..." Lluava tried to defend herself. The general had not seen what had taken place; all she needed was a chance to clear this up. Silent, Yamir looked at her and shook his head in warning.

"Quiet!" barked the general. "Now you dare interrupt your superior! The insolence! The disrespect! I knew allowing one of you into my camp was a horrible idea. Kentril—what does that idiot know about warfare? He has always wanted to disgrace me and my camp's reputation. Look what he sent! A newly whelped country brat! And you!" His stare was so enraged that Lluava had to look away. "You are going to complete your earlier punishment, but instead of using a rake, you will use your hands. Yamir!" the goliath turned to his other prey. "You will help her. Go, now, before I change your punishment into something much worse!"

As soon as they were dismissed, Yamir and Lluava hastily made their way to the arena, closely followed by the general. Entering the arena, Lluava saw several cloth sacks lying in the center, along with a rake. The grand master chief grabbed the rake and stormed out.

What little moonlight they had proved useful, aiding in their already enhanced night vision. Together, Yamir and Lluava began to scrape the blackened patches of earth with their hands. Because the ground was so dry, only the top layer came away. It was going to be a long night.

"Can I help?" a small voice squeaked from the entryway.

Still kneeling, the two turned to look at Chat who, wide-eyed, awaited a response.

Lluava smiled. "Come on, grab a sack." Chat, with his rodent-like smile, scurried to help.

The moonlight illuminated the youngster, and Lluava could see how much baby fat he had lost around his face. His slenderness was intensified by the height he had gained. Buck teeth still poked from his mouth in that familiar way as he concentrated on scraping the ground.

"I have an idea," Yamir said as he stood and stretched. "This is taking too long. Stand back."

Lluava watched him curiously as he shifted into animal form. Spiked hair lengthened and hardened while pointed quills sprang from his back, became rigid, and locked into place. Soon Lluava was staring at a porcupine. This unusual animal stumbled and somersaulted several times. As he rolled on the ground, a few of his barbed needles stuck in the earth. Moments later, he changed back.

"Use the needles to pick at the ground," he said, grabbing one and scratching at the hard surface.

"Oh, yeah?" replied Chat playfully, melding into a red squirrel. With his tiny, needle-sharp claws, he quickly scraped the soil. Yamir shrugged with a grin, then both he and Lluava changed into their dual forms, and all three animals dug at the stained earth with their claws. Even with their hard work, hours passed before they were finished. The moon was nearing its highest point as three dirty bodies left the arena with three neatly tied and very heavy bags on their shoulders.

After wishing the boys good night, Lluava began the lengthy trek to Thowcelemine. The night guard at the gate looked questioningly at her as she returned to the camp; half-asleep and longing for bed, she did not even notice. Without changing clothes, she threw her aching body on top of the sheets.

"Ow!" Lluava had landed on something hard. Reaching under her lower back, she pulled out Berkley's vial. She had forgotten about it. Sitting up, she pulled out the cork stopper and let the soothing liquid drip into her wounds. The serum warmed every spot it hit. She sank into a dreamless sleep.

All too soon, Lluava was gently shaken awake. Her eyelids were heavy. As she forced them to open, Ojewa's smooth, dark face appeared before her.

"Time to wake up," he almost purred.

Grumbling, Lluava slowly lowered her sore body to the ground. Though it was still too early for the girls to rise, she spied Rosalyn standing next to Ojewa.

"Lluava, what in heaven's…?" Rosalyn stared, awestruck, at her bunkmate.

Lluava looked down at herself. She was a wreck in every sense of the word. Her clothes were stained. She knew her hair was disheveled, and she reeked of stagnant water, blood, and sweat. It surprised her to see her wounds scabbed over and well on their way to healing; in several places, you could not even tell that she had been hurt.

"Do I have time to wash up?" asked Lluava, her voice hoarse.

"Not a lot," Ojewa coolly informed her.

Without another word, Lluava grabbed a change of clothes and her white swimsuit and jumped into the shower. Clean, awake, and refreshed, she was ready for the day. Before leaving for Durog, she briefly filled in the eager Rosalyn on yesterday's training and gave quick updates on Yamir and Chat.

Lluava arrived just in time for the morning run. Afterward, the troop did calisthenics before grabbing a five-minute breakfast. She kept close to Yamir, afraid that some angry person might want to pick a fight with the girl who had lost them meal time. He showed her an unused loft area where he and Chat preferred to eat. For the three of them, this niche would become a refuge.

***

The next few weeks passed as smoothly as could be expected. Although the specific schedule might change, the basic format of each day stayed the same. The grand master chief came and went as he pleased. Skipe, aloft in his kestrel shape, kept track of all that lay below and supervised their dual-form sessions. Lluava began to discover that she could speak fluently in her felid shape. On days when they did not practice fighting in their animal forms, the recruits worked out in the gym with weightlifting equipment.

There was always a water class, in which recruits learned a dozen different strokes. Sometimes they swam laps as humans, other times as animals. Unfortunately, some animal forms, like Chat's squirrel, were not good swimmers. Lluava was fortunate that tigers were very comfortable in water. Eventually, she was as much at home in the water in her human form as she was in her tiger form. Sometimes the group split up and completed tasks, such as collecting a certain number of sunken items in a limited time. Lluava actually enjoyed these sessions.

The recruits were expected to become adept with a variety of weapons before specializing in one or two. In training, weapons were rotated often. Although Lluava was competent with the short sword and twin daggers, the broadsword was still a bit of a struggle. Skills like archery or throwing the javelin were more difficult to learn, but she worked hard and adapted quickly.

Lluava did have a few problem areas. She struggled to control her instincts in her dual form. On several occasions, she had to be separated from the others. The troop had daily exercises on a course that constantly changed as well as increased in difficulty. Soon it was impossible to complete on an individual basis; the recruits had to work in groups of two or three to succeed. Regardless, with the exception of Chat and Yamir, the other recruits ignored her and refused to give her any aid. This not only hurt Lluava's individual performance score, but it also damaged the troop's formerly perfect score. Although it was obvious that Lluava was not the sole cause, most of the troop blamed her for holding the team back.

To make matters even worse, the grand master chief constantly criticized her, even when she performed a task or challenge as well or better than others. He took every opportunity to humiliate her publicly and continually meted out punishments for her and sometimes for her friends as well. He made no attempt to disguise his hatred of this female who was the primary source of all his problems.

Every night, Lluava dragged her aching body to bed, yearning for the good night's rest that always seemed to elude her. She found herself truly debating whether or not this pain, this struggle, this humiliation was worth it. She was not sure.

Some changes were positive, however. Lluava was becoming close, really close, to Rosalyn. She had never felt such a connection with another girl. Each morning, Rosalyn woke extra early to have a private talk with Lluava; in turn, Lluava looked forward to their early-morning confidences, their sharing of dreams and hopes with one another in quiet whispers.

Changes were also occurring within Lluava. Her body had become toned and sturdy. She did not bruise as easily, and she healed faster. The sun had darkened her olive skin while bleaching out what color remained in her platinum hair. She was faster and more flexible. Transforming no longer hurt or slowed her down.

She became more comfortable wearing her swimsuit during training. Layers made her too hot in the summer's heat, and sweat made her clothes sticky. On overcast days, she still wore a short-sleeved shirt and shorts, but the weather was usually too dry even for clouds to form.

During the middle of one of the hottest weeks, all the troops received a new set of instructions. All eyes were trained on the burly grand master chief. Clearing his throat, he announced, "You will be divided into groups of four or five. Outside your regular training time, each group will give a presentation explaining how you would command an army in different scenarios. Each of you must participate in both the research and the presentation. This is an important assignment; not only will you learn to negotiate with your group, but you will also learn valuable military tactics. Presentations are in one week. We have a fully stocked library; use it. Listen up! Group One is composed of…"

Lluava's mind raced. She would prove that she was a valuable asset to her group. She knew Kentril would let her use the books in Thowcelemine to help her team with their research. Her ears perked up when she was placed with Talos and two others.

That evening, Lluava met up with her partners. One was Findley, the fox-boy; the other was a heavyset young man named Truden.

Talos read their scenario aloud: "Your army has lost ground and fears being cut off from the main force. The opposing side outnumbers you eight to one. Your location is seven miles northeast of the southern training facilities. What do you do?"

"Since we are in the southern camps," Truden responded with a snort, "that should be helpful for us, since we already know the area."

Smiling, Lluava offered, "I can use the resources from Thowcelemine to look up local topography and current military strategies."

"We don't need any help from your friends in Thowcelemine. We have everything we need in the library here," retorted the redheaded Findley.

Lluava quieted at that remark. Apparently her help was not wanted.

"Actually, Findley," began Talos, "I think any outside resources would be beneficial to our project." He turned his handsome face to her. "Lluava, please bring any information you can dig up to our next meeting tomorrow night."

"Of course," she replied. She couldn't help looking into his sparkling brown eyes.

Returning to Thowcelemine that night, Lluava immediately made her way to its library. This was the first time she had actually entered the room. Numerous shelves were jammed into the tiny space. Had she been human, the waning light would have made it too dark to read, but thankfully, she was a Theriomorph. Skimming the titles of the leather-bound books, she pulled half a dozen from their shelves and carried them to her bunker.

At the following night's meeting, having toted the heavy books in her shoulder bag all day, Lluava placed them on the table. Both Findley and Truden were already deep into their own research.

Talos remarked, "Wow! Thanks." He grabbed one volume Lluava remembered pulling from the upper corner of a tall shelf and skimmed its pages. Lluava opened another on the geography of the kingdom.

"Hey." Lluava felt Talos's hand on her shoulder. "Check this out." Crouching next to her chair, he placed the timeworn tome in front of her. On the yellowed pages were diagrams of Durog and the master workmanship that had created its unique buildings.

"Look." Talos pointed to a drawing that showed a much older layout of the camp. "This place used to be some sort of ancient fortress." On the next page, another drawing indicated an underground tunnel leading from the one of the buildings in the western quadrant to a rocky inlet by the sea.

Both Lluava and Talos regarded each other for a moment, and then she spoke. "We can use this for our project. This is great!" Smiling at one another, they began to formulate their strategy.

On the morning of the presentation, Lluava woke up before Rosalyn. She showered and dressed and then grabbed her pack, which contained her speech. As she was leaving the barracks, Rosalyn called to her.

"I have not seen you in the past few days," Rosalyn sighed. "Where have you been?"

It was true. Lluava had been running between training and her project. She had barely seen Rosalyn, much less taken time to speak to her friend.

Lluava had missed their talks. "I'm sorry. I've been really busy. I have a group presentation today, and I've worked on it all week. I promise, once this is over, things will settle back to normal."

In her silky voice, Rosalyn replied, "I know you will do splendidly today. I just miss talking to you. You have not heard that I am first in our class. I am now responsible for setting up the quarters for special guests. I am actually going to Durog today to set up the guest lodge for General Jormund."

"I can't believe it! I mean, well, I can, but—wow! First in the class—congratulations! Do you want to walk with me to Durog?"

"Oh, yes," the elated Rosalyn responded. "I was not looking forward to walking there by myself."

As both girls headed to the other camp, they talked incessantly, catching up on the past week. Rosalyn passed through the gates of Durog in awe. Lluava smiled, remembering the feeling. After pointing Rosalyn in the right direction, Lluava, feeling rejuvenated, went to meet her troop.

Lluava looked forward to the presentations. Surely her group must have one of the most intriguing demonstrations. The morning seemed to drag on forever. When Skipe finally led the recruits to the large arena, she began to become nervous. She wished her team could have met earlier and rehearsed their parts one more time. As it was, Lluava had not been able to speak to any of her teammates.

As she sat down on the stone benches of the coliseum, she watched the first team set up a display of several maps of the northern section of the kingdom. The grand master chief soon arrived, clipboard in hand.

"I finally found my slate chalkboard," huffed Truden as he took the seat behind Lluava.

"Good. Do you have your part of the speech memorized?" she asked.

"I hope so," he replied nervously.

"You better have," whispered Findley, as he slid in next to Truden. "I want to win...I mean, I want our team to win." Quickly changing the subject, he added, "Hey, have either of you seen Talos? He's supposed to bring the diagrams he had drawn up. I don't see him."

Lluava scanned the stands. Findley was right; Talos was definitely not here. Where could he be?

As if reading her thoughts, Findley said, "Talos better not be wimping out on us. We need him."

"He'll be here. Just wait," Truden said hopefully.

The first group completed its presentation on offensive attacks for sea-based warfare, but Talos had still not arrived. Lluava stood up and turned to her partners. "I'm going to look for Talos."

"You'd better find him fast," snapped Findley. "There are only six other groups before ours, and who knows how long they will take."

Lluava slipped from the coliseum as the second team began its presentation. She was furious. How could Talos ditch them like this? How could he work so hard all week and then just abandon his team?

Where to begin? She backtracked to the small arena, only to find another troop practicing with bolas. Next, she ran to the lake. She made it in seven minutes—her fastest time ever—but found only still water. Turning back to camp, she made her way to the library, but it was deserted.

Time was running out. Her temper was flaring. A low rumble emanated from her core, one that she could not stifle. Her felid form tried to emerge as she checked one empty barracks after another. Her enhanced senses heard beetles burrowing into the wooden walls, tasted the scents on the breeze. Suddenly, she caught a whiff of tangy musk: whitetail deer.

"Talos!" exclaimed Lluava. She followed the scent through the camp to the guest lodge. Swiftly and silently, she took the stairs to the second floor and sniffed the air one last time. Stopping near one of the rooms, she took a breath to calm herself and then swung the door open.

Talos was inside, but he was not alone. Two bodies embraced in the center of the room. Lluava caught her breath as her mind rapidly tried to process what she was seeing. Hearing her gasp, Talos and Rosalyn quickly released each other. Lluava stared at them, aghast.

Talos cried out, "Lluava, wait! You don't understand!"

At the same time, Rosalyn implored, "Lluava, please! We are engaged…"

Chapter 12
Whispering Walls

The words reverberated in Lluava's mind. Shock, anger, and hurt made her head spin. The rush of mixed feelings, the overwhelming sense of betrayal, threatened to engulf her as she struggled to understand what had just occurred.

"You!" Lluava looked at her bunkmate, who was now in tears. "How…why didn't you tell me? I thought we were open about everything, yet you kept something like this from me? Didn't you trust me?"

Sobbing, Rosalyn tried to speak. "No, it was not that…."

"What was it, then?" Lluava cut her off. "Why keep this a secret?"

"Lluava, please," interceded Talos.

Somehow that enraged Lluava even more. "I'm not talking to *you*." She glared at him and then turned back to her bunkmate. "Rosalyn, I asked you a question."

"I…" Rosalyn began. She clung to Talos as if he were supporting her. Almost inaudibly she whispered, "I was afraid."

"Afraid? Afraid of what? Of *me*?" Lluava couldn't keep the hurt from her voice.

"I was afraid of what they would do"—Rosalyn paused for a moment to calm her shaking voice—"if they found out."

Lluava observed Rosalyn's tears glimmering against her pale skin.

After a long silence, Rosalyn began to speak. "We did not want anyone to find out because we feared that one of us would be transferred to a different region of the kingdom to train."

Talos joined in. "It is known that the commanders disapprove of couples; they claim such bonds are a distraction and hinder progress."

Still holding tightly to Talos, Rosalyn stepped forward. She spoke again, this time with passion. "I love him. I love him, and I always will. With the draft, we knew we might not be able to see one another again. But just the thought that he was nearby, that there was some sort of hope that I might see him, even if only a glimpse, kept me going. When I was told that I would be the one sent to Durog to help prepare rooms for guests, I had to see him again."

Rosalyn turned to Talos, and a wordless understanding swept between them. Lluava felt like she was spying on something very private.

Talos broke the silence. "I know it was wrong to slip out on all of you, but please understand, I have not spoken to Rosalyn since I arrived here. I had to be with her again, if only for a moment."

Lluava did not know what to do or even what to say. Finally she commanded, "Come, Talos. We need to go before anyone discovers we are missing. Our presentation and our team are depending on you."

Thus assured that the secret was safe, Talos followed Lluava from the room. As he left, he mouthed the words "I love you" to Rosalyn, who had begun to sweep the floor.

They slipped into the coliseum just as their group was called. Talos pulled the diagrams he had drawn from his satchel and laid them on the table. Truden propped up his slate board. After a nod from Skipe, they began.

Lluava thought it went perfectly. Their well-prepared and eloquent speech kept all the onlookers intrigued. Each one of them took a turn to talk while throughout, Truden illustrated their military strategy on his board. Many recruits leaned over the edge of their seats as Talos used his beautifully drawn diagrams to explain how the troop could retreat into the confines of Durog where the walls of the fortress would protect them from the oppressor's forces. Talos explained that, even if the enemy surrounded the camp, they could send scouts to alert the main army by using the underground tunnel.

Excited by the news of a hidden tunnel, the onlookers began to talk among themselves. Quieting them down, Talos finished by explaining that the main force would secretly surround the enemy camped outside Durog and capture them. The recruits applauded the team as they cleared off the table and reclaimed their seats.

The other presentations were not nearly as intriguing as theirs had been. When everyone had finished, the recruits filed out to complete their remaining classes and exercises. All were curious. Who had won the competition?

At day's end, under a darkening sky, the entire camp, eager to hear the results, lined up in formation. The grand master chief read out the top four teams. Theirs had been awarded a disappointing fourth place. Lluava believed they deserved better; on the other hand, she had missed the other groups' presentations.

After they were dismissed, Lluava caught up to Colonel Skipe. She had to know what mistakes they had made.

"May I ask a question, sir?"

The hook-nosed man regarded her. "You may, recruit, and I have something to tell you."

Lluava asked, "What did my team do wrong in our presentation? I'd like to know where we lost points and how we can improve next time."

The colonel responded. "I wanted you to provide your answer to the problem assigned to you in a logical, realistic fashion. Interesting as it was, I do not care for imaginary solutions. You are lucky to have received the grade I gave you."

This accusation angered Lluava. "What false information? Everything we said was pulled together from research."

Sighing, Skipe continued with sarcasm. "Recruit, do not insinuate that I am naive. There is no secret tunnel leading to the sea. As entertaining as that idea is, such a tunnel does not exist."

Lluava was taken aback. "But what about the book we found? It had diagrams, detailed drawings, everything!"

Skipe turned to her, suddenly attentive. "What book?"

"Um," Lluava responded, "we found diagrams in a book I borrowed from Thowcelemine. They are there, I swear."

"Show me the book, Lluava. Then I will change your team's score."

Lluava was pleased at the news. "I put it back, but I will bring it to you tomorrow."

She was headed toward the gate when she heard the grand master chief call to her. She turned to see the menacing figure advancing toward her.

"You never fail to disappoint me."

"Sir?"

"How dare you disrespect your troop and leave during presentations! I do not know why you always seem to want to give me a headache. You will wash both corridors in the general's barracks tonight."

Lluava's jaw dropped. How had he noticed? Oh, well, no use complaining. The punishment once given would remain.

A voice spoke from behind her. "It was not Lluava's fault but mine."

She had not noticed Talos approaching them.

"What did you say, recruit?" huffed the intimidating man.

Respectfully, Talos continued, "I, uh, well, I...I panicked about making the presentation and ran off to my bunker. Lluava came and found me. It was she who calmed me down enough to give that speech. Lluava saved our group."

The general's face showed his disappointment. Talos had been his favorite recruit. "Because you abandoned your group, *you* will clean the floors." He turned to Lluava. "You, too. You should not have run off to search for him without first informing your superiors."

After the grand master chief had gone, Lluava thanked Talos. "You could have let him just punish me, you know."

"No, I could not," remarked Talos. "That would be a poor way of showing gratitude to my new friend."

That evening, instead of having dinner with her troop, Lluava raced back to Thowcelemine to retrieve the book from the library. Reaching up to the dusty shelf, she pulled it down. As soon as she did, she knew something was wrong. This book was new. There were no battered edges, no dog-eared pages. Flipping through it, Lluava was shocked to find that this one contained neither drawings nor diagrams, only information on the procedures used to convert the ancient structure into a military facility. She skimmed through the entire book but found no mention of the tunnel. She and the rest of her team would have to accept the grade they had received.

Lluava barely made it back to Durog in time for evening laps; already tired, she struggled to keep up with the rest of the troops. Afterward, she made her way to the general's barracks. The two-story structure loomed in the night sky. Opening the thick oak doors, she looked down a dimly illuminated hall. Several candles, in stands attached to the wall, were already lit. Portraits of military leaders hung in heavy ornamental frames. Talos was already there, holding a bucket of sudsy water and a pair of scrub brushes. He handed her one, and they went to work. On hands and knees, the two scrubbed the hallway. The brushes were small, so the task took a long time. After a while, Talos called out to Lluava, "Hey, look at this portrait."

Lluava saw a painting of a young woman in her early twenties. A black ribbon and silver star were pinned to her uniform. Lluava recognized the North Star, the medal given to a soldier who has died in action while saving one's comrades. The young woman had an elegant face with high cheekbones complemented by wavy burgundy hair. The eyes seemed loving and kind although the face was serious. In the lower left corner, a cougar looked off into the distance. Lluava assumed this to be the dual form of the woman. Underneath the picture was a silver plaque that read,

In Memory of
Sergeant Illena Zethra
1259–1281
Awarded the North Star posthumously after sacrificing herself
to protect her commanding officer and twelve comrades.
Graduated with honors at the top of her class from Durog.
First female sergeant since the Merger.

"Look at the date, Lluava," remarked Talos. "She was the last woman to have walked the halls of Durog until you came."

It was true. According to the kingdom's calendar, Illena might have stood where she was standing now...some twenty years earlier. *How did you do it?* Lluava silently asked. *How did you make it through this training? Did you have to put up with the same discrimination that I face? More importantly, how did you accomplish so much in such a short lifetime?*

Lluava followed Talos to the painting opposite Sergeant Zethra's and read about Bruddar, a foot soldier, who had captured two dozen humans during the Landon Wars. Thereafter, Lluava and Talos paused in their work when they reached each pair of portraits and studied the metal plaques that explained the honors those pictured had received.

Halfway down the hall, Lluava stopped to admire the grand master chief's portrait. Without the stress lines that now marked his face, he looked a good ten years younger. Several medallions, including one denoting the commanding officer of a military camp, were pinned to his uniform. The portrait gave him an air of confidence. Lluava studied his strong features and realized for the first time that he was, in all respect, a handsome man. The animal displayed in the lower corner was the fierce mountain bear that Lluava had come to fear. His plaque was golden-hued as were those of all commanding generals. On it was written,

General Promethian Argon
Commanding Officer of Durog
1258 –
Graduated from Neody with honors at the top of his class.
Led the most successful scouting missions in the Outlands.
Youngest officer to command a southern military training facility.

"Neody," Talos explained. "Is one of the northern training camps. I thought I recognized his accent."

"Where is the grand master chief, anyway?" Lluava asked, rubbing her aching knees.

Talos pushed a strand of honeyed hair behind his ear as he knelt down. "He is in a meeting with some other general sent from the capital. I think his name is General Jormund."

"What's it about?"

"Beats me. I have no clue," claimed Talos as he scrubbed the hickory floors.

Upstairs, Lluava had to light all the candles they could find in order to see what they were doing. The hall was a duplicate of the one below. After another hour of scrubbing, their knuckles raw, they were finally finished.

A covered portrait at the end of the hall had aroused their curiosity, and they decided to take a peek before leaving Talos carefully slid off the deep magenta drape to reveal another portrait.

As soon as she saw it, Lluava announced, "I know this person! It's Kentril."

"Who?" asked Talos as he admired the gentle features of a man much younger than the one Lluava knew. The black hair was not yet streaked with gray, and the wide grin lent him a youthful demeanor. A silverback gorilla's head and shoulders were profiled proudly in the corner.

"He is the commanding general of Thowcelemine," she explained.

Talos bent down to read aloud the plaque's inscription:

General Brout Kentril
1253–
Respected Military Officer
Only survivor of the Osmund Discovery Mission
Endured three years in solitude on an unknown island
Advisor to King Thor

"Wow," Lluava exclaimed. "I didn't know any of this."

"He sounds impressive," said Talos as he stretched. "Let's get out of here."

"I agree."

As they slipped the drape back into place and made their way downstairs, Lluava felt crisp folded paper in her pocket. She remembered the letter Rosalyn had secretly given to her before leaving Thowcelemine that morning.

"Oh, Talos, wait. I have something for you."

The young man stopped halfway down the hall. "Yes?"

Carefully Lluava pulled the envelope from her pocket. She noticed that the corners of the paper, forgotten all day, were wrinkled from being carried about. She handed it to Talos. "Here you go."

Lluava watched as he carefully pulled out the note and silently read it. As he did, his face seemed to glow in the dim light. After he reread it, his face lit up even more.

Turning to Lluava, Talos asked, "I do not want to impose, but would it be too much to ask you to give her a note from me?"

Without pausing, Lluava agreed. Talos hugged her. Surprised by the affectionate and unexpected gesture, she was unprepared when he released her. As she stumbled into the frame behind her, she heard a snapping sound followed by Talos's gasp.

Turning, Lluava observed that the portrait of grand master chief had shifted, exposing a hidden passageway. The friends peered into a dark, narrow shaft that could barely accommodate a single person crawling on hands and knees.

"Where do you think it goes?" Lluava wondered aloud.

"I don't know. Want to find out?" Talos started down the passageway.

"I'm not sure about this," Lluava responded. "What if you become stuck?"

"Come on," he replied. "It is an adventure."

After a pause, Lluava slipped in behind him. "I hope there's enough room for both of us."

When the shaft widened, they crawled side by side. Soon the tunnel dead-ended in a wall, but they could hear the sound of conversation from the other side. Though the words were muffled, Lluava could make them out. Quietly Talos and Lluava listened in on the heated discussion between the grand master chief and the guest general.

The grand master chief sounded annoyed. "Just tell it to me straight. What in hell's many fires is going on, Jormund?"

A booming voice answered him. "Do you remember Grend Lout?"

"General Lout? The man who oversees the central camps? Yes, I know him."

"Argon, you may want to sit down. The day after overseeing the aqua exam for Camp Corbin, General Lout was discovered floating face down on Lake Cherin." Jormund sighed.

"Lout? Dead?" The shock in Argon's voice was obvious through the wall. "How?"

"We do not know for sure, but I suspect foul play. He had recently passed the health exam with flying colors. We both know he was one of the best swimmers, dolphin or man. He was also one of our best leaders and the second most trusted of King Thor's military advisors, therefore a primary target for assassination. Our enemies want to take out those close to the king in the hope of weakening our kingdom. Or perhaps I am jumping to a false conclusion."

Argon disagreed. "No. It does make sense. I would do likewise if I were in charge of the enemy. It is logical to assume that they are already attacking the pillars of our country."

"I am glad that you agree," Jormund boomed. "This is why we must speed up the training process throughout the nation. Although the High Council does not think that a major attack is imminent, we feel it best to prepare as quickly as possible."

"What?" growled the grand master chief. "There is no way to 'speed up the process' without sacrificing the quality of the recruits who leave here. I will not allow that to happen. Only the best graduate from this institution."

The response was immediate and emphatic. "You *will* speed up your precious process," trumpeted the now unwelcome guest, "and you *will* be done in half the time. That's an order from the High Council."

A roar penetrated the wall and made Lluava's ears ring.

Jormund continued, "The council is sending an overseer to make sure the camps are preparing recruits at the designated pace. He should arrive in Durog within the next cycle of the moon."

Argon seemed to have calmed down a bit, though his distaste continued to seep into his voice. "Who is this 'overseer'?"

"I do not know. All I know is that the overseer for the southern camps has already arrived at Delphine and will soon move to Calitron. Durog and Thowcelemine are next. Until everyone has graduated or the war begins, he will be reviewing these camps. You are my good friend, and I did not want his arrival to come as a surprise. I wanted you to know the reason behind this push."

"Thank you, Jormund. You are a true friend," the grand master chief said coolly. There was an audible scuffling of chairs being moved.

Lluava and Talos had only a moment to glance at each other before scrambling back through the shaft. There was just enough time to right the picture in its frame before the two generals stepped into the hallway.

The grand master chief glanced only briefly at Talos and Lluava before escorting the even larger man up the stairs. Lluava recognized the seven-footer from the meeting at Thowcelemine.

After storing the cleaning supplies in a closet, the two friends left the barracks. They were unusually quiet, preoccupied with many thoughts: secrecy, murders occurring in the heart of the kingdom, a mysterious overseer who would soon arrive. Something was brewing underneath the surface of this calm empire, and only time would reveal the truth.

Chapter 13
The Tucala

As the next week flew by, Lluava passed a flurry of letters between the engaged pair. Even with the intensified training schedule, Lluava's friends still found a few fleeting moments to have fun. In addition, despite her own demanding regimen, Lluava found her rhythm, one that she could depend on.

There were also new discoveries. Rosalyn explained that Selphy had been her best friend since childhood and that she had fallen in love with her friend's twin brother, Talos. When Talos realized it was Lluava who had saved his sister's life, he was even more grateful. He began to spend time with Lluava and was eagerly welcomed into the group by the ever-trustful Chat.

One evening, after another day of grueling labor, the entire camp assembled in the large coliseum. As Lluava took a seat between Talos and Yamir, she heard whispers among the swelling crowd. As usual, Chat peppered Yamir with questions. Why were they here? What was going on? Had something happened? Watching the stands fill up, Lluava finally realized what a massive number of people Durog housed.

Silence fell when the grand master chief entered the arena. He stood proudly in the center of the dusty ground and straightened his broad shoulders before speaking.

"The entire camp has worked hard and progressed exceptionally well with their training. As a result, you will be given a free day tomorrow. Think of it as a holiday. There are several rules: You must stay inside the walls of Durog. You will act intelligently and will not destroy anything that is not yours. You will respect your fellow recruits. If you fail at this, you will be severely reprimanded." He paused to let his words sink in.

"This is a reward. Do not make me regret my decision." He scanned the crowd then dismissed them.

The recruits in the stands stood and applauded. Young men whooped and shouted as they pushed through the doors and headed to their barracks.

Yamir played with the spikes of his dark hair. "How much are you willing to bet there is some other reason for this 'free' day?"

"What do you mean?" inquired Chat as he kicked a small stone and watched it skid across the cracked earth.

Yamir spun around and faced the trio. "You really think whatshisname, Argon, would just award us a day off? I mean, really. The man has no soul and wouldn't care if we dropped dead of exhaustion. There has to be another reason, don't you think?"

Talos conceded. "It is odd, but what does it matter? A day off is a day off."

"I agree," chirped Chat. "What do you want to do tomorrow? We have the whole day to ourselves!"

"Sleep!" chorused the other three. The four friends laughed before going their separate ways for the night.

As soon as she entered Thowcelemine, Lluava heard that a similar free day had been declared there. Rosalyn could not contain her joy. "I do not know what I am going to do. I can finally read, or swim, or sleep! Lluava, we can even *sleep*!"

"I know," said Lluava, smiling. "I intend to do a lot of that."

As the women of Thowcelemine drifted off into the realm of dreams, Lluava pondered Yamir's question.

She awoke early the next morning to a sky still speckled with stars. After a moment of groggy awareness, she remembered that she did not need to report to Durog, and turned over to go back to sleep. Finally waking at noon, Lluava and Rosalyn indulged in a leisurely lunch with the rest of the girls, during which Shenne and her twin, Sonty, wanted to know all about Durog and the young men Lluava had met.

Around midafternoon, Lluava decided to visit Chat and her other friends. When Rosalyn saw that Lluava was about to leave, she stuffed a folded piece of parchment into her friend's hand and silently mouthed her thanks.

Entering Durog, Lluava listened to a sound she had not heard in the camp before: laughter. In the quad, as the king's flag snapped in the wind above Durog's, several recruits kicked a small ball. Others climbed the scattered trees, while youths in groups of twos and threes sat talking together on the front steps of their barracks. To Lluava, Durog had undergone an enormous transformation overnight.

Lluava didn't know where to look for her comrades, but she soon spotted Chat and Yamir, towels slung over bare shoulders, heading to the woods at the back of the camp. As soon as Chat noticed her, he ran over.

"Lluava, do you want to go swimming with us? Talos is waiting for us at the lake."

"Sure," she replied, glad she had worn her bathing suit under her clothes. "Just as long as there's no pressure to finish forty laps."

"No pressure," said Yamir, smiling. "Here, hold these." He dumped a half-dozen pears he had been carrying into her arms.

"Okay…" she said tentatively, looking at the yellow-green fruit.

As the three started down the trail into the shaded woods, Chat explained. "The mess hall is open all day, so we decided to have a picnic by the lake. That's why we're bringing all this food." He motioned to the overfull pouches they carried. To prevent impending calamity, Lluava grabbed the pears that perched precariously atop Chat's pouch and added them to her own armload.

Listening to the liquid song of the many birds perched in the canopy above them, the friends made their way to the lake. When they arrived, they saw they were not the only people that had come to swim. Talos awaited them on the beach, which was already crowded with towels and sunning, recumbent bodies.

"Come this way," said Talos, waving at them to follow. He led them through the woods and emerged at a secluded cove at the east end of the lake. Large white oaks shaded the inlet, which was much cooler than the main beach. Talos had already tied a rope swing to a tree that leaned out over the water. Now, he stretched out a large blanket for their picnic.

"How did you find this?" Lluava asked as he helped her place the pears on the blanket.

"I spotted it a few weeks ago during one of our diving missions. I've wanted to return ever since."

A splash was heard as Yamir tried out the rope swing. Soon, all four were splashing and spraying each other with water.

Before they knew it, they had worked up an appetite. Back on the bank, Yamir unpacked some jerky and a wedge of cheese from his pouch. Chat had brought several small loaves of rye bread. As they began to eat, Lluava discreetly handed Talos the letter Rosalyn had given her. He quickly tucked it away.

Lluava turned to Yamir. "Yesterday, you thought there was some other reason for this day off. I think there's something to that."

"What changed your mind?" inquired Yamir as he spat on his hand and twisted his wet hair into little spikes.

"Thowcelemine has the day off, too, and since this is not an official holiday, I think the camps must have needed an excuse to…I don't know," she tapered off uncertainly.

As the expert at creating conspiracy theories, Yamir continued for her, "…to allow all the officers to have a chance to congregate for some secret meeting of the highest importance. That sounds about right."

Chat spoke out with his mouth still full, spewing half-chewed cheese and bread everywhere. "You really think so? I just thought they were being nice."

"Hmm," pondered Lluava. "How is General Argon doing today?"

"I do not know. I have not seen him at all, actually," said Talos. "Come to think of it, I have not seen any of our officers except the two guards at the gate."

"I knew it!" exclaimed Yamir. "They are up to something!"

Lluava was finally intrigued. "Well, don't you want to find out what?"

"I do not think that would be wise," said Talos rather authoritatively.

"And why not? You scared?" teased Lluava.

"No, but I am not an idiot."

Lluava was offended. "So I'm an idiot because I'm curious?"

Talos backpedaled. "I didn't mean…"

Sneering, Lluava cut him off. "I may be a female, but I am just as smart as you." The words, once out, felt so good. Before Talos could interject, she continued, "My instinct is telling me something is amiss, and I will find out what." Turning away from Talos, she asked, "Is anybody else with me?"

"How do you intend to discover what is really going on, if anything?" inquired Talos disdainfully.

"By using that passage we found. If there is a meeting, that is the best way to find out," replied Lluava.

Talos gave her a look of warning. Though she could feel trouble reverberating in her bones, it only challenged her.

Seeming to read her thoughts, Talos cautioned, "That is not smart. We were nearly caught last time. If there is some huge secret meeting occurring at this moment, they would surely increase security. I do not like this."

Lluava rolled her eyes.

Talos went on, "I think if we were meant to overhear what was being discussed, we would be told. I am not with you on this."

"In and out really quickly? What do you say, Yamir?" prodded Lluava.

Yamir replied, "As cool as that sounds, I would rather enjoy the rest of my day off where I am safe and sound. Sorry."

Chat shook his head though Lluava tried not to acknowledge him.

"Fine," she declared, as she stood up and slipped her clothes on over her suit. "I'll go alone. I can't let this opportunity slide by."

"Be careful," warned Talos.

Lluava did not know why she had such a need to find out what was happening; she simply knew she had to try. Nor was the overheated feeling from her argument with Talos helping.

It was not difficult to sneak into the general's barracks and slip into the hidden passage. Crawling on her belly through the darkness, Lluava strained her ears to pick up any slight sounds. As she neared the dead end, she caught words here and there: *murder, conspiracy, royalty.*

What could be happening? Her thoughts ran wild. Just as she was about to pull her body into the wider area, she felt the movement of air behind her. Concentrating her senses on the sound of breathing coming from the opening of the passage, she tried to pull herself forward silently. But a strong hand clasped her ankle. Then several things happened at once. Her heart skipped a beat, and she was pulled rapidly backward.

As she tried to escape the powerful grasp, Lluava roared. In a single, sudden move, she was flung from the passageway and sent hurtling toward the far wall. Her body hit so hard, it sent vibrations through the wood. Her whole core throbbed as she tilted her head to look at the man above her.

The grand master chief, red with rage, quickly stepped forward and grabbed Lluava by the back of her neck. Jerking her up to her feet, he half dragged her through a small room to the door on the far side and threw it open. The faces of the kingdom's most renowned commanders, Theriomorph and human, stared at her openmouthed. Lluava recognized General Kentril, Major Ojewa, Colonel Skipe, and Admiral Merrow...even General Jormund. Her face reddened from complete humiliation and the lack of oxygen induced by Argon's iron grip.

General Argon almost growled. "We will take a break from our meeting while I show you and all of Durog what happens to those who not only disrespect the privileges given to them but also threaten the lives of all they know. This female whelp I am holding before you has been caught eavesdropping. She is one of the most unruly, wretched recruits I have ever had the displeasure to command." He gave her a little jerk and, without a glance, continued, "Come, everyone. It is time to give proper punishment. It is time for the Tucala."

Solemnly, the commanders stood in order of rank as the grand master chief marched his insolent recruit past them, Lluava regretting more with every step the huge mess she had once again brought upon herself. General Argon marched Lluava across camp to the doorway of the large coliseum.

Releasing her, he commanded, "Stay here until I call you. I want everyone to see you as they walk in." The burly general disappeared through the doors.

After a moment, a high-pitched siren summoned the entire camp's population to the large arena. As officers and recruits arrived, each person gave her a questioning glance. Tartus looked her up and down and with a smirk walked by only inches from her. Among the last to arrive were Talos, Yamir, and Chat. Chat ran up to her.

"What's going on?" he asked.

"Um..." Lluava could not bear to look at his smiling face, so she looked instead at her soft shoes.

The other two arrived right after Chat. Findley, spotting Talos with the small group of outcasts, came too. "Let's go in, Talos. Leave them be."

Talos turned to the redhead. "Findley, I am staying with my friends."

Findley shook his head and glared at Lluava before losing himself in the crowd.

Talos knew something was awry when Lluava did not follow the rest of the recruits. "What happened?" he asked sternly.

Lluava finally forced herself to look up at her friends. "You were right," she said. "I shouldn't have intruded into someone else's business." After a glance at the rapidly filling arena, she explained, "I was caught, and now I'm waiting for my punishment. Something called the Tucala."

Yamir, with a worried tone in his voice, asked, "And you're not afraid?"

"Afraid of what? I am getting so used to the grand master chief's punishments, they don't affect me anymore. The only difference is that this one's public," she sighed.

Talos spoke up. "Lluava, do you not know what the Tucala is?"

"No," she answered. "Why?"

The two older boys glanced at each other before Talos spoke again. "The Tucala is the severest form of punishment that a Theriomorph camp can mete out. It is also one of the oldest forms of Theriomorph military disciplinary action. This is serious, Lluava."

Lluava saw fear clearly etched on the faces of Yamir and Talos. Not sure she wanted to hear the answer, she nonetheless asked, "What's so bad about it?"

"People die, Lluava," stated Talos.

Lluava's throat went dry. She tried to swallow but could not. "How...how does the Tucala work? What happens?"

"When you enter the arena, several things could happen," Talos explained. "You will be offered either a weapon of the other's choosing or none at all. I pray that you at least will have some weapon, for your opponent will be able to pick his own. The point of the match is simple enough. All you need to do is to make one touch on General Argon. I suspect he will be your opponent."

Yamir interjected, "Yeah, he's wanted to take a good swipe at Lluava ever since she encroached on his territory."

Lluava was silent.

Talos solemnly added, "The grand master chief can continue to give hits until the Tucala ends." Another pause, another glance between friends. "There are three ways you can leave the arena: unconscious, dead, or as the winner."

Clearing her throat, Lluava forced herself to sound hopeful. She did not want Chat or the others to worry. "Sounds easy enough. One touch and I win."

"This is not a game, Lluava," replied Talos sternly. "Very few win. Most of the time, they leave in pieces."

"That just means I have to win," she retorted.

Chat looked at her. "Lluava...don't do this."

"I must," she said. "See you inside."

Yamir looked as if he were about to say something. Lluava did not want to hear any more and snapped, "I said, see you inside."

Shaking his head, Talos called to the boys, "Come on." They trudged past and made their way to the stands.

Alone in the sun, beads of sweat formed on Lluava's brow. She struggled to keep her nerves in order. She would have to stay calm to survive the Tucala.

Inside the coliseum, the grand master chief announced to the crowd of onlookers what was about to happen. He gave an edited version of the reason Lluava was being punished in this manner. After several minutes, he commanded her to enter the open arena.

Every pair of eyes in the coliseum was focused on her. The commanders, their expressions solemn, sat in a raised section at the far end. Lluava held her head high. If she was going down, she would give it her all.

The grand master chief stopped before a rack that held several types of weapons. Running his hand over the hilts of various swords and knives, he grabbed a long knife with a double-edged blade at its point and tossed it to Lluava, who caught it by the hilt. He slipped off his shirt and laid it on the rack. Then he grabbed a broadsword and, testing its weight, swung it in the air.

After a nod from the grand master chief, Skipe called out, "Let the Tucala begin!"

With neither salute nor bow of respect, the general swung at Lluava. The blow caught her at the base of her rib cage, knocking the breath out of her. She had only a second to be thankful that the sword's edge had been dulled with black tar before she was struck again. The grand master chief moved amazingly fast. With each twitch of his body, he battered the girl around the arena.

Lluava thrust and jabbed but could never reach her target. With every miss, she opened an opportunity to be hit, which the grand master chief exploited. Even with dulled edges, his sword broke the skin every few hits. Soon Lluava found herself forced to concentrate on defensive maneuvers instead of offensive ones.

She was floundering. No matter what she did, she was at the receiving end. Fear rolled off her in waves. She realized she was in trouble.

Barely catching her footing after leaping back to avoid another swing, she jabbed at the rippling muscles before her. The grand master chief moved swiftly aside, and Lluava struck air; then he slammed the hilt of his sword down hard on Lluava's back. The blow knocked her to the ground. She had only seconds to roll away before the tip of his sword thudded into the ground where she had fallen.

Pain pulsed with each beat of her heart, and Lluava knew she could not last much longer. She was exhausted. Suddenly, a strong kick knocked the knife from her grip; the glinting metal skidded far from her reach.

The next few moments were a blur. Dodging another strike, Lluava dove toward her weapon. Dust from the combatants' quickly moving feet rose from the ground, stinging her eyes and obscuring her vision. As the air cleared, she lay on the ground coughing, waiting for the final blow.

A unanimous gasp arose from the spectators.

Lluava wiped her teary eyes with one hand and saw that the knife she still gripped tightly in her other hand was touching the heel of grand master chief, who towered rocklike above her prostrate form. In silence and shock, the two regarded each other. A roar erupted from the crowd.

Without a word, the huge man let the sword fall from his hand. It clanked on the hard earth. Straightening, looking neither right nor left, the grand master chief strode from the arena, his head high.

Chapter 14
Driven

Lluava lay in the dust, listening to the cheers that thundered around her, watching the camp's proud leader depart. As her eyes followed his retreating form, she began, despite her exhaustion and pain, to think about this man who had made her life such a misery these past few months. Ever since her arrival, the brutish grand master chief had sought every opportunity to force her, a female, and therefore a black stain on the white linen of his camp—to give up and go away. Now she realized that the truth was more complicated. Had he moved his foot before the dust settled, no one, not even Lluava herself, would have known that she had won. He could have done so, but he had not. Had she lost, she would have called it quits and headed back to Thowcelemine. But she had not.

Lluava had thought the grand master chief wanted her to leave because he considered her, a woman, innately inferior to men. She now understood that he thought of women not as inferior, but as too weak for war. Therein lay a telling difference. Inferiority could not be changed, but weakness could be overcome.

To Lluava, the general had never seemed so much an honorable man as he did now, in the moment of his defeat. By allowing everyone to see that he had lost the Tucala, he had relinquished his pride. Perhaps she could gain the respect of such a man. She felt the idea grow, from intent to determination to iron resolve, to prove to the grand master chief that she could handle anything he threw at her. She would push herself beyond exhaustion if that was what it took to become the best. For, once the general realized she could rival any man in Durog, he would not only have to accept her but also respect her.

The insight that came as she lay prostrate on the hard-packed dirt was her turning point. From that moment, she spent hours of her free time working to improve her speed, agility, and strength. After she was dismissed for the day, she drilled herself in sprinting, practicing, learning to shift swiftly between forms in various attack combinations. Sometimes Talos or another of her friends would spar with her for a while, but she continued to practice long after the others had retired for the night.

A few days later, Yamir brought it to Lluava's attention that Talos had lost his status among the ranks when he began to hang out with them. The young men he once befriended had lost respect for him. The grand master chief had even selected a new favorite—Horus, a man in his twenties from a different troop.

Lluava could not help but notice the shift in favoritism. One afternoon, she found Talos and said, "You know, you don't need to stay around us. I will still pass the letters between you and Rosalyn even if you refuse to acknowledge me. I don't want you to lose the grand master chief's respect because of your dealings with me and my friends."

"Lluava," he replied, "If the general's respect toward me has waned due to my choice of friends, then I care not for it."

She persisted, "I don't want you to forfeit the honors you deserve when you graduate. You have worked so hard. It wouldn't be fair."

Talos countered, "Those so-called honors are not as important as true friendship. Remember that, Lluava."

The final tests for their water unit were fast approaching. Lluava turned her spare time to improving her swimming skills. She forced herself to dive more deeply, to hold her breath longer, to move faster across the liquid surface of the lake.

On the day of the water tournament, Lluava tied the straps of her worn swimsuit and sighed at how frayed it looked. She had worn the same swimsuit every day since she began training at Durog, and the once-white cloth was dingy and stretched thin. She had intended to ask for a new one but, having used all her extra hours to train, had run out of time. She crossed her fingers that the suit would hold up for one more day.

Before Lluava left for Durog that morning, Rosalyn wished her well. Outside, the sun's light was just paling the navy blue of the sky. In that lightening blue, cumulus clouds began to build. A male mockingbird sang to his sleeping mate and their young from the top of a tree by the side of the road. Lluava admired its ever-changing melody as she passed. The dew that sluggishly slid down the blades of grass dampened her endun shoes.

She was the first to arrive in the quad. She stretched her limbs while she waited for the rest of her troop. When all had arrived, they made their way to the lake. Peeling off shirts and shoes, the men waded into the cool water.

Admiral Merrow silently watched as the group lined up in formation. Showing his razor-sharp teeth, he smiled, as though he sensed the nervousness of those awaiting his command and relished the terror felt by the recruits who knew their futures were in his hands.

"Welcome to your final challenge in the water segment of your training." The admiral scanned the recruits. "You will be graded on three components: speed, teamwork, and endurance. First, everyone will swim one lap across the lake and back. This will be timed from the moment I whistle to begin until you crawl up on the bank.

"Second, each troop will be divided into groups of five and will complete a diving task like those we have practiced. Teams must find the hidden metal cubes like this one." He held up a cube, simple in design, painted a dull brown color. He continued, "There is one cube for each group scattered around the lake. You will be graded on how long it takes your team to locate and retrieve a cube and how well you work together. I will be watching all of you in my dual form. After each troop competes, the next will be divided up as the cubes are rehidden.

"The third and final task will involve endurance. You will swim in place in the center of the lake, where the water is deepest. The longer you stay afloat, the better your grade. Let's begin."

Grabbing the whistle that hung around his neck, Merrow blew a high-pitched starting sound. At once, the troop swam for their lives to the opposite side of the lake. Lluava started in the middle of the crowd of men. She became more and more agitated as she closed in on the far side of the lake; with so many recruits competing, she was crowded out of the lead. As she made the turn and began the return lap, she knew she had to make a move.

Taking a deep breath, Lluava dove beneath the bodies of the swimmers. The murky water made it hard to see the kicking legs and stroking arms only inches above her. The dark form of a three-foot pike disappeared in the dim distance. She forced herself to move faster.

A pressure formed in her center as the air in her lungs was used up. Kicking up from the lake floor, she shot up near the front of the line. The only recruit ahead of her was the small, sleek twenty-two-year-old in his otter form. With a quick jerk, the otter dove deep, emerging several yards from the finish point. Lluava would not come in first, but she was quite content with her second-place finish.

Merrow seemed to nod his approval as she made her way onto the beach. As the rest of the troop straggled to shore, the admiral jotted notes on his parchment. Then he divided the troop into groups for the second test.

Lluava was teamed with Yamir, Findley, and two other men whom she did not know well. She tried to talk to the others about how to approach this task, but, once the whistle was blown, they dove in without even a second glance at her. Lluava appreciated that Yamir stayed long enough to shrug at her before he started his search.

Diving into the water, Lluava swam deeply to search the thick water reeds growing on the bottom of the lake. Nearby, the dark forms of her fellow recruits moved frantically in search of the cubes. Lluava spotted one cube wedged between two half-buried boulders. She tried to tug it loose, but it would not budge. She kept tugging but was finally forced to the surface for a breath.

Propelling herself upward, Lluava took a huge gulp of air. A glance at the bank told her that no one else had recovered a cube. She dove back down to the lake floor. When the boulders came into sight in the clouded water, Lluava saw the otter-youth with her cube in his paws, swimming toward the bank.

Lluava wanted to scream but, instead, pushed herself forward. There were still six cubes left. She had to find one. Minutes slipped past as wriggling bodies scrutinized the lake's depths. Every so often, the slick form of a bull shark slid eerily past. Lluava's ears began to throb with the changes in water pressure. Ignore it, she told herself. When she spotted Yamir in the distance, her heart jumped—in his hand was a cube. They were done! Lluava was excited as she swam back to the shore. Her team finished third, behind the otter-youth's team and Talos's team. Wet and tired, they rested on the sand until the last group returned.

Before long, they were ordered back into the lake. It was nearing midday, and the sun glared down upon them. Tired now, Lluava hoped she could make it through the endurance test. They were told to line up in formation. This Lluava found hard to do. Anyone who shifted in the water would bump into those around him, causing a ripple effect down the line of recruits.

Lluava concentrated on the fact that all she had to do was keep swimming. The hours passed. During midafternoon, Chat swam toward shore, the first of many to accept defeat. At first, it was a slow trickle of men; but, as night approached, only a dozen remained in the water.

To keep her mind off her aching legs, Lluava admired the beauty of the night. In the darkening sky, stars began to appear, reminding her of the flickering fireflies that floated around her face. Moonlight glinted on the surface of the water. The soft sound of leaves rustling in the faint breeze was soothing, and the chirping of crickets on shore calmed her.

The slow progression of the silver disk across the night sky was the only way she could gauge the time. Eventually, she found it no longer seemed to matter. She closed her eyes, all her energy devoted to keeping her head above water. In that blackened world, time was irrelevant. The sounds around her were all that kept her from sinking into a watery slumber. From time to time, she heard the water stir around her or felt the movement of someone shifting position nearby.

Eventually, Lluava began to think of home. She pictured her mother cooking in the kitchen, Lamb running around the front yard with a toddling

Mouse in her wake, her grandfather sitting on the rocking chair watching the children play. She longed to be with them. She did not want to be here.

Lluava could not breathe. Opening her eyes, she realized she was sinking deeper and deeper under the water. Her exhausted limbs would not move as she willed them to. Her stiffened legs, like lead, could not be forced to kick. She was drowning.

With a jerk, Lluava felt her body pulled upward. The shark that had swum up behind her changed form and carried her to the surface, where she simultaneously gasped for air and spat up liquid. She felt herself being dragged onto the sandy beach. On her knees, trying to catch her breath, she slowly became aware of dark forms standing around her.

Noise. There was so much noise. Clapping. Applauding. Recognizing the faces of Merrow and her fellow recruits, Lluava saw that they were smiling.

A voice said something indistinct. She shook her head to clear her ears. What she heard could not be true. Yamir stood next to her and was saying something.

"What?" she asked, disbelieving.

Yamir looked her in the eyes and said, "Lluava, you won!"

Chapter 15
Gossip

The words kept repeating themselves in her head. She won. She won? But what did that mean?

Yamir seemed to read her mind. "You're the overall winner! You came in second during the race. Our team tied for first in the dive because Admiral Merrow saw you find the first cube, even though you could not free it." He laughed. "Lluava, you outlasted the entire troop during the endurance challenge by hours! Did you not realize everyone else had left? Or did you want to see how long you could last? Either way, you are the number one recruit."

Lluava was shocked.

Yamir helped her to stand on her shaky legs. "You not only won the aquatics training challenge, but you also set a record for the entire camp in the endurance challenge." He turned to the admiral, who was drying himself off with a towel. "I think she should get a plaque or something."

Wiping off his bald head, Merrow said, "Do not push it, recruit. Escort our winner to the infirmary. Make sure that old goat checks out her sunburn and inspects her lungs for water. The rest of you go to the mess hall. A *very* late meal has been provided for you."

Before she could leave, the rest of her troop swarmed over to her, shaking her hand or patting her on the back. Every one of them wanted to let her know how well she had done and how impressed they were. Finally, with Yamir on one side and Talos on the other, Lluava was helped to the infirmary.

As soon as her friends had settled her on one of the low cots, Berkley emerged from the back to see his late-arriving patient. He shuffled up to Lluava, the two tiny braids in his beard swaying as he walked, and began to inspect her blistering sunburn.

Yamir started babbling about Lluava's accomplishment as the elderly man rubbed green salve on her tender red skin. Exhausted, Lluava merely listened to Yamir's version of the story. She had to admit that he was a great storyteller; he embellished and stretched the truth so much that she would not have recognized her own story had she not just experienced the milder but true version.

When Yamir had finished, Berkley looked him over. "Still clumsy, I see," he said, peering at a particularly nasty bruise on Yamir's right arm. "Let me take a look." The old man pushed his half-moon spectacles farther up his nose. Yamir extended his arm for Berkley's inspection.

Lluava knew that Berkley found Yamir's clumsiness exasperating. If he only knew the truth, she thought. Yamir was not actually accident prone; he had become a living punching bag for others. The bruise on his arm had been left by several large men from another troop who had mocked Yamir's deliberately frayed clothes. The boy unraveled his clothes to express his individuality, to rebel against uniformity. Lluava was angered by the harassment that she and her friends endured. If it continued, she would find a way to end it. Talos sat down next to Lluava and asked how she was feeling.

"I'm fine. Just very, very tired," she said with a sigh.

"That's exactly what I would expect. You were really impressive out there today," he said with a smile.

"Do you have any of the serum left?" Berkley interrupted.

"No, I used it up last week."

Berkley pulled another small vial from one of the deep pockets of his long, loose coat and handed it to Lluava. The ancient healer's knobby fingers showed a slight tremor.

As Lluava stood up to leave, Berkley added, "You really have given your suit a good wearing. I will make you a new one." Pleased, she thanked him graciously.

When she and her friends entered the mess hall, the entire feasting crowd turned to look at her. It felt strange to know that, once again, so many others were watching her. After filling her plate with food, she climbed up to the space near the rafters where Chat was already eating. Lluava thought it was the most delicious meal she had ever tasted.

Over the next few days, Lluava realized that a new status had been accorded her. She was accepted, now—even respected. The members of her troop no longer gave her grief, nor did they harass her friends. She was finally treated as an equal without regard to her gender. Recruits from the other troops acted differently as well. Each in his own way, the commanding officers, too, acknowledged her rise to the top of the class—all, that is, save the grand master chief, whose constant scrutiny of her had not abated. Nevertheless, Lluava continued her extra training. With her help, Lluava's troop rose to the top—along with Troop 12, led by Derrick, the human named twenty-two-year-old leader. Derrick and his gang-like friends were some of the toughest brutes in Durog. Derrick's troop was known simply by "The Pack" since they all had dual forms of wolves. None were seemingly pleasant people.

A few nights later, as Lluava climbed into her bunk, she found a new, two-piece swimsuit lying upon her pillow. The small note next to it was written in deep violet ink: *I hope you like it.*

Berkley had outdone himself this time. The suit was special in several ways. First, it was not a solid color like all the other outfits. This one was made from white cloth with an overlay of black stripes. Lluava realized with surprise that the stripes matched those of her own dual form. Also, this endun cloth was thicker than the other sort used by the ancient warriors. Flexible and light, it was remarkably comfortable yet strong enough to act as a thin shield. She had heard about clothing like this, but now she was actually holding it between her fingertips.

Finally slipping under the sheets, she anticipated the slumber soon to arrive.

"Lluava, come here," called a voice quietly from the doorway. Recognizing it as Kentril's, she immediately arose.

"Walk with me," he said simply and headed to the main part of camp. Lluava wanted to ask the reason for the late-night visit but knew it was better to wait.

The wise commander finally inquired, "How are you feeling about your choice to transfer to Durog?"

Lluava did not know what was meant by the question. She paused. "I think it is making me a better person, both physically and mentally," she ventured.

Kentril studied her. "What I meant is, do you ever regret leaving Thowcelemine? Have you considered returning?"

She chose her words carefully. "There were times I thought I could not persevere through all the trials set for me. But I have learned that I am stronger than I thought. I am, in a strange way, happy to be training there. Why do you ask? And why now?" She had been training for several months; if he were concerned about her happiness, why had he waited so long?

A sigh slipped past Kentril's lips. "Things have been happening," he began. "Things that have jeopardized the stability of the nation. In our kingdom, suspicion of treachery is spreading faster than summer's wildfires. The world is tense, like a bowstring ready to snap; the High Council is ready to accuse anyone it can for the slightest idiosyncrasy, for any variation from the norm." He stopped walking and turned to face her.

"Lluava, due to your recent…," Kentril struggled to find the right word, "…*escapades*, you have now made yourself a very suspicious person." Lluava had known that being caught eavesdropping on the grand master chief would cause enormous trouble at some point. "You must understand that I am one of your biggest supporters, and I know you meant no harm. The moment you arrived in Thowcelemine, I recognized that you were an overly curious individual. Nevertheless, the fact of the matter is, the rest of the world does not understand that. Twice, now, you have been discovered in the center of strange, even questionable, events."

Twice? What did he mean, twice? Lluava wondered. Before she could ask, Kentril continued. "When the bridge collapsed, you survived what should have been a fatal accident. This caused a stir among the authorities. I did my best to persuade them to regard it as a fluke.

"Then you became the center of attention again. You were not only caught eavesdropping on a highly confidential meeting, but also discovered in a secret shaft whose existence is known to only a handful of people."

"It's not what you think," Lluava interjected.

"I know," Kentril said soothingly. "But you have raised many questions. You must understand that many of the High Council members have been waiting for a chance to justify their attempts to pass anti-Theriomorph restrictions. You have gained their attention. I fear they will use you as an example for the rest of the human-controlled government. Some have even suggested that you may be a traitor."

Lluava could not speak. Her heart pounded. How could she have gotten herself into this mess? She would never turn against king and country. What would happen if she were accused of aiding the raiders from across the sea?

Kentril broke the deadly silence. "For now, I have convinced those who have become suspicious that it is merely a coincidence. But I felt you should know that everything you do will be scrutinized. There are people waiting for you to make a mistake so they can toss you into some godforsaken dungeon. I am offering you advice."

Lluava listened attentively.

"As long as you are in Durog, you will call attention to yourself. You are the first woman to have entered its gates in twenty years. You have a commanding officer who dislikes you greatly and who will not come to your aid if anything occurs. Furthermore, while you are in Durog you are out of my jurisdiction; I cannot protect you. I implore you to consider returning here, to Thowcelemine. It is safer. Please consider it."

Kentril's brown eyes looked intently into hers before he turned aside, indicating their meeting was at an end. Bemused, Lluava managed to thank the general for his advice, but he was gone, swallowed by the shadows.

Deep in thought, she headed back to her bunk. She had plenty to sort through before she could fall asleep. One thing she was certain about was the gratitude she felt toward Kentril. Until now, Lluava had never seen him as anything but an authoritative commander. When did he slip into the realm of advisor? She didn't know although she liked it. Having not only Ojewa but also Kentril on her side was comforting. She hoped that one day, she and Kentril would call each other friend.

The next day, Talos and Yamir noticed that Lluava seemed distant, but it was Chat who asked how she was feeling.

"Oh, I'm fine. Just a little stressed, I guess."

"If you want to talk, we're here, you know," said Yamir.

She nodded, and the quartet headed to the gym to lift weights. By the end of the day, she had made a decision.

Lluava found Kentril making notes in his office. She knocked on the doorframe and waited for him to put down his pen and invite her in.

"Sit down," he said, waving to the small chair across from him. "Have you thought about what I said?"

"Yes, I have." Looking him in the eyes, she made her declaration firmly. "I'm going to finish my training in Durog. I won't be scared away by unfortunate coincidences. If I were, I would never again regard myself as courageous. And when this war begins, courage is what I will need."

Kentril regarded her for a long moment. "That is not what I hoped to hear, but it is your decision."

As she stood up, Kentril cautioned, "Lluava, be careful."

**

In the morning, Lluava was pleasantly surprised to find Rosalyn ready to accompany her to the men's camp.

"Two people are to arrive at Durog today," her friend explained. "I will set up their room."

Lluava was aware that since the draft had been instituted, small groups of male volunteers had arrived at the camp at irregular intervals. These men usually fell into one of three categories: those driven by honor, those driven by the desire for glory, or those driven by guilt or family pressure. The original recruits, the ones who had been drafted, often shunned the newcomers. However, to Lluava, they were just more people against whom she had to prove herself.

Rosalyn looked excited. "Since I do not have to be in uniform, I have the rare opportunity to dress nicely today. Which should I wear?" Her pale hands held up a deep blue dress and a white dress with pale blue embroidered flowers.

"The one with the flowers. It brings out the color of your eyes." Switching the subject, Lluava inquired, "I gather they are commanders of some sort?"

"I do not have the faintest idea. Lluava, why do you think they are commanders?"

"Well, you said they will have their own room, so they must not be staying in the barracks. If they aren't staying in the barracks, they must be important enough to receive special treatment."

"I see what you mean. However, all I was told was that this pair would stay in the newer barracks that have small private rooms for two people."

Lluava had not realized the newer buildings were being used. Built to handle overflow from the recent draft, it was logical that their doors were finally open. "If it's just two people, why didn't they make room in one of the occupied barracks? Do you know why these men are arriving so late? It must be almost time to merge the human and Theriomorph camps."

"Lluava, you now know as much as I do."

By the time Rosalyn and Lluava arrived that morning, Durog was buzzing with news. Lluava went in search of her troop to find out what the hubbub was about. She found her friends in front of the flagpole, stretching before their morning run. Chat, of course, was the first to fill Lluava in on the rumors.

"Hey, Lluava, did you hear who's arriving next week?" When he smiled, Chat's two front teeth looked enormous. He had grown in his time at the camp, and his clothes were inches too short. His brown knit skullcap was cocked to one side, and Lluava impulsively straightened it.

"Who's arriving?"

"I'm not exactly sure. Most people think they're royalty. Maybe Duke Petrarch and one of his sons. Isn't it amazing? Royalty here!"

Yamir snidely remarked, "Royalty have no place here. They are too rich to notice any problems beyond their banquet tables."

"A touchy subject, huh?" remarked Lluava. She was surprised by Yamir's opinion.

"Think about it. Royalty don't take the military seriously. From what I remember, and correct me if I'm wrong, humans in power don't actually fight. Command, yes, but they control their armies from a tent, far away from any real danger."

Talos raised his eyes at that remark. Lluava smiled and shrugged at him as Yamir continued. "When was the last time you heard of the upper classes truly fighting for their country? Hmm? They don't. Even during the Landon Wars, King Landon did not actually fight. He sent his soldiers to do the dirty work while he watched from the sidelines."

That was true. It was not human policy to send leaders into the midst of the fray. To protect them, the high command was kept separate. Once again, Lluava was struck by the unfairness of their government.

"Even today," Yamir continued, "the wealthy will send their children to train. They miraculously move up through the ranks, earning honor after honor, before becoming camp commanders or returning home to run their estates. I am not sure any of the aristocracy has sent their children to these camps since they found out there was to be a war. It has been rumored that some have paid government officials to keep their children out of the draft.

Personally, I think royalty are snide, haughty, and self-centered."

Lluava had never seen Yamir truly passionate about anything so serious. Suddenly, Talos began to laugh.

"What's with you?" asked Yamir.

"Yamir, did it ever occur to you that I am of the aristocratic class?"

Yamir's eye grew wide. "I'm so sorry. I didn't mean anything..."

"That is fine, Yamir. It was just interesting to hear what you really thought about people like me."

Yamir's face turned a light shade of red. Talos reached out and playfully slapped him on the back before becoming serious again. "You are right about some things, though. I do know that some aristocratic families avoided the draft. I could have, too, but there is no honor in that. I feel it is not worth living without honor."

It made sense to Lluava now—Talos's gallant demeanor, his well-groomed appearance, even his perfectly crisp way of speaking. This also explained why Rosalyn was so similar. Both must come from wealthy families who, as expected, had brought up their children in the human culture. It was apparent in the way they talked, dressed, and spoke.

As the day progressed, Lluava and the others entertained themselves by guessing who their guests might be, from influential government officials to members of wealthy families from the kingdom's capital. They laughed, picturing pompous aristocrats trying to stay in the general's barracks.

Heading to the gym, Chat said, "What if it's the prince himself?"

Both Lluava and Yamir laughed.

"The prince?" Lluava repeated. "The last time I heard of the prince, he was filling his days dancing at balls and courting every pretty woman he laid his eyes on. Of all the people in our country, he would be the very last one to come here."

"Well, I think it would be neat if it was Prince Varren," sniffed Chat.

"You've been quiet, Talos," said Yamir. "What do you think?"

Talos had removed his shirt and began to work with dumbbells. Lluava could not help but enjoy watching his muscles flex. She was glad Talos and Rosalyn were a pair, as they were obviously meant for each other, but she saw no harm in admiring Rosalyn's fiancé.

After he finished his set, Talos put down his equipment and asked, "Why not? Stranger things could happen."

The group finished their workout early. Talos and Lluava went to find Rosalyn while Yamir and Chat left to eat a quick lunch. As they wove through the maze of barracks, they encountered Skipe walking toward them.

Turning to Talos, Skipe said, "I need to talk to you for a moment."

Talos told Lluava to go ahead without him. "Tell your bunkmate hi from me," he said, and walked off with the Colonel.

As Lluava went in search of Rosalyn, she thought about the mystery guests. She was eager to tell her friend whom they suspected, but, when she calculated the time by the position of the sun, she knew she would have only moments. She did not want the grand master chief to punish her for being late.

Jogging in the heat, Lluava poked her head into several barracks before she found her roommate. As she walked quickly down the hallway, she heard Rosalyn's voice discussing the living quarters. Though hot and sweaty, Lluava had no time to waste in the cool building. She felt as if she would explode with her news, so she dispensed with the formality of knocking and stepped into the room.

Rosalyn was talking to two young men around twenty or so. The men were dressed like villagers. The taller one looked to be about six-two with dark, wavy hair. The other was smaller, his dusty-blond hair brushed neatly like Talos's. Both seemed physically fit, and both were taken aback at Lluava's sudden entrance.

"Lluava?" Rosalyn questioned, embarrassed.

Lluava butted in. "I've got to tell you something."

Before Rosalyn could respond, Lluava continued, "You know I told you that someone was coming to oversee the progress of our training? Well, we think that person is some sort of royalty, and he'll be arriving next week. I'm not certain who it is yet, but Duke Petrarch is a good possibility since he has always been a benefactor of the military."

Again, Rosalyn politely attempted to interject but failed.

"You wouldn't believe who Chat hopes it is. He wants it to be Prince Varren. The prince, gods above! Could you imagine that? His Majesty's grandson coming here, to the kingdom's hellhole, to watch us learn how to fight!"

Lluava started to laugh but then continued. "I'm sorry, but if, for whatever reason, it's the prince—no, it can't be. Prince Varren is a womanizer who's grown up in a fantasy world where there are no problems. Though I agree he needs a reality check to learn that not everyone in the world dotes upon him, he wouldn't stay a day in hell's sanctum if it were the only way he could get the crown!"

One of the men chuckled. Rosalyn, on the other hand, stood open-mouthed. Maybe she's one of Varren's fans, thought Lluava, feeling a bit sorry for her friend.

"I need to run before the grand master chief finds me missing. He'll have my hide on his wall. We'll talk more tonight." As the words left her lips, Lluava took off. She really could not afford to be late.

Lluava was lucky in that both the grand master chief and Skipe were also late. Running around without getting caught gave her a lightheaded feeling. No matter what happened today, she was sure she would enjoy it.

In her barracks that evening, Lluava found Alison and the twins huddled in a group around her bed, listening to Rosalyn talk about some cute boy. Was Rosalyn actually opening up about Talos? As Lluava approached, the girls fell silent.

"Who's cute?" asked Lluava.

Alison whispered something to the twins. They stood up and slowly went to their beds. Lluava looked at Rosalyn, who was now staring at the floor.

"Rosalyn, what's happened?"

Slowly and sternly, Rosalyn asked, "How *could* you?"

Lluava stared at her.

"How *dare* you?" Rosalyn said, even louder.

This confused Lluava. "What did I do?"

Rosalyn looked up. Her eyes were big pools of blue crystal. "Do you not know what you have done?"

"No, what did I do?" Lluava was irritated by her friend's barrage.

"Did you not see those young men I was with today?"

"Yes, what of them? Tell it to me straight; what's going on?" Lluava was becoming more and more distressed.

Tears formed in Rosalyn's eyes. "Lluava," she said. "You insulted the prince to his face."

Chapter 16
Regarding Redemption

Lluava could not speak. How could she have let this happen? Kentril had warned her to watch her step, and she had immediately turned around and insulted the prince to his face. Would she be accused of treason? Viewed as a traitor? Dragged off to trial in chains? Why had she said those things? What had possessed her to be so mean?

Rosalyn seemed as frightened as if she herself had committed the act. "You have done some unintelligent things in the past, but this—why can you not just use reason when you decide what to do or say? One of my best friends has already been sent away. I do not know if I could bear to see another forced away from me."

Tears streamed down Rosalyn's pale cheeks. "Lluava," she sobbed. "I had to tell him your name when he asked me. I am sorry."

The sight of her friend's ebony hair covering her face like a funeral shroud unnerved Lluava. "It's okay," she murmured as she sat down next to Rosalyn. The two girls held each other close.

That night, Lluava dreamed of cold, damp walls in deepest dungeons. Several times, she awoke wondering if guards were coming to take her away during the night. She was more tired in the morning than she had been the night before.

For the first time, Lluava actually dreaded going to Durog. Would the Obsidian Guard, the ones who served as personal bodyguards to the king, be waiting for her? With no way to communicate with her family, she hated the thought of her mother hearing rumors that her daughter was a traitor.

The walk seemed long; this was both a blessing and a curse. Lluava had time to dwell on her future and the million possible punishments she might receive. She savored the last few moments before walking through the gates of Durog.

The guards nodded to her as they did every morning. No soldiers awaited her. The normal sounds of the camp met her ears. The clanking of swords, the chanting of marching soldiers, and the shouting of commands soothed her.

Lluava joined her troop for their morning run. No one looked at her strangely or treated her differently. After they had completed their laps, Lluava shared with her friends what had happened. Talos gave her a stern look. While Yamir made a coughing sound, Chat's mouth was wide open.

Talos was first to speak. "Well, what is done is done. I know you did not mean any harm, and hopefully Prince Varren will understand."

"I can't take that chance," exclaimed Lluava, exasperated.

"What do you mean?" asked Talos.

Lluava confided in her friends what General Kentril had told her. They were as shocked as she had been. As she explained her predicament, she watched the young men's expressions change from intrigued to questioning to astonishment. It would have been amusing but for the seriousness of the subject.

Always sensible, Talos remarked, "You should have told us about your problems when they began."

"Yeah, we're here for you no matter what," Yamir added.

Lluava smiled. "Thanks."

"So, what do you want us to do?" asked Chat.

"I just want to lie low as long as I can," declared Lluava.

Yamir looked at Chat and said with a grin, "No problem. We have that covered." Chat seemed to get a glint in his eye.

"I won't say I like your choice to hide out, but know that I have your back," stated Talos.

Lluava was more than relieved to have such loyal friends. Maybe the day would not be as bad as she feared.

After dual-form training, the group made their way to the gym. As they passed the weapons armory, Talos shushed them. Voices could be heard around the corner, voices Lluava did not recognize. Squatting close to the ground in a defensive position, Talos peered around the corner; Lluava did the same. The two young men walking toward Colonel Skipe were the same two who had been with Rosalyn. Dressed as recruits, they blended in with other youth training in the camp.

"Colonel Skipe," the shorter, blond man called out, "May we have a word with you?"

Lluava regarded the young man. She tried to picture him wearing royal garb and sitting on an intricately carved throne. It was hard. Both he and his friend wore huge smiles. They seemed at ease not only in the clothes they wore but also in the camp's rugged environment. The blonde's playful look made it even harder to picture anyone taking him seriously.

"You may," replied the colonel, snapping a salute at the approaching men.

The shorter one then asked, "Do you know where the female recruit known as Lluava Kargen is at the moment?"

Lluava whipped her head back around the corner of the building, and her heart began to pound. If they were searching for her, she could not risk being spotted. Chat and Yamir moved closer to the edge of the wall, but she motioned them to be still. She could not be caught like this. Listening for the colonel's response, all four were quiet.

"I can't be certain, but she usually works with weights in the gym at this time. Is there some sort of problem?"

"We just want to talk with her."

Lluava realized she was holding her breath. Releasing the air in her lungs disturbed the red-hued dust, which tickled Chat's nose. He let out a loud sneeze.

A long moment of silence elapsed.

In the next instant, Chat and Yamir jumped out from behind the wall, in clear sight of Colonel Skipe and the royal guests, who were surprised at the sudden appearance of the recruits. Talos signaled silently to Lluava. As they slipped away, they heard the colonel ask if they knew where Lluava was.

"You want to know where Lluava is?" Yamir repeated the commander's words slowly as if he were really trying to think hard. "Um…I think she is in the gym."

"Really?" questioned Chat, "I was sure she was eating in the mess hall."

"Now that I think of it, Lluava did mention something about sparring in the coliseum. The large one, I think."

"You sure? I thought it was the small one."

While the two bickered about their friend's location, Talos led Lluava to his barracks. "We can stay here until it is time for our group task." He paused, and then stated what was on his mind. "Lluava, honestly, how long do you think you can keep this up? You know if they really want to find you, they will. All the prince has to do is give the command and the entire camp will be searching for you. Maybe…maybe you should think about facing Prince Varren. It may be beneficial for you in the long run." Another pause. "It is just a thought."

As the two sat in silence until it was time to meet the troop, Lluava's fears began to consume her. She had insulted the prince. He would send her away somewhere dark and closed off from the world. In that place, her life would be scrutinized. They would discover that she was suspected of being a traitor. She would be tried at court and sentenced to life in a dungeon, probably Tarturus, the worst one of all. And her family! Her family would live in disgrace because they had raised a traitor. Or worse, they would be punished, too.

Lluava tried to focus all her energy and concentration in the group exercises. First, they completed a timed relay race and then climbed a steep cliff at the far side of the camp. Lluava had never been this close to Burok Dûr, the solitary mountain that marked the far boundary of Durog. Lluava stared at the dark peak; it seemed to have a proud, almost indignant look. Although the Verta Mountains formed a semicircle around the kingdom, connecting with the Borren Mountain range to the north, Burok Dûr stood alone and far removed from the rest of the range. An ancient Theriomorph legend told how the hero, Sihad, had been imprisoned in this stone monument until his debt to the Theriomorph race was paid. It was this rocky pyramid that blocked Durog from the cool sea breezes.

Their troop worked quickly and efficiently as they moved in concert up the sheer cliff face. After the lead climbers discovered the best handholds, the others followed easily. Working as a team, the better climbers helped those who struggled. When Chat nearly lost his footing, Lluava grabbed the back of his shirt and prevented his fall. Talos and Yamir hoisted others up. At the top, they viewed the panorama of forest and camp below and celebrated their record time with a unanimous cheer. But even in this moment of elation, Lluava's heart was not at peace. Fear prevented her from being swept up in her comrades' proud feelings of accomplishment.

The grand master chief spotted Lluava as she reentered camp. She had no time to hide her worried demeanor.

"I need to have a word with you, Lluava. In my office. Now."

Lluava had hoped to slip away into the dusky evening without being questioned by anyone, not to mention General Argon. There was too much on her mind, and she was fed up with her commanding officer's harassment. As she faced his look of contempt, she sensed something inside her give way.

"Not now," she snapped. "I'm sick and tired of the demeaning jobs you order me to do and your unfair punishments for things I've not even done. I don't know how any king could allow someone like you to run a military training camp when you hold personal grudges against your recruits. I'm done taking your crap. I'm done!"

The words were out of her mouth before Lluava had time to think about what she was saying. There was no taking it back. She stared up at the general, who stood as rigid as a life-sized statue.

"Large coliseum. Now!" snarled the commander through compressed lips. In a daze, Lluava moved in the direction of the large arena. She did not ask what was to happen; she already knew.

Standing in the center of the arena, Lluava's eyes seemed to glaze over as the siren sounded and the camp members made their way to the coliseum. Chat, Yamir, and Talos beheld their friend. Each kept his anxious thoughts to himself. They knew this female standing in the center of the arena had finally broken the boundaries that protected them from the Tucala.

Lluava did not need to watch the grand master chief and a lieutenant position a fully stocked weapons rack at the far end. She did not need to see the two young men, the prince and his companion, take their seats in the raised box, or hear Admiral Merrow explain the Theriomorph ritual punishment for insubordination. Lluava did not need to hear the grand master chief announce the purpose of the Tucala. She knew that she had insulted the camp's head commanding officer and that she would need to make two touches. Moreover, she knew that she was not going to be as fortunate as she had been before. This time, the general could choose any weapon he wished, and she would not receive one.

Turing to the bare-chested man before her, Lluava mentally prepared for the worst. Glaring, he snarled, "I will give you one word of advice. Transform."

"What?" asked Lluava. Caught by surprise, she stared as the grand master chief shifted into his dual form. The great mountain bear raised itself on its hind legs and belted out an enormous roar.

Once again, the beast growled, "Transform!" before he swiped at his prey with sickle-sharp claws. Lluava ducked as the five deadly blades swept over her head. The bear drew closer. Lluava dropped and rolled as the beast clawed the air where she had just stood.

The audience gasped and yelled. Many cheered for the massive hulk, reaffirming his authority as camp leader. After the fourth swing, several recruits joined with Lluava's trio of friends, shouting for her to transform. Lluava paid no attention to the shouting voices. She could only concentrate on her next move.

A dark claw hooked her shoulder, ripping her shirt, tearing into her flesh. One flick of the giant's matted, fur-covered wrist sent her sprawling across the arena floor. In that sheer moment of panic, she at last reverted to that primeval side she kept hidden deep within herself.

In the next seconds, the audience began to go wild. The enormous beast pawed the ground several times; then, with a snort, it charged at the still prostrate girl on the ground.

As Lluava watched the bear race toward her, a hazy trail of dust rising in its wake, she transformed. In the blink of an eye, a crouching tiger now waited for the brute to come and crush her. The bear thundered toward the snarling cat and then dove at its prey. The tiger, a blur of black and white, leapt off the ground. As the bear hurtled past toward an almost certain collision with the wall before it, the tiger landed upon the beast's back and then jumped off.

"A touch, a touch!" The roar of the crowd was astounding as the bear and tiger circled, each waiting for the other to make a move.

A twitch of muscles from the golden brute's shoulder signaled Lluava to leap to the right—a bad mistake. The bear had only feigned its movement; now it seized the tiger's neck in its giant maw.

In pain, Lluava cried out, a high-pitched, screeching sound. Attempting to claw her captor, she was flung to the center of the ring. Twisting her body, the feline tried to spot her opponent. Suddenly back in his human form, the sweat glistening on his bare back, the grand master chief pulled a large, double-headed battle-ax from the weapons rack. He wiped the moisture from his brow and then resumed his attack.

Lluava watched the general effortlessly swing the heavy weapon with one arm. She stayed out of reach of the slicing blade whenever it came near her. Though her dual form was dangerous, it was no match for an ax. In the end, her large form hindered her. She was too big a target with nowhere to run.

Leaping, she pushed off from the wall just as the ax smashed into stone a hair's breadth from her hind legs. In the air, she shifted her form, landing in a somersault several feet from the wall. Sand coated her sweat-drenched body as she rolled across the hard-packed earth.

Through the settling dust, the hulking form of the general approached. A glint in the sun, and suddenly the head of the ax split the ground at Lluava's feet. She pushed herself backward, her body flat against the wall. Another swing; this time the tip of the ax met stone. With a heave of the grand master chief's muscles, the ax bit through the wall. Lluava's sense of time slowed; she could see the blade moving toward her head. Sparks jumped where metal met stone. The black tar cracked and splintered off, revealing the weapon's deadly point.

It was time. Lluava sprang between the legs of the general and took off across the stadium. The ax slashed at her leg, mercifully only grazing it. She could not fight him, but maybe she could outlast him. She could not afford a backward glance, for she knew the hulking man was on her heels. She heard his footsteps; he was gaining ground. In a desperate attempt to shake off her adversary, she quickly shunted to the right.

Pain! The broadside of the ax slammed into the back of her head and sent her spiraling. The faces in the stands blurred together. Lluava stumbled, trying to focus, as the edge of the ax caught her shirt, ripping and tearing it. But the blade did not pierce her flesh.

It happened suddenly. She heard the snapping of her knee as the general kicked it, the thud of the ax handle hitting her back, and her own cries of pain. She landed hard on her shoulder. The pain wrapped around her. She became dizzy, and tears blurred her vision.

Struggling to move, Lluava pulled herself forward, but the general stood over her. She could not move to avoid his strong kick. Rolling onto her back, she gripped her stomach in pain. Coughing, she gasped for air. The arena was absolutely silent. Lluava longed for an end. Looking past the towering man, she saw the sky above and wished she could fly away.

The general raised the butt of his ax to slam it into her face. As the weapon began to move in an arc toward Lluava's dazed eyes, a solitary sound was heard.

"HALT!"

The general's final swing was instantly arrested. Everyone turned toward the voice. Lluava craned her sore neck to see the dark-haired guest who stood in the raised box.

"I, Prince Varren Mandrun, order you to put an end to this immediately! This recruit has had enough."

One thought came to Lluava's mind as she fought for consciousness. The prince himself had stood up for her.

Chapter 17
Infiltration in the Mist

She was saved! But why? Wasn't the man who had just saved her the same man who should be condemning her? Lluava was confused, but she had no time to mull it over. An uproar erupted in the stadium as people jumped into the arena and rushed up to her. She was helped to her feet and moved toward the exit.

Lluava realized that her entire troop was helping her to the infirmary. It did not matter that she had broken protocol and insulted their commanding general; they had come to their injured comrade's aid. She was one of them, and they would not leave her hurt and in pain. She had finally earned their respect.

Glancing back quickly as they passed through the doors of the coliseum, Lluava spotted Prince Varren and his blond friend talking to the grand master chief, but she was whisked away before she could wonder what they were discussing.

At the infirmary, Berkley was waiting for her as the crowd pushed through his door. Three men carefully laid Lluava on a cot and watched while the healer examined her injuries. When the onlookers came too close, Berkley asked them to please give her air; yet it was Talos who took the initiative to clear the room.

"Everyone, out!" He ushered the recruits to the door. When several balked, he gave a sharp command: "Now!"

When the room had emptied, Talos returned and sat down next to Lluava. Berkley had finished administering salves and wrapping open wounds. Feigning seriousness, Talos asked, "So, what is the prognosis? Are you going to live?"

Lluava wanted to laugh, but her ribs hurt when she inhaled. "I'm going to be fine. I just have to stay here overnight to make sure I don't have any internal bleeding." She paused. "Um, Talos?"

"Yes?"

"What should I do about the grand master chief? I shouldn't have blown up like that, and I know it. It's just that I have been trying so hard to make him accept me, and, no matter what I do..." She looked away. The realization was hard to bear. "He'll never accept me, no matter what happens. I don't know what to do any more."

Talos thought for a moment before he responded. "My father is the Lord of Cremwell," he said after a moment. Cremwell was one of the biggest estates in the southern part of the kingdom, Lluava knew, encompassing several small towns and the inland city of Amargo, a distinguished center of knowledge. She had never imagined that Talos came from such a noble bloodline.

Talos continued, "When I let him know that I was going to be drafted, he took me aside and told me about a great man I would meet. He said that this man was the most renowned general alive and also one of the most just. When our country was threatened by outlanders from beyond the Verta mountain range, it was this man who organized the resistance and won. He is one of the few military leaders to actually see combat, and he has felt the loss of many a friend. My father told me these things because this man was to become my commanding general.

"The man is General Argon. He may seem harsh, but he has had a rough past. Lluava, I think you should talk with him, have a civilized conversation. I believe he is an honorable person, and I know he believes in duty before personal bias."

"I hope you're right," said Lluava. "I'll do that. I'll try to reason with him tomorrow."

The door to the infirmary swung open, and two men entered. As Berkley shuffled over to welcome the guests, Lluava recognized them. Prince Varren spoke kindly to the elderly man, while his companion walked straight to Lluava's cot. Turning to Talos, he asked, "May I have a word with your friend alone?"

Lluava's heart began to race. She looked at Talos in a pleading manner, imploring him not to leave her.

Talos stood up and formally bowed. He then bent down and whispered in Lluava's ear, "I will be outside if you need anything." He bowed once more to the prince and his companion and left. Berkley also left, pleading more important things to do in his back room.

Once alone, Varren's friend gave Lluava an enormous grin. "Congratulations! You are my new role model." He grabbed her hand in a firm grip and shook it.

Lluava was totally lost. What was happening?

"Nobody, and I mean nobody, has ever talked to Varren as you did yesterday. It truly took my breath away. Your guts, your nerve!" The young man's smile stretched from ear to ear. Lluava had never seen such a big smile. The prince walked over to them, but his friend continued, "Varren has needed to hear that for years. I have been waiting for someone to show him that the whole world—what was it you said? Oh, yeah, 'not everyone in the kingdom dotes on him.' "

Laughing, he slapped the prince on the back, but Varren's face remained solemn. Lluava was mortified; it was torture to listen to the young man ramble on about her insubordinate behavior.

"And then you stood your ground against your commanding officer. Do you have *any* fear? It amazes me. You are a wonder and, quite possibly, the death of modern hierarchy."

"I don't want to overthrow anything!" Lluava protested. She looked back and forth between Varren and his talkative friend.

"Don't back down now," urged the prince's friend. "You were doing so well!" Finally noticing her agitation, he switched subjects. "Anyway, I am Thadius Sihia II. Call me Thad." He bent down and kissed the back of Lluava's hand. "And, of course, you know Prince Varren. He is rather quiet outside formal settings. Don't mind him."

"Nice to meet you," said Lluava hesitantly.

Thad sat next to her. "Your performance in the ring…"

"Arena," corrected Varren.

"Whatever." Thad's eyes remained fixed on Lluava. "It was really good, considering the odds, you know? And your form! A tiger! If I could change into something else, a tiger would be one of my choices—or perhaps a giant eagle. Yeah, an eagle; it can soar over everything, watching the business of life yet separated from it." He gazed off for a moment then looked up at his friend. "Well, are you going to say something to her, or just stand there like a statue?"

"Yes," said Varren neutrally. "I will have my say."

Thad looked almost shocked that his friend had finally spoken.

"I have one question," said Varren, staring at Lluava. "Do you have any respect for authority? Since I have arrived, you have insulted both General Argon and me. I have never dealt with anyone who would dare say such things."

Lluava bent her head and tried to sound deeply apologetic. "I never meant to offend you. I'm sorry. I know I can't take back the things I said. I just hope you will take into consideration the fact that I have learned from my mistake before you issue your punishment."

The prince raised an eyebrow. "Punishment? I never said I would punish you. I just want to make sure that you are careful whom you choose to insult, whether to his face or behind his back." Without another word,

Prince Varren turned and headed out the door.

Thad, too, stood up to leave. "Once he learns to know the people around here better, Varren will warm up. He's actually quite nice."

This hardly seemed believable to Lluava. Clearly, Varren was nothing more than an entitled young man of the aristocratic class who thought he was too good for a conversation with a simple commoner. She rolled her eyes as Varren's friend disappeared through the doorway. At least Thad seemed pleasant.

Lluava was the only patient in the infirmary. Talos, Yamir, and Chat visited her briefly several hours later. They brought some food and listened to her account of her conversation with the prince. Soon, telling them Lluava needed her rest, Berkley shooed the three companions away and then retired to his own rooms.

Lluava was half asleep when she heard a small bang. Immediately, thick black smoke began to pour from the back room. Berkley stumbled out, hacking and coughing; his beard was charred. Lluava struggled to stand up, but the old man motioned her to stay where she was.

"What was that?" she exclaimed.

Berkley licked the tips of his fingers before pinching out the still-smoking ends of his beard. "I have been working on mass-producing a concentrated version of flashbang."

Lluava recognized the word but could not put her finger on the meaning. "Flashbang?"

"Yes. It was used by our kind in the Landon Wars to scare away the human invaders. Flashbang was banned after the war, but I have gained permission from King Thor to restore it to our arsenal." He brushed a layer of grey dust off his shoulders. "Actually, I am trying to make it more potent. It used to be perfectly harmless, but, if I can develop a more powerful concentrate, it could be used as an explosive weapon. At least, that's what I hope."

"Good luck with that," said Lluava, trying to suppress a yawn. With the room cleared of fumes, Berkley, trailing wisps of ash and smoke, returned to his chamber. Lluava was suddenly exhausted. If there were any further disturbances, she never heard them; instead, she slept unusually well for the remainder of the night.

Next morning, after promising Berkley she would take it easy, Lluava rejoined her troop. The grand master chief did not attend any of the day's events. His presence was replaced by the observing eye of Prince Varren, accompanied once again by Thad.

"I don't get them," commented Yamir after dual-form training. "They have all the money in the world, yet they wish to dress like us." He looked appraisingly at the prince's crisp, white uniform and Thad's bronze outfit.

"Maybe they don't want to seem intimidating," commented Lluava, glancing back at the two guests. They had seemed quite pleasant to her. Well, Thad had.

"That could only happen if it wasn't blatantly obvious who they were," retorted Yamir.

Afterward, Lluava spent her free time trying to find the grand master chief. She finally spotted him instructing another troop on wrestling techniques in another part of the camp. She approached and stood quietly within his line of vision.

When the general noticed Lluava, he ordered one of the men to take over and then turned and headed toward her.

"What do you want, recruit?" barked the grand master chief.

"Sir, I have come to apologize for my behavior, sir."

Wiping sweat off his brow, he demanded, "Well?"

Dispensing with the formalities, Lluava began, "I'm sorry for what I said to you the other day. I have been under a lot of stress lately, but that is no excuse for blowing up like I did. If you want to finish the Tucala, you can."

General Argon considered this for a moment. "Lluava," he responded, in an informal manner that matched her own, "There is no need for another Tucala. You are an unusual individual, but you must learn to deal with opposition. You must not let this annoy you so much. There is a war brewing on the horizon. When it arrives, you will have to endure much more than what you have dealt with inside Durog. You have the potential for greatness, but you must honor those above your rank even if you do not respect them. It will make your life much easier. Trust me."

The general's praise astonished her. Making sure her mouth was not hanging ajar, she stood at attention. "Thank you, sir," she managed to say, and saluted smartly before turning away to head back to her daily work, thunderstruck.

Over the next few days, the grand master chief continued his harshness toward Lluava, but it was the same harshness he directed toward all the other recruits. On occasion, she even got a brusque nod of approval.

Five days later, Lluava and her friends observed Thad and Prince Varren shaking the hands of Argon, Skipe, and Merrow. In the dim evening light, the visitors mounted a pair of beautiful thoroughbreds that pawed at the dusty earth, Varren's a black stallion with a star on its forehead and Thad's a chestnut mare. With practiced grace, the two rode off, disappearing through the gates with full packs attached to their saddles.

"I wonder where they are going," speculated Lluava.

Yamir was indifferent. "Who cares?"

"I gather they are heading to Thowcelemine," commented Talos, rubbing the bristles on his chin.

Lluava wondered at the sudden departure. "Already? But they just arrived." For some reason, she felt dismay as she watched the riders leave.

"Well, what did you expect?" questioned Talos, only half paying attention to the conversation. His fingers fidgeted in his pocket. "Durog is the most renowned training camp in the kingdom. It is run by the best, and there really is no need for someone to try to perfect what is already near perfection, especially in this day and age. Wartime is not the time to take it easy. If I were the prince, I would visit Thowcelemine next."

"Not to totally change the subject, but I'm really hungry." Chat tried not to sound like he was complaining, but his stomach was talking for him.

Yamir turned to his young friend. "I'm with you there. Let's eat."

The next day, the entire camp, hoping to hear the announcement they had been waiting for since arriving at Durog, congregated in the stands of the large coliseum. The chatter of excited men stopped as soon as the grand master chief entered the arena.

Standing at attention, the general announced, "You have all done well with your training so far. It is time for each of you to be graded on your skill level as an individual and as a part of your troop before we place you with a permanent partner. It is time for your finals. Next week, you will be tested on weapons and dual-form training on consecutive days. On the third day, your troop will compete in the Challenge of Burok Dûr.

"Once your scores are tallied, the commanding generals from the southern camps will assign you a partner of the opposite race with whom you will work during the rest of your time in these camps. That person will be your partner throughout the war and throughout your time in military service."

The emotion in the air suddenly changed from excitement to disgust. The possibility of human partners had been discussed during their arrival in the camps, but the recruits found the reality abhorrent. Many had even forgotten those rumors in the grueling humdrum of daily training. Sullen faces appeared throughout the stands as they listened to the grand master chief.

"You and your partner will train to become virtually one entity. You will become bunkmates. You will work together, eat together, and even sleep together. Eventually you will respect each other. Half of you will be assigned to Calitron while the other half will remain here. We will try to keep individual troops together.

"Now go and prepare. You are dismissed."

Two days before finals, Lluava woke up early. Sliding off her bunk, she grabbed a candle, flint and stone, and the two letters she had brought with her from home. Sitting down outside her barracks, Lluava lit the candle and began reading her father's letters. Yearning increasingly for the man she would never see again, she continued to think about him for the remainder of the day.

When evening came, she decided to take a walk by the lake to clear her head before heading back to her barracks. Lluava picked a few moonflowers and tossed them onto the lake's surface, watching as the current caught them. She whispered to herself as she watched the last flower float away, "Happy birthday, Father."

Suddenly she sensed a presence. Alert, she scanned the landscape. At first she did not see anything unusual, but a second look revealed a form standing in the darkness across the lake, so still it blended almost completely into the surrounding shadows. Only the gleam of its eyes gave it away.

"Hey!" Lluava called out.

The figure slid deeper into the shadows and was gone, leaving behind an uneasiness Lluava could not explain away. It was too late for the men of the camp to be about; she herself should have been back in Thowcelemine by now. Also, whoever had been watching her had done so in secret. And was still out there. She could sense him.

Lluava began to make her way back through the forest. The moon was too new to light the path; the only way to stay on the trail was to use her felid senses. She once again wondered how humans could survive as well as they did without a dual form. She was thankful for her acute night vision.

Twigs snapped in the distance.

Turning around, all Lluava saw was darkness. After a moment, she continued, now on high alert. A soft breeze toyed with the dried leaves around her. A rustling of a different sort made the hairs on the back of her neck stand on end.

Spinning around, she glimpsed movement in the darkness. Without hesitating, she ran after the figure in the woods, bolting past several climbing walls and other training objects scattered about. Sniffing the air, she could not discern any unusual scent.

Just as she was about to give up, something moved in the shadows to her left. Turning, she lunged ahead. As she shifted to her huntress form, her black-striped paws trod the ground. Just beyond sight, she heard someone running.

All of a sudden, the ground seemed to drop away right in front of her. Lluava made a giant leap to clear the wide trench. Her paws barely caught the edge on the far side. Hoisting herself up, she tried to spot the figure, but only darkness and silence greeted her questing senses.

Without warning, there was a hissing sound, followed by an enormous cacophony of crackling bangs. Brilliant white light temporarily blinded her. A gust of smoldering hot air blasted her. The force of the blast slung her across the trench, and she tumbled backward onto the ground.

Shifting back to human form, Lluava righted herself and touched her bleeding ears. All sound seemed dull and indistinct. Flames danced in the treetops; smoke was building and making her cough. She carefully made her way toward the spot, now marked by charred ground, where the explosion had occurred. There were no footprints to show who had ignited it or where the person had gone.

One question ran through Lluava's mind: "What in Valcum's fire just happened?"

Chapter 18
The Race to the Summit

What could have done this, Lluava wondered as she looked at the blackened earth and the charred bark of the nearby trees. Smoke arose from the center of the indented ground and wisped away in the canopy. Birds angrily screeched from the top of the forest as they flew away from the area of the explosion.

Even before the siren began to scream its warning, shouts could be heard from the camp. Soon a small crowd of people came running toward her. Lluava was too stunned to move as men, carrying buckets and splashing water on the smoldering ground, passed her. Several yelled for assistance. One called to Lluava to help, but her mind could not process what to do. The grand master chief shouted commands, and a chain of people began to pass buckets from hand to hand to douse the flames.

After the hectic scramble to contain the fire, most of the men were sent back to camp. General Argon, the other officers, and Berkley stayed behind to discuss what could have been responsible for the explosion. Lluava was ordered to remain, too.

"What in the names of the gods happened?" cried the grand master chief. He turned to look at Lluava, who still seemed stunned. "What were you doing in the forest after hours?"

It was several moments before Lluava found her voice. "I was…I just…needed a walk. My father's birthday was today. He died a little over a year ago. I just needed some time…."

"Look at her," interrupted Berkley, who hobbled over to the girl. He had grabbed the quilt from his bed on awakening; now he wrapped it around her shoulders. "She is still in shock. No more questions." He shooed the general away and started to walk Lluava back to camp.

"How do you feel?" he asked her.

Before she could answer, there came a shouted command: "HALT!"

They looked back at the glaring grand master chief, who clearly had not been able to contain his annoyance at being pushed aside. The message was obvious: he needed answers, and he needed them now. This was not time to pamper a recruit's emotional needs.

"Lluava! Lluava!" The general's strident tone brought Lluava back to the present. "What happened here?"

"I don't know," she responded. "I was heading back to camp when I spotted someone else in the forest. No, wait…." She paused, thinking back. "No, I spotted the other person when I was still at the lake. I was sitting on the beach when I saw someone watching me from across the lake. When I called out, he vanished." Her eyes closed as she remembered the dark figure.

Merrow inquired, "Are you sure it was a person that you saw? The lake is wide, and it is dark."

Lluava looked up at the bald admiral. "Yes! It was definitely a person, standing on the far side. He was watching me." Lluava looked from one person to the next. "There was someone out there with me. I heard him when I was on the trail, and I tried to follow."

The grand master chief thought this over. "Did you see who it was? Do you remember anything about him, any specific details?"

"Um. He may have been wearing a cape. I don't know. It was dark and he was fast." Lluava desperately wanted them to believe her. Several faces looked skeptical. She waited as they whispered among themselves.

Berkley finally spoke up. "Can I take her back to check her out now? You can finish questioning her later."

"Go," said General Argon, waving them away. As they turned, she heard him order the rest of the group to examine the area for clues.

At the infirmary, Lluava sat down gratefully on one of the cots while Berkley inspected her ears. With a damp cloth, he first wiped the crusted blood off her face and then tested her hearing. Fortunately, he found no permanent impairment.

Lluava felt drained. All she wanted was to curl up between the sheets and fall asleep.

"Can I leave now?" she asked, when it appeared Berkley had finished his examination.

"Yes, I suspect so," replied the elderly man as he pushed his spectacles farther up his nose.

"Thank you," she replied and left the building without a second glance. As she headed for the gates, Lluava yearned for the day to finally end. But it was not to be, at least not yet.

A voice rang out. "Lluava! Come here!"

It was the grand master chief, standing not far from her. From the look on his face, Lluava knew that the sleep she craved was not likely anytime soon.

"Lluava, I cannot let you leave until this whole situation is sorted through," the commanding officer told her. "You are to be detained here tonight. You will stay in one of the spare rooms in the general's barracks. Let's go." Brusquely, he motioned her to follow.

She wanted to contest these new orders, but she was too weary even to try. It would do no good to argue anyway—that much was certain. She followed the towering man to a tiny room in the general's barracks. He admonished her not to leave and then strode away down the hall.

Once alone, she inspected the small upstairs chamber, which was barely large enough for a cot, a nightstand, and a timeworn oak wardrobe wedged into the far corner, its left door slightly ajar. On the nightstand stood a porcelain pitcher and washing bowl. A small oval mirror above the stand reflected the face of a tired young woman. The curtains flanking the window were a dull gray; the other walls were bare. It was apparent that the room had not been used in a while.

Lluava peeled back the surprisingly crisp sheets and laid her head on the smooth pillow. She did not want to think about anything.

It was not till she awoke the next morning that she started to worry about her predicament. Would she be allowed to rejoin her troop? She opened the door to her room and was surprised to find two armed guards on either side of the doorway.

When the guards saw her, the taller of the two said, "I am sorry, miss, but you must stay in your room until orders are changed. Please step back inside."

Backing into the room, Lluava remembered Kentril's warning. Was she actually suspected of treason, of being a traitor to her country? For the rest of the day, she paced around the room, fearing what was being discussed elsewhere in the camp. She was not even allowed to use the lavatories but was handed a chamber pot when the need arose.

Around midday, the door was opened, and Lluava was given a tray of food. She took the tray and sat down on the bed, the tray on her lap. She looked at the piece of salted pork and three carrots but could not make herself eat. She set the tray on the floor, lay down on the bed, and stared up at the ceiling. After a while, Lluava lost track of time.

Sometime later, she heard the voices of people, two men in heated discussion, walking down the hallway. The gruff voice, which Lluava recognized as that of the grand master chief, was lecturing.

"I know Berkley's batch of concentrated Flashbang was stolen last night. I also know that Lluava is the only recruit in Durog who knew of its existence. That is why I want her in confinement. All the evidence we have points to her."

"And how long do you expect to keep her in there like a caged bird?" snapped Kentril's angry voice. "I demand that she be moved. You cannot keep her in there. Be fair! Let me take her, and she will not be in your hair anymore."

Kentril was pushing General Argon to free her, just as he had said he would. Lluava silently thanked him for his support. At least he did not want to see her taken to court and sentenced to life in some dark, dank cell. Why was the grand master chief refusing to let Kentril take her back to Thowcelemine? She thought he would be pleased at the opportunity to be rid of her.

As these thoughts and more ran through Lluava's mind, Thowcelemine's commanding general continued, "You are not helping her by keeping her here."

"*I'm* not helping *her*?" Durog's leader sounded as if his patience were stretched dangerously thin. "How dare you consider taking Lluava away! The incident happened within this camp's walls, thus making her case mine and mine alone. End of discussion."

It was not the end, however, for Kentril continued to importune the grand master chief to change his mind as the two men headed down the stairs and far from earshot. The idea that General Argon once again wished her ill was deeply disturbing to Lluava; clearly, this camp was unsafe for her.

For the next day and a half, those thoughts consumed her without distraction.

On the evening of the second day of her confinement, the door opened, and Lluava was summoned to General Argon's office. It felt strange to be escorted by one uniformed guard marching in front of her and another behind. The men assumed their positions on either side of the door as Lluava stood at attention waiting for permission to be "at ease." Argon, preoccupied with paperwork, did not look up. Lluava waited silently for him to finish.

Finally, placing his quill pen aside, the grand master chief acknowledged Lluava. "You are a very lucky lady," he began. "It would have been unfortunate if you had been condemned for treachery. Yet again, you have slipped by for lack of incriminating evidence. Lluava, you are being released from lock and key and will return to your troop tomorrow."

He noticed Lluava's desire to speak. "What?" he demanded.

"You thought I was guilty the other day. What changed your mind?"

"If you would only learn patience! I was coming to that. A witness confirmed the sighting of another person in the forest."

"Who?" Lluava butted in.

"Patience," the general repeated and then looked at the door behind Lluava. "Let him in."

A youth, whom Lluava recognized as Horus, the grand master chief's new favorite, stepped inside. He glanced at Lluava before locking eyes with the commander.

General Argon demanded, "Tell me what you saw the other night."

Without taking his eyes off the general, Horus began. "I was taking my night flight, as I routinely do before I go to bed, when I spotted movement. Swooping low, I saw Lluava Kargen walking on the trail back toward the camp. I was about to fly off when I spotted other movement not far from the recruit. It was a caped person slowly following Lluava. I decided to land in the nearby clearing so I could shift and then confront Lluava and her follower. As I proceeded to do this, I heard the explosion. Taking wing, I tracked a dark figure running away from the fire. I tried to follow but lost him in the thick canopy near the base of the mountain. When I heard that Lluava was suspected of foul play, I came to you."

"Thank you, recruit. You may go." The grand master chief waived Horus off, and the young man left without so much as a glance at Lluava.

Turning to Lluava, General Argon said, "As you heard, your story of another person has been confirmed. You are free to go." After a pause, he said a bit louder, "I said, go."

Lluava did not wait but hurried from the building where she had been held for far too long. Her first thought was to find her friends.

She found their barracks and was welcomed inside by the entire troop. Everyone clamored to know what had happened. Several recruits left during Lluava's third retelling and returned with food; she ate rapidly as Chat filled her in on all she had missed. Finals were two days away. She would need to catch up quickly.

Over the next few days, Lluava was pushed to her limits to acquire the new skills she needed to complete her exams and to build on the skills she already had. Talos drilled her on the different styles of hand-to-hand combat while Yamir demonstrated the latest dual-form combat formation. The new material made Lluava's brain ache, and she fervently hoped that she could remember it all.

On the day of the dual-form exams, Lluava was not scheduled until midday. She tried to sleep in, but her nerves awakened her even earlier than usual. Meeting her friends, she ate a decent meal and went in search of a place to practice. It seemed the whole camp felt the urge to squeeze in extra practices before the exams. Because both coliseums were being used by the examiners, they were off limits; recruits were shifting back and forth from humanoid to dual form in the gyms, on the fields, even in the barracks.

In the largest gym, Lluava spotted Horus. He and the members of his troop were changing into an assortment of birds and practicing aerial dynamics. Before Lluava could call out, Horus transformed into a golden eagle and proceeded to do several hairpin turns and dives. Spiraling around the rafters, the giant bird dove almost vertically toward the ground. Only a feather's width away from impact, the eagle turned and landed at Talos's feet.

Changing back into his humanoid form, Horus wiped the sweat from his face.

"Hey," he rasped.

The young man, although sturdily built, was actually smaller than Lluava. His nose, in keeping with his lean features, was thin and unusually straight. His round, burgundy eyes flicked from person to person.

Lluava fumbled for words. Did she need to thank him for his earlier testimony, in Argon's office? It was his duty. She was not sure she needed to say anything at all, so she settled for a simple "Good luck today."

Offhandedly, Horus replied, "Yeah, you too." After a glance at her, he leapt into the air and transformed and then flew off to rejoin his comrades.

"Well, that was awkward," announced Yamir as he turned his attention to three pigeons flying around each other in a braided motion.

When the sun reached its zenith, Lluava and the rest of her troop met in the small arena for their exam. Spectators, glad to have finished their own tests for the day, sparsely filled the stands to watch the torment of other recruits' exams.

Colonel Skipe and one of the first lieutenants stood watch over the scene. Without the competing sounds of clanging metal, the cicadas' low, metronomic drone was loud. The late summer heat was fierce, and by the time the troop had completed the first task, they were blanketed with sweat. After three hours under the blazing sun, the band of men was tired, sore, and parched. Glad to be finished, they slowly trekked to the mess hall, where they consumed what seemed like enough liquid to fill a good portion of the lake.

Sitting in their loft area, Lluava spoke to Chat, who ravenously gnawed on a chicken leg bone. "You got a good bit of sun today. Does your face sting when you touch it?"

Chat poked his cheeks with a greasy finger. "Kinda," he said, then continued to suck on the bone.

"You know," Yamir interjected, "You can always go down and get another leg."

Chat replied, "Yeah, I know. I just like to savor every bit of the flavors. It's really good."

"Well, I'm going to turn in. I'm hot and tired, and I crave a long shower," Lluava said as she descended the ladder. "I'll see you all bright and early tomorrow."

"That is true," Talos said. "I am surely looking forward to our hand-to-hand combat exam first thing in the morning." There was no way to hide his sarcasm.

It was early, too early for their liking, when their troop gathered under a cloudy sky for the second barrage of testing. A loud whistle announced the beginning of the exam, and the group was given weapon after weapon with which to demonstrate their skills. They began with hands-on defense maneuvers and then moved to daggers. After several hours of sword fights and archery tournaments, they were released. With sore arms and tight backs, the group trudged out of the small arena as another troop marched in proudly.

As they passed the other troop, Yamir shook his head at the freshly rested men entering the arena. "You think you are something now, but wait till they are done with you," he said, more to himself than to the passersby.

There was little wind, and the sweat slowly slid down the backs of the four as they headed off to eat. Lluava was thankful the day had not been sunny like the previous one. Cumulus clouds had been building up all afternoon; the dark underbellies of the fluffy beasts promised rain.

After briefly nourishing their bodies, Lluava headed back to Thowcelemine. There really was no way to prepare for the final challenge, the Challenge of Burok Dûr. They had no idea what to expect. All Lluava wanted was to lie down and rest.

When she awakened from her long afternoon nap, Lluava wrote a letter to her mother. She borrowed a quill pen and a vial of deep blue ink from Rosalyn, as well as a few sheets of crisp, honey-colored paper. She sat in the library among the rows of dusty books and began.

Dear Mother,

I hope you are doing well. I do miss you very much, and I am truly sorry that I have not written to you as often as I would have liked. I have been very busy with all this training. It has been incredibly hard, and sometimes I have found myself questioning whether I should really be here. I am now training in Durog because I was told that it would help me reach my potential.

The commanding general here is very strict. I believe he hated me in the beginning and wanted to make my life a living hell. I have been through so much, and the war has yet to begin. I have been persecuted, insulted, falsely accused, and physically beaten to the point where I did not wish to continue.

At times, I felt that it was useless to stand up to those who opposed me. I really miss your reassuring presence. I miss Lamb's nagging questions and Mouse's cries and Grampy. Oh, I miss him and all his wisdom! I miss our house and our stable and our decrepit mule.

Thinking about all of you now makes me realize how much I want to go home. I want to go home! I am tired of this place.

Your miserable daughter,

Lluava

Looking at the drying ink, Lluava found herself tearing the letter to pieces. Her mother did not need to worry about her any more than she already did. What was she thinking? How could she even conceive of letting her mother know about such dark happenings?

Throwing the shredded pieces of paper away, she began again. This time, she wrote about the people she had met and befriended. She told of the constantly curious Chat and the playful yet almost wiseass Yamir. She described Talos's thoughtfulness and his charming demeanor and Rosalyn's elegance, grace, and unending kindness. She talked about how much she was learning and expressed her newfound respect for those who willingly chose the life of a soldier. She ended by saying how much she looked forward to seeing her family soon and promised to write again shortly.

This was the sort of letter her mother would want to receive. She folded the paper into an envelope and sealed it with wax. Tomorrow she would send it off. Tucking the letter away in her pocket, she headed out of the building to eat an early supper.

It was finally time for the last exam. Lluava and the others stood at the forest's edge. They had waited all day for their troop's turn, and now that it was time to begin, they were becoming anxious. There were only a few more hours of sunlight left. Night would only make the challenge harder, so they had to hurry if they could.

They were now aware of what was expected. Each troop was paired with another troop that matched its own level of training. Lluava's troop was neck and neck with another led by Derrick; both troops vied for the top position. They would be sent to the summit of Burok Dur simultaneously. Their goal was to capture a chest that contained a silver sphere. The troop that succeeded in bringing the prize back to camp would be declared the winner. There were no rules, no guidelines about what the troops should or should not do to retrieve the item. In addition, the area was rigged with moving obstacles they would need to circumvent.

The overcast sky grew darker as they waited for the signal to begin. A distant rumble warned of an impending storm. A steady breeze began to build and raced through the canopy. The recruits waited in silence.

Finally, there it was—the signal. A fire-tipped arrow soared into the ashen clouds, and the troops were off. They ran at pace toward the looming mountain.

It was not long before someone to Lluava's left shouted, "Watch out!"

Before those in the lead could stop, the ground underneath them gave way, and they fell into a sixteen-foot pit.

"Are any of you hurt?" Talos, bending over the edge of the pit, asked.

A voice, coughing from the dust in the air, called out, "No!"

Without a second's hesitation, the group aligned themselves in formation and hoisted out a half-dozen men from the pit. As soon as the last man was up, the troop resumed its march toward Burok Dur—this time more cautiously.

Once they reached the base of the mountain, the troop silently split into two groups. One group headed to the north face while Lluava's group began to climb the western side. The gradual slope still allowed them to move quickly through the thickening trees. The wind picked up dramatically as they climbed upward, and the tall white pines creaked and groaned as they swayed.

A crackling sound was heard above them. The group had only a moment to split apart as a widowmaker crashed down. The large, dead limb rolled down the slope, ricocheting off the trunks of other trees.

Halfway up the mountain, Lluava's hopes soared; for an obstacle course challenge, this one appeared not to offered many. However, this thought occurred a bit too soon, for suddenly Yamir jerked Lluava down; she fell on her back and slid a few feet down the slope. She had no time to wonder why; a huge tree trunk, tied with two thick cords, swung from the canopy. If Yamir had not shoved her to the ground, she would have been impaled.

Peering into the treetops, Lluava realized it was not the only one. The canopy was filled with deadly logs waiting for someone to set them off. Lluava did not understand the trigger mechanism, but she knew they had to be very careful from this point forward. Slowly rising to her feet, she pointed out the booby traps riddling the trees.

"Please be careful," she cautioned. "And watch your step!"

Declaring that he, for one, was not going to risk setting off one of those swinging battering rams, Chat changed into his squirrel form and leaped from tree trunk to tree trunk.

Suddenly they heard a distant cry—the lonesome call of a wolf.

"It's Derrick and his pack of wolves," Talos shouted. "They are nearing the summit. If he retrieves the chest, his team is sure to win!"

It was time to do something. Fast.

Chapter 19
Among Wolves

There was not a moment to lose. Lluava would not let Derrick win so easily; they had worked too hard and too long. It was time to make their move.

"Let's go!" she shouted. "On the double!"

Shifting into their animal forms to give themselves more speed, they charged up the mountain. Missing them by a hair's breath, tree-trunk missiles hurtled past. The whooshing and swishing sounds of the plummeting trees made her fur stand on end. Lluava could feel the rush of air around her as she dodged the flying wood.

The forest was left behind as she forced herself up the steepening slope. The rocky ground made it easy for her paws to slip. She dug her claws into any bit of earth she could find. The air was thinner near the top, and she began to pant with her struggles.

Beside her, the sound of sliding rocks made her head turn. Loosening pebbles under his sharp hooves, Talos, a prancing stag, bounded from one rocky surface to another. On the other side, a bull, trudging up the steep, stony ground, snorted. It was Tartus, with Truden right behind him in the form of a wild boar.

As they neared the top, Lluava made a long leap to a flat ledge, sending a cascade of small rocks tumbling downward. Hoping they were not too late, she scanned the panorama in front of her.

Please let it be here, she desperately thought. It has to be here.

Lluava and the trio with her began their search as the other troop members made their way to the top. She had seen the return of a successful troop earlier that day and knew the chest was fairly small, about the size of a loaf of bread, and appeared to be made of dark mahogany.

Come on, come on; where is it? Lluava's desperation was catching up to her.

"It's here! I found it!" Truden shouted triumphantly. He was so happy he snorted. He had shifted back into his human form, but his pudgy fingers could not pull the chest free, for it was tightly wedged between two boulders.

Shifting along with the others, Lluava grabbed the chest and pulled. It would not budge. Time was of the essence. Derrick and his troop would soon be breathing down their necks.

"Help me move the boulders," ordered Lluava, wrapping her arms around the smaller one. The others followed suit, and, after several heaves, they pried the rocks apart and the chest slipped out.

As Truden picked it up, they heard a low rumble.

"Here, piggy, piggy, piggy."

A tawny grey wolf crept slowly toward them. It was not Derrick, but Lluava knew that he would arrive any second. The wolf bared its teeth and snapped at the petrified Truden, who had begun to sweat.

Between breaths, Truden gasped out, "What...do...I...do?"

"Remember the formation we practiced in training?" asked Lluava, not taking her eyes off the wolf.

"Which one?" whimpered Truden.

"The one with the hot coal."

The wolf raised his eyebrows—or at least the skin where Lluava expected his eyebrows to be.

"Oh, yeah, that one." Truden sounded a little more assured. He looked down at the wooden box in his arms and suddenly shouted, "HOT!" He tossed the chest into the air. It was caught by Tartus, who took off at an angle to the left.

The wolf sprang after him in a second. The rest of Lluava's troop ran zigzagging all over the place. At the same time, the entire troop tossed their hands in the air and shouted "HOT!" as Tartus lobbed the chest.

This time, Talos caught it. The wolf skidded to a stop and then hurtled toward his new prey. As Talos passed in front of Lluava, the group again raised their arms in the air, and Lluava grabbed the chest.

She took off down the side of the mountain. In a few moments, she passed the prize to another teammate, who handed it off to another, and then another. After only a few minutes, the wolf was thoroughly confused and no longer knew whom to chase.

He let out a mournful cry, which was repeated by other voices. The pack was on their heels.

Lluava knew her team had to pick up the pace. Half running, half sliding down the slope, the chest was passed to her again.

The moment she caught it, the blackening sky gave birth to a thick wall of rain, a torrent so heavy Lluava could barely make out the trees before her.

She concentrated on not crashing into any of them. The wolves, close behind, howled in the stormy air. She feared to glance back, lest she see the gaping maws of a dozen angry canines.

As lightning flashed, Lluava glimpsed a shadowy form but did not have time to stop. The large black wolf, white teeth gleaming in the flaring light, leapt in front of her. Lluava tumbled straight into sopping ebony fur.

The wolf righted itself and circled the girl sprawled on the ground.

"Well, well, well. Look what we have here. If it isn't the she-tiger herself! And look; she bears a gift." The dark beast had found the chest that had been jarred from her arms when they collided.

"Oh, Derrick," Lluava called out in an exceptionally sweet voice as she transformed into her felid form. "Come play with me."

"Woof, woof," he replied in his deep voice and then howled with laughter.

Lluava snarled, and the dark beast snarled back. In a way, she thought, it was strange that Derrick had so much confidence. He was only a wolf and barely half Lluava's size. She knew he was smart and would have already calculated his chances which, at the moment, were not exactly great. But why was he so sure that he could take her on? There was not even the slightest hint of concern in his glowering eyes.

As the wolf took a step forward, the guard hairs on his back sprang up, making him look quite a bit larger than he truly was. Was he crazy? Lluava's four-inch claws could shred him easily. She did not want to hurt him. He was one of the top ten soldiers in the camp, and they needed him. Was he mad enough to attempt to fight her?

Another step closer and the canine cocked his head to the right. His eyes burned into hers. Lluava tensed. She was definitely missing something. What was it?

The flicker of movement in the reflection of Derrick's eyes let her know what she had overlooked. Too late! There was no escape, nowhere to go; she was surrounded. How could she have been so stupid? Wolves always hunt in packs.

More than a dozen snarling, snapping canines encircled her. Lluava's training told her never to leave her back open to attack, yet there was no way to protect it.

Derrick barked once, and a small timber wolf with reddish fur trotted up and grabbed the chest in its strong jaws, then took off down the mountain. As the wolf disappeared from view, her hopes of winning went with it.

Lluava did the only thing she could. She shifted her position to avoid presenting an easy target. Then she waited. With each passing moment, she wondered why none of the wolves tried to attack her. Maybe they knew a tiger's wrath could severely injure them. Or maybe....

With a quick glance at Derrick, Lluava understood their plan. They never meant to attack her—only to keep her trapped inside their circle, to prevent her from escaping and retrieving the chest.

But that was exactly what she intended to do. Lluava turned and charged two silver wolves, but just before she reached them, she turned and sprang at three of the pack opposite them. She spun a third time and charged a small, white-pawed wolf. At this point, none of the canines had any idea what was going through the tigress's mind.

The fourth time, Lluava did not stop. Vaulting over one small wolf, she landed clear of the circle and took off down the slope. She was fast but not fast enough. Lluava knew that even at top speed she could not catch up to the canine with the chest. But she was not going to give up.

Trees blurred as Lluava sped onward, the deep green of pines blending with the cooler greens of oak and maple. Suddenly, she glimpsed a bit of yellow at her side. She tried to speed up. There was no way she would let the wolves catch her.

There it was again. Lluava risked a glance at the flashing, tawny-yellow creature—not a smart move; she rammed her left shoulder into a tree. She spiraled around. No! She wanted to scream. The wolves would soon be on top of her.

Stumbling back onto her paws, Lluava heard a familiar voice shout, "Where is the chest?"

The cheetah leapt to her side and asked again, "Where is it?"

Lluava had forgotten the rest of her teammates. Panting, she replied, "It's with a timber wolf—one of Derrick's men—heading down the mountain...."

Before she could say more, her comrade replied tersely, "I have this." The feline took off after the prize in a blur of tan and black. And not a moment too soon, for the wolves emerged from the rainy haze behind Lluava.

Bolting down the slope, Lluava made a last-ditch attempt to evade the opposition. She knew she was reaching the halfway mark, but there was something she needed to do first.

She doubled back, shaking up the angry pack at her heels. Skidding down the muddy incline, they tried to turn and follow her. She headed up and to the left, straight toward the mass of booby traps. Although all of them ran headlong into the thicket of danger, only one was prepared for what was to come.

All around her, the ferocious canines snapped at her fur, trying to grab hold of her and bring her to a halt. Reaching for a second wind from gods-knew-where, Lluava forced herself to speed up. She needed as big a lead as she could create; every stride counted.

Lluava zigzagged through the thicket of trees, trying to touch as much ground as she could. Soon, she heard the whirring and whooshing sounds, but she did not look back at the web of swinging battering rams wreaking havoc upon the pursuing pack. An occasional yelp was heard when an unfortunate wolf was struck by a log or had an uncomfortably close encounter with one. As its members retreated to safety or were felled by the treacherous obstacles, the sounds of the pack soon faded.

Now Lluava could concentrate on finding her teammate and the chest.

To her surprise, she soon discovered the box lying on the ground. A few paces away, the timber wolf stood over the body of the beaten feline. The cheetah's fur was bloody, but Lluava could see that it still breathed. The cat had risked its own life to halt the wolf. It was an unfair match. There was no way the wolf could have lost, but their struggle had given Lluava enough time to reach the chest.

With her loudest war cry, Lluava seized the wooden box between her teeth and hurtled down the slope. The poor wolf did not know what had happened; by the time he turned around, Lluava had disappeared among the trees, along with the chest.

She was home free. There was no further opposition as she raced down the mountain. Excitement coursed through her body as she entered the last stretch of forest. She was going to make it.

And then she heard the long, piercing howl.

Derrick. Somehow, the wolf leader had made his way to the base of the mountain and was heading right toward Lluava.

A black mass of fur erupted from the bushes behind her, and Lluava knew she could not sustain this pace much longer. Her rear legs had begun to cramp, and it was increasingly hard to catch her breath. Then movement ahead attracted her attention.

A squirrel leapt from a tree, landed on the ground, and transformed. It was Chat. "Over here!" he shouted.

With a strong jerk of her neck, Lluava flung the parcel from her mouth to the youth's open arms. She then turned to face her opponent. Derrick tried to swerve around her, but Lluava hooked his rear leg with her dark claws.

Derrick yelped, and Lluava pulled him toward her. The wolf could only watch as the boy ran off with the chest in his arms.

Another flash of fur passed, loping after Chat.

"Chat, watch out!" cried Lluava.

She tried to push Derrick out of the way so she could protect her friend, but a third wolf arrived and sank its teeth into her flank. Between the two, Lluava could not tear free. She lay pinned between the two bodies as Chat stumbled and dropped the chest. It slid away from the boy, rolled through the mud, and stopped at the feet of…Yamir!

Grabbing the wooden treasure, Yamir broke for the finish line. He was almost upon it when the rest of the pack arrived. He had no chance. The mass of wolves tripped him, jerked the chest from his hands, and crossed the finish line in a blur of fur and flying legs.

Lluava could hear the cheers in the distance as two dozen wolves proudly loped from the forest's edge to the clearing where the rest of the camp waited.

It was over. They had lost.

Chapter 20
Issaura's Claws

The two wolves holding Lluava down released her. As they transformed, the dark-skinned Derrick paused. "You fought well," he acknowledged. "Perhaps next time." The wolves walked off toward the roaring onlookers.

After Lluava reverted to her human form, Yamir and Chat helped her to her feet. Listlessly the three trudged into the open area behind the camp where Derrick and The Pack were being congratulated. As the best team in Durog, they were eligible to be paired with the top soldiers from Calitron.

Lluava's pang of disappointment was more distressing to her than her physical pain. She had wanted her team to win so badly. And they almost had. She kept envisioning the chest in her arms. She had held it, felt its smooth, polished surface.

As the rest of her troop gathered around her, they watched the elated faces of Derrick's comrades. The grand master chief smiled at Derrick—the man could actually smile!—and shook the hand of each person on the team.

"We have our winners," he announced in his husky voice. "Troop 12 has successfully brought back the silver sphere."

"That's not exactly true," a small voice called out. The happy cheers of the crowd almost—but not quite—drowned out the words. The cheering ceased.

The grand master chief scanned the onlookers to spot the person who dared say such a thing. All eyes turned to the young boy who stepped forward.

The youth, whose rusty brown skullcap matched his hair, spoke again. "They did not bring back the sphere. If that is what it takes to win, they did not succeed."

Yamir stood with his mouth agape; both Talos and Lluava could only

159

stare as Chat looked intently at Durog's leader. *What is he doing?* thought Lluava. *Please don't get yourself in trouble, Chat.*

The general replied coolly, "They brought the chest containing the sphere, recruit. That was all it took for them to win."

Chat shook his head. "No, they didn't."

At this moment, most of the onlookers started to question Chat's sanity. Had the poor boy lost it? He was too young for war; maybe this event had pushed him over the edge. Surely he saw the chest that the grand master chief held under his arm.

General Argon unlatched the wooden box. Flipping the lid open, he quickly turned the chest upside down and shook it. People gasped as nothing fell out. The silver sphere was gone.

Eyes turned to the boy, who reached into his deep pocket and pulled out the small orb. Looking up at the general, Chat announced, "As you can see, I have the sphere."

Deathly silence followed. Everyone seemed to hold his breath.

Durog's leader waved Chat forward. The boy approached and handed his prize to the tall man. Holding the silver orb at eye level, Argon inspected it, as if looking for imperfections. He then placed the item into the chest and turned to the waiting crowd.

"Today's overall winners are..." he began.

Lluava's heart pounded. She glanced around; everyone seemed hypnotized.

"...Troop Seven."

A great roar erupted from the onlookers. Everyone went wild. Lluava took a couple of big breaths; she could not believe it. Talos came up to her and slung her around in a huge hug. People crowded around Chat and bombarded him with questions. "How did you do it?" "What made you think of removing the orb from the chest?" "When did it happen?"

Yamir shooed the throng away, saying, "Give the guy some air."

Chat began to speak, and everyone quieted down. "It happened right before the wolves crossed the finish line. Lluava threw the chest to me." Heads swung toward her for a moment. "I started running with it, but I tripped. The chest hit the ground and skidded away from me. As I started to stand, I noticed that the sphere had fallen out." He turned to the grand master chief, who was also listening. "I grabbed it, intending to put it back in the chest—I swear. But by that time, Yamir had already run off with the chest."

Yamir, standing near Lluava, mumbled to himself, "So that's why the lid was ajar when I picked it up."

"Congratulations," the grand master chief said again. His face revealed no emotion. "By that simple accident, you have won your team victory."

Several members of Lluava's troop hoisted Chat on their shoulders. Soon he was being paraded around like a large trophy. The onlookers cheered, "Chat! Chat! Chat!" Watching, Lluava knew this was probably the happiest day of Chat's young life.

Derrick sought out Lluava. He gave her a congratulatory nod. "You and your team have proven themselves worthy opponents."

"Thanks," she replied. "Yours as well." She followed the parade of people heading back to the camp where all competitors would be inspected and treated by Berkley.

That evening, the troop celebrated. Several small kegs of draft mead had been smuggled into the barracks. It was Chat's first experience with fermented drinks, and he soon passed out on his bunk. Nevertheless, the night was filled with singing, gambling, and all sorts of foolish camaraderie.

The next morning, Lluava could spot those who had enjoyed themselves a little too much. She was glad she had called it quits relatively early. Unlike the rest of her troop, she had to return to Thowcelemine. Chat complained of a stomachache, but other than that, he looked thoroughly rested. Unfortunately for Yamir, it was a different story. He appeared exhausted as he trudged up to the group, one hand shielding his eyes from the sunlight.

"You look wretched," said Talos, almost laughing at Yamir's plight.

Yamir feigned a laugh and then suddenly covered his mouth with his other hand and ran to the side of the closest building.

"Poor guy. I warned him to stop, but he just continued." Talos looked as if he truly felt sorry for his friend. "I hope he is ready for this afternoon."

"Oh, yeah," Lluava said, remembering. "That's right. We meet our partners today." She looked around at her group. Most appeared like the living dead. "For the best troop in Durog, we sure are in bad shape."

"This will be an interesting day," commented Talos.

After their midday meal, the troop packed up their belongings in the event of reassignment to a different camp after the pairing. Lluava became nervous as she realized that she could be separated from those she knew and cared about. But, she sternly reminded herself, this was a time of war, and individual feelings did not matter.

The group marched several miles up the dusty road leaving Durog's silhouette looming behind them until they reached a makeshift stage with rows and rows of log benches. A walkway split the seating into two sections; the Theriomorphs were seated on the right-hand side. Behind the stage, four armed guards watched over a stack of crates. Lluava wondered what was stored in them.

The recruits took seats. Then they waited for the human men to arrive at this halfway point between the camps.

They had been sitting for half an hour in the humid heat before spotted a band of people marching down the road. They were led by a short, stout, dark-skinned man in uniform. Several other people of rank accompanied him. The procession entered the crude theater and, after dumping their satchels and bags on the ground, took their seats. The leaders had separate chairs at the back of the stage.

At the center of the wooden platform were two empty seats. The grand master chief sat to the right of the empty chairs, and the squat black man sat on the left. Before Lluava had time to wonder for whom the empty chairs were intended, a clatter of hooves was heard down the road from the direction of Durog and Thowcelemine. In moments, a chestnut mare trotted forward, and the rider slid off as a guard took the reins from him.

The rider was Thad. He walked up to the stand and addressed the group. "I apologize that I have delayed this ceremony and must sadly announce that Prince Varren will not be attending. He is working to procure reinforcements for the southern camps."

Lluava wondered if this had anything to do with the intruder at Durog. Additional guards would be beneficial.

As soon as Thad had taken his seat, the grand master chief stood up and introduced himself and the dark-skinned man. "I am Grand Master Chief General Argon, the chief commanding officer at Durog, and this is Chief General Miller, the commanding officer of Calitron. We have worked hard to match each of you with a partner best suited to your skills and your level of training. Unfortunately, we could not find perfect matches for everyone, and since we do not believe in pairing people just for the sake of pairing, not all of you will leave with a partner. Do not be ashamed if this happens to you. This is the case every year. You will be paired with someone at a future time.

"Because we Theriomorphs have a wide range of dual forms, each recruit is assigned to one of three groups: aerial, marine, or terrain."

Lluava realized that her troop consisted only of land animals, while other groups, like Horus's, were composed solely of flying creatures.

Chief General Miller began to speak. "It is preferred that Theriomorphs who trained as a troop stay together. Humans paired with Theriomorphs will train with the Theriomorph troop and will be split from their own."

Quiet grumbles were heard, and several humans glared at those responsible for separating them from their friends. The squat man, who had a bit of a paunch, continued, "Once you are paired, you will split up. Those with Theriomorph partners from Troops One through Eighteen will train at Durog. The rest will return with me to Calitron. Is that clear?"

A unanimous reply resounded: "Sir! Yes, sir!"

General Argon began to call recruits to the stand. He began with Theriomorph Troop One. The first recruit walked to the stand and was presented with a weapon from one of the crates behind the platform. As the young man held his bright new sword, the grand master chief told him the weapon's name. Then he called up the human recruit who would be partnered with the dark-haired Theriomorph. The human received his weapon. The two recruits gave one another dark looks before moving off to the side.

The pairing continued for the rest of the afternoon. Lluava zoned in and out of the ceremony, her attention caught here and there by the name of a familiar Theriomorph or an interesting weapon. For the most part, her mind was elsewhere. Trying to read their faces, she kept scanning her friends. She wanted to know what they thought about all of this. She was thankful that her troop would stay together, but that did not change the fact that they would double in number. It was strange to think that each of them would now have a human shadow.

What was to happen next? After today, it would not be just Lluava and her three friends, but eight people living and working together. Would she and her friends have time to enjoy each other's company anymore? Tomorrow, they would have to form a connection with their human partners and begin to train as pairs rather than individuals.

And what if they did not get along? What would they do then? Lluava could tell by the expressions on many of the newly paired recruits that they were not thrilled at partnering with someone of a different race. One thing was certain: if the commanding generals hoped for a smooth blending of the two races, they were going to be disappointed.

As soon as the first person's name from her troop was called, Lluava became fully alert. Talos was the third to be summoned. He walked proudly to the platform and graciously accepted the long sword, Heldrien, and a small shield from Berkley. The old man seemed pleased to be presenting the weapons to the new soldiers.

When Talos's partner was announced, Lluava could not help but let her jaw slide open. Byron arose from one of the back rows and walked up to his new partner. Since he already carried a weapon, there was no need to give him another.

Lluava remembered Byron mentioning that he had not been paired with a Theriomorph partner. He must have been one of the few who had not found the perfect match upon completion of his training. Lluava was excited that she would be reunited with another friend.

Soon, Yamir made his way to the stage, receiving two spears and a long, thin dagger. He stood admiring them as his partner was called forward. To Lluava's dismay, it was the one person she had hoped never to see again. Though the training had toned his body, Lluava instantly recognized Malnus. His dark hair looked greasy, almost gleaming in the sunlight. He nodded his thanks after receiving a bow and a quiver filled with newly fletched arrows.

Lluava waited for her name to be called. Team member after team member was summoned to the front and paired with another. Soon, only she and Chat remained from Troop Seven.

The boy was called first. He proudly held his weapon, Zepher—a sword so short it could have been a long, wide dagger. Or maybe it was.

The grand master chief looked almost kindly at his small recruit and then requested, "Please leave the stage, Chat."

Chat's eyes grew wide at the implication. Sadly he slunk off the stand. He was not to be paired with anyone this time. Lluava's heart sank; Chat would have to fight alone.

As Lluava rose, the next name was called. But it was not hers. The first man from Troop Eight went up to be partnered while Lluava was left standing confused. She slowly sat down and watched recruit after recruit leave the benches around her and greet their new partner.

What could this mean? Was she not paired with anyone? If she was not, shouldn't General Argon have called her up at least to receive her weapon? Did this have anything to do with her gender? Lluava was upset but refused to cry. Observing those around her from beneath lowered lids, she sat in silence.

Lluava tried to smile as Horus was partnered with Thad. Horus should feel honored to have someone of such noble rank fighting next to him. They would make a strong team.

By evening, Lluava was the last person sitting on the benches. Inwardly, she pleaded for someone to give the word to return to the camps. She was miserably embarrassed and felt that everyone was looking at the girl who sat alone.

Chief General Miller called the names of those that would return with him to Calitron. He took notice of the solitary girl and motioned Argon to lean over; then he whispered in his old friend's ear. Argon nodded, which was all the consent needed. The dark-skinned man called out one last name. "Lluava Kargen, come to the stage."

When she heard her name, Lluava's spirits rose. She quickly made her way toward the waiting generals. She did not know what would happen, but she was glad to leave the bench.

General Miller was several inches shorter than she, but that did not make him any less formidable. She waited for someone to say something, anything.

It was Berkley who pushed past the generals and, in his smoky, almost gravelly voice said, "Here you go, my dear." He then handed Lluava two small golden weapons unlike anything she had ever seen. They were similar to the brass knuckles that seafarers carried in case they entered into a scuffle at the docks. But unlike the knuckles, each had three golden claws that branched out and curved away from the metal base.

Berkley saw the admiration in Lluava's eyes. "You are a very special individual, and a normal weapon would do you no justice at all. These are known as Issaura's Claws. They were made centuries ago and have been stored away in the castle's vaults for the past fifty years. It took time to gain approval to remove these relics. They were made by Theriomorphs for a

Theriomorph. Use them well."

Lluava was awestruck. She did not know what to say to the sweet old man. Throwing her arms around him, taking care not to bruise his frail body, she gave him a long hug.

When she finally released him, Lluava turned back to the generals. "I guess I don't have a partner, then," she said.

It seemed as if the grand master chief wanted to console her.

"It's okay," stated Lluava. "Really, it is."

A kind voice spoke from behind her.

"You *do* have a partner."

She turned around and saw a disheveled Prince Varren. His face was flushed from the heat, and he was slightly out of breath from his long horse ride. "He just had not arrived yet."

General Argon stepped forward and announced, "Lluava Kargen, meet your new partner, Prince Varren Mandrun."

Chapter 21
Shattered Glass

Lluava's mind froze for a moment as she floundered to find words. She wasn't dreaming, was she? It really was Prince Varren staring at her with his gentle blue eyes. The prince, her partner, stood there waiting for her to react. How could this be?

A loud rumbling from the road distracted her. More than a dozen uniformed riders galloped into sight. They halted as soon as they reached the crowd and dismounted in unison.

The compassionate voice of the prince broke in. "I am truly sorry that I kept you waiting, but I was required to complete my assignment."

"I know. You left to request reinforcements to protect the southern camps." Lluava said this without looking at him. Something was not right with this pairing, and she could not pretend to be happy about it. Turning to the grand master chief, she asked, "Sir, I am staying with my troop at Durog, right?"

The general nodded, and Lluava walked off toward her troop. She did not need to glance back to know that Varren was following her. Her friends wore dazed expressions from the proclamation. None of them spoke to her. What could they say? Although she was still the same young woman who had trained with them all along, things were different now. The prince was her partner.

As soon as the generals ordered the two newly formed groups to travel to their assigned camps, the recruits began to make their way back down the road in silence. Though no one spoke, humans and Theriomorphs alike felt the tension. They could take no comfort in the fact that they now had someone to watch their backs when they went to war; that did not matter. What did matter was their almost instinctive distrust of the other race.

Lluava did not care about that. Her reason for unease with the pairing was different from the others'. None of her friends would understand. She let her thoughts consume her until she said her goodbyes to her friends at the gates of Durog. Thankfully, she would not have the inconvenience of reassigned sleeping quarters. The idea of partners as bunkmates may have sounded good to the camp's leaders, but Lluava expected that it would only heighten the tension between Theriomorphs and humans.

"Lluava, please stop!" the voice of her new partner called out as she headed toward Thowcelemine. Slowly she turned. For some reason, she felt drained.

The prince made his way toward her. "You seem angry. I apologize if my late arrival embarrassed you in any way. I would like it if we could start out tomorrow on good terms."

"Your Majesty, I—"

"Varren. Just Varren, please. I want you to think of me as an equal and to disregard my birth status. And maybe, just maybe, you can one day look upon me as a friend."

Much as she appreciated the sentiment, Lluava could not shake the feeling that something was just amiss. "As you wish," she replied. Then she headed toward the women's camp without giving her rudeness a second thought.

That night, Lluava did not speak to Rosalyn, and she ignored the other girls' excited banter about the next day's pairing with the ladies of Delphine. All she could do was stare at the thatched roof above her and meditate on the day's events. After several hours, she finally came to a conclusion: something had to be up with this pairing. There was no other way the prince would be partnered with her.

Rising early from an uncomfortable sleep, Lluava was the first to arrive for the new partners first day of training. When the rest of her troop had gathered, they started their daily laps around the camp. These were completed in record time, in part because both Theriomorphs and humans wanted to test each other's strengths, each race showing off and trying to outdo the other. Rising with the heat, tensions were high throughout the day. By midafternoon, several brawls had broken out, although they ended quickly when the drill sergeants intervened.

As Lluava and her new troop walked from the small coliseum, they saw four men fighting. The dusty haze that surrounded the tossing bodies prevented Lluava from recognizing who was involved. Without officers around, no one stopped it. A man was flung to the ground and landed in a heap. Two others attacked; one kicked the helpless man while the other held him down. The fourth person jumped onto the kicker's back and tried to pull him over.

Unable to watch any longer, Lluava ran toward the brawlers. Prince

Varren did the same. Lluava wondered if he was following her. Her pondering was cut short by a swinging arm intended for another target. As she tried to pull two of the men apart, she was shoved roughly away.

"Stop!" shouted the prince. "I order you to stop this instantly!"

The men seemed to suddenly take note of their surroundings. All four gawked at the prince before standing up and brushing themselves off. Lluava recognized two Theriomorphs from Troop Four and their human partners. As she had expected, the hatred between human and Theriomorph could not be pushed aside, even in the face of an oncoming war. The two races would tear apart the camp, if not the kingdom, before the raiders even arrived.

As the blood-spattered men slunk away, Prince Varren stared after them. "I do not understand. Why are these soldiers acting like that? This camp has been so orderly and professional."

Although Varren was talking aloud to himself, Lluava felt the need to respond. "What did you expect? That everyone would be happy at this turn of events?"

His expression a mix of shock and sorrow, her partner turned to look at her. "I cannot understand what is going on. We should all be working together to save our kingdom. Where is their honor? Their valor?"

His words surprised her. Did the prince actually know so little about his people? Could he really have been that sheltered all his life? Clearly, he needed to know the way things really were.

"Humans, in general, distrust Theriomorphs," Lluava began. "That's the way it has been since the beginning. As a result, Theriomorphs are not friendly toward humans.

"There are some who try to fit in with your kind," she added, thinking of her mother, "because they think they will be accepted if they act, dress, and believe as you do. And then there are those who are firm in the old ways and feel that humans are forcing them to change."

"Why do they feel they have to deny their own heritage and accept our culture as their own?" the prince asked.

Lluava considered him. As far as she could tell, he sincerely wanted an answer. Perhaps he actually cared. She responded, "The only way most of us have any chance of truly being treated as equals is to blend in. In a sense, to disappear."

"How can this be?" questioned Varren. "My grandfather decreed that the two races were to be as one and to have equality. There are laws that prevent both humans and Theriomorphs from forcing their beliefs upon each other. Everyone was given a fair say, and it was decreed by the High Council itself that we should look upon the other race as our own."

After a pause, Lluava spoke. "Hundreds of years of fighting one another, hating and killing each other, don't just go away after the creation of some law. It's true that there can be no open violence between the races, but the distrust of generations is still there. Crimes against one another are committed every day, and the only reason people get away with them is that they call them by some other name." She looked at the young man before her. "Someone's house can be broken into, and it is called a robbery, when, in fact, it is the result of pent-up loathing for a people different from oneself. Look around you," Lluava waved her hands at her own troop, now seated on the steps of the mess hall, awaiting their turn to enter and eat. For the most part, the races had separated into two groups that exchanged only dark looks, not words. "Your kingdom is far from perfect."

The prince's eyes grew wide as he absorbed this darker reality. After a moment, Lluava turned to follow her troop into the mess hall.

"Is that why you hate me?"

Lluava turned back to the prince. "I don't hate you."

"The way you act around me, the way you looked at me when you found out that I was to be your partner. You have barely spoken to me at all. Your dislike is obvious."

"I don't hate you," Lluava said again, a little louder as her annoyance grew.

"What is it, then? You do not trust me?"

"No, it's not that." She paused, searching for a way to word her fears. "It—it's just that I don't trust that you trust *me*." Once she had said it aloud, Lluava felt much better.

"What?" Varren appeared to have no idea what she meant.

"Why are you my partner?" Lluava demanded.

Varren did not take his eyes off her. "You have the most outstanding scores of anyone in Durog. You have proven yourself to be strong, resourceful, and a true leader. Your team won the competition through your help and quick thinking. It is an obvious match."

They regarded each other wordlessly, each hoping for an answer to their questions. Lluava finally broke the silence.

"No, it isn't. I'm the worst possible choice for you."

Confusion showed on Varren's face. "What do you mean by that?" he asked again.

"You can't be so naive or so oblivious as not to know that I have recently been accused of potential treason. Of all the people in the kingdom, why would you, the king, or the High Council ever risk the life of the one and only prince by pairing him with a suspected traitor? *That* makes no sense!"

Varren smiled. "You were proven innocent. Is that not right?"

"Yes...."

"Do you not believe that once proven innocent, past suspicions should be pushed aside? I do."

Lluava was stunned. What he had said was true, but could she really believe that he meant it? That he fully trusted her? To be partners, they would have to place their lives in each other's hands. If there was even the slightest bit of suspicion, both lives could be lost. Although Lluava wished she could put her faith in Prince Varren, something prevented her from doing so.

During the following day's training, Lluava, waiting for the moment when her partner would not be where he said he would be, kept herself on high alert. Her second-guessing distracted her and opened her up to a series of attacks from opposing pairs. The contagion of doubt and distrust seemed to have spread throughout the camp. It did not matter which group had started it; it was here and would not go away.

After the troops had been dismissed for the night, Prince Varren caught up with Lluava as she headed out through the gates. "Come with me," he said. His tone was undemanding, yet he seemed confident that she would obey.

"Where?" she asked as he motioned for her to follow.

His eyes locked with hers. "Trust me."

There was a moment of hesitation. Lluava ran through several scenarios in which she would be led into some sort of trap. Dismissing her thoughts as foolish, she followed as the prince led her around the outskirts of Durog's wall. She had never explored the camp's perimeter and had not a clue where they were headed or what Prince Varren intended.

Soon she could not contain her curiosity. "What are we doing out here?"

Without stopping, the prince replied, "You will see when we are there."

"Where?" She really wanted to know what was going on. "Get where?"

He glanced back at her, the corners of his lips curled slightly. What was he up to?

They finally rounded the back part of Durog. A thin strip of land lay between the walls of the old fortress and the sheer cliffs that jutted over the ocean. The sound of waves crashing against the towering cliffs soothed her, and Lluava suddenly realized how much she missed being able to walk down to the docks, close her eyes, and listen to the surf. Those peaceful days of summers past were now only a memory.

As Lluava gazed off into the distance, Prince Varren announced, "We are here."

Trying to discern what was so important that she had been asked to walk this far out of her way, Lluava looked around. There was nothing spectacular about this spot; the cliff, jutting out over the sea for long stretches and then retreating to form small inlets, seemed to wind like a snake.

Several trees of the forest that wrapped Burok Dûr lay beyond the walls of the camp. One such tree had fallen across one of the inlets. Varren climbed up and broke off several small limbs as he made his way to the bare trunk.

"What are we doing here?" Lluava demanded.

"Come." The prince took her hand and helped her up onto the fallen tree. "There you go. I think it is time for the two of us to partake in a true test of trust."

"Trust test? I—I don't think we need to do that." Craning her neck to look over the edge of the cliff, Lluava observed the powerful breakers pounding the base of the cliffs. Fallen rocks and shattered stones were scattered over the seabed like broken bones.

"I think we do." The prince smiled calmly. "This is what we are going to do. Each of us in turn will blindfold the other and lead him or her across this tree to the far side. Our lives will be placed in the other's hands; one wrong move, and the blindfolded one will—well, you can guess. I am hoping that after tonight, whatever doubts you have about me can be tossed aside."

Lluava was *not* happy. This was the perfect place for a convenient accident. Staring down at the watery rocks below, she became dizzy. The image of her broken body washing out to sea was not appealing. There was no way she would participate in this mad request.

"I will go first."

Lluava looked at Varren as if he were insane. He was already removing a cloth he'd worn tied around his waist like a belt, refolding it as a blindfold.

"What? Wait, no! You can't be serious!" How could he do this? If he slipped—for whatever reason—the heir to the throne would plummet to a salty death, and it would be her fault. Lluava could not afford such a risk.

But the prince merely took several steps onto the log and tied the cloth around his eyes. "Now, where do I place my foot?" he asked.

"Please get down from there!" Lluava's voice cracked. The situation was far too dangerous, and she did not like losing control.

The prince tried to scoot backward but almost lost his footing. Swaying for a moment, he righted himself and said, "It would be easier for me to move forward than back. You can do this, Lluava."

Pushing the numerous fatal scenarios from her mind, Lluava carefully climbed onto the tree trunk and gingerly stepped around the prince. Standing before him, she began to direct his movements. Slowly and meticulously, the pair made their way across the fallen tree. Lluava's eyes flickered rapidly as she gauged her footing as well as that of the man whose life was now in her hands. She studied every twitch of Varren's muscles; even the slightest wrong movement could offset his balance. Smooth and toned, he reminded her of a jungle cat prowling in the moonlight.

The minutes dragged on as the pair took one slow, precarious step after another. Lluava longed for the torment to be over. Finally, she reached the far ledge. In seconds, both she and Varren were safely on solid ground.

"See. That was not too bad," said Varren, slipping the blindfold off and handing it to Lluava. "Now it is your turn."

The cloth in Lluava's hands felt heavy. The very essence of her being resisted placing it around her head. Yet Varren had trusted her; shouldn't she trust him? Could he really be conniving enough to pretend to put his faith in her and then kill her? That didn't make any sense, but did logic have any place in reality?

"Here, let me help you," said Varren. Careful not to catch her hair in the blindfold, he tied it around her head. Lluava's last glimpse of the world was now blocked by an artificial wall of cloth.

"Take a step forward." Varren's lips were next to her ear. His breath was tinged with fennel and rosemary, the herbs her mother often used in cooking; the familiar scents comforted her. Slowly, Lluava slid her left foot forward along the rigid bark. Carefully shifting her weight to her outstretched leg, she slid her other foot around the first. She did not trust herself or her companion enough to lift any part of her foot off the prostrate trunk.

Step by step, the pair made their way across the chasm. Although her senses were on constant alert, Lluava eventually allowed herself to relax as Varren guided her. She knew she must be nearing the far side, when suddenly she felt a chunk of bark loosen under her weight. She had no time to react; the bark slipped off the trunk and plunged to the watery basin below. Lluava felt herself toppling sideways as Varren's arms wrapped around her, steadying her.

"I will not let you fall," he reassured the shaken girl, and steered her smoothly the rest of the way.

As Lluava set foot on solid earth, she realized that against her better judgment, her attitude toward Varren had indeed changed.

In silent understanding, the two partners made their way back to Durog. Before parting, Lluava turned to Varren. She wanted to apologize for her earlier actions, but before she could say anything, he spoke, "We understand each other now." Then he headed to his bunker.

With the dawn came the forging of trust from the raw iron of the pair's relationship. Throughout the day, the change was marked as Lluava and Varren worked together to complete their training assignments. In partner combat sessions, each strove to become attuned not just to the enemy but also to the other's presence. They helped each other traverse obstacle courses. Reaching a barricade neither could negotiate alone, they combined their skills and strengths in order to succeed.

Lluava was learning to use her gilded weapons. Issaura's Claws were strong but very light which enabled her to swing them around her with great ease. To be effective, she had to be virtually next to her adversary. This close-range fighting was unnerving at first, but, as time went on, she became more confident.

As Lluava learned to read her opponent's body language, she actually began to prefer being close to her aggressor. The fluctuation of an enemy's heartbeat could reveal fear, helpful information in close combat. Fear diminishes the ability to fully concentrate which causes one to become an easy target. Lluava could also sense anger, another factor affecting a person's focus. The twitch of a muscle, the flicker of an eye, even the smell of sweat—all were telltale signs of what an opponent was about to do. The skills Lluava gained with her weapons were honed as she and Varren practiced together.

Although both Lluava's and Varren's prowess increased, the situation around them worsened. Fights between races were commonplace. By the end of the first week, the hatred between humans and Theriomorphs seemed to have reached a climax. Lluava knew the situation could not continue much longer.

One evening, Lluava and Varren discussed this problem as they walked along the forested path near the base of the mountain.

"We must do something to prove to the troops that they are only hurting themselves by not trusting their assigned partners," Lluava said with a sigh. "If this continues, we will have a blood feud on our hands."

Troubled, Varren replied, "I know. I know. I have been racking my brain, but I have not come up with an answer."

Both were silent as they sat on a fallen log. They stared at the forest around them and at the objects, scattered about seemingly at random, that were used as obstacles on the ever-changing course.

"I wish we could force the entire camp to do what we did." Lluava paused, contemplating the newborn idea.

Varren shook his head. "If only it were so simple, but it is impossible. Even if it were, the races hatred of each other is so severe that I fear some might actually let their partners plunge to their death."

A sly smile slid across Lluava's face. "But we can…" she began, and then proceeded to explain her idea.

The next morning, the camp was abuzz with news of a break from the daily schedule. For an undisclosed reason, the grand master chief led the recruits to the forest. Varren, with Lluava at his side, stood on a makeshift platform in front of the recruits. The crowd quieted instantly once the prince began to speak.

"I have observed and noted the events of the past week and have been thoroughly disappointed. You were given a chance to become forerunners in the fight for equality that still persists in our kingdom, but, so far, all I have seen is that you have failed miserably."

Theriomorphs and humans alike were quiet. This is exactly what Lluava had hoped for.

"At this point," Varren went on, "We are like shattered glass, shards of some ancient object that would be beautiful and awe-inspiring if it were whole. As long as we act as separate entities, we have no chance to defend ourselves effectively against the onslaught that will soon be upon us. We must unify. We must become one great beast that will cause all before us to quake in our shadow."

Although the troops roared and cheered at the speech, Lluava was unsure whether they were truly ready to place their trust in one another or were merely swept away in the moment. Varren continued, and everyone quieted once more.

"I have set a challenge for all of you. To complete it successfully, you will have to put your full trust in your partner." Grumbling erupted at this comment. Varren ignored it. "I have arranged a special obstacle course, one with moving objects as well as auditory warnings. One of each pair will be blindfolded, while the other will have pieces of wax-coated cloth stuffed in his ears. The missing sense emphasizes you as you are now: only a weak individual. Neither partner has a chance of finishing the course without the help of the other. You must work together, combining your senses, in order to survive. Only when you fully trust your partner will you become, in a sense, whole. Once you and your partner have completed this task, you can continue your training. You will repeat this course until you have succeeded. The course will continually be altered, so do not bet on trying to outsmart this challenge. Good luck to all!"

The challenge began as predicted: everyone fought its purpose. Lluava hoped that when the challenge was completed, the two races would face each other, eye to eye, with respect and trust. But that hope was waning.

Chapter 22
Emerald in the Rough

Although the sun blazed brightly above the recruits, their mood was dark. Every five minutes, the grand master chief sent another pair through the obstacle course.

The entire course took a good half hour if there were no mistakes; but as expected, very few of the partners worked together to pass the test. Many actually argued about which partner should be blindfolded and which earplugged. Often the sighted partner bolted ahead of the other, leaving the latter behind to wander off course or fall into the first obstacle, a pit. Three ropes were tightly stretched across the pit's opening: two at shoulder level for support and the third at ground level to walk on. The sighted partner traversed the pit on the base rope while holding onto the top ropes for balance. Several obstacles could be navigated successfully before the sighted contender was knocked out by weighted sacks that swung from behind or above him. Hollowed, pierced water reeds tied to the sacks caught the air as they swung and emitted a high-pitched warning sound. However, with waxy plugs stuffing his ears, the sighted partner was unable to hear the alarm. By the end of the first round, only half a dozen pairs—including Talos and Byron, Horus and Thad—had completed the course.

Lluava found herself disheartened at the dearth of successful partners. As the day continued, a trickle of pairs made it through successfully; by evening, a quarter of the camp had succeeded. As a reward, these were allowed to rest and watch the other pairs struggle to complete the course. When it was too dark to continue, all were sent to their barracks to rest. It was midway through the third day before the last, straggling pairs, including Yamir and Malnus, finally finished. That afternoon, Varren made a congratulatory speech.

Regular training resumed the following day, and the change was phenomenal. The once common brawls and scraps had disappeared. A sense of unity replaced feelings of distrust. Over the next few days, the pairs embraced the idea of working with one another. Those who had once thought of themselves as individuals now believed they were a part of a ferocious entity that would protect their kingdom when the time came.

Walking across camp at dusk among her friends, Lluava was comforted. Even the sounds of the camp as it quieted for the night seemed more united. The clanking sounds of metal weapons seemed structured and deliberate; the boots of marching troops resounded in step with a certain beat. This was the music of the military. Somehow, she felt at home.

A band of recruits marched by, singing a martial song to keep time. As the friends admired the men's precision, Talos congratulated Varren and Lluava. "Your plan really paid off. Everyone is now working together—even developing respect for one another. The drastic change has an almost miraculous feeling to it. It was a wonderful idea."

"I do not know about any of you, but I thought the entire challenge was actually quite fun," added Thad. "I would not mind repeating the whole course again. How about you, Horus?"

Horus looked down his sharp nose and then said with a pleased expression, "Fun might not be the word I would have chosen, but I have always enjoyed a challenge."

"In a way, I wish I could have had my try at the course," said Lluava absentmindedly.

"Do you, now?" responded Varren, one eyebrow raised. "Well, enjoyable or not, it accomplished its purpose."

"If it worked here, wouldn't it work elsewhere, too?" questioned Malnus. Recently, even he had seemed to become aware of how badly he had treated the Theriomorphs. This was a miraculous transformation in Lluava's eyes.

Yamir, still not thrilled with his assigned partner and obviously happy with Malnus's silence, was curious enough to ask, "What are you proposing?"

Malnus, his voice scratchy from a week of self-imposed silence, explained his train of thought. "That trust-building exercise worked here, with the exception of a couple of irretrievably prejudiced men. Don't you think that it would work in Calitron and even in the ladies' camps? I know many of the men who left to train in Calitron. The blatant displays of hatred between our two races would be the same there as well as in the girls' camps. I think that exercise would work for the others. Just a thought...."

Lluava remembered how Rosalyn had expressed her distress at the lack of progress in Thowcelemine since the camp had paired with the women of Delphine. "Thowcelemine is having similar problems."

"Then this is settled," stated Varren emphatically. "Tomorrow I will ride to Thowcelemine and then make my way to Delphine and Calitron and order them to construct similar obstacle courses. As soon as I see that the order is followed, I will return."

"Do you want me to join you?" inquired Lluava. She had not been to the human camps and was curious to see what they were like.

"No. You need to stay here and continue training. I will go alone."

"What about this so-called partnership?"

"Lluava," Varren shook his head and smiled, "I have been training for war my whole life. You have only thought about it these past few months. You need to learn as much as you can. The battle could begin next month, next week, or—god forbid—tonight. You will stay."

Although Varren's decision made her unhappy, Lluava knew he was right. She shrugged and nodded her understanding.

"I'll be your temporary partner," piped up Chat's mild voice. The boy, now only a few inches shorter than Lluava, glanced at Varren. "At least until you return."

Varren laughed and tousled the Chat's hair. "I like that idea."

Lluava grinned at them both. "Me, too," she said.

After dinner, Lluava set out on her usual return trip to Thowcelemine. As she headed toward the gates, Varren waylaid her.

"Come with me," he said mysteriously. Without further explanation, he led the way back to the forest of Durog.

He stopped at the woods and pulled a piece of black cloth from his pocket. "You wanted to try your hand at the obstacle course, so here is your chance. Do you want eyes or ears?"

Lluava did not know how he had received approval from the general, but she was thrilled at the chance to test their skills on the course. "I would prefer to see."

Varren handed her a small pair of wax plugs. Placing them in her ears, she helped Varren tie the luxuriously soft strip of cloth over his eyes. She had never seen dark purple velvet before and could not believe that Varren would use such a fine material for this occasion; but then, she was not from the upper class.

Lluava glanced around her now silent world. The sun had slipped away beyond the horizon, and the haze of night had overspread everything. Although she could not hear it, a slight breeze rustled the dry leaves and blew gently over her skin. It was a truly pleasant evening. Standing beside Lluava, Varren waved to her. It was time to begin.

The order of the obstacles had been changed, although the first still consisted of a pit; this time a ladder stretched over it. Lluava guided Varren as easily as she had on the cliff. She told him the exact placement of each rung and when to shift his weight; they used each other to keep balance. The next few trials were fairly simple, while the climbing wall was one of the harder ones. It took several tries before Lluava figured out how to steer her blind partner to each handhold and over the top.

Lluava guessed they must be halfway through; the mobile obstacles lay just ahead. She still wondered how Varren had arranged for them to be here this evening and would have liked to ask, but she needed to focus on the course. Anyway, with her ears plugged, there was no point.

As they rounded the corner of their designated path, Lluava could see that it was a straight shot to the climbing ropes. She told Varren to hurry, and they began to jog forward. Her thoughts were now on breaking the fourteen-minute record of completion.

To her dismay, Lluava suddenly found herself flung sideways. Varren had pushed her hard, and the two slid down the slope, where he landed on top of her, his face a mere mouse's length above hers. Simultaneously, a large battering ram swung through the treetops and skimmed over their heads. Lluava saw the whistles strapped to the top of the massive tree trunk.

Lying on her back, staring at the dark canopy above, she spotted Thad sitting on a limb holding the device's pull cord. Thad winked, then slipped into the shadows, no doubt to arm the next mobile obstacle. So that's how it's done, Lluava thought. She couldn't help but laugh. Varren had rolled off and sprawled beside her, laughing too. As Lluava observed her partner, she found herself appreciating his pleasant smile.

When they finished the course, the record was still unbroken, but it no longer mattered to Lluava. This night would be one that she would remember for a long time to come.

The next morning was also memorable. The entire camp was called to the large coliseum for another announcement. Looking grimmer than ever, the grand master chief stood in the center. Lluava's heart began to race as it had when Varren had knocked her down the night before. The troops were quiet in anticipation. Could this be it? Had the war against the Raiders finally begun? Varren was nowhere to be seen, and Lluava began to worry.

It was Thad who put her mind at rest. "Remember, Varren left to spread word to the other camps about this new way of unification."

With a sigh of relief, Lluava turned her attention to the arena's center. As if awaiting some secret signal, the general seemed to pause before he finally spoke.

"Surprisingly, you have all been doing well. If you keep working at it, you might actually make something of yourselves. I have talked with General Kentril, the commanding general of Thowcelemine. We are rewarding you for your hard work by arranging a dance in ten days' time, to be attended by the ladies of Thowcelemine and all of you ruffians."

The entire stadium was dead silent. Everyone wanted to burst into conversation, but nobody dared speak while the grand master chief had the floor. The idea crossed their minds that this was some kind of hoax, but the thought of a dance, of meeting and mingling with the ladies of the southern camp, entranced them. Lluava did not know what to think.

For the rest of the morning, Lluava's stomach was in knots, but not for the same reason as the rest of the camp. She needed to ask Talos a question but was forced to wait until they met at the gym.

While Chat and Yamir were climbing the ropes, she pulled Talos aside and whispered into his ear, "I don't know how to dance."

"What?" Talos raised his eyebrows.

"Shhh!" She could feel her face turning red. "I said, I don't know how to dance."

"Really?" inquired Talos.

"I was wondering if you would teach me since you probably have been taught, being— you know."

"I should know because I am upper class, right?" He laughed; then, sensing her distress, said, "Sure, I will help you. It really is not that hard. There are several styles, both human and Theriomorph, that I can show you."

"Can I learn, too?" inquired the deepening voice of Chat, from behind Lluava. When she realized that she was not the only one who could not grace the dance floor, Lluava felt better.

Talos chuckled. "Sure. What about you, Yamir?"

"I know how to dance," scoffed Yamir. "Why would you think I didn't?"

"I am sorry," said Talos. "I did not mean to insult you."

"It might be good if I were to sit in and make sure you teach them correctly," he retorted quickly. Malnus nodded in agreement. Lluava and Chat exchanged smiles.

Talos grinned. "Of course, you can," he said.

As a result, the group met at the gym during their free time. Yamir and Chat had balked at being paired together, but there was only one female. Talos demonstrated how the woman places her left hand on the man's right shoulder, and then extending her right arm out to one side, elbow slightly bent, she places her right hand in the man's left hand. Talos made sure Lluava kept her form rigid and her lines straight as he taught them the appropriate footwork for the human's waltz.

For a dance that looked so easy, so effortless, it was surprisingly hard to follow Talos's lead. Lluava's arms tired of holding the same position for a long time. Around her, Yamir and Chat spiraled in an ungainly manner. They enjoyed goofing off and weren't taking this seriously. Malnus, on the other hand, would not even consider dancing with another male; he sat and observed.

Byron also gave instruction in the art of dance. Though clearly less structured than Talos, he gave the group several important tips. As there was no music, Talos sometimes sang. If they knew the song, the others joined in, but it was Talos's crisp voice, keeping time for the dancers' movements, that carried the tune.

Over the following days, whenever Lluava was not practicing for combat, she and her friends danced until their feet hurt too much to stand. On the second day, Talos introduced some Theriomorph styles. Faster and less rigid, they were no less hard to master. All in all, the group learned the five most popular dances in the kingdom. Talos thought that that should be sufficient for the camps' simple celebration.

One evening after returning to Thowcelemine, Lluava realized she was missing a very important item for the upcoming dance. Her feet ached as she slipped off her worn endun shoes. She rubbed her feet as a swarm of freshly showered girls, abuzz with excitement, came into the barracks.

The girls gossiped about the dresses they were going to wear for the dance and how they should style their hair. "I think I might curl mine. Curls would match the ruffles on my dress, don't you think?" Alison said, shaking her strawberry blonde hair.

"That would look lovely," the twins replied in unison. Shenne continued, "I am wearing the canary-yellow dress while Sonty will wear the lemon-yellow one."

"Or do you think the canary-yellow would look better on me?" asked Sonty while Shenne waited for an answer.

Alison looked at both of them. "Let me see the dresses."

The twins each pulled out a beautifully sewn gown from the chests under their bunk.

"Hmm...." Alison paused; the colors and the styles were almost identical.

Rosalyn politely asked, "May I say something?"

"Sure," replied the twins.

"I think that Shenne should wear the canary-yellow, for it brings out the color of her eyes, and Sonty should wear the lemon one. It would go well with that pair of shoes you showed me, Sonty."

The girls seemed pleased and began chatting about the jewelry each would wear.

Sitting cross-legged on her bunk and listening to their banter, Lluava admitted a very unfortunate fact. "I don't have a dress. What do I do?"

Alison laughed but stopped when she realized that Lluava wasn't joking. Lluava, for her part, pondered how she had changed. Did she actually want a dress? Was conformity becoming part of her belief structure?

"You do not have *any* kind of dress?" questioned Alison.

Lluava shook her head.

"Not even a nice skirt?"

"Nope."

The girls looked at each other in amazement. They had never met anyone who did not own at least a common working dress.

"We don't have one in your size," said the twins, as if they were one person.

"Neither do I," commented Alison.

Lluava was disheartened, but Rosalyn spoke up. "I think I can help. Actually, I think all of us can help."

As the girl with raven-black hair shared her idea, everyone crowded around her; even Lluava jumped down from her bunk to listen. Later, after the other girls had made their plans and climbed into their own beds, Lluava discovered that she was once again excited about the dance.

When the day finally arrived, Lluava found it hard to focus on her daily training. She was not the only one who felt this way. Many of the recruits' performances were under par. Only after the grand master chief threatened to cancel the whole endeavor did the troops focus on their work. Unfortunately for Lluava, the men were not released early. It was seven in the evening by the time she was finally free to run back to Thowcelemine, where the ladies had been preparing themselves since three o'clock that afternoon.

When Lluava, entirely disheveled, burst through the doors of her barracks, the girls swarmed around her to hurry her through the grooming process. After Lluava showered, Alison and the twins worked on her hair and makeup. She had no idea that so many powders and oils could be smeared on one's face. The twins moved on to groom Lluava's hands and feet as Alison finished the partially upswept hairdo. For the first time in her life, Lluava's hair was elegantly waved.

Finishing the final touches to Lluava's dress, Rosalyn sat on the bunk next to her. Lluava joined in the excited chatter.

"Wouldn't it be simply lovely to bring home a soldier, maybe even a war hero, after all this is over? My parents would be thrilled," sighed Alison.

Shenne replied, "I just hope to dance with someone who is tall…"

"…and has dark hair…" chimed in Sonty.

"…and hazel eyes!" they exclaimed in unison.

That night, Lluava and her girlfriends were the last to arrive. The group asked Lluava nonstop questions about Durog until they were about to enter the camp. Their excited banter increased once they could hear the melodious strains of a well-known song, *The Ballad of Necanel*, coming from the large building that was the weapon's storage facility.

When the doors were swung wide by several uniformed officers acting as stewards for the night, Lluava thought the change that had occurred within the building could only be described as enchanting. The dividers had been removed along with the entire camp's weaponry, leaving a wide, open space. Candles illuminated the perimeter of the room while paper lanterns, the likes of which Lluava had never seen before, hung from the ceiling. Hickory benches had been brought in to line the walls. A string quartet played in one corner; Lluava spotted Chat and Yamir pouring punch from a table in another corner. A crowd of twirling twosomes completed the picturesque scene, the image of a royal ball.

Lluava and the rest of the girls took seats on the closest bench and watched the spinning couples.

"Look how handsome they all are," sighed Alison, glancing at a group of several young men chatting among themselves.

"I hope one asks me to dance." Sonty stared at the crowd before her.

"And me as well." Shenne's excitement was obvious.

"Lluava, is the prince here? If so, you should introduce me," Alison said with a demanding tone as she tugged at one of her curls.

"I doubt that he will make it," Lluava replied. "Varren is probably working with the ladies of Delphine or the gentlemen in Calitron." She tried not to sound as disheartened as she felt.

"That's too bad," said Alison, touching up her lips with the red stain from the small tin she carried in her purse. "From what I saw when he visited us a few days ago, he is *very* handsome."

While the three other girls chattered about each and every man they saw, Lluava could not help but glance at her bunkmate. Rosalyn sat quietly next to her, ankles crossed and back straight. The obsidian-haired girl kept peering around anxiously, scanning the crowd. Lluava knew whom Rosalyn was waiting for, and she, too, looked about for the young man.

It was not Talos but Byron who first asked the ladies to dance. Dashing in his formal uniform, he approached; the girls quieted, wide-eyed, to see which one he would choose.

Byron smiled at all of them. "Ladies, you look so elegant. I am Byron, son of Teckner, and I would be more than honored if each of you would grant me the pleasure of a dance at some point tonight."

The three on the end nodded their heads, trying to control their excitement.

He continued, "As it is too hard to pick with whom to dance first, I will be glad if my friend and comrade, Lluava, would join me on the dance floor."

"It would be my pleasure." Lluava stood up and let Byron lead her through the crowd. Once in the center of the floor, she remarked, "You are surprisingly smooth with the ladies."

Byron clasped her hand in his and led her into the waltz. "It is a gift," he said with a smile. "And you look beautiful tonight."

"You do not need to flatter me, Byron. Tomorrow I will be merely your comrade-in-arms again."

"But, you see, that is where you are wrong. I am not just whispering pleasant words to the wind. I am stating the truth. Did you not notice how, upon your entry, the majority of the men had to force themselves to keep from staring at you? You are a shimmering emerald with that dress, that necklace, and your eyes. You are exquisite, and you must see why I felt compelled to be the first to dance with you."

Lluava felt herself blush. "Byron, you should be a poet instead of a soldier."

Lluava spotted Rosalyn dancing with Talos. Her head was resting on his shoulder. Talos, wearing a finely tailored suit, looked handsomer than ever. They truly seemed made for each other. Soon other pairs of dancers blocked Lluava's view of the engaged couple.

Lluava relaxed. She felt beautiful as she danced with man after man. She knew she would have to thank Rosalyn again for making the dress, a deep green linen layered under a sheer, pale-green material that gave the dress the ability to shimmer in the light. Instead of the typical puffed sleeves, two long pieces of cloth extended from the low cut V-neck to tie around her neck. The back of the dress was cut low, to save what little material with which Rosalyn had had to work. To minimize the bareness, forest-green lace crisscrossed the back for an elegant effect. A sash made from the spare cloth wrapped her midriff, blending the tight-fitting bodice smoothly with the pleated skirt. Between dances, Lluava absentmindedly fingered her mother's emerald necklace, but she never had to wait for long before the next dance. She even made sure to dance with Yamir and Chat.

A little before midnight, Thad took his turn with Lluava. "You are surely the catch of the night," he said, spinning her around.

"What do you mean by that?"

"It has taken me several hours to manage to dance with you. You are breathtaking this evening."

"Why, thank you." Though she felt a little downcast, Lluava changed the subject to more serious matters. "How do you think Varren is doing at the other camps?"

"Knowing Varren, I think he is doing just fine. He can be quite the diplomat when he wants to," Thad said with a smile.

After their dance, Lluava passed Thad off to the waiting Alison and took a seat on the bench for the second time that night. Watching, she was happy to see that all the girls were now dancing. The song changed to one with a slower pace; Lluava was captivated by the way Rosalyn and Talos danced together.

"I cannot believe that you are just sitting on the sidelines. I expected you to be the center of it all."

Lluava could not help but smile as she turned to look at Varren. Her partner wore a crisp white suit with a double row of gold buttons at the top. His sword was sheathed in an embossed silver scabbard at his side. He looked like a figure out of a dream.

Fitting her hand into his as they made their way among the dancing figures, she replied, "I've been waiting for the right partner."

The night continued with a series of dances, each more perfect than the last. Lluava felt as if she were floating on the dance floor as Varren spun her around. He knew just how to lead her when he introduced her to new dance styles. She found herself laughing as she attempted different steps. When the music finally stopped, Lluava noticed that many couples had left the room. She and Varren smiled at one another and walked out into the night air.

In an almost dreamlike state, Lluava started to head back to Thowcelemine, but Varren seized her hand.

"Wait, I want to take you somewhere. But before we go, we need to change."

Without hesitation, Lluava followed the prince to his room in the new barracks. Once inside, he pulled out two black training uniforms and tossed one to her.

"You can change here; I will use the washroom."

Slipping on the pants and shirt, Lluava could smell the cedar from the chest where they had been kept. The uniform was too big for her, so she rolled up the cuffs of the pants. Lluava decided to go barefoot rather than struggle with the too-large sandals.

Varren returned wearing a similar black outfit. A slight smile tugged at the corner of his mouth when he looked at her. "It is time for us to go. Come with me."

The two trekked through camp, the woods, and at last up the side of Burok Dûr. A pregnant crescent moon shone high in the sky, illuminating their way to the top with its milky light. Just before they reached the rocky precipice, Varren veered off toward the far side of the mountain. The surrounding pines stopped at a cantilevered stone ledge.

From this vantage point, they had an exquisite view of the ocean and the forest below. In the distance, Lluava could almost see the dark outlines of Calitron, near the ocean's edge. Several faint lights still flickered within its walls. Beyond lay Delphine, the walls seeming to sink into the sea itself.

Varren spread a blanket he had carried with him on the ground, and the two sat down. They were quiet for a while until Lluava broke the silence. "I thought you weren't going to arrive in time."

"Lluava," he turned to look at her, "I would not have missed this for the world. You are my partner, and I want you to know I will always be there for you."

"Your partner..." Lluava repeated thoughtfully under her breath.

"Yes, my partner. And the best one anybody could ever wish for. I am sorry that I am developing a habit of being late."

Looking at him, Lluava replied, "As they say, better late than never."

As the pair gazed at each other, a glimmer of light like a shooting star illuminated them. Varren's eyes left hers, and he scanned the horizon. Lluava watched his sweet smile slip into something more worrisome. It struck her at this moment that the light around them had not disappeared. Almost in unison, the partners turned to the horrid image before them just as an explosion of sound bombarded their ears. The cacophony that followed made the mountain tremble.

Far below in the distance, Calitron and Delphine were being consumed by flames. Large spheres of fire rained from the heavens. On the ocean's horizon, dim shapes of numerous oar-ships emerged from the darkness. Suddenly, one of the flaming orbs roared through the sky toward them. Falling short of the summit, it exploded against the side of the mountain, setting trees afire. Faintly, they could hear screams from the burning camps below.

The war had begun and laid claim to its first victims.

ISSAURA'S CLAWS

PART II

Chapter 23
A Secret No More

The flaming projectile blasted past them by a hair's breadth before it crashed; its incredible heat singed Lluava's hair. Burok Dûr groaned under the impact, and the resulting tremor sent several large boulders tumbling down its sides. Varren grabbed Lluava's arm and pulled her off the protruding lip of rock where they had been sitting. A second blazing ball careened towards them. Bits of rock whistled past their faces. The pair ran for cover as the once solid ground began to crack and crumble.

Lluava could not stop to consider how close they had come to a fiery death. The quiet night blared with noise. Continuous explosions competed with the screeching of Durog's alarm. Screaming flocks of disrupted birds took wing, while shouts and cries echoed from the camp below.

Lluava's senses were on high alert. Her ears rang from the bombardment of sound. Fires began to spread. As black smoke billowed around them, Varren and Lluava forced themselves toward the camp.

Running and coughing through the smoky gusts, the two of them startled several people desperately fighting flames encroaching on the woods. Following her partner, Lluava joined a throng of recruits forcing their way through the doors of the small coliseum. They entered the arena, and Varren strode up to the furious Merrow and Skipe. Standing as if born for this particular day, the grand master chief towered over them with fierce concentration and commanding focus. Varren quickly related what he had observed from the top of Burok Dûr, then he and Lluava took their seats with the rest of the recruits.

"Attention!" Colonel Skipe shouted. It needed only to be said once.

The grand master chief growled out, "Congratulations, all of you! This is your graduation day. You are no longer recruits; you are now soldiers in

His Majesty Thor's army. The sound you awakened to this morning was the sound of the Raiders' catapults assaulting our seaside wall. Thankfully, Burok Dûr is our natural defense against such attacks.

"As of today, all of you will follow my commands precisely. You will do what I say, when I say it. Any hesitation could risk not only your own life but also the lives of those around you. Doubt and fear will not be tolerated. Is this clear?"

Voices rang out in unison, "Sir, yes, sir!"

"I regret to inform you that according to reports, both Calitron and Delphine have been breached by the attacks."

The humans were distraught at this news; their partners tried to calm them as the grand master chief solemnly continued.

"I am sending a small band of elite soldiers from this camp to reconnoiter the area and to search for survivors. After dismissal, the following pairs will meet Colonel Skipe by Durog's gates: Thadius Sihia II and Horus Ethril; Derrick Urbane and Trintan Brenders; Varren Mandrun and Lluava Kargen."

Excitement and fear welled up within Lluava; her whole body trembled. She forced herself to pay attention.

"The rest of you have ten minutes to change into uniform, pack your weapons and gear, and line up with your troops in the courtyard, where you will receive your orders. Dismissed."

Immediately Lluava and Varren began to make their way through the crowd to the gates. Simultaneously, Talos was shoving his way through the tightly packed bodies. Lluava tried to wave him down, but he pushed past unseeing, forcing his way to his destination: the grand master chief. Detouring, Lluava followed Talos. Varren did the same.

Talos spoke to the general, desperation in his voice. "What are we going to do about Thowcelemine? Should we send a group to bring back the women? We cannot leave them to be attacked."

"I am glad you have so much compassion for the ladies you met tonight, soldier," responded the general, "But you are out of line. Thowcelemine is far from the ocean; the Raiders' projectiles cannot possibly reach them. The other two camps are under siege, so they are the ones in need. Once we have responded to them, we will proceed with caution and provide safe passage for those in Thowcelemine, but only when I say so. Is this clear?"

Without answering, Talos turned abruptly and almost knocked Lluava over.

"Talos, calm down! Talos, wait!" Lluava grabbed him as he tried to sidestep her.

"You do not understand," he snapped. "I am the reason she is here. She enlisted just to be near me. I will do anything, *anything*, to make sure she is safe. I have to help her…" Talos's voice cracked.

"Listen to me. I know you want to be a hero and save Rosalyn, but the grand master chief is right. We need to attack the problem in a level-headed manner. Promise me," implored Lluava, "that you won't do anything rash, and you'll wait till we return. *Promise* me!"

With a yank, Talos slipped free of Lluava's grasp and strode off toward the barracks.

"Lluava, we have to go."

Varren's voice drew her attention, and she turned reluctantly. Varren was right. They had an assignment, and the others would be waiting for them. The pair hurried off to their impatient comrades.

Along the way, Varren retrieved his sword. At the meeting point, Lluava was issued a pair of daggers to compensate for her missing gear. She yearned for her own weapons, which she had left behind at Thowcelemine, but now was not the time to complain. She still wore the clothing Varren had lent her and now Yamir's spare pair of shoes. Her discomfort with the current situation continued to build.

Colonel Skipe's tone was brusque. "Here is the plan. Since we do not know whether the Raiders have landed, we must be very cautious. Roads are unsafe. We will use the nearby fields; the grass and grains are tall enough to hide us. Move fast. Don't stop until we reach Calitron's gates. Keep your partner in sight at all times, and stay alert. Let's go!"

The gates of Durog opened just enough to allow the small scouting party to slip out. Lluava tried to remain calm as the group headed across the road at a steady run. For once, she wished the moon were covered by clouds; unfortunately, it shone bright as ever. She felt safer when they had ducked into the overgrown fields. The rough edges of the long blades of grass, choking out the last remnants of wheat from a long-ago harvest, tugged against her oversized clothes. A barrage of explosions could still be heard ahead of them. She tried not to imagine what they would find.

Soon, however, something more ominous became apparent: the bombardment had stopped. What did that mean? Could the camps have been breached? What was happening? Lluava tried to shake the dark images from her mind.

In the silence around them, crickets were chirping a little ways a head of them. Although this was a good omen of calm, the quiet was bad news for the scouting party. Crickets quieted when people were near. Anyone paying close attention would know that something was moving in the field.

By the time the small party finally neared Calitron, tensions were high. They had to be very careful to approach the camp undetected, and daybreak would come within the hour. More worrisome was the fact that the only sound coming from inside Calitron's walls was the hiss and crackle of dying fires.

Colonel Skipe led the group up the road, inspecting the camp's perimeter to get a sense of the situation inside. What they observed was distressing. Large holes had been blasted into Calitron's stone walls. Portions of the camp had collapsed. Large-rock debris was scattered everywhere. Thick plumes of smoke billowed over the walls like writhing maggots consuming a meal.

Slowly the group crept ever closer. As they ducked behind the wreckage of the once mighty stone wall, Lluava detected a scent. The odor was one that anybody might smell in the kitchen at home, but the knowledge of what caused it made the scent unbearable. The stench of burning flesh made Lluava's head swim and her stomach churn. Derrick, crouching beside her, could not keep one corner of his lip from twitching. He, too, was repelled by the odor.

Skipe motioned them forward. Soon they reached a section of wall that had been entirely blown away. Thick cracks branched from the central hole like an intricate spider web. Squeezing close together, the group had their first look at the destruction wrought upon Calitron. Most of the buildings were defaced with blackened scorch marks or were still ablaze. Barracks had been flattened by debris or shattered from the catapults. It was a wonder that any buildings still stood. The worst thing about the whole scene was the absolute lack of movement.

One at a time, the group followed their leader through the gap in the wall. Careful not to trip over fractured boulders and shattered wood, Lluava safely traversed the devastated terrain until she had safely reached the back of a more or less intact barracks. Ever so slowly, they advanced toward the center of the camp.

Suddenly Varren froze. His fists clenched tightly, and his gaze traveled off to the right. Lluava followed his line of sight until she spotted the blackened body of a man sprawled on the ground. Thin wisps of smoke rose from the charred bits of cloth. His head was turned to one side, his mouth open. He was too badly burned to be recognizable.

Did her legs just waver? Was she actually dizzy all of a sudden? Horus tugged at her wrist releasing Lluava from her thoughts. Slowly, they moved forward. More burned and dismembered bodies were discovered, some half buried in rubble, others lay on the road. There was no sign of life.

Finally, the party reached a point from which they could clearly see the central courtyard of the camp. There, in Calitron's heart, Lluava first glimpsed a sign of life. About twenty men knelt, bound, before a group of Raiders twice their number. The men of Calitron struggled in vain against the tightly knotted ropes. Their captors wore thick layers of fur-trimmed cloaks draped over bulky shoulders. This strange garb was ill suited for the summer's heat. Arrow-shooting devices were strapped on their backs along with fully stocked quivers. Their horned helmets and thick, unkempt beards gave them a wild, demonic look. At their sides, sharp blades—bringers-of-death—

glinted in the early morning light.

One Raider, a man of average height, stepped out in front of the rest. He pulled off his helmet and laid it at his feet. Horns protruded from either side of the dull metal; one was unusually long, while its counterpart was broken in half. The man's hair, like his beard, was dark, but as he stepped into the torchlight, a hint of red could be seen. He was only middle aged, Lluava guessed, but prematurely gray hairs massed over his ears. He wore a cloak made from the pelts of two silver wolves, their snarling heads resting one on each shoulder.

He spoke with an accent so thick it was almost unintelligible. "Your time is up," he said to the kneeling captives.

Instantly, his companions pulled out their swords and quickly ran each and every man through except one. The survivor had to listen to the gasping and groaning of his dying comrades.

Lluava leaned out as far as she dared to obtain a better look at the survivor. It took her a moment before she recognized the unfortunate captive. Half of General Miller's face was covered with bubbling scars. She did not want to know whether his burns came from the attack or from torture. It was clear that he was in excruciating pain.

The leader of the Raiders spoke again. His hostile expression and threatening demeanor made it utterly clear that he was absolutely serious. "You answer me, yes?"

General Miller replied slowly and almost inaudibly. "What do you want to know?"

His captor did not smile. "Now we get somewhere. Where are others hiding? I do not believe for one second that we disposed all of them. I want to know what are th' weaknesses. Surely, they have weakness? Is some way to easily identify them? Well?"

Though General Miller was a small man, he had probably never looked fiercer than at that moment. Spitting on the Raider's boots, he proclaimed, "May god have mercy on your soul!"

The captive general did not move, struggle, or try to resist his fate. At a quick nod from the Raiders' leader, a red-haired man stepped forward, jerked the general's head back by the hair, and slit his throat. A crimson tide spewed from the wound and was almost instantly absorbed by the parched earth. The general of Calitron died on his knees before his kingdom's greatest threat.

Lluava swallowed bile. Despite her dizziness, she forced herself to concentrate on the lead Raider as he pushed the corpse of the once proud man onto its side with his boot. He whistled, and a white and gray bird of prey flew down to land on his extended wrist. His thick gloves protected his hand from the razor-sharp talons, which held a twitching mouse.

Turning to his men, the Raider commanded, "Go! Find anything that still moves, and kill it, whether man or horse or rat that crawls beneath floorboards!" He glanced down in disgust at the now still rodent being consumed by his pet. "Slay anything that breathes. They will not escape. We keep no survivors."

The whinny of a horse reached their ears. From a stable, one of the invaders led a pair of balking steeds to the courtyard where, without a second thought, two men slit their throats. The other men scattered and began to search the camp. One headed toward the spot where Lluava and the others crouched.

Colonel Skipe signaled a retreat with a silent wave. Quickly and quietly the group withdrew to the hole in Calitron's wall. Lluava peered around; every shadow made her heart leap. Trembling all over, she forced her legs forward. Once safely away from the camp, they hid behind large boulders and debris.

Horus was first to speak. "They knew about us. How could they know about us?"

"We can't be sure that is what he was referring to," said Trintan optimistically.

His more realistic partner spoke up. "What else could he have meant?" Derrick's tone was stern. "We are not a secret anymore. We must now expect that they have come prepared to fight Theriomorphs, too."

"So what do we do now?" Trintan asked.

Colonel Skipe broke in. "We head back to Durog at once."

At this, Varren was distressed. Cutting the commander off, he said, "We have to help Delphine! We cannot leave them to die! We…"

"Varren, listen to me." Thad's was the voice of reason, trying to reach his lifelong friend. "It's too late. They are gone. The time we spend here could risk the lives of others. We need to focus on Thowcelemine. They need us. We must go."

"They were my people," whispered the prince.

Thad placed his arm on Varren's shoulder. "I know."

The others began to leave, but when Lluava tried to move, her limbs felt weak, and she found herself unable to stand. Was something wrong with her? Then the strong hands of Skipe lifted her up and propelled her along.

The trek back to Durog seemed endless. Lluava found it difficult to concentrate. As soon as they entered the gates, they were ushered to the general's barracks.

Entering the meeting room, Lluava and the others found Admiral Merrow and the grand master chief strategizing over a map of the southern part of the kingdom.

General Argon turned to look at the disheveled scouts. Lluava was clearly in shock, and the rest did not look much better. Their news would not be good. "What have you found out?" he asked tonelessly.

"Calitron and Delphine are both lost. The Raiders killed those who survived the bombardment," Skipe said bitterly. "And they know about us. Somehow, they found out about Theriomorphs. I think you were right; someone must have tipped them off."

They were silent while the grand master chief digested the information. At last he spoke. His voice was remarkably calm. "So, we are a secret no more. That is too bad. Ah, well, no time for tears." He straightened his shoulders and continued, "We must concentrate on retrieving the women of Thowcelemine. Colonel Skipe, there is no time for rest. Take several troops to Thowcelemine immediately. Admiral Merrow and I will lead the rest in a counterstrike, which will also function as a distraction."

"Yes, sir," replied Skipe. "Permission to choose my own troops?"

"Of course," the general answered.

"Then I want Aerial Troop 16 and Terra Troop Seven."

"Then it's settled." The grand master chief turned back to the map. "The rest of you can rejoin your respective troops. We move out in twenty minutes."

Outside, the humidity had risen, an abrupt change from the dry heat they had experienced all summer. The pre-fall rains would be upon them soon. Lluava looked at the brightening sky and watched as clouds, like saturated tufts of lambswool blanketing the fading stars, began to build upon each other. Nothing will ever be the same, she thought. Everything is changing.

Shouts from her friends broke her reverie. She saw that her troop had gathered by the flagpole alongside others. The flag hung at half-mast. Chat called her name and ran toward her.

"What's going on? Is it time to leave already?" she asked as the boy approached.

Chat looked at her worriedly. "You have been standing and staring at the sky for a while. They told me to let you be." He nodded toward Varren and the others, who were talking among themselves. "They said you needed time."

Joining her troop, Lluava saw that one of her friends was missing. "Where is Talos?" she asked.

"Lluava, we tried to stop him," Yamir answered apologetically.

"Where is he?" she demanded.

"I swear to you that we tried," Byron replied. "He wouldn't listen to reason."

Lluava glowered at Byron. "You're his partner! You should have stopped him!"

"I tried," snapped Byron, turning his head to face Lluava directly so she could see his bleeding lip and the bruise under his right eye.

"Oh," she gasped. "I'm sorry, Byron."

Varren stepped to her side. "In a few moments, we will head after him.

We can only hope that he has made it safely to Thowcelemine." Varren's face was grim. "One of the Raiders' ships has been spotted at the docks beyond Thowcelemine's walls."

Chapter 24
The Nocturnal One Takes His Rest

Lluava fidgeted impatiently, barely keeping her place in line, as she waited for the order to move out. They needed to hurry. Talos, alone against the Raiders' army, was somewhere outside Durog's walls.

The thick gates groaned as they were opened wide for the first time since the recruits had arrived. With a fearsome war cry, the grand master chief led the first troops from the camp. He was followed closely by Admiral Merrow and the second half of Durog's. Soon only Troop Seven and Troop 16 remained. Moments passed as they anxiously awaited Skipe's signal.

At last, the colonel waved them forward. The air was still cool, but the humidity made their clothes cling to their bodies. Lluava felt weighed down by the oversized outfit she still wore. Without the benefit of Theriomorph-made material, she could not shift without bursting the sewn seams, so she had to push herself in human form to keep up the quick pace of the fresh troops around her. As before, Skipe led them into the tall grass on the far side of the dirt road. Crouching low, the band made its way to the silent gates of Thowcelemine. Lluava felt dismay at the absence of signs of life inside the camp. Could they really be too late?

Lluava watched Skipe signal Horus to change form. The eagle took wing and flew over the gates. All waited, hoping their comrade would evade whatever trap the enemy might have set.

Movement. The gates were opening. A single form stood in the sliver-sized opening and beckoned them inside. Horus had successfully flown over the gates to warn the camp. The two groups quickly marched inside, where the young women were already packing essential supplies and medical equipment. Some were lining up in troop formation near the gates with full army packs strapped to their backs.

Without asking permission, Lluava went in search of any news of Talos; Varren followed like her shadow. She knew that if he had made it here, he would be with Rosalyn. As she headed to her own barracks, a familiar voice called her name.

Turning to the swarthy man behind her, Lluava asked, "Major Ojewa, do you know if a young man entered Thowcelemine?"

"If you are talking about the one known as Talos, yes, he did."

Lluava breathed a sigh of relief.

Her former commander recognized Varren. "Your highness, Talos is the one who notified General Kentril about the morning's events. He told us that General Argon was consolidating all four camps and that we should expect escorts from Durog. And here you are. As you probably have noticed, we are almost ready to depart."

"Major Ojewa," Lluava tried to keep her calm. "Delphine and Calitron are no more. It is up to Durog and Thowcelemine now." She choked back the sudden tears. The images of that morning played before her eyes. She could not shake them, even with Varren standing reassuringly by her side.

"Go find your friend, Lluava." Sorrow written on his face, Ojewa looked down at the young woman before him, "We will be ready to depart soon."

"Go ahead, Lluava," agreed the prince. "I need to speak with Major Ojewa. I will catch up to you in a few minutes."

As they parted, Lluava spotted the two figures for whom she had been searching. Talos and Rosalyn were lugging overstuffed packs on their backs as they headed from the barracks that had been Lluava's home. In her relief, she forgot the harsh words she had for Talos and his rashness.

Rosalyn caught sight of her and hurried toward her closest friend at the camps. "Lluava, I am so glad that you are all right. Talos told me that you were one of the few who was sent to rescue the poor souls at the other camps. Have you retrieved all of them? How many are injured?"

It was clear that Rosalyn's training as a healer had left its mark. Lluava shook her head and felt herself begin to be sick. There was no point in saying more. The couple's expressions became dark. Rosalyn gripped Talos's arm. They stood quietly for a moment, a reverent silence for the dead.

Blinking suddenly, Talos said, "We have to leave soon."

"Oh, Lluava," Rosalyn spoke up before she forgot. "We packed your things already, including your uniforms, letters, and your book."

Before Lluava could thank them, Talos interjected, "You might need these." He removed Lluava's shoes, a white uniform, and her weapons. Passing them to her outstretched hands, he said, "I think you will be happy to have them back." She thanked him and ran to change.

Once back in her own clothes, Lluava felt a new sense of confidence. With the familiar weight of Issaura's Claws in her hands, a wave of energy enveloped her. When it was time to leave, she was ready.

Although the sun was just beginning to rise, the heat had dried up all the moisture in the air. Compared to Durog's, Thowcelemine's gates opened quietly. Lluava gave one last look at her first training camp before leaving its grounds forever.

The men of Durog formed a small protective ring around Thowcelemine's female regiment. Officers on horseback were scattered throughout the formation as sentinels. Because there was no possible way to hide this many individuals, General Kentril decided it would be best to march back along the road. The clear path would make traveling faster, and speed was what they needed now.

They were barely halfway back but making good progress when the strident trumpeting of a war horn was heard. That single, solemn blast was followed by several dozen others. Kentril and Skipe shouted to the convoy to move faster as the unholy sounds came nearer. Despite their frantic pace, the trumpeting drew steadily closer.

The wind picked up, blowing dust from the road into a swirling cloud around them, slowing them down. Loss of vision was the last thing they needed. Lluava, at the front of the regiment, automatically clutched the Claws. Sensing Varren's presence, she backed up next to him.

Suddenly, a sharp noise sounded a short distance in front of her. The regiment halted instantly. As Lluava peered into the dust, trying to make out what lay ahead, a form emerged. The horned helmet gave the sturdy-looking, silhouetted shape an unnatural appearance. A double-bladed battle-ax was slung over the man's shoulder.

Another gust of wind caused the man to be enveloped in a cloud of dust. By the time the air began to clear, the man had disappeared, and the war horns were silent. Lluava scanned the fields around them and sniffed the air. The long grass tossed in the wind, and the stench of sweating bodies wafted up from the field of yellow and green.

The Raiders were using the fields as cover, just as Lluava's troop had done earlier. Had they been in hiding the whole time? Were they waiting for the moment when all of Thowcelemine was out in the open? Had they just walked into a trap?

Although Varren could not distinguish the sour smell of the Raiders from the hot bodies of his own troop, he understood what had happened. Grasping the hilt of his sword, he waited, body tensed, for some sign of the attackers. He appeared surprisingly controlled. Lluava wished she had his composure.

Like specters rising from the surrounding grasses, the Raiders, with weapons ready, charged. At Skipe's shouted command, the aerial fleet took wing. The rest of the troop moved into formation, weapons drawn, and prepared for the attack. Then chaos erupted.

The clanking and clattering of metal on metal shattered the silence.

Shouts rang out everywhere. Lluava's friends, her comrades, were fighting for their lives, defending themselves from the Raiders' offensive maneuvers. The tumult made it difficult to hear Kentril's commands to push forward. In the air, talons bared and beaks ready, the winged fleet attacked from above.

The group heading for Durog outnumbered the Raiders eight to one, but the females had not been trained for combat, and the Raiders had brute strength on their side. Lluava feared that the point of this attack might not be to kill but to distract the regiment until reinforcements arrived.

Lluava positioned herself near Chat. The boy was sweating profusely. Fortunately, there were only a couple of Raiders fighting in front of them; most had attacked the army's flanks. While Varren charged from Raider to Raider, Lluava and several others kept the young women moving forward. The troop forged ahead slowly; it did not help that their enemy was putting up a formidable fight.

The Raiders' surprisingly fast, cross-shaped bows shot down several birds. Lluava's heart sank at the sight of falling feathers. People were dying; they would never return home. Colonel Skipe soon ordered his aerial fleet to transform and, using what weapon's they could scavenge from the dead, finish their fight on the ground.

Although their opponents were exceptionally strong, one at a time they began to fall. Lluava's regiment had begun to move forward again when a shape in the grass charged her. A haggard monster slung the huge, double-bladed battle-ax that Lluava had glimpsed earlier. Instinctively, she blocked the blade with the golden Claws. The force of the man's swing sent a shock wave through her body, and she was flung backward.

People shouted and screamed around her. Lluava heard nothing, saw nothing but the beast of a man before her. The great brute pushed his body close to hers. She smelled the stagnant breath that whistled through smokeweed-stained teeth. Bits of moldy bread were tangled in his amber beard. Spraying tainted saliva on her, the man stepped backward just far enough to slam the handle of his ax into her chest. She tumbled to the ground.

Coughing from the cloud of dust that rose around her, Lluava struggled to stand upright. She had only a moment's warning; a glint of polished metal swung at her, and she dove to her left into the tall reeds, hoping the thick grass would shield her. The man used his razor-sharp weapon like a scythe, chopping a swath through the grass. Spotting her, he took aim and threw his ax. Once again Lluava caught the blade with the Claws but was knocked down by the force of his strike.

All she could do was stare at the man looming over her. His face was devoid of emotion as he raised his weapon to deliver the death blow. Suddenly, red liquid oozed from his lips, dripping onto his amber beard. He looked down, an amazed expression on his face, at the bloody tip of a sword protruding through his chest. The ax fell to the ground as the dead Raider slid off the iron blade.

Varren, his clothes peppered with red, stood behind the slain man's body. Grabbing Lluava's arm, he pulled her to her feet and rushed her back to the now fast-moving troops. In formation, the group headed toward Durog at speed. The attack had made it clear that there was no time to waste.

Despite its hectic pace, the march back to Durog gave Lluava a chance to reflect. For the first time in a long while, she doubted the choices she had made. War meant death and blood and carnage. Was she capable of inflicting such pain? Would she be able to take a life when she needed to? Could she live with herself if she did? Could she survive if she didn't? Could she have killed the Raider who had attacked her? As these questions and more hurtled through her mind, the realization of what she was expected to do, of what she *must* do, appalled and sickened her.

As they drew closer to the camp, the sounds of war reached their ears once again. The clatter of metal, the shouts and cries of men, and the screams of dying war horses would become their bedtime lullaby; right now, it was simply a new and terrifying cacophony.

Once inside Durog's gates, the recruits of Thowcelemine wasted no time in setting up nursing wards. The injured and the dead arrived in a steady stream, and the women put their training into practice. Lluava felt helpless; she could only watch as injured men, men she knew, were brought into the new wards. Some had lost limbs; others were lost in the recesses of their minds. Blood stained the ground red.

Admiral Merrow met them almost immediately. "How did it go?" he inquired.

"We were attacked a mile down the road," General Kentril replied. "There were not many, but they inflicted heavy damage. We lost fifteen, I think. Twice as many are injured."

"I see. General Argon wants you to meet with him."

In an odd tone, Kentril asked, "Where is the general?"

"Where any commander ought to be—on the front lines with his troops." Merrow's thin smile displayed his pointy teeth.

"Well, then, that is where I must go." Kentril glanced around. "Lluava will escort me to the general's tent."

"Um...I don't know where the general's tent is," Lluava protested.

"I assure you, soldier, that you will find his tent easily," responded Merrow.

"Wait. What about the rest of us?" chimed in Byron, who had been waiting nearby. "We should be doing something."

Merrow looked at the young soldier. "When your troop has time to regroup, then I will give you your orders. You can fill Lluava in later."

"Sir, yes sir!" the new soldiers replied. Varren caught Lluava's eye and nodded to her as she left.

On the front line, the noise of war rang out. The ground was blackened and bare where fire had scorched it. The vast fields of grass that had stretched over the miles of ground that separated Durog from the now demolished Calitron no longer existed. The closer Lluava and Kentril neared the battleground, the thicker the air became with dust and smoke. Grit filled their noses and mouths.

Lluava observed the different lines of defense. The back line had erected a rudimentary fence from splintered wood and field thorns. The line in the middle was busily digging trenches, while those in front stood ready for an attack. Then came row after row of offensive troops. One large tent stood alone at the back of the army lines. Lluava and Kentril made a beeline toward it.

The tent seemed to shudder in the increasing wind. Thick cords strained to keep it taut and bound to the ground. Two lieutenants, their uniforms almost camouflaging them against the mossy green cloth of the tent, stood sentry. They were as rigid as posts, unmoving, uncaring— living weapons of destruction waiting for a sign to spring into action.

Pulling aside the tent flap, Lluava saw the grand master chief bent over a map unrolled on a small table. From his commanding presence and assertive, even defiant expression, it was clear that Argon was in his element. He was conversing with several of the officers and pointing to different parts of the map. Without an upward glance, the general waved them inside.

"They will try to attack us from different positions," he told the officers. "We must secure the entire perimeter around Durog. It is crucial that they not enter the camp, just as it is crucial that they not force us back into it. I need you to lead Troops Five, Eleven, and Nineteen to the other side of Durog to start building defenses as soon as possible. The remaining troops will force the Raiders back toward the ocean and their ships. We must not allow them to gain any more ground than they already have. Go."

After the officers had hurried out, Argon turned to the two figures still standing at the tent's opening. "I gather the evacuation of Thowcelemine was successful?"

General Kentril replied, "Thanks to the early warning of that young soldier of yours, Talos."

"That, at least, is good news. Are your women preparing themselves in Durog?" Without waiting for an answer, the grand master chief continued, "Well, Kentril, you must be put to some use while you wait for your troops. You and Lluava are to go to the front lines. Make yourselves useful."

Kentril tensed subtly at the demeaning command but nodded wordlessly and stepped outside the tent. Lluava at his heels, the general led the way through the harried troops. All around them, young men were running. Lluava could almost taste the emotions that hung heavily in the air.

The thrill of the fight, the fear of death, the dedication to country, the overbearing sense of duty all blended together. Lluava tried to filter the emotions out of her thoughts, but the constantly mutating presence of so many conflicting feelings was overwhelming.

Nearing the front lines, Lluava could no longer contain her doubts and fears. "General Kentril, I can't do this," she said, gesturing toward what lay before them.

Without a look at her or a pause in his step, Kentril replied, "Don't be foolish, soldier. You have prepared for this day long enough."

"No. I mean—I can't make myself kill anyone. I'm not ready or able or...." Lluava's voice was almost inaudible over the clamor surrounding them. "I just can't do it."

A dust cloud created from the ash of the now barren earth swirled before them. Kentril stood his ground as he tried to peer through the grainy murk. "Have your weapons ready," he commanded.

Lluava clenched her fists. Her body automatically tensed, and she had to concentrate on making herself breathe. Kentril shifted form to the silverback gorilla. He stood up, roared, and beat his chest, threatening all who dared oppose him. Then the dust cloud engulfed them.

Ash and sand stung Lluava's eyes as she desperately tried to make sense of what was happening. She strained her ears to pick up any sound that would signal an attack. Through the dark blur, she glimpsed vague images: the clawed paw of a Theriomorph swiping at an unseen villain; the tip of a horn from a Raider's helmet; the glint of a weapon.

Somewhere to her right, the bestial war cry of Kentril rang out. He must be fighting one of the invaders. Lluava hated that she could not force herself to help. She wanted to curl up and hide. She could not bear the thought of her friends being injured and killed by the Raiders, but there was nothing she could do. Lluava was rooted in place in the center of the cloud of soot and dust. She was waiting, but for what? Screams of pain surrounded her. She wanted to stop up her ears but knew that would be a fatal mistake.

Suddenly she felt the air bend as a spear whistled past her right shoulder. Instantly she crouched, waiting for someone to charge her. A presence appeared from behind, and she saw a gorilla lift a massive stone above her. Kentril flung the stone over Lluava's head; it crashed into the chest of a Raider, knocking him back into the thick blanket of swirling dust, where he disappeared from sight.

Kentril picked up a sister stone to the one he had just tossed and grunted at Lluava. "You are making it all too easy!"

Another assailant charged from the gloom, battle-ax in hand. Kentril turned his attention to this new opponent and left Lluava alone once again. She had to do something other than crouch in the dirt. Then she heard the cry.

"Chat!" The name slipped past her lips, and, without a moment's pause, she ran in the direction of her young friend's voice, forcing her way through the grappling bodies. Anyone who stood in her way was quickly pushed aside. Seeking Chat's silhouette in the dust-choked air, she peered out in all directions. The wind shifted slightly. For a brief moment, she spotted the boy. They looked fearfully at each other. Then dust enveloped him once more.

"Lluava! Lluava!" His voice pierced the darkness.

"Chat!" Lluava called back. "Chat, stay where you are!"

She ran blindly toward the area where she had sighted the boy.

"Lluava! Help me! Help me!"

She spotted the youngster. He had fallen backward and dropped his dagger, and was crawling toward it. A short, stout Raider swung a broadsword menacingly as he advanced on Chat. To distract the man, Lluava shouted, "Hey! Leave him alone! I said, leave him alone!"

The Raider did not turn but lifted his sword and began to swing. Using the Claws, Lluava swiftly sliced at the shield strapped to the Raider's back. The shield hit the ground with a heavy thump. Chat's attacker felt the jerk as the leather straps holding the shield were cut, and he turned toward her.

The brute had ruddy whiskers. His face was pockmarked, and his nose looked as if it had been broken at least twice. His drooping eyes looked over Lluava's figure while, in a coarse accent he muttered, "Pretty, pretty, pretty."

Behind him, Chat grabbed his knife and charged the Raider. The dagger struck the hide but did not puncture the thick layers of garb encasing the man. The attacker twisted his form quickly and snatched up Chat by the arm. He made a tsking noise.

"Bye-bye, boy," he said with relish.

Lluava hooked the Raider's blade with the golden claws on her left hand. The seafarer's eyes sparkled.

"Pretty girl plays, huh?" said the Raider. He twisted Chat's arm hard enough to make him cry out. The boy struggled, but the man paid no attention. He just stared at Lluava.

The Raider was toying with her. Lluava knew she needed to free Chat so both of them could flee far from their assailant. To buy time as she struggled to come up with a plan, she stepped in front of Chat to block an oncoming blade. This made the man smile. His grimy teeth were twisted in a nest of enamel. His breath was foul enough to wake the dead.

"Is girl's insides pretty, too, pretty girl?" The Raider pulled back his sword and thrust again, this time at Lluava.

Instinct took over. Shifting form, the full weight of the tigress sprang onto the squat man. Unable to release Issaura's Claws from her grip, they shifted with her, coating her claws in a metallic sheen. Impossible as it was, her gilded claws easily deflected his blade. In a motion that flowed like liquid, the Raider's throat was slit. His lifeblood spurted out over the felid's fur.

There was no time to ponder the phenomenon that just had occurred. The wind had died down and the air was clearing. Multiple apparitions seemed to rise from the atmosphere. A seafarer ran through the slowly settling ash and then another. The enraged tigress made easy victims of both. Chat stared wide-eyed at her as if she were a creature ordained by the gods. The tigress, standing in pooling blood, turned to the boy. He saw humanity flicker in her slitted eyes, and the creature transformed back to the woman he knew, bloodied weapons in hand.

Lluava beheld the carnage. The milky eyes of sightless corpses stared at her as the memory of what had just occurred came flooding back. Unable to prevent it, she bent over and vomited. Her legs were shaky, and she felt as though she might pass out. She remembered what had happened, but not why it had. Lluava could not ponder that thought for long. Chat steadied her and then told her to follow him.

As the two carefully made their way toward Durog, Chat explained, "Our troop was commanded to hold off and fight in the morning shift. Since you had already left, several of us went in search of you." After a pause, he said, "Thank you for rescuing me out there. I wish I was as strong as you. You were amazing, and I failed. How am I supposed to fight when I can't even protect myself?"

There was no response.

"How did you make your weapon's shift with you?"

Chat looked at her. "Lluava?" he inquired, "Lluava, are you feeling all right?"

When she still did not respond, Chat fell silent. They passed Yamir and Malnus, who had also reached the safety of Durog's walls. Soon they met Talos and Byron, who began to ask questions.

"So, Lluava, what happened?"

Chat spoke up. "She was amazing! Out there in dust so thick you couldn't see your nose, she came out of nowhere and saved me from one of the Raiders. She came right up to the man and started swinging, like this." Chat made wide motions with his arms. "She transformed and so did her weapons and killed that man and two others!"

"Wait—what?"

"All at once?"

"That's amazing!"

"Very impressive."

"Issaura's Claws did what?"

The men gathered around Lluava, waiting for her answers. Hearing Chat describe what had happened forced her to live through it all over again. Her friends crowded closely around her; she felt smothered. It was too much. She had to break free.

Not caring where she was headed, Lluava ran. She ran past the barracks and the camp buildings. She ran until she was deep in the woods of Durog. She ran until she reached the edge of the lake where, sobbing, she finally collapsed. Tainted by the blood now drying on her face, her tears fell red after mixing with those crimson stains. Alone with the relative silence of the forest around her, she cried until her eyes burned.

Afterward, Lluava sat facing the lake. The day passed leaving her to ponder in solitude. At some point, she fell asleep though little rest was gained by this. Upon waking, she pulled her knees close to her chest and watched as the moon rose up from the water. Its reflection danced upon the surface of the lake, unhindered by the bloodshed still occurring within earshot of the clearing.

There was a rustle behind her, and soon the reflection of Varren appeared in the water.

"You're shaking." He spoke kindly.

Lluava had not noticed until that moment that her whole body was indeed shaking, even though the night air was mild. She could not force herself to stop.

Quietly, Varren knelt next to her. Carefully he took one of her hands and slid the golden Claw from it. He dipped the triple blades in the lake, rinsed off the gore, and laid the shining weapon at her feet. Then he did the same with her other hand. He took out his handkerchief and dipped it in the water. Gently he moved Lluava's hair off her shoulder and proceeded to wipe the dried blood from her face.

Lluava did not resist. She did not move. Her unfocused eyes gazed into the distance. When Varren finished, he sat next to her in silence. The faint clanging of metal on metal receded until it seemed to disappear into the darkness.

Lluava broke the silence. "Does it get any easier?"

"Hm?" Varren turned toward her, but she still stared into the void.

"I mean, do you ever become used to the knowledge that you have taken someone's life? Do you ever become accustomed to the killing?"

There was a long pause, and then Varren replied, "Some say they do."

Another pause.

"How about you? Are you used to it?"

"Lluava, I was raised from childhood to fight. I have known for a long time what to expect if war came to our shores." Varren looked at the stars glinting above them. "But to answer your question, no. I have not become accustomed to taking another's life. I am not really sure that one could ever be untouched by that fact. I fight so that another does not have to. I bear the burden so nobody else should. In order to protect my people, I must kill others. It is not a pleasant reality, but it is the only reality I know."

The two sat silently side by side. At last, Varren stood up and said, "You need rest. Our troop returns to the field at midmorning. You need to lie down for a while. Let us make our way back to camp."

At last, the young woman stirred. Varren lent his hand to help her up and then he picked up her weapons and handed them to her before walking her back to her new barracks. Exhausted both physically and mentally, Lluava quickly fell asleep.

***

When midmorning arrived, Lluava washed up and grabbed a quick bite to eat at the mess hall. She had not eaten in over forty-eight hours.

Rosalyn sat down at the table beside her.

"I am truly glad that you are safe," Rosalyn said as she regarded her best friend. "When we heard that General Argon had sent you to the front lines, we began to worry."

"Yeah," Lluava said. "Who went to look for me? What happened yesterday?"

Wiping her mouth with a napkin, Rosalyn answered, "Well, Chat went along, with that young man, Yamir." Lluava nodded and Rosalyn continued. "Both Yamir and his human partner left with Prince Varren. The prince looked really worried."

Trying to catch Lluava's eye before finishing, Rosalyn paused. "I think that may be the reason he took so long to return. As soon as he came back, he asked me if I had seen you. I told him you had run into the woods to be by yourself. I told everyone, including the prince, to give you time and to leave you alone. The prince was most reluctant to obey. I had to take care of a medical emergency, so I left him after that."

She smiled, and Lluava did the same.

"Thank you," said Lluava.

"You do not need to thank me," Rosalyn replied. "Everyone copes differently."

"Where is Talos?"

Rosalyn sighed. "He is being disciplined for disobeying orders."

"What?" exclaimed Lluava. This time the grand master chief had gone too far. "If it weren't for him, we could not have rescued you so quickly."

"That was acknowledged. He has been banned from fighting on the forefront until further notice. Until that time, he will help me tend the injured."

"Well, I don't think he will complain too much about that," Lluava teased.

"He did not," giggled Rosalyn. "Oh, I do have something to give you before I forget." Reaching into her new nurse's apron, Rosalyn pulled out an envelope.

"It arrived the morning before..." Her voice drifted off at the memory she did not wish to vocalize.

Lluava did not need to ask from whom it came; she immediately recognized her mother's untidy handwriting. She took the letter, and, after quickly thanking Rosalyn for keeping it safe, left the mess hall to find a quiet place to read it.

Hiding in the gym, Lluava broke the wax seal that bore her father's crest.

My Little Girl,

How are you? How is your training going? I haven't heard much from you since you transferred to Durog. I do hope you are well.

How is my writing? I am really working hard on it. It may never be as nice as yours, but I am trying.

Mary constantly asks about you. She tells everyone about her sister who has gone off to fight. Tom, the way he is at it, will be walking before we next see you again. On that note, are you able to come and visit us any time soon?

Lluava, the reason I am writing you is that your grandfather has died. He passed away peacefully in his sleep. I do not want you to be upset by this, but it would not have been right to keep this from you. Your grandfather loved you so, although he was becoming more and more confused. It was strange. Near the end, he kept referring to you as Issaura. Maybe you can make sense of this and explain it to me one day? He always claimed that you would be the one to save Elysia. Oh, how he loved you.

Please take care of yourself, my dear one.

Your Loving Mother

Outside the window, the sun was rising. Lluava forced back her tears. She had shed too many lately, and she knew her grandfather would not have wanted her to cry for him. He would want her to remember him as he was—the old owl keeping watch over her. It was time to face her fears and the Raiders once again. But this time would be different, for she had found her reason to fight. Her family.

As she joined her troop and headed to the front lines, Lluava slipped Issaura's Claws, and their mysterious capabilities, over her hands. She might not be a goddess, but she would show the Raiders a force that they had never expected.

Chapter 25
A Tactical Strike

The morning air was already thick with humidity. Though this weather usually made Lluava perspire more, it was a pleasant change from the dry heat of midsummer. Rain would usher in the autumn season. She hoped that the people of Elysia, like the changing weather, could wash away those who threatened them.

Her troop, along with several others, was gathering at the gates. Just beyond the walls, fellow soldiers were laying down their lives to fight off the invaders. Lluava lined up next to Varren, who was sheathing his sword.

Glancing at her, he commented, "You seem to be feeling better this morning."

"I am, thank you," she replied. "May I ask—"

"Attention! Attention, troops!" Colonel Skipe's barking call filled the yard. "Head to the battlefield immediately! The lead partners from each troop will report to the general's tent for your troop's orders. Go, now! There is no time to waste!"

"Let us go," Varren said. He walked rapidly through the gates toward the general's tent. More tents had been erected since she was last outside. The ladies of Thowcelemine were busily treating the injured as they were brought up from battle. The less critical cases were laid on blankets in rows outside the medical tents.

Lluava followed Varren across the barren field and into the general's tent. Just as they had the day before, two sentinels stood at attention, guarding the opening. Admiral Merrow motioned the partners inside.

"Welcome, welcome, all of you," said the admiral in his slippery voice. "I'm glad that you are here and ready to face the day. Unfortunately, the general is already on the front lines and will not be giving you your orders.

207

Troop Seven will fight on the left wing…here." Merrow tapped a spot on the map with his finger. Varren and Lluava studied the location for a few moments and then left the tent to return to their waiting troop. This was not a time to inquire about Issaura's Claws. Would it happen again? Could it? Weapons that shifted along with their Theriomorph owner were impossible. Right?

Although the wind had picked up, the humidity kept the dust low to the ground, improving visibility. Scanning the skirmishes, Lluava found it quite easy to pick out the Raiders. They wore their heavy garb of layered furs; several used visible metal breastplates, and most wore horned helmets. By her best guess, they were from some northern kingdom. Lluava wondered why they hadn't stripped down in order to be lighter and cooler in the southern heat. But even if they altered their clothes, they would still be easy to identify with their grisly beards and over muscled, stocky bodies. It seemed they cared nothing for good hygiene. To Lluava's heightened sense of smell, the Raiders gave off a foul odor dankly reminiscent of spoiled fish innards and burnt water reeds.

Suddenly a Raider stood before Lluava with his double-bladed ax in hand. How had such a large man snuck up on her? And within striking range? As he charged toward her, Lluava willed herself to go wild. From this point forward, it no longer mattered which form she took.

Releasing her feral animal nature, she became an unstoppable force. Raiders fell before the enraged tigress with golden claws like stalks of wheat before a scythe. In this attack state, Lluava's conscience was blurred and muted; she could recognize her comrades and understand when people called to her, but her feelings and emotions were dissipated, almost nonexistent. If a blade or an arrow broke her flesh, it would register, somehow, that she should move away, but she felt little pain through the adrenaline.

At night, Lluava struggled to cope with the knowledge of the lives she had taken. Guilt and sorrow would overwhelm her until she wanted to scream. She soon realized that she could not dwell on the death and destruction of the battlefield. She, Varren, and the others were doing what they must do to survive and to protect their kingdom. The only thing she was certain of was that Issaura's Claws were special, and somehow they gave her the strength to continue.

On the third day of the battle of Durog, Lluava, in her human form, was defending herself against a particularly fierce Raider when an opposing archer caught her eye. The seafarer was crouched behind one of the briar fences. He aimed his weapon, and Lluava saw that he had a clear shot at Thad, who was completely unaware of the danger. Lluava started to shout a warning, but she had to dodge an unusually complicated set of offensive maneuvers. At the next glance, she saw the arrow flying toward its mark.

"No!" roared Lluava, as she dropped and rolled behind her Raider. With a quick flick of the golden claws, Lluava slit the tendons of the unprotected backs of his legs. As the marauder toppled forward, she glimpsed the quick flash of feathers that stopped the arrow short of its intended mark. An eagle plummeted to the ground in a tumble of dust.

Without pausing, Lluava pierced the heart of the Raider with the Claws and then leapt toward the broken body of Horus. When she reached down to pick up the bird, Horus stirred, dropped the arrow gripped in his talons, and flew to Thad's gauntleted arm. With only a moment to make a respectful nod toward the partners, Lluava turned to counter another Raider's attack.

General Argon's earlier efforts at building partnerships appeared to be succeeding. All the pairs were working together, not just efficiently but with great trust, placing their lives in one another's hands. Each was well suited to the other. Varren and Lluava could easily fight side by side in human form; just as effortlessly, Lluava could protect Varren when he rode out on his stallion, the tigress by his side.

Even Yamir and Malnus managed to work well together. Regardless of the bickering that occurred off the battlefield, they had each other's backs. Yamir, like Lluava, watched over Chat in combat. If the boy was not with her, Lluava knew that Yamir and Malnus would not be far away from the youngster.

On the evening of the fifth day of battle, Lluava and Varren were summoned to the general's tent once again. The wind blew more strongly than it had in a long time and whistled as it gusted past the tent. Inside, candles illuminated the interior, for building storm clouds blocked out most of the sun's waning light. The small space was crowded. Those of highest rank were present, Ojewa and Kentril on one side of the table, Merrow and Skipe on the other. The grand master chief positioned himself at the far end of the table. Four other pairs of soldiers who headed up different troops were also present, along with Berkley, who seemed to have aged even more.

General Argon struck the tabletop with the palm of his hand. "It has been five days since we made our stand against the Raiders. Five days have come and gone, and what have we to show for it?"

"We have taken out their southern convoy, which would have attacked Thowcelemine," reported Major Ojewa. "In addition, the warship that made landfall has retreated and is now moored offshore with the rest of their fleet. We control the entire area south of Durog."

Colonel Skipe continued, "The aerial troops have scouted several miles up the coast and saw no other attack sites. This may be the only point of attack by the Raiders."

"Our oceanic troops have uncovered some interesting information, as well," Merrow informed them. "The Raiders keep at least half their troops on board their ships at all times. This not only allows them to protect the vessels, but also and more importantly, it provides them with fresh troops to replace their exhausted land-based ones. In addition, they have several sentries on Hulme island."

Berkley spoke up. "They are unusually adept at identifying Theriomorphs, and so we have been unable to approach them. We have reason to believe that before they send fresh troops into battle, their men smoke something similar to our smokeweed. This is the cause of the foul odor that many of you have noticed."

The grand master chief studied Merrow and inquired, "Can we not gain access to their vessels?"

"No," said the admiral with a sigh. "Those who tried were harpooned in the water. It is unsafe and imprudent to continue leading troops to slaughter."

"Unfortunate," muttered the general. "Good job on procuring this information." The grand master chief gave a nod of approval to the other commanders.

"Major Ojewa, you also should be praised for your work. As for your comment, Berkley, you must take into consideration that the human sense of smell is far less acute than ours." Argon glanced at the others before continuing. "The reason we have convened here this evening is this: What we are doing is not working. Although we have not lost ground in the north, we have not gained any, either. This is unacceptable. We need a plan to force the Raiders out to sea and back from whence they came."

Hoping to clear Talos's name, Lluava verbalized a suggestion he had previously put forward. "What if we could attack the Raiders using a flanking maneuver, attacking from their rear?" She reached forward and traced a path on the map with her finger. "If they are defending both sides, they will wear down twice as fast. They would be forced to release their hold on the area they now possess. Furthermore, if we attack from the rear, we can prevent them from moving their forces up the coast."

The grand master chief deliberated for a moment before he answered. "The suggestion you make seems sound," he said.

"It was Talos's idea," confessed Lluava.

With a nod, the general acknowledged this. "It's time for the private to face the battlefield. Tell Talos that he has orders to fight. Tonight I will lead four of our strongest troops to attack the far side of the Raider encampment." Looking up at his favorite rival, the general continued, "Kentril, you will follow with another troop. When we reach the opposite side, break away and head north to Fort Brinsdale. When you arrive, tell them to send messengers to the other camps and the capital informing them that the war has reached our southern borders. Order them to send reinforcements as swiftly as they can."

"Why Fort Brinsdale?" questioned Kentril rather disrespectfully. "Why not head directly to Cronus, the capital?"

Grand Master Chief Argon looked rather disappointed in the other general. "Fort Brinsdale is centrally located between all three training camps. It is also relatively close to the capital," he said in a tone one would use to explain to an untrained recruit. "Brinsdale is the ideal location to send word to the other camps as well as to Cronus.

"I request Troop Seven to come with me," Kentril abruptly demanded. He slipped a glance in Lluava's direction.

The grand master chief grunted and then retorted, "No. I need that troop with me; they are a mighty force, and we will need them on the attack. Take Troop Eleven. It has some of the fastest trainees in Durog. You will need swift feet, for even at full march it will take the better part of half a moon to reach Fort Brinsdale."

Kentril made no reply.

"May I have a word about my weapons, Grand Master Chief?" questioned Lluava. She hoped to finally having a chance to talk to the general.

"Have they malfunctioned?"

"No," noted Lluava. "They…, they do strange things."

General Argon gave Berkley a sideways glance. Berkley responded in his raspy voice, "They were made by a Theriomorph for a Theriomorph. They were specifically chosen for you. Use them well. "

With no other further explanation given, Lluava remained quiet. When everyone else was certain of their orders, Argon dismissed those in the tent. They would move out within the hour.

As Lluava and her partner headed toward the rest of her troop, she heard Kentril call after her. "Lluava, I would like a word with you alone, please."

Varren looked questioningly at Lluava, but she told him, "It's okay. Go ahead. I'll be there soon."

The former leader of Thowcelemine waited until Varren was gone from sight. "I know you have heard things—suspicions—that were speculated upon before this siege began. Am I not right?"

Lluava hesitated and then admitted that she had.

Not sure for what he was looking, Kentril glanced nervously over his shoulder. When no one appeared, he continued almost inaudibly. "Although I am not completely certain, I am *almost* certain that I know who our mole is."

"Who?" Lluava inquired eagerly. This subject had eaten at her for a long time.

"At this moment, that knowledge would place your life in danger." Kentril peered into the dark once again. "What I will tell you is that there are men in power who cannot be trusted. They have become corrupt."

Kentril's cryptic statement left her impatient for answers, but she knew the general was risking his own life in suggesting that such treason existed.

"Why are you telling me this?" she demanded.

Kentril looked sternly at her and then relaxed, his tone kind. "You are the best recruit I have had in all my years at Thowcelemine. You are smart and strong, even fierce. I trust you—more than many of the men we work closely with now. Take care of yourself while I am gone. Watch your back. Not everyone who wants to see you dead crossed the ocean."

Kentril strode quickly away, leaving Lluava to ponder alone in the darkness. This information was unsettling, but she had no time to let it consume her thoughts. She had to find Varren and prepare for the night attack.

Exactly one hour later, the troops moved out with General Argon in the lead. The grand master chief led them in a wide arc to avoid attracting attention. The moon was making its descent through the cloud-filled sky when they finally reached the forested outskirts on the north side of the camps. The storm broke. Thick sheets of rain swept over both armies and washed away the bloodstains on the ground. A signal was given, and the troops began to crawl toward the opposition's camp. They began their slow progress up a ridge and then waited for the order to attack—an order that never came.

Those fighting below on the barren plain heard the ungodly war cry emanating from the woods. The fierce sound put a smile on the faces of the Raiders engaged in combat.

In the forest, General Argon and his troops turned to face a swarm of oncoming Raiders that had been hiding in the woods. It was a trap, and they had fallen victim to it. The grand master chief grabbed Kentril and growled a command: "Go...now! We will distract them."

With a look of remorse, Kentril retreated with Troop Eleven. Lluava did not watch them leave; she was already fending off several marauders who slashed at her with their heavy blades. Next to her, Malnus yelled out, "I can't believe how easily we were ambushed! It was like they were waiting for us the whole time."

He was right, Lluava thought; it was all too convenient. How could the Raiders have known where and when they would arrive? A dangerous idea entered her mind, but just as quickly, she rejected it. There was no possibility that the betrayer, the mole, was General Argon. No, it had to be another. But who?

"Retreat!" The call of their leader was heard and passed from soldier to soldier. "Retreat! There are too many of them! Fall back!"

In the darkness, countless numbers of Raiders swarmed from the forest like ants from a disturbed mound. Leaving no gaps, the brutes attacked from all sides. With a sinking feeling, Lluava realized that they were trapped. But wait—General Argon was muscling his way through the enemy's blockade.

Even in his human form, he presented a fearsome opposition to any in his path. Around the general, a gap was made by other, unfortunate forerunners. Suddenly, the soldiers of Durog broke free and made a mad dash to safety. The grand master chief held the enemies at bay until every last soldier had escaped the fray.

Lluava sprinted through the breach with Chat by her side. Yamir and Malnus were ahead of her. She feared for Varren and the others whom she could not see, but her first priority was to insure Chat's safety.

Then it happened. A dark form emerged over the ridge and jumped down at Yamir. In the dim starlight, Lluava could see the thin, spiked mace raised high above the Raider's head. Malnus saw it, too, for he leaped forward, shoving his partner away from danger.

A swishing sound and a heavy thud preceded a howl that ended in a shriek. Lluava ripped into the enemy, leaving a corpse upon which the ravens would feed. Yamir frantically rushed to help his fallen partner. Lluava moved nearer as the expression on Chat's pallid face indicated that something terrible had happened.

Malnus bent over his arm, screaming. Yamir tried to move him forward, but Malnus stumbled, and Lluava saw the horrific wound he had taken in that heroic moment. Just below the elbow, his arm had been torn nearly in half; two thin strips of flesh connected the upper part of the limb to the lower. Blood gushed out at an appalling rate, the red liquid spewing over his uniform as well as Yamir's.

"We have to stop the bleeding," Lluava said aloud as her training from those first days at Thowcelemine emerged. Tearing a strip of cloth from her shirt, she spoke more loudly and with assurance to Yamir. "We have to stop the blood!" Moving to the shaking Malnus, she ordered, "Yamir, hold his arm still."

Without questioning, Yamir immobilized Malnus's arm while Lluava tied the cloth around the joint. She tied it as tightly as she could to try to stop the flow, but blood continued to drip onto the damp ground.

"We need to return him to the camp now," Yamir said as he helped his partner up. "Chat, warn them that we have injured coming. Go!"

Lluava supported the other side of Malnus, and the three made their way to the medical tent as quickly as possible. Rosalyn was waiting when they arrived and waved them over. "Hurry," she said, holding the flap up. "He is losing too much blood."

Four cots had been set aside for those who needed critical care. Rosalyn helped Malnus onto the one remaining open cot. With agile fingers, Rosalyn retied another piece of cloth around the mutilated arm, slowing the blood to a trickle. "I sent Chat for water. The way he described the wound, I knew this would not be good. Truthfully, I did not want him to see what is about to happen." Grabbing a wooden stake from the cot's side table, Rosalyn said,

"Here, I am going to place this in your mouth." She slipped it in the already grinding teeth of her patient. "Bite down on it when it hurts."

Rosalyn tucked a stray hair into her bun and then inspected the gruesome break. The bone was shattered; splinters of it were embedded in the muscle. Shaking her head, she muttered to herself, "It needs to be a smooth break."

The others followed Rosalyn's instructions. "Yamir, I need you to help hold Malnus down if he moves. The same goes for you, Lluava."

"What are you going to do?" Yamir asked worriedly.

"What needs to be done."

The flap of the tent was pulled back, and Talos stepped into the candlelight. With a quick look around, he asked, "What do you need me to do?"

The three held Malnus while Rosalyn picked up a butcher's cleaver, holding it over the small fire in the tent floor until the metal glowed orange. Positioning herself in front of the broken arm, she said, "Hold him tightly."

Malnus started to squirm, and muffled noises slipped past the wooden bit in his mouth.

"Still!" Rosalyn ordered. "I need him still!"

With great effort, Talos and Yamir regained control of Malnus's writhing form. Rosalyn quickly grabbed the wrapped end of his arm with one hand and pressed it against the edge of the side table. With the other, she lifted the burning blade and let it fall precisely as intended. The severed part of the arm slipped off the table and fell to the floor with a thud. Malnus moaned and passed out. With the wound already cauterized, Rosalyn quickly wrapped the nub in a clean swatch of cloth. Lluava watched in sickened awe as her friend worked.

Rosalyn was tying the knot when Yamir spoke. "He isn't breathing right."

"What?" inquired Rosalyn, turning to listen to the sporadic inhales and exhales of her patient. "There are too many people in the tent. I must ask you men to leave. Lluava, help lift up his shirt."

Lluava and Rosalyn gently removed Malnus's stained shirt, revealing his badly bruised and swollen chest. Patches of flesh had been scraped off where the mace had struck his chest. Rosalyn swiftly cleaned the wounds and gingerly felt the bruised areas.

"Many of his ribs are broken," said Rosalyn as she inspected Malnus's body. "I think one may have punctured his left lung." She ran her fingers over his chest once more. "Yes, his lung is deflated."

"What do we do?" asked Lluava.

"In the far corner, there is a stack of water reeds. Grab one, please."

Lluava moved around the other nurses carefully so as not to disturb them or their patients. As she reached for one of the reeds that stood in a basket, the patient in the nearest cot clutched her arm.

The young man was a human whom Lluava did not know. His face and skin were blanched. His other hand, holding his unbound organs inside, protected the gaping hole in his torso. In a hoarse voice, he cried, "Help me! Please!"

Another nurse ran to him, pushing him back down on the cot. Jerking her arm from the man's grasp, Lluava half stumbled back to the other side of the tent. She felt weak and wanted to be rid of the smell of blood and guts that wafted through the tent. The stench was provocative; she could feel the beast stirring within her.

"Lluava." Rosalyn's voice was grave and commanding. "Stay with me. I need you to stay focused."

For the first time, Lluava recognized her friend's great strength. She nodded and handed over the reed. Using a small blade, Roslyn cut the reed into a mouse-sized piece with a few swift, precise movements.

"Hold his shoulders down," she said. Lluava obeyed.

Rosalyn found the spot she sought between two of the ribs and jabbed the reed into Malnus's chest. He jerked once, moaned, and then was silent.

"Listen," she said. "He is breathing better."

It was true. Malnus was indeed taking in full breaths. As the pair looked over their patient, he shifted and coughed. A bit of blood rolled down the corner of his mouth. Rosalyn wiped it with the corner of her nurse's apron.

"Will he be all right?" Lluava finally dared to ask.

Rosalyn propped Malnus's head up with a pillow as he hacked up more blood.

"I do not know. All we can do is wait and watch and pray for the best. Thank you for helping me. You can go now. Please let Yamir know that he may come in if he is ready."

Lluava took the message to Yamir, who waited anxiously just outside the tent. She and the rest of her friends chose to stay nearby in case anything was needed. She was relieved when Varren appeared and grateful when he refused to leave her side. The night seemed unusually long. Impatiently, they waited for word of how their comrade was faring.

When the sun had just begun to creep over the vast expanse of ocean, Rosalyn stepped out, looking disheveled. Her glossy black hair frayed from her bun; dark circles tinged the porcelain skin below her eyes. Remorsefully, she looked at the waiting group and shook her head and then returned to the tent.

Lluava could not sift through the strange combination of feelings that took hold of her. A man who had been so connected to her childhood, one whom she had first learned to loathe and then came to respect, was now dead. After the war, her home would be different. Her life would be different. Never again would she be a Theriomorph schoolgirl, butting heads with the local human boys. Never again would she listen to the stories of her grandfather by the fire. Lluava wondered if she could ever again be content with that simple country life.

Silently, she mourned the loss of her comrade along with the death of the life she had once lived.

Chapter 26
At Cliff's Edge

Without a word to the others, Lluava turned and made her way back to her barracks. The blood of the dead was still on her hands and clothes; it had to be washed off before she was summoned back onto the field.

When Lluava returned to her companions, Yamir solemnly asked his friends, "After our shift today, would you help me bury Malnus? I don't want his body placed in one of the group burials. He deserves his own grave."

"Of course," they replied. Talos placed his hand on Yamir's shoulder and gave him a quick squeeze before lining up with their troop.

While they waited for orders in formation, Lluava whispered to Varren, "What will happen to Yamir now that his partner is gone?"

Quietly Varren replied, "Until the war is over or there is a sizable moratorium in the fighting, he will have to fight as an individual. It is harder that way, but it is all he can do until a reassignment can be arranged."

Lluava felt queasy at the thought of ever having to fight alone. She had become so accustomed to Varren as her partner that he was like an extension of herself.

The day was reasonably cool, due in part to the still overcast sky. The fighting was more treacherous, for the waterlogged ground made for slippery footing. Suffering fewer accidents and fatalities than the other groups, Troop Seven was fortunate.

When evening came, Lluava and her friends began the dismal process of digging the grave. It did not take very long to dig a hole of respectable depth; however, the emotional reaction to what had occurred drained the strength of those who shoveled the slightly damp soil. Nearby, a raven pecked at the insects uprooted by the displaced earth. Lluava wondered if the creature could somehow understand the preparations they were making.

Yamir, Varren, Talos, and Byron served as pallbearers for the crudely created stretcher upon which they laid the body of Malnus. The light that flickered from their candles did nothing to relieve the darkness of the hole they had dug. In resolute silence, Lluava watched the men lower their fallen comrade. She stared as Malnus's body was consumed by the darkness.

After a moment of reflection, Talos asked, "Would anyone like to say something?"

Yamir grabbed a shovel and solemnly answered, "I will." Scooping up a pile of dirt, he addressed his fallen partner. "Though we might not have understood why we were assigned to each other initially, I came to realize why you and I were well suited. At first, it seemed that we came from different worlds, but we began to overcome our differences. You were like a bratty brother, as irritating and vexing as a mosquito on a summer afternoon. Nevertheless, I trusted you. You saved my life and, in doing so, sacrificed your own. I'm eternally grateful to you. May your god now watch over you. Farewell, my friend." He shook the dirt into the mouth of the hole and then passed the shovel to the next person.

When it was Lluava's turn, she remembered how Malnus had mistreated her and thought of the rebukes she had always wanted to say. None of that mattered anymore. Instead, she spoke about his brotherly protectiveness of young Thane, his ability to command others well, and his self-sacrifice. Her speech was suitable if not elegant.

After everyone had had a chance to speak and to sprinkle a bit of earth over the body, the men filled in the grave with the remaining soil. Then they gathered stones and piled them over the mound to protect it from wild animals.

The raven ignored the vulnerable insects exposed by the disturbed earth. Cocking its head first to one side, then the other, it observed the unusual activity, then hopped atop the mound. In a flash, Yamir seized one of the smaller stones and threw it like a lance at the obsidian scavenger.

"Get away from him, you filthy bird!" Yamir's projectile hit the creature directly in the head; the bird tumbled, twitching, to the ground. Seeing the bird convulse, Chat ran up to it and swallowed a cry. The boy picked up the bleeding raven, wrapped it up in his shirt, and held it close. Yamir scowled but merely went on collecting stones to add to the pile.

When the grave was safely protected, the comrades returned to their barracks for a restless night's sleep. As they trudged back, Lluava overheard Yamir apologize to Chat for injuring the raven. The boy still held the injured bird tenderly. After a pause, Chat replied, "I'd be your partner if you ever want one."

The next few days posed a challenge for Durog's defenders. A new swarm of Raiders, fresh and ready for action, slowly began to push General Argon's troops back toward the walls of the fortress. To add to their trouble, heavy rains arose rapidly, stopping as quickly as they had started.

One afternoon, only a few hours after one such storm, Lluava and Varren were battling several particularly ugly seafarers whose troop was stationed near the cliff's edge that so abruptly broke off above the sea. Lluava's attacker attempted an evil smile, but his lack of teeth made him look more like a masticating cow. In a different situation, his visage would have been humorous.

As Lluava used the Claws to dispatch her opposition, she spotted Thad on his chestnut mare galloping after two Raiders who had broken past the last line of defense. Like a professional cattle driver, Thad rounded up the two men near the cliff and began to herd them back into the fray. Waterlogged from the heavy rains, the ground was oversaturated and unusually soft. The weight of horse and rider was too much for the fractured rocks; suddenly the earth gave way. In a flash, Thad, his mare, and the two unfortunate marauders tumbled from sight toward the waiting sea.

Varren saw what had happened and made a mad dash to the cliff. Lluava was close behind him. Transforming, she began to make her way down the side of the rock as Varren led the way. Fortunately, the stone wall was not as sheer as it had seemed, and the slight incline allowed them a decent grip on its surface.

Terrified that she would see the mangled bodies strewn upon the sliver of rock-encrusted beach, Lluava was afraid to glance below her. Leaping to the ground, she spotted the impaled forms of the two Raiders. Several paces away, Thad's mare had collapsed. The poor beast struggled to rise, but its injuries were too severe. The rider was still in the saddle.

"Thad!" shouted the prince as he ran to his oldest and dearest friend.

The body moved, and hope sprang into Lluava's chest as she resumed human form.

"My leg," moaned Thad. "It's trapped under Icius. I can't free myself."

"My god, you are lucky!" exclaimed Varren as he and Lluava lifted the heavy horse so that Thad could slide his leg from under the animal. All around them were jagged boulders. Somehow Thad had fallen between them. With the exception of a few scrapes and bruises and a very tender leg, he seemed fine.

Thad turned his attention to his wounded mount. "Oh, Icius," he sighed. "I have owned you since you were a sprightly filly. You have been a true and loyal companion over the years. Look at you, now...." Thad ran his hand over a break in the horse's right foreleg. Icius whinnied and tried to stand, but after a bit of struggling, the animal lay quietly once more.

Thad drew the head of Icius onto his lap and stroked the chestnut mane. With his free hand, he pulled his small dagger from its sheath and slit the horse's throat. There was a last cry of death and then silence as the mare's eyes glazed over. Thad bowed his head in reverence.

Looking up, he exclaimed in horror, "Oh, God!"

Upon the precipice of rock stood a pair of Raiders, who had forced the unarmed Horus to the edge. They were unaware of those who watched from below. As the two assailants moved toward him, Horus inched backward. In a moment, his feet had reached the crumbling edge. Small clumps of soil and bits of stone tumbled down onto the beach below.

Lluava and the others stood absolutely still. There was nothing they could do for their friend. Lluava knew that even if she tried to spring up the cliff, she could not reach him in time. All she could do was look on in terror as the scene played out.

With the Raiders' thin swords pressed against his uniform, Horus leaned back as far as he could. For a brief second, he seemed to teeter on the ledge; then he plunged backward toward the waiting rocks.

The Raiders peered over the edge to watch their victim die. To their utter dismay, they observed the young man transform before their eyes into a magnificent eagle that swooped up and flew over their heads. The bird took wing back toward the battleground, the angry Raiders in pursuit.

In her fear for Horus, Lluava had momentarily forgotten his dual form. Now, more than ever, she was grateful to be a Theriomorph. Silently cheering, Lluava, Thad, and Varren hurriedly climbed back up the cliff.

When they reached the battlefield, the trio quickly noted that the winds of war had changed. General Argon and his troops were in full retreat. Their squadron was among those making a hasty run for Durog's gates. Varren urged the others to follow suit, and they soon entered the vast gateway.

"What could have happened? We weren't on the beach that long," Lluava panted.

"It must have been something terrible," guessed Thad, "to cause the entire army to withdraw behind these walls. I have to find Horus. I'll meet you later, Varren." The young man limped off into the disorderly midst of the soldiers.

Once his friend had gone, Varren spoke sternly. "Let us find out exactly what occurred. I need to know the reason for this hasty retreat."

The camp was in utter disarray. It was difficult to maneuver through the jostling crowd. Nobody knew the whereabouts of the grand master chief— or anyone of authority for that matter. Finally, Lluava spotted General Argon heading into the general's barracks.

The grand master chief did not stop when he saw the pair making their way toward him. They followed him silently, like a double shadow, as he entered his meeting room and took a seat. The small space was filled with the other commanders. Argon waved the young pair to the last vacant seat. Varren sat; Lluava stood behind him, as dictated by his rank.

"For those who might not know," said the grand master chief, looking straight at Lluava, "We have been forced to withdraw from the outer battlefield. This decision was made for several reasons, but primarily because the Raiders' reinforcements have arrived, and their ranks vastly outnumber our own. They have steadily forced us back toward these walls. I made the call to pull what is left of our forces inside Durog for their own protection."

Varren looked displeased. Undeterred, the commander continued. "We have lost too many of our soldiers in the effort to defend ourselves against their mighty onslaught."

The prince rose. "You would let the Raiders go about the countryside as they please? Keep us at bay, caged like dogs? Until our own reinforcements arrive, we are Elysia's only defense."

The grand master chief barked back, "All we can do now is distract the Raiders from splitting their forces and attacking other locations in Elysia. We must stall them until we either come up with a viable plan or receive reinforcements from the other camps. There is no other option. I will not continue to lead my men to slaughter."

Varren sat down slowly. The commander looked at Colonel Skipe. "I want the aerial troops to continue attacking the enemy throughout the day. Major Ojewa, take charge of securing the camp. Assign sentinels at any strategic position you deem important in order to protect Durog against any attempt to breach the walls. As for everyone else, use this time to rest and recuperate."

Dismissed, Lluava asked her partner and prince, "Varren, what do you know of Issaura's Claws?" Their unusual properties had not left her mind or those of her friends. She already dealt with their questioning and knew they talked about her and the Claws when she was not around.

"If you are inquiring if I knew they transformed as you do, the answer is no," responded Varren. "They, like many war relics, had been locked away since the Landon Wars ended. Their true nature and original purpose was forgotten long ago."

"By Theriomorphs for Theriomorphs," muttered Lluava under her breath. Yet she was happy she possessed the golden treasures. Regardless of their origin, having weapons that could shift with her was a great benefit. She would make sure she used them to their full potential.

Lluava retired early and, for the first time in many nights, slept well. For the next few days, she and her friends rested while those in charge debated military tactics and strategies. Thad began to spend time with them while his partner continued fighting in the aerial attacks. He would remain near Varren until dusk, when Horus and the rest of the flying Theriomorphs swooped back over the walls.

One evening, Lluava walked by herself among the barracks; the weather was noticeably cooler and the air crisp. The stars seemed to dance above her head, and a wisp of moon floated lazily in the satin sky. It would have been a perfectly pleasant night but for the sounds of the Raiders doing who knew what beyond the walls.

As she turned the corner of one of the buildings, Lluava spotted Thad sitting on the small porch of his barracks. Walking over, she asked, "Where's Horus? He should be back by now."

"Hello, Lluava. Horus is grabbing a bite to eat. He will be back before long. What might a lovely lady such as yourself be doing wandering around the camp all alone?" Thad motioned to her to take a seat. Lluava knew that there was no romantic intent behind his words; Thad was simply a natural charmer.

Taking the bait, she said with a smile, "I just felt it was a nice night for a walk, which fortunately brought me to you. How are you dealing with having a partner who fights without you?"

Thad shook his head. "Oh, Lluava, it really is quite horrible for me. I just sit around becoming fat while Horus does all the work."

"That doesn't seem too bad," she commented, laughing.

"One might think not, but waiting and wondering if your partner will return alive is torment enough for any man," he said earnestly; certain topics were not to be treated lightly. "You and Varren are always together. But what would you do if Varren left to protect this kingdom while you had to sit here and hope for the best? I do not like it."

"Oh, I see." Lluava acknowledged the truth of his words. The two sat silently next to each other for a bit. Lluava wondered if this might not be a chance to learn things about her partner that she could not ask him about directly. "What will Varren and you do if—I mean *when*—we win this war?"

"Well, in due time I will assume my father's title and inherit his property. Before too long, I hope to have a family of my own. I will also serve as counselor to Varren when he becomes king." Thad smiled as he envisaged his future. "As for Varren, he will inherit the throne from his grandfather upon His Majesty King Thor's death. He will be expected to marry and father an heir. He would have been married this past summer had it not been for the events that ensued. The wedding has been postponed."

"Wait," Lluava responded hastily. "Varren is engaged?"

"My dear," pointed out Thad as he rolled up the cuffs of his shirt, "The proper term is *betrothed*." Looking up, he saw the shocked expression on Lluava's face. "Lluava, you must understand that it is the custom of the upper class to have their children, actually even their future children, betrothed to one another. Varren, as prince, has been paired with another since childhood. I, myself, was betrothed to my wife in childhood."

Lluava had not realized Thad was already married and that Varren was betrothed. This unexpected information was too much for Lluava. She looked aghast. Thad chuckled. "It is all right. I know the customs of our race might seem strange to you, but that is the way of our culture. We are born, are paired off by our fathers, are wed, and then spend the rest of our lives getting to know our mates."

"How many times did you meet your wife before you were wed?" Lluava wanted to know.

"I had not even seen her before she walked into the church on our wedding day. Lluava, please do not look at me like that. It really is not as bad as it sounds. We do not need, or even expect, to love the person we marry."

"How could you marry someone you do not love?" Lluava's head was spinning.

"Just because I might not have loved my wife before our marriage does not mean I do not love her now. Over time, you learn to love the person you are with. Emily, my wife, is a splendid woman. She might be plain of face, but she has enough personality to fill the whole kingdom."

"And what of Varren?" inquired Lluava. "Will he meet his bride before they marry?"

"Actually, he has met the girl—her name is Illia Alcazar—on several occasions. I think he is quite taken with her. She is a pretty little thing—polite, elegant, beautiful. She will make a lovely queen one day."

"I…I hope they will be happy together," Lluava said in a whisper as she stood to bid Thad farewell for the evening.

Only later did she feel bad about her abrupt goodbye. For some reason, she felt an inner disquiet. Before going to bed that night, Lluava found Rosalyn and asked the question that was nagging at her.

"Rosalyn, were you engaged to Talos recently, or were you betrothed to him?" she asked.

"I have been betrothed to him since I was a child, but I have been fortunate to grow up knowing him. Since our love began to grow, I have deliberately chosen to refer to it as an engagement, for that term seems more appropriate. Why?"

"Oh, I was just curious," Lluava told her friend, resolving to think no more about it. Nonetheless, she found the information unsettling.

Almost two weeks had passed since Kentril's departure for reinforcements. Another council of the commanders was called; as prince, Varren was invited. As his partner, Lluava was allowed to accompany him.

The gravelly voice of the grand master chief sounded even rougher than usual. "Thus far, mighty Durog has been able to withstand the Raiders' onslaught. We have prevented them from scaling our walls, and Colonel Skipe has successfully kept the enemy occupied with his aerial fleet. However, unfortunate news has come to my attention: our food supplies are greatly depleted. Housing two entire camps was never factored into our original plans, and Durog was unprepared when the attack forced us to evacuate Thowcelemine. It is a mixed blessing that our losses have allowed us to apportion what is left in greater magnitude, or have at least provided us a bit more time. But the fact is that even if we ration our food, we will exhaust our resources in approximately two weeks. This is not enough time for reinforcements and supply wagons to reach us. Fellow commanders, we are facing starvation."

This news was deeply unsettling to the camp's leaders. There was muttering, and concerned looks were exchanged. His dark brow furrowed, Ojewa inquired, "What do you wish us to do?"

"We will ration what we have to the best of our ability," responded the general. "We will not divulge the reason for this action to the camp at large; we haven't the time to deal with a mass panic. Instead, we will treat the situation in a logical and straightforward manner; that is, we will continue as usual, with the exception of training exercises. These will be curtailed to reduce the need for extra food." The grand master chief paused. The muscles in his jaw twitched in agitation before he continued. "There is nothing we can do at this point other than to hope that backup arrives before our supplies are gone."

A sullen murmur followed the announcement. The commanders filed out according to rank.

Lluava turned to Varren, "What shall we tell the others?"

"Nothing," he answered. "We tell them nothing. Were you not listening to what was said? We cannot risk a widespread panic. We will tell them *nothing*. Is that clear?"

Lluava had never seen Varren this rigid before, nor had she ever had to keep secrets from trusted friends. She was both shocked and disappointed. If this was how Varren intended to one day rule the country, she would have none of it. She turned away from her partner.

A few nights later, there ensued a ruckus on the grounds of Durog. Lluava and the others left their barracks to discover what was happening. They saw people yelling and gathering at the gates, many with their weapons ready.

"What in the names of the gods is going on?" demanded Talos as he strapped on his sword. His small shield had been discarded long ago.

Byron stood beside him looking disheveled, his hair unbrushed and his shirt only partly tucked in. "I wonder if we are finally being ordered back onto the field."

Lluava spotted Major Ojewa standing not far from the massive door. As usual, he looked like he knew what was going on. She made her way toward him.

"We received a signal that someone wants entry into the camp. We will open the gates shortly," Ojewa explained.

"Is it a Raider? What if it's a trap? How can we trust anyone beyond these walls?" Lluava asked her questions rapidly.

"Always inquisitive," noted Ojewa, his accent unusually thick. "It is a lone person, but it is too dark to recognize him. The general has granted him entry. Whoever he is, he will be thoroughly questioned."

As Major Ojewa finished speaking, the gates began to move. Groaning, they slowly split open to allow a single figure to step through. All stared as an enormous silhouette emerged from the darkness. The man wore a horned helmet and carried a double-bladed battle-ax over his broad shoulders.

The figure stepped into the light, and a gasp escaped the crowd as they watched a grisly-looking General Jormund stumble and then catch himself with the butt of his ax. Through his cracked lips slipped one word: "Water."

"Fetch water! Somebody fetch water now!" cried voices as the onlookers gathered around the weakened general.

Ojewa quickly ordered everyone to step back, while a full canteen was thrust forward. The massive Jormund took several long gulps, then grabbed Ojewa by his collared shirt and demanded, "Where is the commanding officer? Where is Argon?"

As if magically summoned, the grand master chief forced his way through the crowd. Kneeling next to Jormund, he asked, "What is it, my dear friend?"

"The Raiders," rasped Jormund. "They are on the move! They are heading north..."

Chapter 27
Hope Subterranean

Panic spread through the growing crowd. Even before the gates closed, the officers of Durog had lost control. Many recruits, both men and women, were yelling and running around to no apparent purpose. Those who had weapons gathered them and sought a way out. Only when the grand master chief and his fellow commanders forcefully took control did the soldiers form some semblance of order. The troops were ordered to return to their barracks and remain there until summoned in the morning.

In the dark of the bunker, Chat shakily asked the question that was on everyone's mind. "How are we going to stop the Raiders?"

No one had an answer. Restlessly the troops of Durog waited for morning's light and the call to action. When someone finally rapped at their door, all leaped from their beds and stood at attention.

"Troop Seven, you are permitted to eat your breakfast rations. Afterward, return directly to your barracks. You have no further orders at this time."

As the troop filed out the doors, Byron asked the officer, "What are we doing about the Raiders? Do we have a plan to stop them yet?"

The officer looked at the young man. "We have yet to finalize plans. Until further notice, you will follow orders without question…and that is an order."

In the mess hall, Lluava and her friends discussed the situation in hushed voices. "They have no plan. That is the problem," stated Talos. "If they did, it would already be in force."

"We have to do something!" Yamir's voice rose. "We can't just sit around and let those seadogs escape. Who knows where they are going. They could be headed straight for the capital, for all we know." He quickly added,

"I'm sorry, Prince Varren."

"No, you are perfectly right," responded Varren. "Tactically it would be a smart move to take out the capital as soon as possible." The prince ran his fingers through his wavy hair.

"Why can't we just go back out and fight what is left of the Raiders' army?" asked Chat. Seeing the dismay on the others' faces, he slid low in his chair, careful not to disturb his satchel.

"I wish it were that easy, Chat," said Varren. "The problem is that the army has positioned itself outside our gates. It would be easy for them to kill any who try to leave, for even when the gates are wide open, only a small portion of our army can pass through at one time. We are trapped inside like caged animals in a traveling fair."

Chat's bag stirred; the movement caught Lluava's eye. She briefly glimpsed a dark feather through the opening at the top and then perceived the almost undetectable scent of a carrion eater. The idea that Chat was still toting the injured bird around in his satchel would have been comical had the present circumstances been different. She returned her focus to the current problem.

Talos said sadly, "If only there was a second doorway—one unknown to the Raiders."

"That's it! Talos, you're a genius!" exclaimed Lluava. The others stared at her as she quickly swung herself off the bench. Was she mad? Trying to jog her friend's memory, she said, "Remember that project early in our training? Remember? We found those old maps of Durog with the secret entrance?"

"The *supposed* secret tunnel," Talos corrected her.

Lluava would not be stopped. "If we could just find the opening, we could use it to move our army out of Durog and attack the Raiders by surprise from behind!"

"Lluava, don't you think that if such a door or tunnel or whatever existed, one of the commanders would have known about it and used it already?" asked Byron.

"I'm certain they would have used it if they'd known about it." Lluava looked at the skeptical expressions of those around her. "The maps....We found the maps in a book in the back of Thowcelemine's library. I don't know if anyone here even knows they exist. Even the grand master chief didn't know about them."

"But remember, Lluava," Talos interjected, "you could not find the maps when we had to prove our research's validity."

"That's true, but you can't deny that you saw them with your own eyes," Lluava countered.

Sighing, Talos admitted, "You are right about that. I did see the maps."

"Lluava, don't you remember what happened the last time we tried to attack the Raiders from the rear? That ended badly," noted Byron.

"Yes. But they were expecting us to try something along those lines. This time, we can take them completely by surprise."

"Well, I say it's worth a try," Chat piped up assuredly. The bag beside him convulsed and cawed. With everyone's eyes riveted on the satchel, the bandaged head of the raven poked out. Chat carefully pushed the bird back inside and tightened the drawstrings.

Varren finally spoke. "I agree. We should not pass up any opportunity at this point. The question is, what are we going to do about this?"

"Those two officers standing by the doors won't be too happy if we do not return to our barracks. We need some sort of distraction," commented Byron.

Chat stood up and nominated himself. Taking a deep breath, he strode up to one of the officers and began to ask questions, one after another, nonstop. Annoyed, the officer ordered Chat to return to his barracks. Nevertheless, the boy continued to talk. Then Yamir stepped up and began to do the same. One by one, the others peppered both officers with questions until the officers grew angry at the disrespectful behavior.

Talos, Varren, and Lluava slipped past the distracted guards and hastily made their way to the general's barracks. Recognizing Prince Varren, the flustered guard allowed the trio inside. They raced into the meeting room, where, as expected, the grand master chief and several officers were arguing strategy.

"Well, well, well! What do we have here?" asked the general when the three burst into the room.

"Lluava has come up with a solution to our current predicament," stated Varren authoritatively.

The general turned to look at the young woman. "Well?"

Lluava reminded General Argon about the hidden tunnel to the sea. The grand master chief looked highly skeptical as Lluava explained her idea. When she finished, the fierce commander said, "Lluava, even if this tunnel you speak of does exist, you seem to have purposefully omitted its exact location—leading me to believe that you do not actually know where it is. Am I correct?"

Lluava hesitated. "The map was old, and it was hard to make out specific details. I do remember that it seemed to be located under one of the buildings on this side of the camp."

"I am sorry, Lluava, but we need more substantial proof than a cryptic guess based on a map nobody can find."

Talos interjected, "But what if it is true? What if there *were* a tunnel that could help us change our present situation? Do you not think that would be important enough for us to look into it, rather than disregard this information?"

"I agree with Talos that this possibility should not be ignored," asserted Varren.

"Hmm." The grand master chief pushed back his chair and stood up. "There is one major problem that you face. This camp was renovated a dozen years ago, and very few of the original buildings remain. If the map is indeed as old as you seem to think, the building that marked the entry to your tunnel might no longer be standing."

Disheartened, they hung their heads. Lluava was angry. What good was a way out if they could not find it in time? Just as the general motioned for them to leave, an idea occurred to her.

"Wait!" she called out. The grand master chief paused.

"Don't you think that workers demolishing the old buildings would have found the opening? If so, don't you think they would have made note of it? That would have been important to document. And if they had, you would have access to this information as the commanding drill sergeant for the camp." Pointing at the grand master chief, Lluava spoke as fast as her thoughts came to her. "So, unless you are keeping this a secret—and, all things considered, this would not be the time to do so—you have no knowledge of it. Since you know nothing of this tunnel, it has not been discovered and must still lie under one of the untouched buildings!"

Lluava stopped to catch her breath. General Argon returned to his chair.

"Well, Lluava," he said. "Let's take another look at your supposed tunnel." Shuffling though the papers and plans on the table, he retrieved a blueprint of Durog. The others gathered around to look at the diagram.

The commander pointed to different parts of the camp. "Here are the two coliseums. They are the oldest buildings in Durog."

Lluava could not remember the tunnel's location. Fortunately, Talos had a better memory. "No, those are too far from the interior of the camp," he said. "The tunnel was in this area." He pointed to a series of buildings near the wall. Lluava tried to determine which building was which, but, to her, they all appeared to be barracks.

The grand master chief tried to make sense of the rectangular shapes. "The only building near that area that has not been altered is this one." He gestured at one structure that was much larger than the others.

"Which facility is that? It is hard for me to tell," said Lluava.

The general laughed. "You're standing in it."

As the others digested this information, the grand master chief asked, "What do you want to do now? Are you going to tear down the whole place searching for this fantasy?"

"Maybe," replied Lluava, deep in thought.

"Do we have the original plans for this building?" Varren asked.

Without a word, the grand master chief left the room. When he reentered a few minutes later, he carried a small scroll. He spread it out on the table, and everyone bent to study the blueprints. At first glance, there was nothing unusual, but when Talos skimmed over it again, he paused, one finger on the map.

"Why is the entryway shown on the opposite side from where it is now?" The others moved in closer. "Look. The main doorway is at the back of the building—not the front. And here." He tapped the spot on the blueprint. "There was a large room where the porch now stands."

The general spoke up. "That's right. When Durog was being renovated, the master builder relocated the front of this building so it would face toward the camp, not away from it."

"Does anyone else think it strange that this building was the only one in the entire camp that faced away from the center?" asked Talos. "Perhaps something prevented the front from being where it is now—like the entryway of a tunnel. The general's barracks might have been built over it to keep it hidden and safe. Over time, it was forgotten."

"Would not the master builder have found the tunnel when he built the porch?" asked Varren.

"That section of the building was destroyed during an unusually strong tempest," explained the grand master chief. "The master builder might not have found the passage if the opening to it had been damaged in the storm. The tunnel might be buried under the porch."

Grins broke out around the table as new hope pervaded the room.

Soon, after a few unusual orders were issued, the demolition of the porch was underway. Wood snapped and splintered as two teams of Theriomorph oxen pulled the porch beams down. On the opposite side, General Argon and other large land mammals threw their massive weight against the now tilting column.

"Heave!" the commander yelled. "Heave!"

Spectators crowded around as the structure finally collapsed. The loose timbers of roof and columns were removed, as were the platform and steps. Once the debris was cleared away, a collective gasp arose. A small black hole stared back at them. It was just large enough for a grown man to slip through.

"Well, Lluava," the commander acknowledged. "You were right. I was wrong."

Before Lluava could feel pleased about the grudging apology, Major Ojewa pointed out, "Look! Look at the ground around the hole. It looks as if somebody has dug out from the tunnel."

"From the inside," observed Byron, kneeling by the side of the opening. He pointed to the edges. "The marks are at an angle, indicating that someone *inside* the tunnel dug out. Someone could have entered Durog using the tunnel and emerged from under the porch."

"He is right," said Colonel Skipe, as he, too, inspected the hole. "Thankfully, this was not done recently, so I do not believe that the Raiders yet know about it."

A sigh of relief escaped the onlookers.

"We must send someone down to see if the tunnel has collapsed," Admiral Merrow declared in his slippery voice, craning his neck to gain a better view of the abyss.

"Let me go," Lluava volunteered.

"No, I can't let you do that," said the grand master chief. "We need someone who understands tunnels and subterranean construction."

Lluava's disappointment showed. She had discovered the tunnel, and yet she would not be the first one in it. All she could do was watch as a human who had worked in the mines descended into the darkness.

For several hours, everyone waited for a sign and prayed that the man was not trapped in a collapsed shaft. Finally, a voice shouted from the depths of the hole, and the miner was hoisted up.

Shaking his head to remove loose bits of soil and rock, he said, "The tunnel is older than any I have seen, yet it's in better shape than any I have built. It is unusually tall. I suspect it was created to move horses and riders in and out of Durog. The opening is not far from Thowcelemine's beaches. Nearby, a small path carved into the stone leads up the cliff. The path is so crude that I almost did not recognize it for what it is. The problem is that the opening would be completely covered by water during high tide. If you want to use the tunnel, you'll have to factor in the tides."

After thanking the man and dismissing the onlookers, the commanders positioned two sentries at the mouth of the tunnel before they carefully reentered the building to make new plans. Varren and Lluava were among them.

"We can't send out the entire army." The grand master chief pondered silently for several minutes. "The tunnel is too narrow; only a few soldiers could stand side by side or exit together at one time. I will not risk the Raiders' picking off my men one by one. Instead, we will use the tunnel to send someone to warn the camps and the capital that the Raiders are moving north. To minimize the chance of discovery, only one pair will be sent. Moreover, a smaller number means greater mobility. The Raiders will be moving slowly, as many are on foot, so whomever we send should ride the swiftest horses."

Heads nodded in agreement. Then Major Ojewa spoke up. "Just to be extra careful, we should send at least one other pair to guard the messengers until they are safely beyond the Raiders' encampment."

"I am in agreement with you," stated Skipe. "I urge you to consider Thadius Sihia II and his partner, Horus Ethril, as messengers. Sihia is adept at public speaking and will express well the direness of the current situation. His partner Ethril's dual form is the eagle. In this form, he can fly alongside his partner, which will save the resource of an additional horse. Furthermore,

Ethril can keep an eye out for the band of Raiders moving north and steer his partner around them. This will help prevent capture. They are both highly trusted and respected among the troops I command."

After a moment, General Argon agreed.

Varren stood up. "I would like to volunteer Lluava and myself as guards for Sihia and Ethril. By now you know of our prowess on the battlefield. I believe we would be the best suited for this assignment."

The general was adamant. "I cannot allow the sole heir to the throne to take such a risk."

Varren stood silently.

Lluava was unusually upset. She was losing this chance because of her partner's pedigree. Solemnly looking at Varren, she caught his eye. The muscles in his jaw twitched; then, hesitantly, the prince countered, "I must insist."

If the grand master chief was unnerved by such arrant pulling of rank, he did not let on. Stoically he announced, "So be it."

Lluava glanced at her partner then quickly turned away. She wondered if he knew just how much she wanted to explore the tunnel.

Their orders were to depart at dusk, before the tide began its steady movement toward the shore. They would have only a short time to travel through the tunnel, scout out the Raiders' encampment, insure Thad and Horus were safely on their way, and return before the tunnel's entrance was submerged.

As evening approached, Lluava met the others at the tunnel's entrance. Soldiers had enlarged the hole and were completing a gently inclined slope by which a horse could enter the dark pit. Varren, holding the reins of his steed, arrived moments later.

Turning to Thad, he handed his best friend the reins. "Take Ulder."

"I can't take your horse, Varren," Thad protested.

But Varren insisted, "He is the fastest horse in Durog; you will need his speed to get to Fort Brinsdale. Please, ride him."

Honored, Thad replied, "Thank you."

Colonel Skipe shook hands with Horus. "Good luck. May your wings fly you swiftly as the gods."

"Farewell, Uncle," Horus replied.

Ulder pawed at the ground and snorted as Thad walked him toward the tunnel's entrance. The horse shied, not wanting to enter the dark chasm in the ground, but with Varren's gentle prodding, he finally followed Thad into the tunnel. Varren walked behind Ulder; Horus followed, and the last to enter was Lluava.

The darkness engulfed them. Both Lluava and Varren carried small torches. Lluava carefully squeezed past Thad and the horse in order to illuminate the path while Varren positioned himself as rear guard.

The tunnel was lined with boulders. Each piece had been carefully cut, smoothed and meticulously aligned with the others in a perfect and long-forgotten method of interlocking. Even in the ceiling, shaped rocks were wedged one against another with enough pressure to hold them in position. The horse's hooves clinked against the hard surface and reverberated along the corridor. The only other sounds were their own breathing, the rustling of their clothes, and the occasional drip of water from the ceiling.

Running the fingers of her free hand along the wall, Lluava reveled in the cool dampness of the stones. An almost slimy moss grew on many of them. The air was thick and stagnant with the smell of damp soil and whatever lay behind the rock. In the tunnel, time blurred and was almost indeterminate. After an hour, Lluava's torch began to flicker. Moments later, a slight breeze carried the tangy scent of ocean.

"We're getting close," Lluava reported.

She almost missed the slight change in light that signaled the way out. Unlike the rest of the tunnel's careful handiwork, the opening was crudely cut into the cliff wall. She wondered if it had originally been a natural crevice.

Outside, the last rays of light were disappearing. The ocean's waves glimmered as they surged forward. Water was just starting to lap at the edges of the cliff.

"We have to hurry," Horus said. "Soon the ocean will engulf the entrance, and you and Varren will have to find another way back into Durog."

The small band trekked through the spreading water, which glistened in a thin layer over the beach. Searching for the trail that led up the cliff cost them precious time, but Thad spotted it, and they started up the winding path. Lluava was still in the lead, her senses tingling with every smell and sound. Though she tried to prevent it, her muscles tensed. As they neared the top, her eyes darted everywhere. They were indeed near Thowcelemine for she could make out the camp's walls clearly in the distance. Fortunately, only low shrubbery peppered the landscape. Judging it safe to continue, she signaled the others to follow and cautiously crept along the cliff's edge. The sea roared below, and waves crashed against the rock walls.

The wind shifted, and Lluava picked up the stink of sweat and grime—but it was too late. Four of the bushes were moving toward them. Realizing they had been spotted, the camouflaged Raiders had no further need to hide. They charged. Lluava heard the horse's frightened whinny but could not stop to look back. The brute who attacked her swung a short sword, barely missing her midriff. Jumping back, she felt the ground beneath her feet give way. Instinctively she grasped the furry garb of the Raider. The next few seconds seemed to stretch out and slow down as young woman and Raider tumbled over the ledge. Staring skyward as she fell, Lluava saw Varren rush to the edge and scream her name.

Chapter 28
Attack on the Sea Monsters

Lluava was not aware of hitting the water, nor did she feel the rocks crushing her body as wave after wave hurled her against the cliff wall. She did not remember her struggle for air as she was repeatedly pulled under the sea's churning surface. She did not fully compute when she became entangled in a small pile of driftwood floating back towards the vast waters. Her first sensation was of coldness that gently brushed her toes and then receded, only to return moments later. The world was dark, yet she could hear birds singing loudly. Was she blind? She was horror-struck at the thought. No, no, my eyes are just closed, she told herself. But why wouldn't they open?

She could tell that she lay on a beach for she felt gritty sand beneath her and small waves softly rushing over her feet. It had to be close to midday; the heat of the sun was directly overhead. Without the occasional breeze, the heat would have been unbearable.

Lluava lay still and tried to remember what happened. Did Thad and Horus get away? Was Varren safe? Were they looking for her? Slowly she tried to move her toes. They wiggled in the sand that washed up around them. Then she forced her fingers to move. Finally, Lluava attempted to open her eyes; the sun was too bright, and she quickly closed them. Her body felt heavy, and she drifted in and out of consciousness. After a time, she regained awareness. Lluava could not tell how long she had been out.

She turned her head to the side and forced her eyes open. Blinking, Lluava was soon able to make out shapes. She lay on an empty stretch of beach. Palm trees arched their long necks over the shoreline, creating patches of shade. A semitropical forest bordered the pale sand. Where am I? she thought. The place was totally unfamiliar.

Slowly, Lluava turned on her side and propped herself up on one elbow.

The quiet serenity and natural beauty surrounding her almost made her wonder if she had indeed died, but the steady ache and severe pain that wracked her body confirmed that she was clearly alive. Slowly and unsteadily, she rose to her feet. Although badly battered, she did not seem to have any major injuries. Her clothes were shredded but usable. Maybe there are gods watching over me, she thought with a wan smile.

Lluava headed down the beach in search of identifiable landmarks. As she rounded a bend near the end of the peninsula, she suddenly stopped, rooted to the ground. Before her, their presence concealed by the lushly forested land, floated an armada so large as to be almost incomprehensible. Countless rows of snarling, dragon-headed ships, their sails furled, rested at anchor. Elaborately painted with brilliant colors, the fleet resembled sleeping creatures bobbing silently on the waves. On the decks of each vessel, Raiders lolled about. If each craft held as many Raiders as Lluava counted on those nearest her, their army had barely set foot on Elysia. She had stumbled upon a nest of sea monsters waiting to be hatched.

There was no time to waste. Lluava had to return to Durog and warn General Argon of this horror. Quickly she began to retrace her steps, only to be brought up short by the sight of half a dozen Raiders stooping to peer at the footprints she had left in the sand. Without a second thought, the girl dove into the dense underbrush.

Carefully she crept through the bushes and passed the men as they trotted along the beach. She only had a few moments before they discovered her returning tracks and realized she was heading into the forest. Swiftly she ducked under low branches and wove through vines until she reached the edge of the woods. Scanning the shoreline from this new perspective, she spotted the mainland and the walls of Thowcelemine across the waters of a large bay. Suddenly, she knew where she was—the island, Hulme. The crescent-shaped island had blocked the view of the Raiders' navy from Durog. Cautiously, she stepped out onto the beach.

Immediately, a glittering object caught her attention. Drawing nearer, Lluava recognized one of Issaura's Claws. But where was the other one? Time was running out; nevertheless, she had to find its mate. She picked up the single Claw and slipped it over her right hand.

Scouring the beach ahead, she spotted movement. Partially hidden behind a beached tree trunk, a Raider bent to pick up something from the ground.

"Vat dis?" the bearded man barked in a guttural voice. He straightened his helmet over his matted golden hair and lifted the Claw to inspect it in the light.

Lluava felt sick at the sight of the oaf pawing at her weapon with his grimy hands. Silently she edged closer, using the driftwood to hide her approach. She had only one chance; if she failed, he would alert his companions. Marshaling her energy, Lluava jumped over the log and leaped onto the Raider's back. With a quick jerk of her arms, she snapped his neck, and the burly body collapsed onto the sand.

Lluava pulled the Claw from the huge, hairy hands of the corpse. "That's mine, thank you," she whispered to the lifeless form, then turned away and raced to the ocean. Enraged shouts reached her as the scouting Raiders discovered their slain comrade. They looked furiously about for the unknown assassin who had left only footprints, but Lluava appeared as just another white-capped speck among the wind-tossed waves.

It did not take her long to swim to the mainland and reach the hidden tunnel. She was grateful the tide was just beginning to turn. When she emerged from the opening in Durog, she had to dodge a pair of swords wielded by the on-duty guards, who quickly recognized their mistake and allowed her to run straight to the general's barracks to search for the grand master chief. However, the meeting room was empty, and no one replied to her shouts.

Lluava strode hurriedly across the camp toward her own barracks. When she burst through the doors, her fellow comrades stared at her as if she were a ghost.

"Where is the grand master chief?" she demanded.

"Lluava!" gasped a familiar voice. "We thought you had died!" A haggard-looking Varren pushed his way through the others crowding around her.

"Well, I didn't, did I?" she snapped. "Would someone *please* tell me where the grand master chief is?" Everyone just stood there gawking; didn't they realize this was urgent? Frustration surged in her belly.

"I'll take you to him," answered Varren. His voice was hoarse, but Lluava paid no attention to it. She had more important things on her mind.

Varren led Lluava into the small coliseum where the general was sparring with two other men. He had removed his shirt, and his rippling muscles gleamed with sweat. In a swift combination of moves, the leader of Durog forced back his two opponents and then returned his long sword to its waiting sheath. He glanced briefly at Varren and Lluava.

"Enough," he barked at the young men, who were preparing to charge him again. Gesturing to them to leave, he said, "That is enough practice for today."

He turned to Lluava. "I guess the gods weren't ready for you yet."

"No, sir," Lluava replied, saluting. "May I have a word with you? It's of the greatest importance."

"Are you trying to insult me with the informality of your address, or are you just ignorant of the proper way to address a superior?" grumped the grand master chief as he slipped on his shirt. Lluava felt a twinge of embarrassment, but this was not the time to worry about formalities. She waited anxiously until given permission to speak.

"I am sorry, sir, but hiding behind Hulme is a fleet unlike anything we ever imagined. Thousands of Raiders are lying in wait on their ships." The words tumbled from her as she tried to give a full account of the past few hours.

Argon was taken aback by her news. "This," he half-whispered to himself, "is dire." Staring silently into the distance, he scowled deeply and shook his head.

Nothing more was said. The three stood like statues, in the middle of the coliseum, under the sun, waiting. Lluava wished for something, anything, that would change the course of events for the better. But what? She closed her eyes.

That's when the idea hit her.

"I know how to take out their army," Lluava said quietly.

"What did you say, soldier?" rapped out the general.

Lluava looked at the two men and smiled. "I know how to destroy their fleet," she said again, louder this time. "We need Berkley."

Something in her manner must have convinced him; for once, the grand master chief did not waste time questioning her. "Lead the way," was all he said.

Half-running, half-stumbling into the medical ward, Lluava found the old man caring for a soldier with a head wound. Berkley flipped his long beard over his left shoulder as he bent over the wounded man to inspect the bandages he had recently set.

"Berkley," Lluava panted as she paused to catch her breath and waited for the other two men to follow her inside the building. "Can Flashbang ignite when it's wet?"

The wizened healer rubbed his knobby hands together. "The new variation can. I mixed it in an oil so it floats above the water's surface. But it still works better on dry surfaces."

Lluava's heart beat with excitement. "How much have you made?"

The old man cleared his throat. "Well, not as much as I'd like," he said. Then he looked up at Argon. The general's expression was enough to make him understand the seriousness of the questions. "Enough to demolish a mountain if need be. How much do you need?"

"All of it," was Lluava's reply.

By the end of the following day, Lluava's plans were ready. Admiral Merrow gathered the entire brigade of aquatic Theriomorphs; each packed enough Flashbang to destroy an entire barracks. At the front gates of Durog, the aerial and terra divisions, along with the aquatic Theriomorphs' partners, lined up in large regiments, each composed of four separate divisions. As Lluava's troop began to line up, she slipped away and headed toward the mouth of the tunnel where the aquatic regiment was preparing to leave.

"Where do you think you are going?" asked Varren testily. So far, Lluava had managed to avoid her partner. Recently she had found that she preferred to distance herself from the prince. Although she did not understand her own behavior, she felt better away from him.

"You're supposed to be lining up with the rest of our troop," she replied.

"As are you," he said in a tone she had come to dislike.

"I have been posted with Admiral Merrow's regiment for this battle. He needs Theriomorphs who can maneuver quickly in water. As a tigress, the water is a friend to me. You will stay with the rest of our troop," she stated flatly.

"The admiral has enough troops. You are *my* partner, and we are supposed to fight together," Varren replied, disapproval written on his handsome face.

Admiral Merrow had come up behind them. "I am sorry, Your Majesty," he interjected. "Lluava is correct. She is not only an unusually agile swimmer, but she knows exactly where to lead my regiment. She is coming with me."

Varren glared at Lluava, turned on his heel, and headed toward the gates. She watched him leave, and then joined the aquatic regiment who were entering the dark underground tunnel.

When the regiment had traversed the passage and reached the cliff opening, Lluava peeled off her uniform, revealing her swimwear. She slipped the strap of the sealed horn that contained her portion of Flashbang over her shoulder. Then she motioned to the waiting troops to follow.

One by one, the soldiers waded into the surf, transformed into their dual forms, and headed for Hulme. The seawater flowing past her fur made Lluava shiver with exhilaration. Dipping her muzzle under the water, she savored the feeling of liquid droplets sliding down her whiskers.

In the deepening night, Lluava silently steered the group toward the far side of Hulme. She did not look back as half a dozen troops split off toward the beach. They would take out the Raider sentries posted on the island with great efficiency.

Rounding the bend, the regiment did not stop to assess the massive amount of opposition asleep aboard the ships. Instead, the troops split up, disappearing among the moored vessels, and began their dangerous work. A shark's fin sliced silently through the water an arm's length from Lluava. The image was eerie. The fur down her back twitched involuntarily.

Once in position, the Theriomorphs shifted back to human form. They carefully smeared the oily Flashbang around the base of the ships just above the water level and dripped some into the surrounding water before moving to the next ship. Once the entire fleet had been treated, the remaining Flashbang was poured onto the ocean's surface.

As the horns of Flashbang were emptied, the soldiers transformed again and swam back, undetected, to the rendezvous point on Hulme.

Lluava had one final task. She found Merrow surveying their progress. In the dim moonlight, the ocean gleamed with subtle colors of Flashbang's oily sheen. It was a strangely beautiful sight.

"Admiral Merrow," she began. "Do not ignite the Flashbang yet. I need twenty more minutes." The admiral frowned, but she continued. "We need to take care of the ships moored near shore. If we are going to destroy their fleet, we must demolish *every* ship."

"Twenty minutes?" He pursed his lips in thought. "I'll try. But if they grow suspicious, I will have to light the flames. You will be on your own."

Lluava started through the forest, emerged onto the beach, and dove into the water. As quickly as possible, she swam toward the ships nearest the shore. Their dark forms rose and fell on the waves; the carved jaws protruding from their bows seemed to snarl and snap among the shadows. Wispy clouds veiled the moon, hiding the night's events from her ever-watchful gaze.

Lluava smeared Flashbang onto the sides of one ship after another. She wished she could coat their oars, too, but these had been pulled from the water and stowed deep in the ships' holds, leaving rows of open ports like a multitude of eyes on the ships' sides.

More than once, she had to halt her work when she heard footsteps on the deck above her. When this occurred, she flattened herself against the side of the boat and let the waves wash over her. Once, a lantern was held out over the edge of the vessel, and she had to duck under the surface of the water to escape the aura of light.

Soon Lluava had sabotaged all but the last ship. That vessel was anchored a short distance away from the others on the far side. She spotted several men standing guard, constantly searching the water with their lanterns. She would have to be extra careful with this ship; there was something about this one that was special.

As Lluava swam toward the ship, she heard a crackling sound behind her. The hissing and snapping rushed right toward her, and she had only a moment to dive under the waves before a blazing conflagration spread across the surface of the ocean. The salty liquid burned her eyes, but she forced them open as she watched the bright light of the flames coating the water above her. The fire signaled the downfall of the Raiders' fleet, a signal that would be seen by those waiting in Durog.

Lluava ran through her plan once again. The Raiders taking refuge on the ships would be burned alive or, if they abandoned the flaming pyres, would succumb to Merrow's merciless aquatic regiment. The fire and screams would distract the Raiders encamped on the mainland; when they attempted to go to their comrades' aid, the gates of Durog would be thrown wide open, and Elysia's southern army would attack the landlocked Raiders from their rear. Once Durog's forces had a decent foothold on the battlefield, General Argon and General Jormund would lead four troops north to attack the Raiders who had branched off north. Soon, she hoped, this war would finally end.

Although Lluava was elated that her plan was actually succeeding, the lack of air in her lungs brought her back to grim reality: she was trapped beneath a ceiling of fire. Desperately, she swam underwater seeking a surface not blanketed in flames. Her lungs burned, and she was becoming lightheaded. If she could not find a clear spot quickly, she would have to risk the inferno above.

At last, her straining lungs at their limit, she glimpsed a gap in the blaze. Kicking upward, she resurfaced, gasping. Instantly the heat of the fire slapped her face; swirling cinders and acrid fumes made her eyes water. Trying to discern shapes through the thick columns of smoke, she saw nearby ships crackling with flames. Sailors shouted and screamed as they tried to save their dying vessels. Some attempted to lower rafts but took too long. Risking death on shore or in the ocean, others jumped overboard. Sails caught fire like flaming torches marking some horrid sacrifice. Not far from Lluava a ship suddenly exploded; debris rained all around her. Another ship spewed flames from its open ports.

On shore, the Raiders fared little better. Durog's regiments swarmed out and surrounded the enemy; many Raiders had not even brought their weapons with them when they ran toward the cliff's edge to see what was happening to their companions.

Through the crackling of the flames came the sound of voices. Lluava turned to see a small vessel rowed by six Raiders plowing through the fiery water next to her. The eyes of all six were riveted on her.

"Oye, looky here vat I find," grunted a man with a shorter beard than the rest. "A sea wench to harden our hearts!"

He and his friends laughed as the closest one reached down and grabbed Lluava by her hair and pulled her, screaming, into the small boat. In the narrow vessel, these massive creatures could sit only one to a seat, so Lluava was slung into the middle of the boat.

Fire began to lick at the wooden sides of the small craft like a starving animal. The men rowed through the inferno. Lluava struggled to free her hair, but the man held it in a death grip. There was no escape. Even if she transformed, where would she go with the conflagration upon them? Lluava squatted in the bottom of the boat and bided her time as she headed into the den of the enemy.

Chapter 29
In Spider's Web

Lluava could only watch as the small boat encroached upon the shore. Refusing to think about what they would do to her upon landing, she sat solemn and unmoving, her hair like reins in the swarthy Raider's fist. Her weapons had been confiscated and lay in the lap of the man who steered the boat. Salty mist stung her eyes, and the heat from the fires dried the sea crust on her clothes. She forced herself to calm her breathing and struggled to devise an escape plan.

Suddenly, the air was filled with the sound of cracking and splintering wood and the astonished gasps of the marauders as, seemingly out of nowhere, a vast form sprang upon the narrow craft. A gigantic shark crashed through the rear of the vessel, tearing off the rudder, a screaming Raider clamped between its massive jaws. The gaping hole took in water at a rapid rate, and the force of the attack sent the boat rocking sideways. Lluava, the man who gripped her hair, and the rest of the brutish lot toppled overboard.

Her captor released his vile hold to save himself, and Lluava dove after Issaura's Claws, which were quickly sinking into the depths. Moments later, she resurfaced with the weapons in hand and gulped the smoky air, relieved, now, that the boat had been so close to shore.

The small craft was completely under water. The few men unravaged by the huge shark swam frantically toward the beach. A dark fin sliced through the floating carnage straight toward Lluava. When it drew abreast, the sea monster shifted into human form and gave her a relieved smile. "You did not return as agreed. Why must you always disobey orders?"

Lluava suppressed a giggle. "Admiral Merrow," she replied, "Don't you know by now that I love to push the limits?"

After reaching shore and scaling the cliff, Lluava went in search of

General Argon. Despite the pandemonium, it was clear that the army of Durog had gained the advantage. The enemy was surrounded, and the Raiders were being forced to the cliff's edge.

On the far side of the battlefield, Lluava found Major Ojewa, in his dual form, locked in combat with several brutes. As the black leopard screamed and roared, the marauders backed up uncertainly. Following Ojewa's lead, Lluava transformed and helped force them back. With two wild cats on the attack, the men were desperate to escape.

"Where is General Argon?" inquired Lluava, after the pair had herded the Raiders toward the others.

"He has already left," said the ebony cat, "But I'll take you to him. Follow." Major Ojewa commanded several privates to take over their positions, and the two felids loped off toward the forest to the north.

They caught up with the small regiment crossing the ruins of Calitron. When Argon spotted the two Theriomorphs running toward him, he called out, "Well done, Lluava! Major Ojewa, you must return at once. I am trusting you to lead our army to victory."

Ojewa nodded to Lluava and turned away toward the battlefield. The grand master chief made his way to the front of the regiment, and Lluava followed respectfully. Finding her troop marching in front, she shifted and rejoined her friends.

Varren did not acknowledge her as she took her place at his side. Why was he angry at her? Wasn't she the one who had risked her life to save them all? Had she not sabotaged the other ships, twice as many Raiders would have attacked Durog. Varren should be pleased that she was so fearless. Was he upset at her for leaving him? How could he expect people to respect him when he acted so immaturely?

The troop trekked in silence toward the devastated remains of Delphine. The massive stone walls had been reduced to piles of boulders and mounds of rubble that stretched across a vast area. Tall grasses had already begun to take over, and weeds stretched their tendrils into the crevices of broken stone. Not one building remained standing. Only carrion eaters roamed about the wreckage.

Looking again upon the devastation the Raiders had wrought, images of the first attack flashed before her eyes; Lluava could almost sense the dead, smell the blood. She felt suddenly drained and realized she was near exhaustion. She must rest soon. But not yet.

As Lluava passed the ruins, large forms emerged from the tall grass behind her. Once again, they had walked into an ambush. Soon, the marching regiment was under attack by a squadron of some of the fiercest fighters they had yet encountered. Lluava and a handful of others who had been in the front lines, including both generals, managed to break through the line of savagely hacking battle-axes; the rest of the troop was cut off and trapped to the south.

"General Jormund, take those who are left with you and head north," ordered the grand master chief. There is no time to waste on frays like this."

"And what in Ullr's name are you going to do?" trumpeted the hulking Jormund.

"I am going to show these sea brutes a thing or two. Afterward, the rest of the troops and I will catch up with you." The leader of Durog turned back toward the fighting.

"You're mad," General Jormund bellowed after Argon. "You can't just barge through all those warriors to rescue your men!"

"No commander abandons his men. Go, General! Leave now!" exhorted the impressive Argon, who was soon enveloped in the skirmish.

Lluava's first instinct was to charge after him. Varren, seeming to read her thoughts, grabbed her arm and shook his head. They both knew that the grand master chief might be a little mad himself, but he would never ask others to follow him into a fray and needlessly risk their lives.

And so the small squad pushed northward. Lluava looked around to see with whom they were traveling on this trek. There were more soldiers than she had originally thought. At least half of her own troop was with her as well as a few men from the other groups. It was not a large band, but enough to inflict respectable damage if it came to a fight.

After hiking through the woods in silence for several hours, Talos spoke to General Jormund. "Should we take the main road to Fort Brinsdale? That route would certainly be quicker and easier to travel."

"The enemy could be using the road. They would be able to spot us from a distance. It is much safer to travel in the woods near the coast. At least here we have cover."

"It will take us longer to march through uncut forest," Talos pointed out. "We are wasting valuable time." The years of poring over his father's maps during the tedium of his studies and listening to his father's counsel had finally paid off.

"Since I am the commander, I will make the decisions. I believe it is safer for us to take the extra time than to risk calling attention to ourselves."

Talos glanced at the future king's complacent face, hoping to find support for his logical argument. He gained none. The discussion was over.

For the next two days, there was little talk. Even at night, Lluava and her friends were relatively quiet. On the third evening, the small band of soldiers was on high alert. In the distance, the snapping of twigs and rustling of fallen leaves could be heard. This was soon followed by the sound of numerous feet treading heavily on the ground. Sickly slivers of moonlight slipped through the dense canopy and silhouetted horned forms moving in massed formation toward Lluava and the rest of the squadron hiding amid the underbrush.

Lluava's thoughts were dire. Something terrible must have happened to the grand master chief and the rest of the regiment. Why else would an organized group of Raiders be tracking them? There was nowhere to take refuge. Lluava realized that, once again, it was time to fight for their lives.

General Jormund must have realized this, as well, for he shifted. The massive elephant rising before them had two great spears of ivory that almost touched the ground. The enormous beast trumpeted its war cry and charged into the approaching enemy ranks.

Like a plague of locusts, the marauders swarmed Lluava and her comrades. Swords and daggers were wielded, iron striking iron. Arrows and spears streaked through the air. All around her, men were dying, yet there was nothing anyone could do to stop it.

A man nearly thirty years old stood over his fallen partner, heroically defending the body from any Raider that approached. He was not from Lluava's troop, but he clearly recognized Varren. He waved them closer, then spoke rapidly.

"We are just south of my town, Therial. There are ravines not far from here. If you lead the men north, you might use the ravines to your advantage."

"You sound as if you won't be joining us." Lluava looked questioningly at the man.

His jaw twitched, then he firmly replied, "Go."

Lluava looked more closely and saw the yawning wound that streaked his back. She respectfully nodded at him before turning and running to her partner's side. Byron and Talos were nearby as well, and the four took shelter in a grove of large trees as arrows flew through the spaces between the trunks.

When Varren repeated the dying man's words, Talos spoke with confidence. "If we could lure the Raiders into the ravines, we could attack them from above. The only problem is allowing time for most of our regiment to move past the ravines without those sea brutes grabbing at our ankles. We don't want them to corner us as we cross the chasms ourselves."

"We need a distraction," interjected Byron. "Something that will attract the attention of the enemy long enough for us to cross."

"I know the perfect distraction," Yamir added smugly. He had just reached a nearby tree. Chat was on his left.

After a moment's pause and another volley of arrows, Lluava asked, "Well? What is it, then?"

"You're looking at it. I'll be the distraction." Yamir appeared confident his plan would work.

Talos thought otherwise. "No. They would pay no more attention to you than to any other person here." There was a pause as the gears in Talos's head turned. Yet it was Varren who added, "Except one."

Everyone looked at their future king as if they wanted to question him. Yet Talos's glance at Varren expressed his understanding.

"What better bait than the prince of the kingdom they hope to conquer, the sole heir to the throne?" explained Varren. Lluava was skeptical.

Byron grimaced and quickly argued against the idea. "I don't advise such a reckless move. You're the heir and thus shouldn't be placed in jeopardy. We should be protecting you."

Their plan needed to work. Varren asserted, "How would it look if our future king dared not risk his life for his people? How would it appear if he asked others to do something that he himself would not?"

"I don't think that would be enough," Lluava hastily replied. "I mean, one man acting as the sole distraction?"

Quickly thinking it over, Talos added, "Maybe not, but Varren will have to do, for we have nothing else."

Lluava could not understand why Talos, of all people, was advocating such an idiotic plan. How could it ever work? Looking at the men around her, all of whom had already made up their minds, Lluava could tell further argument was useless.

"Fine," she bitterly consented. "But I will follow Varren closely, since I am his partner."

Varren gave her a strange look as Talos and Byron carefully crept from the safety of the tree trunks and put the plan into motion. Yamir and Chat had already slipped away. Varren was determined. His stern features expressed that he believed this to be the only option.

"So what do we do now?" asked Lluava, after the other two had disappeared into the dense forest.

"I need to find a mount," Varren replied. Carefully the pair ran from tree to tree as arrows and javelins whistled past them. Once a barbed arrow flew so close to Lluava's head that it tangled in her hair and yanked a clump out. After that, she was extra cautious when dodging projectiles.

Soon Varren signaled Lluava to join him behind a particularly large oak. She waited for the right moment, then dove from the elm behind which she was crouched toward Varren. Unfortunately, she slipped on the leaf-littered ground and toppled away from the protective shield of the tree. In a flash, Varren grabbed her and yanked her back just as a thick spear was hurtled at the spot where she had fallen.

The two took a moment to catch their breath. Lluava shrugged out of Varren's grip and softly thanked him. "Now, why did you call me over?"

But Varren signaled her to be quiet, then pointed some yards off at a saddled gelding without a rider. Though she didn't recognize the breed, Lluava could tell the hickory steed had not been bred to be a warhorse; it was too scrawny. Rather, it was built for speed. Its elegant limbs were so beautifully sinuous that it seemed more like a work of art than a living, breathing animal. Its mane was a lighter shade of brown, almost a deep honey, and black speckles dotted its flanks. Lluava wondered if it was one of the Raider's mounts that had been shipped over with them. Either way, Varren needed it in order for their plan to work.

Without a word or sign, Varren stealthily approached the horse. Though aware of the arrows falling around him, he focused only on reaching the steed. When the gelding spotted him, it did not run or seem afraid. Instead, it stepped toward the prince as if wanting Varren to ride it. Varren had a special connection with equines, a certain aura that comforted the beasts.

Mounting the gelding, Varren let it rear up once; then he gave a shout, and the two forms became one as they galloped away. Lluava shifted into her dual form and loped after her partner, making sure to keep enough distance between them—neither on top of the horse's heels nor too far away to protect him.

Their plan took effect almost immediately. Varren galloped wildly about, yelling, making as much commotion as possible. Proclaiming himself prince and sole heir to the throne, he shouted that he alone would be their downfall. The Raiders took the bait and raced after Varren. Lluava attacked and quickly dispatched any individual who came within range of him.

With each passing minute, the number of marauders encroaching on the prince increased. Lluava realized that soon she would not be able to protect Varren and his tiring steed. With a burst of speed, she caught up to the horse and shouted to the prince, "Let's head to the ravines!"

"A few more minutes!" he shouted back. Both horse and rider picked up speed once more. Lluava's nerves started to twinge. She did not know how much time they had left. Looking over her shoulder, she saw a swarm of Raiders on horseback not far behind.

Pushing through a copse of small trees, Lluava saw Varren turn northward. Unfortunately, a line of Raiders blocked his path and began to swiftly encircle the young prince. Varren turned his horse and charged the approaching enemy. In a giant leap, horse and rider cleared all but the tallest warriors. With a clatter, helmets were knocked off heads, and the bewildered marauders turned to see the prince ride off.

Lluava bounded after her partner. Although several Raiders peeled off after Varren, others stood their ground as the tigress hurtled toward them. Lluava's muscles were beginning to cramp from the constant tension; she would have to force herself to clear the approaching mob. If Varren had done it, so could she. When she was almost on top of the column of Raiders, Lluava leaped, vaulting up and over. But just as she thought she was going to make it, she fell too early.

There was another clatter of claws and metal as Lluava toppled onto a pair of Raiders standing in the last row. In a fury of movement, arms and weapons targeted the floundering tigress. She batted and struck at anything near her. Regaining her footing, the enraged animal struggled to free herself from the brutes. With a roar of anger, she heaved forward and bounded away from her bloodthirsty attackers.

Varren had disappeared. Lluava desperately tried to regain the ground she had lost in those precious minutes. As she burst through briars and brambles, she sensed a change in terrain; had she not been on the lookout, she would have tumbled into the first ravine. A narrow slice of earth, little wider than a man, sank abruptly into the ground. Lluava leapt easily over the crevice but almost landed in an adjacent one.

Scanning the landscape, she noted that the earth's surface had fractured, like a piece of broken glass, into a delicate web of interconnected ravines. She paused only briefly to wonder what had caused such an unusual natural phenomenon, for, somewhere within one of the embankments, she heard hooves striking stone.

The recognizable scent of the equine's sweat filled her flaring nostrils as she bounded toward the sound. Trying to spot the familiar figure, Lluava peered into the next ravine, but it was empty. She jumped over the chasm to the next one, only to see a shabby Raider hobbling on a twisted leg. The tread of ironclad hooves was so near, yet her senses struggled to pinpoint the exact ravine from which the sound emanated.

Lluava continued to leap over the ever-widening fissures. Behind her, the Raiders were no longer able to clear the rifts and were forced to climb down into the earthen cracks. This slowed them down while the king's soldiers maneuvered into position. Behind every crooked tree and scrap of hedge, the troops tensed, waiting for the moment to spring down into the ravines and attack those who had caused so much pain and death.

Charging forward, Lluava had no time to slow down or veer sideways as a lasso flew up at her from a gap in the earth. Her body jerked as the cord snapped tautly. In an instant, she sprawled on the ground, half off the ledge. Neck throbbing, she shifted to her human form so that her smaller body could slip the noose. But just as she freed her head, a rough hand grabbed her ankle and pulled the rest of her body toward the edge.

Kicking wildly, she hit her mark with a loud cracking sound. The injured man cried out and released her. As Lluava hoisted herself back upon high ground, a bleeding mass of shattered nose and its attached face emerged from the ravine. Enraged, the burly Raider lurched up and desperately tried to grab hold of the creature who had so defiled him. Lluava squealed as the brute laid hold once more. This time, he was prepared for her thrashing feet. The man was clearly too strong for her to pull away, despite her struggles.

Just then, several small flying projectiles impaled the flesh of Lluava's foe. One dug into the front of his jaw; others sank into the crusting mass of the nose; yet another pierced his bulging left eye. The grip on Lluava's leg slackened as the warrior's lifeless body slipped back down into the natural grave. Lluava tried to spot her rescuer, but no one was there. It didn't matter; she knew who it was.   Getting up, she thought, I'll thank Yamir later.

Throwing quills! I never knew he could do that.

Nearby, a horse screeched in terror. Glancing down and back, Lluava caught sight of Varren and his injured steed in the ravine that split the ground next to her. His mount galloped toward Lluava, the beast half mad with fear and pain. A spear's broken shaft had buried itself deep in the animal's rump; as it ran, the shattered end ripped through compacted soil on the wall of the narrow ravine. A pair of Raiders on horseback were gaining ground rapidly; one bugled on a horn-of-war while the other prepared to throw another lance.

Lluava glanced ahead and saw that the two ravines merged to form a bigger gully. With only moments to spare, she began to run in the direction Varren was heading; she could not allow the Raiders to harm the prince. She was only a few strides away from the wider gully when Varren charged past her. As the Raiders raced by, Lluava reached the end of the ledge. With a giant roar, she vaulted into the air, shifting as she leaped. She landed on her mark—the Raider with the spear—and knocked him off his horse. He was dead before he touched the ground.

She charged after the second Raider, who was preparing his own attack. Leaping once again, Lluava dug her claws into the rump of his unsuspecting steed. The horse reared, catching its rider off balance. The freshly strung arrow, shot from the crossbow, barely missed its intended target and buried itself in the earthen wall. Lluava pulled herself up onto the failing mount and clawed at the Raider, catching his heavy fur coat. At her strong tug, he tumbled to the ground where she quickly slew him.

With the immediate threat removed, Lluava took note of how the rest of her comrades were faring. It seemed the plan was working; many Raiders had been tricked into the ravines and then attacked from above by Durog's men. Although skirmishes continued for several more hours, they were victorious, sustaining minimum injuries and almost no fatalities.

"Praise be to the gods," said Talos when it was over.

"I never knew you were religious," Lluava remarked when she saw Yamir make a sign of thanks.

"I never said I wasn't," was his response.

In the distance, a mournful cry rang out, followed by another and another until the whole forest vibrated. "Wolves," observed Byron, peering into the growing dark.

"Derrick and his men!" Lluava exclaimed. "General Argon and the rest of the troops have finally caught up with us!"

"Let's hope so," Byron replied, gripping the hilt of his sword. "Or else we have a pack of hungry, carrion-eating dogs on our hands."

Varren placed his hand on Byron's arm as an enormous ebony wolf leaped from the dark and shifted before them. Blood stained Derrick's dark skin, yet his amber eyes were pleased. He spoke directly to his prince.

"Sorry for the delay. It took longer than we thought it would to break free of that rubbish." He looked over his shoulder as the approaching bulk of General Jormund loomed into view.

The elephant trumpeted, "Where are General Argon and the rest of your troops?"

"The grand master chief and the others will arrive shortly," answered Derrick. "We were asked to scout ahead for you." Derrick looked around at the fractured landscape. "It seems you also had a bit of a scrap to deal with today. Nevertheless, we are here now, and the grand master chief will regain command of all the troops immediately."

General Jormund snorted. "Sorry, I have dust in my trunk," he declared as he sauntered off.

Under his breath, Derrick snarled, "One should never turn one's back on a rogue elephant." Then he and the rest of his pack left to help tend to the injured. Lluava and her comrades were grateful for the brief respite.

Before the light of the sun had fully drained from the sky, General Argon and the rest of the troops arrived. Quickly the grand master chief surveyed the wounded and accounted for the dead. "We will stay here tonight to tend to the injured and let the troops rest. This will also give us time to send off our fallen comrades in the manner appropriate to each individual's traditions. When the sun rises, we will move northward."

No one debated his decision. Even Lluava was pleased that her fearsome commander was showing a compassionate side. He was not so ruthless after all.

Shortly after his arrival, Argon ordered, "Private Talos, come here. I've found something that you might want."

Talos and the others looked in the direction the general pointed and saw a lost-looking young woman. Her raven-black hair was unkempt and fell haphazardly over her thin shoulders. The nurse's gown she wore was torn and muddied at the hem. She looked like a miserable stray dog hoping for some sign of kindness.

"Rosalyn!" Talos exclaimed as he ran to her and kissed her on the forehead. "I am so very glad that you are safe!"

While they embraced, the grand master chief said sternly, "It is important to have a healer among us, Talos. You will be solely responsible for her safety."

"I will protect her until the moment of my last breath," he answered, pulling her close.

The troops made camp just north of the ravines. The Theriomorph and human corpses were buried in crudely marked graves, while those of rank were burned in massive funeral pyres. When these ancient rites had been completed, the solders ate their rations and dispersed to their tents. Lluava's group gathered by a campfire. They had had no time to relax and socialize for weeks. Lluava sat on a patch of ground. Nearby, Chat pestered Yamir, while Varren sharpened his sword.

"Is this spot taken?" inquired Byron playfully as he sat down beside Lluava. "I wanted to give my partner alone time." He nodded toward Talos and Rosalyn, who were whispering to one another, their heads close together. Byron and Lluava stared quietly at the dancing flames. Finally, Lluava spoke.

"Doesn't this remind you of when we first headed to the camps?"

"That seems so long ago," replied Byron with a small smile.

"Remember how you, Chat, and I used to spar together after we made camp each night? You tried to teach us some basic techniques of fighting so we wouldn't look like fools when we began our training."

Byron chuckled. "Do you want to spar—for old times' sake?"

Lluava's eyes flashed with excitement. "I'd love to! Of course," she said with a pause, "I've improved a bit since the last time we played together by light of fire."

"I hope so," he smiled. "Now I do not have to be so easy on you."

Lluava gave him a playful shove and rose to her feet. Byron followed quickly, and the two headed off to find a space. Lluava noted the unpleasant stare that Varren gave her as she slipped away into the darkness.

The pair sparred back and forth for some time until both were dripping with sweat and exhausted. By the time they decided to turn in, the others had gone to bed. Lluava thanked Byron for the chance to distract her from the grim reality of what had occurred.

"You have improved. I'm surprised that I even won a match," he said as he wiped the sweat from his brow.

"Actually, I was being easy on you," Lluava said, laughing, as she tossed away the stick she had used as a sword.

"Oh, really?" Byron retorted with a shove. "Good night, Lluava."

"Good night, Byron."

Lluava crawled into her tent. Although meant to be shared with a partner, she had had it to herself...until tonight. Wrapped in a blanket, Rosalyn was already fast asleep. Careful not to wake her, Lluava lay next to her friend. She had trained herself to sleep lightly; throughout the night, every snap of a twig or rustle of dead leaves made her wonder if it was the sound of an oncoming attack.

Chapter 30
The Therial Oak

Over the following days, the troops moved quickly. Their trek was blessedly dull. The grand master chief ordered rations cut in half to make them last until the army reached Fort Brinsdale. As the soldiers moved north, the forest thinned out a little more each day, although the trees themselves increased in age and size. Here and there, the still-thick canopy was splashed with yellow. At one point, Varren mentioned that the trunks towered like wooden columns reminiscent of those found on marble cathedrals from the largest cities.

Argon steered the army toward the coast, where they picked up one of the larger seaside roads. Now their speed almost doubled. Although the sun's rays were still blistering, the sea breeze made marching throughout the day more manageable. The grand master chief wisely allowed a midday break during the hottest point so that the troops could rest in the shade of nearby elms.

On the evening of the fourth day, General Argon summoned Varren to his tent. Lluava, as Varren's partner, was also admitted. As Argon was a man of rank, the moss-green tent was larger than those of privates. General Jormund and the other officers discussed matters in hushed voices. Lluava was quite aware that due to Varren's birthright, she and her partner were the only privates in attendance.

General Argon motioned Varren to join the circle of commanders. "I wanted you to be here, Your Majesty, since one day you will be the ruler of Elysia. It is not only right that you be invited to sit among the commanders, but also that you have your say in matters dealing with our actions in this war."

Lluava was not acknowledged directly. She sat next to her partner and tried to dismiss the slight. Varren did not seem to notice that his partner had been snubbed.

Turning to the others in the small circle, General Argon announced, "Shortly after midday tomorrow, we will arrive at Therial. We are running low on rations, so it is essential that we replenish our reserves when we reach the town. It is the obligation of every Elysian to give aid to the royal army in time of need. I don't anticipate any problems."

Lluava could not help but smile at the thought of a real meal.

The general continued, "The reason I have called you here today is to gain your opinions on our actions thereafter. We have two options. One is to take the main road inland, which, though an easier route, might delay us several days as it makes a wide arc to the fort. The other option is to cut straight through the forest and forge a more direct route. The terrain is not as level, so this might slow us down. Since our scouts found no sign of enemy activity along this road over the past few days, I assume the Raiders are working their way through the forest."

There was a pause as the commanders mulled over their options. Then Varren spoke up. "I believe it would be better to continue on a main road. I realize that the road inland will cost us several days at most, but we move quickly when on a well-trodden path. Also, we would have the option to rest and replenish supplies at one of the nearby villages. We would not have to worry so much about our reserves."

Argon nodded his agreement. General Jormund, however, frowned. "I hate to be the one to disagree with our soon-to-be sovereign," he grunted, "but I believe the straightest path is the most ideal in our situation. We are not unfamiliar with marching through forest terrain, and every day and hour we save could be essential to our mission. Furthermore, traveling on a main road could make us an easy target for a band of Raiders hiding in the woods. Moreover, this part of the kingdom is notorious for nomadic bandits who attack travelers on the roads. We are much more skilled than they are, so I am not too concerned about them, but, again, any inconvenience that affects us could affect the outcome of this operation."

Looking between the two, the grand master chief scratched his graying head. Turning to the future king, he inquired, "Do you have a preference, Your Majesty?"

Without a pause, Varren replied, "I trust your opinion."

Looking around the room once more, General Argon sighed. "Anyone else have an opinion to share? No? Then I will let you know tomorrow what course we will take. You are dismissed." At the wave of his hand, they all left the tent.

Lluava silently followed her partner back to the small fire around which her friends sat. Chat was using the embers that floated above the fire for target practice with a handmade slingshot. Yamir was doing the same but with a small store of his quills.

"You are getting really good at that," Varren acknowledged with a smile as he sat down next to the buck-toothed boy. Chat grinned, making his teeth protrude even more, and nudged his prickly friend.

"Yamir," continued the prince, "that is just weird." The coppery-skinned youth feigned a look of hurt before wandering off to pitch his own tent.

Still unhappy with her treatment by the general, Lluava pretended that the flames were more captivating than the conversations around her although she still trained a keen ear on her partner.

"Varren, you know a lot about your kingdom, right?" Chat asked, scooting near the young ruler. His pet raven, still bandaged though flying on its own, was tethered by a makeshift creance from one leg to Chat's left wrist. How Chat had kept the bird with him was a wonder.

"Yes, I do," replied the prince whose curiosity was aroused. "What do you want to know?"

"What is Therial like? I mean, I know we will be there soon, but can you describe it for me?"

"Sure," said Varren. His voice, assuming a storyteller's tone and cadence, changed subtly. "Therial is one of the oldest towns in Elysia. Originally, it was inhabited by Theriomorphs, long before King Landon and the humans arrived. It has changed greatly since its original discovery. All the old buildings have been either torn down or destroyed over time, except one, the church on the mound. It was built on the tallest hill on the outskirts of the city. The church used to be one of the Theriomorph temples but has since been rehabilitated to suit my forefathers' monotheistic religion…"

Lluava noted the particular terms Varren used when he referred to her race. He certainly was well trained in politics; yet the cunning of a snake would not ensure that a leader was a good one. The sharpness of these thoughts about Varren surprised her, but she could not deny her feelings. What had changed to make her feel this way? Why did everything Varren say or do anger her so much? He had seemed so kind in the beginning. What had he done? Lluava had no answers to her own questions.

"Other than the ancient church, there is another aspect which makes it a desirable place to visit. An albino oak stands near the front of the church. From the roots to its uppermost leaves, this tree is devoid of all color except a milky white that resembles ivory. No other oak like it exists in the kingdom. It is thought that the Theriomorphs, believing it to be a gift or a sign from their gods, worshiped the oak. I do not know exactly. I have to admit that I am not an expert on Theriomorph religion. Regardless, I must say that Therial is one of the most enchanting fishing villages in the kingdom. It has a wonderful charm, in part due to its ancient heritage."

As Varren described the details of Therial as he remembered them from his recent travels, his passion for his kingdom and his people was clear. Lluava smiled at the sight of Chat listening with the same eager attentiveness that her own sister had shown when her grandfather told his bedtime tales. At a pause in his story, Varren cast a glance in Lluava's direction with his amazing blue eyes. The moment their eyes met, a sickening feeling made her stomach churn. She stood quickly and headed to her tent. That night she lay awake sulking for reasons that eluded her.

Lluava's mood had not improved by the following day; in fact, it was just the opposite. Every little thing seemed to irritate her: Yamir's peppiness, Chat's aimless questions, Byron's cockiness—the list went on. She was annoyed at how little food she received for breakfast and was frustrated at the blisters developing on her feet. The worst was having to walk next to Varren all day. He had been given the chance to ride on horseback, but he let one of the injured ride instead and chose to walk by his partner's side. His attempts to appear perfect agitated Lluava beyond all else. Why did he have to try to be so faultless. Nobody is, so why did he have to seem that way?

When Varren attempted to talk to her, she could only force herself to nod or grunt. Eventually, he gave up and walked silently alongside her. The day plodded on with nothing particularly exciting happening; overall, this was a blessing at the very least. Instead of stopping for a midday meal, the small army lumbered on. With Therial so close, the group marched with an extra boost of energy. There was an unspoken eagerness to finally reach a place where they could eat and rest.

Shortly after the sun had begun to descend from its midday peak, the scouts brought word that Therial could be observed on the horizon. Lluava, like the rest of the troops, strained her eyes to pick up every detail she could as they neared. It would be so wonderful to be in a regular town and not another military facility! As if Therial knew how tantalizing it was to the weary foot soldiers, it allowed a glimpse of itself through the hilly woodland at one point, only to disappear at another. Finally, the troops reached the edge of a man-made clearing where a flock of dark, stocky sheep fed on the last bits of green grass in a yellowing field.

Orderly buildings appeared in the center of the clearing, and others spread out into the distance. Therial was the largest town Lluava had ever seen, actually more like a small city. The town as a whole encompassed several large hills. The houses were built of fine timber, with a few stone buildings here and there. Large, multistory homes, probably those of wealthier aristocrats, were spread over the hilltops. Closer to the valley floor, the houses diminished in size and character. A few tendrils of smoke floated from fireplaces, and a dog barked. Therial's atmosphere of safety and shelter beckoned the weary troops.

Excitement seemed to bubble over; almost at once the soldiers started chattering happily. It was hard to discern which groups were discussing food and which were talking about pretty fisherwomen. The men who so recently had been gloomy and sullen now smiled and laughed. Even Lluava felt lighthearted as they approached the town.

Before long, they were marching through the streets, shouting with joy. But their happy banter and cheerful laughter were quickly silenced by a sharp command from the grand master chief. Stilled, the troops quietly moved into formation without waiting for the command to do so. Ahead, Lluava could see the grand master chief giving orders to one of the lieutenants who began to relay them to the regiments. Since Lluava's troop was one of the first, they did not have to wait long to find out what was going on.

A swarthy lieutenant came up and briskly commanded, "You are to search all of the buildings for any sign of people." He then moved on to the next troop.

"He is right," observed Varren. "Where are the people of Therial?"

Lluava realized that they had not had a single glimpse of anyone as they approached the town. If this was the bustling seaside port that Varren had described so wonderfully, where were the people who should be going about their daily business?

The partners paired off, each pair moving to a house or building. Lluava and Varren headed toward one of the smaller shops bordering the central road. A wooden sign creaking in the breeze served as a swaying perch for a fat crow. Carved into the wood was the image of a wedge of cheese over the name *Crainer's*; over time, the paint had faded in the sunlight until it could barely be discerned. The front window display consisted of small wooden cattle wandering amid a field of hay. Each animal was hand carved, and each was different from the others. All were in unique positions: standing, eating, and even nursing a small calf. The charm of the display certainly would have lured plenty of passersby inside.

The front door was closed. Varren said he would force it open if need be, but it was unlocked and swung open freely. Inside, only the light that streamed through the front window illuminated the room.

"Hello," Varren called out. "Is anyone here?"

There was no response. Both Lluava and Varren kept their weapons at the ready. Once again, Varren called out, and once again, silence was the only reply. The two began to look around the room. Lluava moved toward the counter to her right. It was bare except for a scale and a platter with cheese samples displayed on an embroidered handkerchief. A pair of flies buzzed over the tantalizing treats. The shelves behind the counter held a few stacked rounds of cheese.

Varren had disappeared into a back room, and Lluava followed him into another dimly lit area. She could make out a butter churn, several cupboards, a stove, and a table with various utensils scattered on top. A sour odor forced her to cover her nose and stop in the doorway.

"What's that smell?" she asked as Varren sifted through the cupboards.

"It is coming from over here," he replied as he moved to one corner of the room, "There are several pails of—"

Varren jumped back, his hand reaching for the hilt of his sword as one of the buckets, spilling its contents, toppled over. The culprit, a black feline, escaped by running up the back stairway. The spoiled milk slowly spread over the floor.

After a nervous laugh, Lluava asked, "Upstairs, then?"

Pausing each time a step creaked or groaned, both moved slowly up the stairs. It was uncomfortably dark in the narrow passage. Upstairs was not much better. Lluava was thankful for her feline ability to see fairly well in the dark. As a human, Varren was not blessed with that gift; he stumbled into the single-room apartment and then almost immediately tripped over an overturned footstool.

The curtains over the small windows were closed. Lluava cautiously made her way across the room and opened them, allowing light to enter.

The room was small and seemed cramped despite only being sparsely furnished. A bed was pushed against one wall with a hand-stitched quilt folded on top and a large chest at its foot. A thick, woven rug had been placed so someone could step on it when alighting from bed on a cold morning. Only a common comb and a lantern whose wick had burned down to a sooty nub adorned a side table. A cupboard and two shelves held some plates and crocks. A table and three chairs filled what little floor space remained.

As Varren stood up and righted the footstool, movement in the shadows caught Lluava's eye. The frightened cat scurried under the bed. "Here, kitty, kitty," Lluava called, bending down to peer under the bed. "Come on, kitty." The words had barely slipped past her lips when a projectile of ebony fur shot up and over her shoulder and bolted down the stairs. She tumbled back, and her hand felt something soft.

"That's the second time that cat's caught us off guard," stated Varren, as Lluava turned to look at the object she had picked up.

"Varren," she said, "Look at this."

In her hand was a small rag doll. Its eyes were made from two different buttons, one wood and the other some sort of shell. The hair was a mass of red yarn atop a noseless face, and the stitched lips had a perpetual smile. What made Lluava's heart beat fast was the dark stain on the worn, ragged dress. She sniffed the air.

"Blood," she said, as Varren peered over her shoulder.

"Are you sure?" he asked. "It could have been made by something else."

"It's blood. I can smell it," replied Lluava as she carefully replaced the doll on the pillow.

Finding nothing else of note, they decided to inspect a dwelling behind the little cheese shop. This door was open a crack. Inside, the rooms looked normal enough. The kitchen had a large fireplace in which a cauldron hung. A few tendrils of smoke rose from the embers of a spent fire. Whatever liquid had been simmering in the pot had evaporated; the blackened and burned remnants of soup or stew had congealed on the bottom.

"They left in a hurry," Lluava added before moving on.

Each search had similar outcomes but no explanations: half-eaten food on tables, shops left open, estates abandoned. Only a few houses showed signs of forced entry. Household pets wandered the streets looking for their missing owners, but no sign of any person, alive or dead, was found. When all the structures had been searched, Lluava and Varren met with the grand master chief and reported what they had observed. Reports from the other teams were equally disheartening. Therial was deserted. The most unsettling news came from those who had searched the waterfront. All ships, fishing boats, and other vessels had been sunk.

"What made them leave so quickly? Where did an entire town go?" Lluava asked as she eyed a pair of crows preening themselves on the railing of a nearby porch.

"Those are the questions, but we don't have the answers," grunted the grand master chief as he brushed passed them, startling the birds, which cawed angrily at the disruption.

Sorting through his thoughts, Varren was silent for a few minutes. "If you felt threatened," he asked, "where would you go to feel safe? What place would offer an entire town shelter?"

Taking a moment to think, Lluava locked eyes with her partner and replied, "Those who were religious would go to the church."

"Exactly," Varren responded, then asked the grand master chief if anyone had investigated the church.

"Hm…no," grunted the general. "You two go and look. When I have everyone in order, I will send others after you. Take horses; it will be quicker."

Varren rode a speckled steed, and Lluava chose a small horse fleet of foot. They headed toward the hillside church that was built, as Varren described, on top of the tallest peak near the town. It was too far away for them to make out details, and some sort of smoky haze prevented them from gaining a good view.

They climbed at full speed until they reached the peak. The air was eerily still and held an undertone of something unpleasant. A low humming sound seemed to emanate from the hill itself.

By the time they reached the top, the smoky veil had disappeared, revealing a structure of massive proportions. Varren explained that the temple was made of a milky marble from a distant mine. A columned porch wrapped around the building. The front doors were of heavy wood and carved with intricate designs. Lluava had never seen a building so tall.

"My people built this?" Lluava asked, awed by her ancestors' skill.

"There are several other temples scattered through Elysia, but this is certainly one of the most magnificent," explained Varren as he, too, took in the amazing sight.

The pair dismounted and approached the structure. The closer they approached, the worse the smell became. A fly buzzed in Lluava's ear, and she swatted it away. Her stomach began to churn. The putrid odor became all but unbearable, and Lluava pulled up a part of her shirt to cover her nose.

The pair passed the open doors of the temple. There was no need to look inside. Instead, they followed the growing swarms of flies to the far side of the building. They turned the corner and stopped.

"God…" was the only word that escaped Varren's lips; the color in his skin seeped away, and he sank to his knees. At the sound, a massive cloud of flies, partially obscuring the horrid sight before them, rose into the air.

Like the skeleton of an enormous creature, the gigantic, bone-white oak filled their field of vision. Its base was so large that five adults holding hands could not have encircled it. The massive trunk split into countless branches that rose like beseeching arms to claw at the sky, and almost every twig had been stripped of its tooth-white leaves. Like a plum tree overburdened with fruit, its limbs sagged with the weight of its unholy bounty, the multitude of bodies that hung from the tree. The entire city of Therial—humans, Theriomorphs, men, women, children— several thousand in all, hung all noosed up together like murderers, their rigid bodies swaying in the faint breeze.

Chapter 31
The Mole Is a Mighty Animal

Nausea rose in Lluava's throat. On ungainly legs, she stumbled to the corner of the temple and vomited. On her hands and knees, she heaved and heaved again. After the entire contents of her stomach had been purged, she managed to stand. She wiped her face with her arm, but the bitter taste of bile still tainted her tongue.

Lluava's heightened sense of hearing recognized the sound of hooves, and she moved away to intercept the two steeds and their riders galloping up the hill. Dismounting, the soldiers approached, but she waved them away. She did not want them to catch sight of the grisly scene behind the temple.

"Go back!" she yelled. "Go back! Tell the grand master chief that they are all dead. Everyone is dead. Go back."

The disbelieving horror displayed on their faces was clear even at that distance. One made a sign of prayer, and the other, shaking his head in disbelief, uttered one word: "All..."

"Go!" ordered Lluava. The men still struggled to make sense of the news. Before they could ask any questions, she shouted, "Now!" They jumped on their mounts and rode swiftly back down the hill.

Although it took every ounce of will power to face that horrific sight again, Lluava knew she had to return to her partner's side. Varren was still on his knees with his shoulders slumped and his head down.

"Varren," murmured Lluava as she approached him, "Please get up."

Varren did not respond. He just sat there amid the swarming flies—eyes barely focused, arms limp at his sides, silvery trails of tears drying on his cheek. Lluava's heart ached for the pain he must be feeling. More importantly, she had to rouse him. Nobody should see him, their heir to the throne, like this, and others would arrive soon.

Softly she spoke again. "Varren, take my shoulder. Please, Varren…" Her partner's head twitched in her direction, but he made no effort to stand. Lluava maneuvered herself next to him and placed his arm over her shoulder. Slowly she stood up, hoisting Varren to an upright position. His body, although limp, moved freely with her. Now he was able to stand alone. Yet it was his eyes, the unfocused eyes of one lost in his own mind, that worried her.

"Varren, please say something," she implored, but no response came. In desperation, she slapped him—hard. "Varren!" she shouted.

Slowly he focused on her. Fresh tears ran down his face. He reached for her arm, and in a distant tone whispered, "My people, Lluava. They were my people."

Lluava longed to console him, but how could she? What could she say or do to lessen the horror of an entire city massacred? She felt utterly helpless. Gently she placed her hand on his. Averting their eyes from the image already etched into their hearts, they stood together in reverent silence.

Gathering courage, Lluava gazed upon the scene before them. Even at this distance, bloodied clothing and torn flesh were noticeable. These people had been killed before being hung like some monstrous offering to appease a bloodthirsty god. However, this knowledge gave little comfort.

Once again, she heard hoofbeats and voices over the mind-numbing buzz of the plague of flies. She did not look at the faces of the riders; the horror in their voices was clear enough. The sounds of anger, fear, prayer, and disgust were nothing compared to their anguished cries of utter despair.

The sight humbled even the grand master chief. After several moments, he drew himself up and ordered soldiers to gather wood. They would build an enormous pyre, one large enough to burn the entire town's inhabitants. Others were sent to the village to gather pitch and other flammable materials.

Most of the men had regained their composure, yet Varren remained unfocused and uncommunicative. Lluava caught the general's attention. "Grand Master Chief, please, help Varren," she begged. "I can't get him to respond."

Argon looked closely at Varren. "Take him back to the encampment and have that healer girl take care of him."

Carefully, Lluava helped Varren walk back to Therial. She would not risk his riding on horseback, but the hill was steep, and there were several narrow escapes when they almost lost their footing. Finally, shifting into her dual form, the giant tigress maneuvered Varren onto her broad back. Hunching over, he grasped her fur without conscious awareness as she carried him safely down the dangerous slope.

Lluava shifted again and attempted to hide the prince as they entered the town, but the majority of the army, who anxiously awaited orders, quickly spied them. She did not want the prince's condition revealed and desperately tried to shelter him as they were bombarded by questions about what happened and how everyone had died.

"We'll tell you later!" Lluava cried as she shoved through the crowd. "Please let us through! We need to find Rosalyn!"

Several men shouted for the raven-haired girl. Weaving around the soldiers, Rosalyn came toward them.

"I am here," she said as she approached. "What is the matter?"

Lluava looked worriedly at her partner. "It's Varren. He's...."

A quick glance at the prince was all Rosalyn needed. Turning to a soldier behind her, she asked, "Can you help me with that door?" She nodded at a nearby shop.

Lluava helped Varren follow Rosalyn. Once inside, Lluava retrieved a stool from the back room while Rosalyn began to inspect the young prince. As Lluava sat Varren down, Rosalyn gently shooed away the onlookers who crowded the doorway and closed the curtains.

When they were alone, Rosalyn said in a matter-of-fact way, "He is in severe shock."

"Will he be okay?" inquired Lluava nervously, noting her partner's pallid complexion.

Lluava's former bunkmate smiled at her and began to treat Varren. "Yes, he will be fine. It just takes a bit of time to recover. What exactly did you find up there?"

Lluava walked Rosalyn far from earshot of the prince before explaining, in as little detail as possible, their discovery of the horrible hanging tree. Rosalyn's pale skin seemed to blanch even more, and she wept silently as she listened to the tale. Lluava felt herself becoming sick again as she mentally relived the gruesome spectacle.

When Lluava had finished, Rosalyn returned to tend her ward in silence. Lluava tried to push the evil knowledge to the back of her mind, but over the course of the next hour, she had to repeat the story several times to different groups of questioning soldiers until the entire camp had heard.

As the afternoon passed, a sullen mood engulfed the small army. Lluava remained near her partner, who had begun to regain his senses. Eventually he waved her over to sit next to him. An expression of abject misery stained his face as the two awaited word from those at the top of the hill.

Shortly before dusk, the grand master chief rode back into town. It was clear that he, too, was weary and disheartened by the day's events. Ordering everyone to gather round, he made his announcement.

"Today," he began, "a discovery was made..."

"We already know," a soldier muttered aloud before realizing what he had done. The general's eyes paused briefly on Lluava before calmly scanning the crowd.

"I see," he said and then resumed. "Out of respect for all the lives that have been lost, we will burn their bodies in a fashion similar to that of our honored war heroes. In truth, I do not want you to be there to see this foul sight, but I will not prevent you from paying your respects if you must. Tonight we make camp here and start fresh tomorrow. Try to rest; we will need to increase our pace. Now, I am going back to oversee the rites of final passage for the people of Therial."

To Lluava's dismay, Varren stood up. She chastised him, "Varren, you are still weak. Sit down. They have things under control, and you do not have to be there."

He turned to her. "I have to be there. They were my people, Lluava. I was their protector, and I failed them. They should not have died and not in that way...." His voice began to break. Taking a moment to gather himself, he continued, "I need to be there. You must understand."

Nodding, Lluava said, "Then I'm coming, too."

The two partners, along with a few others, made their way to the top of the hill. A huge pile of branches and kindling had been placed at the base of the tree. The ancient albino oak that had served as a spiritual symbol and mystical site would serve one final purpose— that of funeral pyre for all of Therial.

As the sun set behind the trees on the horizon, torches were lit. Varren faced those who had come to observe this most tragic funeral.

"We are here today to send the people of Therial to their final rest. They were simple folk: humble fishermen, hardworking shopkeepers, dutiful wives, and innocent children. They were our brothers and sisters, people no different from us." Varren paused for a moment to regain his composure. "Their ashes will mingle together, Theriomoph and human, male and female, to be mourned together and remembered as one forever. I vow that a memorial to those slain in this heinous crime will rise from these ashes and will be erected on this site where so many precious lives were lost."

Although it was dark, Lluava saw Varren tremble slightly.

"We must ensure that these lives were not lost in vain. Therial perished under the malevolent evil that has descended upon us, those whom we call the Raiders. They are a ruthless people who care not if their victims be women or children. These marauders from across the sea wish only to destroy and conquer, pillage and ransack. We will not let them win." Varren's voice rose with assurance. "Shall we not show them that treading in the path of a tornado has mighty repercussions?"

A roar rose from the crowd.

"Shall we not show them that the people of Elysia are mighty indeed? It is our turn to strike fear into their hearts!"

Another roar erupted; several minutes passed before it died down.

Prince Varren studied the face of each soldier. "We will not forget the souls that we have lost. Let us take a moment of silence to show our respect for the people of Therial."

For several minutes, the only sounds were the keening wind and the creak and groan of rope on wood. When Varren raised his head, the torchbearers set the pyre alight. At first, the flames wavered; then the kindling caught, followed by the dry wood, until fingers of fire, turning all that hung above into a raging inferno, exploded into the air. It was truly a sight to behold. Yellow and orange blazed against white wood, and the dark silhouettes of the bodies were slowly consumed by the light. Sparks and smoke billowed into the night sky, and the smell of burning flesh forced many a man to turn away. As the oak was consumed in a column of fire, it served as a beacon to those in the town below.

In the darkness, someone muttered, "Have you ever seen anything like that before? The fire...it's unnatural...."

Another replied, "It must be a sign. The gods are angry."

Varren and Lluava watched in respectful silence as the nameless forms, contorting as they broke apart in the flaming jaws, twisted and turned in the fire's breath. When only a mound of ash remained, the pair returned to Therial and a sleepless night in which images of crows fluttered among the shadows of their minds.

Early next morning, Lluava found her friends talking in hoarse voices. It seemed that no one had slept well in this city of ghosts.

"How could the Raiders capture and murder an entire town?" inquired Yamir in a hushed voice.

"If you read the signs they left behind, it's all too clear," Byron stated flatly before explaining. "Many of the houses showed only a few signs of forced entry. The townspeople were probably warned that the army of Raiders was heading their way and went to the church for sanctuary. That was their fatal mistake. Instead of a safe haven, the church provided the optimum opportunity for those barbarians to corner, capture, and slaughter all of them."

"How can you be so certain?" asked Yamir.

"Again, all you have to do is read the signs. Before enlisting, I used to trap animals as a side job. Though I never was very good, it proved to be a necessary skill. With practice, I learned to read the smallest subtleties."

"And how to explain the crows?"

"What of them?"

Yamir whispered, as if to prevent unwanted ears from overhearing. "There are plenty in the town yet they stayed away from the dead. Not one bird neared the temple or that tree."

Byron hesitated, suddenly unsure. This was unlike anything he had ever encountered. "I...um...," he fumbled.

"Maybe there were none around," said Chat, trying to help him out.

"They are here. The dark-winged ones have been following us since we left Durog. They know death is never far from a marching army."

No one else had an explanation for this.

From Chat's bag, a muffled "caw" was heard.

***

Not long after this conversation, the army was summoned in front of the tent of the grand master chief to receive new orders. He, like the rest of his men, did not dare sleep in any of the abandoned buildings in the town.

Their leader began, "I hope you are rested, because for the next few days you will be pushed to your limits. Our plans have changed. Taking the advice of General Jormund, we will no longer head toward Fort Brinsdale. Instead, we will follow the Raiders' trail in order to overtake them. I cannot allow what happened here to be repeated in another innocent village or town. We will move at a pace that may be considered unreasonable by most, but it is essential in order to catch up to the enemy.

"Before we head out, we need to restock our supplies. You will take what we need, and *only* what we need, from Therial." The listeners began to shift and fidget in discomfort. The general continued, "You must respect the town. If I see or hear of any vandalism, those partaking will wish for the same fate as those of Therial. You have an hour to gather what you need. Dismissed!"

Scavenging for useful items, the soldiers dispersed throughout the town. Lluava and Varren entered one of the larger shops. The tables inside were scattered with no apparent order. Displays of goods ranged from small wooden children's toys to clothing, lanterns, and oil. The wares of the well-stocked store overflowed into the narrow aisles.

Lluava's arm brushed against something soft. She turned to look at a pretty dress about her size. An embroidered floral pattern was sewn around the collar, and the short, puffed sleeves were as dainty as clouds blushing in the new morning light. How sad that these clothes would never be worn. No young woman would enjoy the warmth of the sun in this dress. No young man would see his sweetheart wearing it. Waiting for a customer who would never arrive, it would hang on its little stand. Lluava felt unsettled in this place that had once held so much life and now was only a symbol of death. It seemed Varren was thinking the same thing. Taking careful note of all that was around him, he moved through the room slowly.

They found the supplies they needed at the back. Varren began to pick up jars containing pickled vegetables and other preserves. He turned to Lluava. "Can you look and see if they have any jerky or salted meat?"

She nodded and turned to search but could not find any. When she returned to her partner's side, he handed her a tiny satchel filled with goods. She began to reach for it but then stopped.

"This feels wrong," she said.

Without looking at her, Varren replied, "They are dead, Lluava. We are not stealing or committing a theft of any kind. They are dead, and we need the food."

"I know...." She wiped her finger on a dusty counter. "I know it sounds stupid, but it feels wrong—disrespectful."

She watched as Varren pulled off the royal signet ring he always wore. Placing it on the counter, he said, "Our food has now been paid for." He looked at her. "Shall we go? We still need to find some meat."

Lluava began to object, and then stopped. He had given up something valuable and precious to him to soothe her irrational feelings. There was no need to say thank you; he knew she was grateful.

Not far down the road, they found a butcher's shop, and careful to avoid any spoiled items, they gathered what they needed for their journey. This time before they left, Lluava placed on the counter the few coins she still had from the sum her mother had given her.

Quickly checking a variety of shops for any other supplies they might need, the two continued down the road. Soon they ended up near the docks. Looking out over the sea, they spied the half-submerged vessels almost invisible under the water. Nothing but skeletons left for the tides to overtake.

"Let's go back," said Lluava in a quiet voice. "I don't want to be here anymore."

They quickly rejoined the troops who were rapidly organizing the scavenged supplies. As the hour ended, the army left Therial behind and began its forced march after the Raiders.

The drudgery of the next few days blurred into a never-ending cycle. The sights and sounds of the wooded trail seemed never to change. Lluava could almost swear that they were going in circles. Their best trackers were sent out in shifts to mark the trail for the small army. Marching day and night, they stopped only for a few hours of sleep during the darkest part of night. Although rations had been replenished, the supply was still small, and they had no time to stop for a proper meal. Lluava felt they would all go mad if this continued much longer.

On the third night, the trackers announced that they would catch up with the band of Raiders the following day. This bit of good news was unfortunately paired with bad. The Raiders would arrive at the coastal town of Ymen several hours ahead of them. They had to prepare for a gruesome sight. That night the army rested only two hours then began its final push for Ymen.

During the morning march, Lluava, thinking how much Chat had changed during these weeks, kept looking at him. He was taller and thinner now. His reddish hair had grown so shaggy that a couple of days ago, Rosalyn had insisted he let her trim it; it now fell just above his eyes. He was also quieter. Long gone was the curious, inquisitive little boy with the wide grin that elongated his protruding teeth. In his place was a quiet, meditative youth who had experienced pain, hatred, sorrow, and death—far too soon and far too much.

Had it really been only four months since this whole ordeal began? In truth, it was less than that. Just over two months in the camps and six weeks of this bloody horror. The draft had been announced near spring's end. What season was it now? Had autumn already arrived? It was hard to fathom how such a short time could encompass such a large change in a person, a group, and a kingdom.

"Chat, what happened to your cap?" inquired Lluava as she looked at the boy's mess of a head. His bandaged crow, perched on his shoulder, nibbled the ends of one of his rusty tufts. "You always wear it."

"I don't know," was his response.

Yamir spoke up for his friend. "It disappeared several days ago."

"I don't need it anymore," added Chat. "I'm fine without it." Yamir shrugged, and for the next few hours, nobody spoke. Although it was early fall, the heat was still intense; the troops needed to avoid the excess expenditure of energy. The sun was high in the sky when shouts were heard from the scouts. They had spotted smoke billowing in the distance.

Ymen. The name jumped into everyone's mind. Torrents of smoke at midday meant only one thing: buildings were on fire. The town was under attack. Hurriedly, the army pushed forward at a run. They did not want another Therial. Soon the first few structures could be seen, simple houses scattered on the outskirts of town. Sending up plumes of smoke, these had been torched. As the army neared the town, the smoky haze interfered with their vision and distorted the screams and shouts of the townspeople. The hair on Lluava's neck stood on end as the disembodied sound of weeping passed somewhere close to her in the drifting smoke.

General Argon gave the signal to charge and the army ran into the gloom. It was hard to see anything at all, much less to differentiate friend from foe. No one wanted to harm a civilian, but hesitating too long to discern Ymenite from Raider cost several lives. Others reacted too quickly, wounding defenseless townspeople. It was truly a horrible fight. Many houses, shops, and other structures were ablaze. The Raiders attacked townspeople indiscriminately. Desperately trying to douse the flames with buckets of water, a few brave folk risked attack by the helmeted enemy. The army— which would become known as Durog's Legion—ran, headlong and blind, straight toward the enemy.

Thick smoke filled lungs; dulled senses made eyes water. Breathing was arduous; one had to concentrate and not panic. Soldiers struggled to keep themselves from coughing, which might alert an unfriendly of their presence. Worst of all, the thick blanket of ash made it easy to become separated from one's partner.

Not long after crossing the town's border, Lluava realized she had lost

Varren in the turmoil. Stumbling in the semidarkness, a form brushed past her. Lluava swung and sliced the air with the Claws. There was a scream. Between waves of smoke, Lluava glimpsed a woman holding a crying bundle in her arms. The frightened woman clutched her bleeding shoulder and ran off before Lluava could say or do anything.

Calming her racing heart, Lluava focused on her training and let her felid senses take over. If sight was not going to help her, smell and sound would. Moving stealthily in the gray murk, Lluava came upon a burly swine of a man restraining a woman by her arms, forcing her up against the wall of a building. The woman tried to yank her wrists free, but he held her firmly. Locking eyes with her tormenter, she spat in his face. The brute reached for his belted ax, but Lluava was quicker.

Transforming in midleap, the tigress knocked the pair to the ground with the Raider ensnared in a death grip. With Lluava's teeth at his throat, the attacker was dead before the woman had regained her footing. After gasping out her thanks, the woman disappeared into the smoke. The taste of the Raider's blood stayed with Lluava even after she had shifted back.

As waves of smoke blew past, Lluava made out bits and pieces. She spotted the horned silhouette of a Raider but lost him a moment later. Several times Ymenites ran past her or she glimpsed a fellow comrade, but for the most part, she was alone.

Pulling Rosalyn by her arm, Byron appeared.

"Have you seen Talos?" Rosalyn asked worriedly.

"We lost him in this cursed haze," explained Byron in a guilty tone. When Lluava said she had not seen him, they continued their search.

Lluava made her way into the heart of the town, defending it whenever she could. Even the smoke-cloaked Raiders could not withstand the bite of the Claws. As she neared a row of buildings, her ears strained to hear nearby noises, but the only sounds she detected were people crying out in the distance.

Suddenly she tripped. Tumbling to the ground, she found herself looking into the soulless eyes of one no longer in this world. She had fallen between the bodies of two men. The one facing her might have been the father of the other. His jaw hung loose as if he were trying to talk with her.

Lluava sprang to her feet, stumbled backward, and bumped into another lifeless form. A feeling of evil swept over her, and all she wanted was to escape. Not thinking where she might be headed or why, she began to run. As she raced through Ymen, she spotted more bodies. Thankfully, most were face down; she did not want to see their lifeless faces, their dead eyes.

Lluava ran so fast that she began to cough, yet she did not stop until the smoke began to clear. Through streaming eyes, she spied a large tributary, obviously Ymen's water source, and realized she was at the far side of the town. Quickly she slipped down the slope to the water's edge. The forest that encroached upon the banks of the stream shielded her from potential foes. Trying to regain control of her emotions, she splashed handful after handful of water on her face, but images of all those prostrate bodies continued to torment her.

A twig snapped, and Lluava looked up. Across the water, a man stood staring back at her. She recognized him almost immediately as the Raiders' leader. The enemy's sole commander was only yards away. After a moment, the man carelessly turned his back and disappeared into the woods.

Lluava could not let him escape. As commander of those bloodthirsty brutes, his capture— whether alive or dead— might alter the entire course of events. Shifting, Lluava observed her transformation between the ripples in the water—skin sprouting fur, bone structures reconfiguring, ears altering shape and position. In a matter of seconds, the feline, ready to chase after her prey, was swimming across the stream.

As she pulled herself onto the opposite bank, a familiar voice shouted after her, "Lluava, what are you doing?"

"I have to go!" she roared back. There was no time to waste; if the enemy leader escaped, the number of lives that would be lost would only increase.

"Wait!" shouted Varren as he scrambled down the slope. "Lluava, wait!" But it was too late; Lluava was already charging after the Raider.

Scenting a foreign, honeyed smell—the man's perfume—the tigress bounded after the Raider. Weaving erratically around trees, she was hot on his trail. The scent grew stronger, and Lluava picked up speed. Spotting him beyond a bramble bush, she vaulted into the air, ready to pounce on her victim.

The Raider maintained his steady pace. Without any sign that he knew his enemy was upon him, he grasped the hilt of his sword, swung around, and with unprecedented speed slammed the hilt into Lluava's head in midair. The blow knocked the tigress sideways, and she collapsed in a heap.

Sheathing his weapon, the Raider squatted down to look at her. Lluava struggled with her vision. Two of everything fractured into three while her own warm blood drizzled down her muzzle. The man pulled a dagger from its scabbard. His intention was clear.

Just then, an enormous roar resounded, and a massive mountain bear stormed through the briars. Quickly, the Raider stood to face his new opponent. Lluava could not help but smile in her felid way while a low purr rumbled from her sternum.

The most renowned warrior of Elysia was about to face off with the leader of the Raiders. Lluava was confident that General Argon would not only win but also triumph easily. He was the best, bravest, and fiercest soldier in the field. He was skilled in both forms, a magnificent force to behold. The tides had turned, thought Lluava; victory was within their grasp.

Then everything changed.

As man and Theriomorph stared each other down and sized each other up, the unthinkable occurred. In a blink of an eye, the grand master chief was hoisted into the air by a large ivory spear that skewered him through his torso. Behind him, the rogue elephant shook his victim violently before tossing him off the giant tusk. The monster trumpeted and stomped on the ground. In the next moment, he shifted into his most recognizable form.

General Jormund, grabbing his hidden javelin, walked up to the fallen Argon. Simultaneously Lluava shouted and the Raider leader commanded, "No." Lluava leaped to the spot where Argon lay in an attempt to shield her commanding officer from the traitor.

Jormund lit a cigar that almost fell from his mouth when he smiled. Holding Argon's wavering attention, he said nastily, "I want to be honest with you. I murdered Illena."

Argon lay very still, and, for a moment, Lluava thought he had died. Then she noticed the slightest rise and fall of his chest. Turning to Lluava, Jormund taunted, "I have a secret for you, too, but I will save that for another occasion."

The Raider gave the simple command, "Come," and turned to leave. Jormund lumbered in his shadow.

Chapter 32
Lost and Found

Once they were alone, Lluava concentrated on the injured general. There was no time to wonder on why they had been left alive. She tore off a portion of her shirt and used the cloth to keep pressure on the gaping wound. Blood oozed between her fingers as she willed her commander to keep breathing. Although the dense forest shielded them from enemy eyes, Raiders could be heard not far off. In their hasty retreat from the Elysians, a few Raiders almost stumbled over Lluava and Argon. None of this mattered now; Lluava barely noticed. Her whole being was focused on the heartbeats she could feel through the soaked patch of cloth.

She did not know how much time had passed before gentle hands pulled her aside. Rising to her feet, she watched as three Elysians hoisted Argon up and laid him on a stretcher. He coughed and spat blood. Numbly she helped the Elysians carry the stretcher back to the ruins of the town of Ymen.

When they reached the town, the two men in front led the way to one of the larger shops, which had been turned into a makeshift medical center. The local doctor ushered them into a back room. They laid Argon on a large butcher's table from which all evidence of its former purpose had been scrubbed away. The uneven surface was not ideal; however, it was the only available option, all other surfaces being occupied. The doctor insisted that they wait elsewhere while he worked desperately to save the general.

The outer room where Lluava waited was full of injured. Some lay on counters and former display tables, others on the floor. Lluava was carefully picking her way among them when she spotted Byron's familiar face. He was talking with an injured Ymenite woman in a crowded corner. His left leg, tightly wrapped and splinted, was immobilized. The faint hue of blood had seeped through much of the wrappings.

270

"Oh, Byron! What happened?"

Recognizing Lluava, he gave a wry smile. "While I was searching for Talos, a Raider came from nowhere. I jumped in front of Rosalyn, and the brute speared me in my leg. Went right through; didn't hit the bone. Rosalyn says that's a good thing, though she thinks it damaged my tendon. Might not walk the same way again," he said with a chuckle.

Lluava found no humor in the matter. Seeing this, Byron continued in a more serious tone, "At least it was me, not Rosalyn. I'd do it again. It's the right of a soldier to protect a pretty lady."

The Ymenite woman cooed, "You really are brave, aren't you?"

Byron turned his smile on her, and she blushed.

"Did you find Talos?" Lluava asked. "Is he okay?"

The young soldier pulled his attention away from the doting girl. "Oh, yes. He's searching for injured, I think."

"And Varren?" The sudden realization that she had abandoned her partner hit her hard. Her mouth went dry. Had something happened to him? Had she placed him in harm's way? First the grand master chief, then Varren—both people she loved. Did she say love? Surely, that word just slipped into her thoughts. Yet she did care for both men greatly, especially Varren.

"He's around. But I warn you—even though he's usually calm and collected, you sure seem to find ways to distress him."

Lluava left Byron to his unabashed flirtations and went outside to find her comrades, one in particular. The soldiers helped the Ymenites bring in the wounded, gather the dead, and salvage belongings. Some tended the injured, and others brought food to what was left of the army. As Lluava feared, their numbers had been greatly diminished; more than half of Derrick's troop had been killed, as had three fourths of Lluava's. The other troops had suffered similar losses. Only about sixty uninjured men were in fighting form; maybe twice that many had survivable injuries. She was grateful that none of her close friends had been killed; only Byron had been injured. Lluava helped pass buckets of water to throw on still smoldering buildings. Though the work was tedious, it kept her mind occupied. Varren was assisting, too, though clearly he was not yet ready to talk to her.

A group of townswomen made large cauldrons of soup with whatever ingredients had not been damaged or spoiled in the attack. Lluava tried to eat but ended up giving her portion to Yamir and Chat, who greedily accepted it. A bit later, Rosalyn, looking as if she had aged several years, found Lluava and told her that the grand master chief was asking for her.

"Is he....?" Words failed Lluava.

"He is stabilized for now," responded the other young woman. "He wants you to come to him."

As Lluava turned to leave, Rosalyn put a hand on her arm. "But,

Lluava," she said in a low voice, "He will *not* live."

***

When Lluava first looked upon her general, she caught her breath. His torso had been stripped of clothes and wrapped in some gauzy material. A pillow propped his head so he could look at those who entered the tiny room.

"Lluava..." rasped Argon hoarsely. "Come here. I wish to speak to you."

Moving to his side, Lluava concentrated on his strong hands, which lay folded upon his barrel of a chest. He appeared so mighty, yet so desperately weak. Carefully, she placed Issaura's Claws on a nearby table. There was a time and a place for weapons, and this was not it.

"I have a confession to make," began the once mighty general. "I have always mistreated you. When you arrived at Durog, so naive and excited, I admit that I wanted you gone. I treated you unjustly. Whenever you were in trouble, which you always seemed to be, I would give you a biased punishment, trying to force you to leave. But you would not. You are very stubborn. But you know this..."

Argon coughed. It was clear that the pain was unforgiving; however, he forced himself to continue. "I want you to know why I mistreated you so." He sighed and began again. "You are not the first woman to have trained in Durog. When I was a young officer, there was another. Her name was Illena Zethra. She, too, was stubborn and had a way of pushing the limits of her commanding officers.

"Illena was a force to behold. She was physically and mentally strong, smart, and had a gift for commanding others. She moved quickly up the ranks to sergeant. And she was beautiful.

"We were to be wed that summer. Several of us were sent on a routine march through the Outlands. This was during the time when nomadic bands of people often crossed our kingdom's southern borders to escape the desert heat. One of the bands attacked us. A skirmish ensued, and Illena was killed by a nomad's spear while protecting our commanding officer. For years, I thought one of that rubbish had taken her from me, but..."

Argon's words faltered. Lluava had never seen the grand master chief's emotions catch up with him before. She waited silently until he was ready to continue.

"You remind me so much of her. Your looks, your form, and even your personality are so like Illena's. This was the reason I did not want you in Durog—you, who are so much like her. I thought I was protecting you.

"I want you to know, Lluava, you—like Illena— are one who has great potential. If allowed to train further, you might have become the first female general that Elysia has ever seen. I recognized this in you and pushed you to be great, but, fearing to show preference, I ended up being harder on you than on the others. Remember, Lluava, in order to be great, you must understand and follow ethics in war. Just as important, you must never leave your partner's side."

Lluava cringed. She could not help thinking that if she had waited for Varren, the general might not be lying here.

Argon grimaced in pain and continued, "I have seen that you and the prince are at odds much of the time. Whatever the cause, you must put it to rest. In order for you to succeed in your mission, the two of you must work together. Lluava, you must get to Fort Brinsdale at all costs. The fate of the country is in your hands."

With that, Argon turned his head to the far wall and whispered, "Oh, Illena." His breathing became inconsistent and, as Rosalyn rushed into the room, Lluava left. She heard Rosalyn call for assistance, saw the doctor rush in, but she did not stop. She could not bear to see her general struggle with his last breaths. Instead, she ran, instinctively heading toward the woods.

A dark rage began to build inside her; the need to cause pain arose. Anger and frustration mixed with the bitter taste of regret flowed into every muscle and sinew. She cried out in despair. Tears blurring her vision caused her to stumble and fall. Her insides churned, and she felt as if she would burst. Her fury built until she could no longer contain it.

At last, she stopped somewhere deep in the forest. There, in the cool quiet, Lluava screamed and screamed. She grabbed rocks and pinecones, hurtling them at the trunks of trees. Picking up a small broken branch, she slammed it into a white pine, leaving an indentation in the bark. Moving to the next tree, she repeated the gesture. As she moved from tree to tree, her branch shattered from the force. Looking around, she discovered that she had returned to the spot where the double-bladed battle-ax had embedded itself in a pine. The foreign metal seemed to shine even in the murk of the forest.

Attempting to free the weapon, Lluava grabbed the hilt and tugged. The ax did not move from its wooden sheath. Placing one leg on the trunk, Lluava pulled harder, yet the ax would not budge. Enraged, she yanked again and again, to no avail. Finally, she sank to the ground. Her hands still gripped the hilt so tightly that her knuckles were white.

She cried until her eyes hurt and her stomach went numb. The forest swallowed her sobs, which was somehow comforting. She lost all sense of time. She stayed there, in that position, as the patches of sunlight shifted and dimmed.

At some point in that surreal reality, a pair of hands reached out to hers. They gently loosened her fingers' grip, forcing her to release the ax; yet there was tenderness in the force. Her hands were stroked soothingly and then held. Her sorrow palpable, Lluava continued to cry. She no longer cared that Varren saw her misery. She needed him with her.

Leaning toward him, Lluava wept in her partner's arms. They remained there, just the two of them, as the crescent moon rose and cast its silver stare from above. All around, crickets sang and quieted. A few fireflies blinked. An owl glided silently past.

"Lluava," his voice softly said to her. "We will survive this."

"He respected me," Lluava said between sobs. "He cared for me, and I never knew. I treated him like...I reminded him of her."

Varren listened quietly, then whispered as he handed her Issaura's Claws, "You need to rest. Let us go back to camp."

Lluava was suddenly aware of her exhaustion. Her body cried out in weariness. She nodded, and they walked back to Ymen.

As she headed to her tent, Lluava turned to him. "I'm sorry, Varren." He stopped outside her door. "I know."

Next morning, the world seemed a little grayer. The soldiers took longer to awaken and ready themselves. The dead were gathered, counted, and, where possible, identified. The injured were under the constant care of Ymen's doctor, Rosalyn, and local volunteers. Lluava could not tell if her friend had slept at all last night; she suspected not.

Lluava walked down to the river and washed her face in the cool water. Collecting her thoughts and listening to the water gurgle past, she sat on the bank. The uncertainty of the road ahead was hard to grasp. Which officer would step up to command them? Would he be prepared for such a task? Would they reach Fort Brinsdale in time to warn them and spread word of the war to the other camps? And what about the capital?

Clutching her military coat tightly about her to fend off the morning cold, Lluava returned to find her friends fixing porridge for breakfast. Yamir interrupted his conversation long enough to hand her a bowl.

"We don't have many choices," the spiky-haired youth replied.

"No," agreed Talos, "We do not."

"What choices are you talking about?" inquired Lluava.

"Oh, yes. You were not here, were you?" noted Talos, brushing back his golden locks. "I just came from laying out the dead. All the commanding officers were killed except one, and he is missing. We have not found General Jormund's body, which means we have no leader and no order right now." His voice was solemn, and the others looked forlorn.

Varren had been standing quietly behind Yamir. "They intentionally targeted those of rank. Somehow they knew exactly who was in charge."

"Jormund's alive," Lluava stated bleakly now that her grief focused thoughts had lessened slightly.

"What?" exclaimed several people at once. Everyone asked questions: How do you know? Where is he? And the most serious question of all—what happened last night?

It was the last question that made Lluava's stomach turn over again. Varren remained silent seeming to have put enough together to guess what had occurred.

Lluava looked around at her closest friends as she began to relate the events of the previous evening. Their faces mirrored horror as she talked of Jormund's betrayal. They bowed their heads when she told them how she and Argon had remained in the woods until help arrived. On purpose, Lluava omitted most of what the grand master chief had told her as he lay dying on the rough butcher's table. She would not share what he had confided on his deathbed.

"So, Jormund could have killed the other officers?" The shock was clear in Chat's tone. His raven muttered in its avian way and scratched at its bandaged eye with its foot. The bird was the only one not impacted by the implication of the question.

"That could indeed have been the case," noted Varren. "However, we cannot be certain."

"Well, one thing still remains to be decided," said Talos. "Who will become our leader? We cannot stay here while the Raiders move on." The others nodded in agreement. "I think it should be you, Varren. You are our crown prince and will one day rule this kingdom."

"Stop, Talos. I need time to think this through."

"You have an obligation, a duty to your people. Lead them!"

"Everyone would follow you," Lluava commented earnestly.

"I would," Chat added, grinning.

"And you have had as much, if not more, training than anyone here," added Yamir.

Lluava stared at Varren. Why was he hesitating? His entire life revolved around honor and duty. Why was he holding back?

Varren looked directly at Talos. "You should lead them, not I. You are one of our most levelheaded strategists. You are the perfect candidate to step up and command the army."

The prince turned to leave. But Talos was not about to let his future leader escape his responsibility.

"No," said Talos firmly. "This is your right and your obligation. Do not turn your back on your duty!"

Talos had not intended to raise his voice, yet watching Varren walk away agitated him even more. He ran after the prince.

"Varren!" he cried. "Do not walk away from your responsibility!"

Yamir tried to calm his friend, but Talos shrugged him off and grabbed the prince, forcing him to listen.

"You cannot run forever, Varren. It is past time for you to make decisions and stand by them."

Lluava was puzzled by these statements. "Talos, what are you talking about?" she demanded.

"Have you not noticed that our prince has not made one authoritative decision since he arrived at Durog? He is incapable of making choices."

"What?" Lluava's mind spun to all the councils they had attended together. Surely Varren had presented some sort of plan or idea—at least once. Hadn't he?

As Lluava searched her memory, Talos continued, "This is far from the beginning. Whenever my family attended court, Varren was always present, yet he never said a word. When asked his opinion, he always found a way to sidestep responding or issuing any sort of permanent decree. He usually directs attention to someone else or says how much he relies upon good counsel and cherishes the wise advice of others.

"I have to admit that at first I thought he was a genuinely cautious, politically shrewd leader. But after interacting with him on a daily basis, I realize that it was all just a ploy to save face."

Varren shrugged Talos off, but was backed up to a tree and could not run.

"You see, Lluava," Talos finished, "If one never makes a stand, then one can never be challenged or proven wrong. Our prince is no more than a measly, pathetic little coward. He is a disgrace."

There was a heavy thud as Varren struck Talos in the jaw. There was a stunned pause as Talos carefully touched his tender face—and then returned the punch. Varren fell back against the tree. Twisting, the prince agilely escaped his opponent's grip and threw his angry friend to the ground. Talos rolled onto his back and gave Varren a vicious kick, tripping him. The pair rolled through piles of leaf litter as Yamir and Lluava desperately tried to pull them apart.

"Stop it!" shouted Lluava, to no avail. The two men continued to batter each other. Finally, Talos forcefully pinned Varren down. Both panted as they caught their breath. Talos, a sneer on his face and venom in his voice, demanded, "What say you, coward?"

"I did not ask for this privilege," shouted Varren.

Lluava was shocked; he seemed on the verge of tears.

"I never asked to be born to nobility."

"No one does," noted Talos with a touch of sympathy as he began to cool down.

Varren tried to steady his voice. "If I proclaim myself leader, those under my command can and will die because of the choices I make. One wrong decision and countless lives will be lost."

"I know," responded Talos bitterly.

"They will judge me on the decisions I make as well as the outcomes."

Talos loosened his grip on the prince. "Yes. They will. What we are asking of you is unfair—yet you are the only one who can do it. You are the symbol of all for which Elysia stands, and it is the faith in that symbol that empowers the people." Releasing his captive, Talos stood up. "So—will you lead us?"

Varren stood up, dusted himself off, and addressed them. "I do not seek power...but who else is there to take command?" He paused briefly. Lluava wondered if he was hoping someone would take up the responsibility forced upon him. Varren glanced at Lluava then back to Talos. "Very well, I will decide which course to take. Tell everyone one who is able and willing to fight, as well as the injured and the survivors, that their crown prince summons them here at noon."

With that, he walked away from them to be alone with his thoughts, to confront his fears, and to choose the fate of his people. Lluava and the rest of her friends did as their prince commanded.

***

The people gathered shortly before the sun reached its peak. Ymenites of all ages and genders were interspersed among the soldiers. Mothers rocked children on their hips, farmers left crops and animals in the fields, the injured leaned on makeshift crutches. Many swatted at small clouds of gnats buzzing around their faces. All waited for their future king to appear.

A few feet from the edge of the crowd, a crude dais had been constructed from fieldstone and remnants of burnt timbers. Talos and Yamir were testing its stability when Varren appeared.

The prince thanked his friends for their work and waved Lluava onto the platform with him. As his partner, it was her privilege and responsibility to stand near him. She respected his wishes but felt awkward and chose to stand in a corner in the back.

"People of Elysia, I, Varren Mandrun, sole heir to the throne, have called you here today. We have survived so many horrors. We have seen the brutality of the Raiders. We have lost friends and family, homes and property. One thing we have not lost is hope—a hope that not too far in the future, this war, a war that has infiltrated our peaceful borders, will end. In order for this to happen, we need strong defenders who are willing to risk their lives to prevent the Raiders from continuing their vile conquest. We must work as one to accomplish this task. We need a leader whom we respect and trust."

Several soldiers glanced questioningly at each other, although none dared speak. Varren continued.

"I have dismal news to share with you. Last night, we lost our leader, Grand Master Chief General Argon, to the enemy."

Gasps from the crowd could not be stifled, yet Varren went on without hesitation. "Unfortunately, this is not the worst of it. We had a traitor in our midst. General Jormund, in whom we had placed our trust and respect, has turned against us and is in allegiance with the Raiders. He is a traitor who has set us up and has more than likely passed on vital information to the enemy. Last night, in the fray, all of our commanding officers were systematically killed. The enemy removed our leaders in the hope that we will not be able to regroup and prevent them from attaining their main objective."

Everyone was deathly quiet.

"We cannot let them win. Our lives and the lives of our families depend on the actions we choose to take today. As your future king, I am assuming command of this army. The orders I give will be followed, and the actions I decide to take will be respected. Let it be known that the orders I am about to give to you are orders I, too, would follow."

Varren paused, and Lluava scanned the crowd. There was no sign of opposition.

Taking another breath to calm his nerves, the prince continued. "I will ride out tomorrow on the main road to Fort Brinsdale. Five others have been selected to come with me on this journey. We will require six well-rested steeds to take us on this journey. Our goal is to reach Fort Brinsdale before the band of Raiders arrives. Upon reaching the fort, we will warn the other camps as well as the capital of the Raiders' imminent attack.

"Derrick Urbane, come forward, please."

The handsome man Lluava had come to respect stepped onto the platform.

"Urbane is one of the most highly skilled recent graduates of Durog." Lluava felt a pang of jealousy when she heard Varren's appraisal. "Urbane will lead the remaining troops in three days' time. You will track the enemy and keep close watch; however, do not engage them. Since General Jormund knew our plans, I believe he will lead the Raiders to Fort Brinsdale to attack that outpost. If need be, you will stall their progress toward the fort. However, if Urbane decides to fight, you will follow his command.

"Ymenites, you have seen with your own eyes the wrath of the Raiders, and you know what they will do to your neighboring towns. If there is any Ymenite who is willing to fight, join us. I ask only for volunteers, for if you are not willing to fight, you will be of no use.

"I ask you who live here to continue to help our army until they depart. Finally, tonight we will have a memorial ceremony for those who have died. Let us grieve as one people."

Varren solemnly stepped down and headed to his tent. Lluava followed, and he waited until she was at his side. As they walked together, Varren said, "Lluava, I have something I would like to ask you."

"Yes?"

"Would you do the honor of lighting the fire for General Argon's pyre?"

Lluava had not expected this request. She was unaware that her lips moved as she thought it through.

"You do not have to do it," Varren continued, seeming to read her pain. "I just thought…"

"No, I'll do it," said Lluava, through trembling lips. Without looking at her partner, she sensed him stepping closer. She quickly realized Varren was the one person around whom she could not feign strength. If he even touched her, she might break down again as she had in the woods. She turned away, saying, "I'm going to see if Rosalyn needs help."

That evening, lanterns illuminated the main road leading to the field where the dead had been laid. The fertile ground where cattle had grazed only days ago was now tilled, turned into a massive gravesite for Ymen. Men and women had worked without sleep to identify and bury the dead. Each mound had a handcrafted stake with name, age, and status inscribed on it to serve until the stonemason could create permanent markers. For those of rank from the Elysian army, pyres had been erected. The soldier's rank was indicated by the height of the pyre. General Argon's pyre was the tallest and was centered in a semicircle of deceased officers.

Even though the ceremony had begun, Lluava did not dare approach the body of her former commanding officer. Varren had arranged the rites to include rituals incorporating both human and Theriomorph customs. Yemen's priest entreated the humans' god with prayer and vows to allow these souls entry to heaven. The eldest Theriomorphs wore customary cloaks of brilliant colors and chanted to their own gods, especially Nott, the goddess of death. There were dances and song, eulogies and prayer. When the sliver of moon clawed at the night, Varren gave the signal to ignite the pyres.

Custom required the highest rank to be honored first. Lluava lit a great torch from the fire pit centered within the semicircle of dead. Holding the writhing flames away from her so as not to be overcome by the heat, she slowly moved toward the body of her commander. When the light was near enough to illuminate the form, Lluava looked once more upon the figure she now held dear to her heart. He appeared almost as he had when she first met him—hair shaved close to his scalp, the lines of his chiseled physique visible through his clothing. This time, his face held no scowl but rather an expression of calm.

Lluava could hold back her tears no longer. She tried to hide them as she wiped them away. She reached out toward the departed general but pulled her hand back quickly. Her eyesight blurred even more, and she felt herself trembling.

Suddenly a hand was laid over hers, a body pressed close; she felt soft breath on the back of her neck. Lluava let her arm be lowered toward the bundles of wood until the torch's fire began its hungry ravaging, growing stronger as it fed on its new sustenance. She stood watching the blinding heat consume the base that held the platform and the body. She stared as the flames covered the form until only the face remained, haloed in the blazing light. Finally, she turned away, and Varren led her past the other flaming pyres, past the wall of mourners, past the dying lanterns until they reached their encampment.

Exhausted physically and emotionally, Lluava shut her eyes and drifted off into the numbing land of sleep. Varren's words barely registered, "Be rested, for we leave at dawn."

***

The next three days served as break from the struggles of warfare. Lluava had been happy that, of all the wonderful warriors who had survived the battle at Ymen, Varren had chosen her four friends to ride with them. Had he picked them to please her?

When she asked, he replied, "I chose Talos because he has the potential to become a great tactician and because his counsel is invaluable to me. Rosalyn is a healer; we may have need of her. Yamir is not only a skilled fighter but also a decent tracker and, without Byron, these skills are needed. You are my partner, but you are also the best warrior in our troops."

"What about Chat? Why did you pick him?" asked Lluava incredulously.

"Chattern, come here," commanded Varren. The boy rode up to them, although his steed shied away. Even though his mount was only a large pony, he still had a little trouble controlling it.

"Show Lluava what you can do," Varren ordered the youth in a friendly manner.

"Now?" asked wide-eyed boy.

"Yes."

"Okay." The ruddy-haired boy turned to Lluava and asked, "Can you hold my reins?"

As soon as Lluava had a grip on the leather, Chat shifted, becoming the little red squirrel. He leapt off the pony and bounded to a nearby tree. Lluava could hear the small rodent leaping from tree to tree. When the squirrel was far ahead of the group, he began to chatter a warning call. Soon the whole forest was filled with screeching squirrels.

"As you can see, or rather hear, Chat is our alarm system. He will alert us if any Raiders are nearby." Varren smiled. "Thus the reason we need him."

"Huh," grunted Lluava, still wondering what other reasons might underlie his decision. If Byron had not been injured would he have been selected as well?

Using the main road was certainly more efficient than trekking through the forest. They traveled at a fast pace. As they moved inland, the salty taste of the air dissipated. The days were becoming cooler, and afternoon showers became a regular occurrence and thus the damp evenings made everything moist. Knowing they were only days away from reaching the fort, they pushed forward

It was early morning when the sound was heard. At first, they paid little attention, but as they rode on, it became clear that this was no coincidence. Everywhere the trees vibrated with aggravated squirrels. A flash of red fell from a branch and landed on the pony led by Yamir; the small horse spooked and jerked back with a start. Chat shifted form just in time to grab the reins and prevent his mount from galloping off. Wide-eyed, the boy blurted out, "There's a band of robbers heading this way. They'll be here soon."

"Are you sure they are thieves and not Raiders?" asked Talos as he and Rosalyn reined in their horses and moved closer to the group.

"They are definitely not dressed like Raiders, and they sure don't look like Elysians," huffed the excited youth.

"How many?" Varren inquired.

"I don't know for sure." As Chat spoke, his voice became sharper. Fright was starting to take over as he realized how serious this could be. "There were more than I could count. Let's just say they outnumber us."

"We have to ride. Now!" shouted Varren, spurring his mount. The small band rode swiftly up the road. Rounding a bend, Varren forced his horse to halt so quickly that it reared up, nearly throwing the rider to the ground. The others were forced to pull up to prevent themselves from colliding with one another.

A produce wagon was overturned in the middle of the road, and behind it were half a dozen armed men. Varren signaled to turn, but more men emerged from the woods and surrounded them. Behind the group, a score or more thieves rode up on small, densely muscled ponies.

Lluava heard Yamir mutter, "Oh, no," and Talos bluntly declare, "It was a trap." She tried to reach into her saddlebag for the Claws, but a burly man a few feet away said, "Uh-uh" and flicked a barbed whip. The ends snagged Lluava's arm, and he jerked her to the ground. She had to tuck and roll out of the way to avoid the hooves of the agitated horses.

A voice commanded, "Tie them up."

From her position on the ground, Lluava could not see who had given the order. Hands grabbed her roughly, pulling her up. She tried to break free until she felt the hungry edge of a knife licking her back. She turned toward her friends, who had also been forced off their mounts. A plumpish man with a purple sash tied around his brow began to speak—the same man who had given the command. As he talked, the excess skin under his chin twitched like a fattened turkey's wattles.

"Line them up so I can see them."

She was shoved in line next to Yamir. The fat man inspected them as if they were cattle ready for market. Lluava noted his darker skin, not as black as Ojewa's but certainly ruddier than hers. His plump face seemed to sag, and from under his sash a gold-studded earlobe hung low from the weight of the jewels.

Facing his new captive toys, the man asked, "Do ya know who we are?"

"Bandits," squeaked Chat.

The man made a distorted gurgling sound, which Lluava recognized as his form of laughter. "Bandits," snorted the man. "He thinks we are mere bandits." The man laughed again, and those nearby joined in.

"My dear boy," chuckled the man. "We're much more than bandits and common street thugs. We're members of the Cloven-Hoofed Clan, the greatest and most famous band of independents. We refuse the oppressive rule of the crown and proclaim the right of people's choice. Yes, we take what we need from those fattened on their birth privileges, but we aren't killers—unless we must be."

Ignoring the captives' scowls, the man walked down the line of prisoners. Lluava could smell the sour odor of garlic on his breath as he approached. She let loose a low growl, which made him grin, displaying his smokeweed-stained teeth. Lluava turned her head, trying to escape his raunchy aroma. When he reached Yamir, the man stopped abruptly. With a flick of his wrist, the bandits released the captive.

Speaking directly to Yamir, the man said, "Hello, Son." Ignoring the scowl on Yamir's face, he turned toward his followers. "It seems that our lost sheep has finally come home."

Chapter 33
The Cloven-Hoofed Clan

"Father."

That one word changed Lluava's entire view of Yamir. Looking closely, she saw the similarities between the two. However, although they shared coppery skin and slanted oval eyes, all their other features were different.

"Yes, Son," the man replied.

On behalf of his friends, Yamir implored, "Let them go. We are on an urgent mission. We must be at Fort Brinsdale as soon as possible."

"Mission?" questioned the older man. "When ya abandoned us for the tyrant's service, how do ya think it made us feel?"

Lips pressed tightly together, Yamir stood in silence as a crooked smile seeped onto his father's face. "Why, we felt pushed aside like garbage. An' after all we did for ya. Ya weren't easy to raise, my young child."

Exasperated, Yamir raised his voice. "Don't you understand? The enemy of the king is our enemy, too! If they conquer this land, they won't take too kindly to us!"

"Oh, Yamir," sighed the mammoth man. "We've lived like this since the beginning. Kings old and new have tried to thwart our lifestyle, but they always fail. This is the way it's been, an' this is the way it'll stay."

"But the Raiders are different. They are stronger and…"

"Hush!" barked the big man, cutting Yamir off. The muscles in Yamir's jaw twitched as he forced himself to hold his tongue.

The large man began again in a calmer manner. "Yamir, you are my son and always will be. You're young, and your ideologies have only begun to take form. What kind of father would I be to keep his own child from chasing his dream? I'll let your friends go if ya stay with us tonight."

As his father turned away, Yamir sent an apologetic glance in Lluava's direction. Suddenly, a dark sack was thrust over her head and secured. She heard Rosalyn cry out.

"Don't fight—it will be okay. Just do what they ask," shouted Yamir.

Trapped in darkness, Lluava allowed herself to be led to a horse and thrown onto it. She barely had time to balance herself when the animal left the road in a trot.

They traveled for some time before the horse halted. Lluava was pulled off the horse, steadied, and freed from the sack. They were in a large clearing in the forest. Talos was helping Rosalyn from her mount; Varren was scanning their surroundings with Chat at his side.

Lluava took note of the strange encampment. Traveling wagons were arranged in a circle, some covered in brightly dyed cloth, others open to the sky. Half a dozen were entirely enclosed on three sides, with bars on the fourth. Lluava's first impression of cages on wheels was exactly right, for each wagon held a rare form of wildlife. A bonfire, presumably from the night before, still burned in the center of the circle. A pair of women tended the flames, while others roasted a wild boar on a spit.

All around them, people stared, peering out from makeshift tents and the curtains of wagons. Several ragged children stopped playing with an inflated pig's bladder to inspect the newcomers.

Every person was dark-skinned, though not completely black. Most had slanted, oval eyes and smooth, hairless features. They all seemed to have either a plethora of piercings or large, elaborate tattoos on their bodies; a few had decorative scars from homemade brands. Their dark hair was unusually styled; some had short spikes, like Yamir, or one long strip of hair that stuck up in the middle of the head. Others grew their hair long and had woven bits of colored cloth or bright feathers into it. Many wore once-fine garments, now several decades old. Although he sported a new outfit, one man in his mid-thirties seemed to have deliberately shredded the edges. Overall, they seemed a disheveled lot.

Lluava studied Yamir as he chatted with two fellows his own age. She realized his eccentric behavior and unique appearance fit in perfectly with the members of the Cloven-Hoofed Clan. There was an odd sense of belonging in the way he stood and moved and conversed with the others. He was as much a part of the scenery as the clan members around him.

Noticing Lluava's gaze, Yamir turned toward her. He took leave of his brethren and made his way to her side.

"Why didn't you tell us about your family?" asked Lluava when he was within earshot.

"Didn't see the need," he answered tersely. Realizing that she had touched a tender spot, she left it at that.

Yamir led his friends beyond the circle of wagons to a clearing just large enough to allow them to make camp. They did not need to build a fire since they were guests of the clan that night. After pitching their tents and tethering their horses to graze, the group split apart to explore the vagabond village.

Lluava wandered toward the wheeled cages. What she found was pitiful. One held a pair of flea-infested wolves whose only interest was to gnaw at their tiny tormentors. Another imprisoned a tawny mountain cat whose skin stretched tautly over its bony skeleton. Its hollow eyes stared blankly at the far wall. The poor animal did not even lift its head as Lluava approached; the only sign of life was the steady rise and fall of its rib cage. In the last cage was a small valley bear, its dusty fur patchy from mange. Fur from its snout had fallen out, as had half of its teeth. Its mouth hung loose as if it were panting, and its pale tongue draped over one side. One forepaw was held up at an unnatural angle. Like the other animals, it wore a heavy iron collar around its neck. The weight of the piece forced its head to hang low. The animal's sad eyes caught her own, pleading for release. Lluava absentmindedly reached her hand between the bars, and the bear limped forward.

"I'd pull my hand back if I was ya," a dry voice warned. "He likes a fresh catch."

As Lluava retracted her hand, a lanky man stepped out from the shadows between two of the cages. He must have seen Lluava start, for a thin smile twisted his bristly face. He nodded at the bear.

"He's one of our main attractions. Him and Grandmother. He dances, ya see."

"It would be hard to dance with a hurt paw," replied Lluava cynically.

The man's smile grew wider, which angered her. "You'll see tonight how good he dances." He slipped his hands into his coat pockets. The tattered material barely held as he did so.

"No, thanks," Lluava responded.

As she turned to leave, the man called out, "Then ya should pay a visit to Grandmother. It'd be worth your while."

Lluava quickly moved away from the cages; she did not need to look to know the man was smirking at her.

Away from the animal keeper, Lluava watched the children play in the inner circle of the caravan. The shirtless young boys concentrated on their ball-kicking game. It had some similarities to castle crashers, her favorite childhood sport. One of the boys asked if she would like to join in, and, after listening to a brief explanation of the rules, she was running after the ball with the rest of them. Soon she was laughing and giggling along with the youngsters. At one point, she kicked the ball a bit too hard, and it skidded off toward the wagons. She and one of the youths ran after it.

Lluava spied the inflated bladder resting by the makeshift stairs of a faded red wagon. The boy who had come with her halted and told to her to leave it be. Laughing, Lluava went to collect the toy.

The boy called out, "Grandmother might get mad."

"And why would she do that?" Lluava asked as she bent down to pick up the ball. When she turned around, the boy had vanished.

"Hey!" she called, but there was no sign of the child.

A crackling voice behind her made Lluava spin on her heels. "Come in, dear girl," said an elderly woman.

She was *very* old—older than anyone Lluava had ever seen. Her small face was host to countless wrinkles. Thin hair trailed like silver snakes down her back, almost touching the ground. A milky film covered her sightless eyes. Knobby fingers waved Lluava forward; for some reason, she followed the old woman into the dark wagon.

In the gloom, a few flickering candle stubs placed here and there emitted enough dull light to illuminate untidy bundles of dried herbs and jars. Lluava did not want to think about what they might contain. The woman led her to a small, square table at one side of the wagon and then motioned her to sit down on a tiny wooden stool. The woman sat on a small bed that served as the other chair for the table.

Running her fingers over the midnight-blue tablecloth, Lluava inquired, "Are you Grandmother?"

"That is what they call me."

Lluava paused for a moment. "What do you want of me?"

"That is not the right question," said the woman in her cracked voice.

"What do you mean?" asked Lluava, confused.

With a smile almost as toothless as that of the caged bear, the old crone asked, "What is it you want to know?" Then, without waiting for a response, she said, "Give me your hands."

Hesitantly, Lluava slid her hands across the table into the elder's surprisingly strong grasp.

"Ah, yes," crooned Grandmother as she traced the lines on Lluava's palms. "It is touching how much you miss your family, especially your little sister. It is odd that ya refer to her by her dual form—but not so unusual."

Lluava gasped. "How do you know that?"

"Why, ya told me so," said the peculiar woman, turning Lluava's hands over. Lluava wanted to inquire further but held her tongue as the Grandmother began to speak again.

"You have been through much since your small-town days. You've seen great loss and questioned many things. You're hesitant to place your trust in any particular belief or any particular person. Ya care for many, but there is one you seek affection from the most. Yet ya fear what ya crave."

That was too much. Lluava tersely demanded, "What do you mean?"

"Sweet girl," hummed the elder. "I did not mean to fluster ya. I am simply stating the facts as they are presented. Maybe you'd rather know what lies in the future rather than what ya should already know."

"*My* future?" the question slipped past Lluava's lips before she could conceal her interest. Had not Gramps warned her about dealings with fortune-tellers? Had he not told her to stay away, that the future was not meant to be known?

Lluava rose to leave, but the strange woman gripped her hands forcefully. She inspected Lluava's palms again and hissed, "Don't ya want to know how the war will end and where you will be in the years to come?"

"No," said Lluava, surprised at the meekness in her voice as she tried to jerk her hands free.

"Don't ya want to know which of your friends will die?" hissed the woman.

Lluava paused. "Die?" she whispered.

Grandmother's long nails dug into Lluava's palms, and the woman spoke again almost gleefully. "Yes. One whom you hold dear is doomed to fall within a fortnight. And you, Lluava, you will send him to his death."

At those words, Lluava yanked herself free of the unearthly grasp, knocking over the little stool as she stumbled through the gloom to the door. Reaching the open air, she thought she heard the old woman laugh.

Outside, the sun began to set; long shadows stretched across the ground. Without hesitation, Lluava raced toward the encampment. Turning a corner, she almost slammed into Varren who was staring at the bear.

Trying to avoid a collision, Lluava skidded and fell over backward. Grasping her arm, Varren pulled her to her feet. "Are you okay?"

"Do you believe in fortune-tellers' prophecies?" she asked.

"What?" Varren smiled, almost bemused. He did have a wonderful smile.

"Do you believe in fortune-tellers' prophecies?"

"I believe that people make their own futures. Those who listen to false prophets believe in it so much that they begin looking for any sign that the fortune is true. Often they end up causing the very thing they were told or warned about. I believe that fortune-tellers play with people's minds, nothing more."

"But that grandmother lady," Lluava whispered.

Varren chuckled. "I would not place my faith in people whose life's work is cheating others out of their money. People who like hearing their fortunes sooner or later become addicted to it. And that is how caravans like this one survive."

"She seemed to know so much." Lluava felt herself blush in embarrassment.

"None of it is true," Varren confidently replied. "Come. It is almost dinnertime."

As Varren led the way through the jumble of wagons, Lluava could only think, What if it is? And what if it's you?

When the last rays of light began to fade, the feast began. Wide dishes piled high with heavily seasoned food were served to all the guests. Large goblets of mead were poured and kept full. Around the central fire, dancers spun and capered. Dresses snapped up around the women's waists while men leapt over the flames. Singers sang wordless melodies while tambourines clashed, lutes thrummed, and drums beat a wild rhythm. Halfway through the meal, fire-dancers performed. As the flames flashed and twisted, Lluava was amazed that no one set himself on fire. The sight was spectacular.

Varren, who conversed with Yamir's father on his left, was seated with Lluava on his right. The other friends sat together nearby. Chat had apparently done a bit of trading; he held a cage containing his large raven. The bandages had been removed displaying a face that bore an ugly scar and a blind eye. Knowing Chat was bad at bartering, Lluava wondered who had gotten the better end of the deal, but then her attention shifted to the dancers and the poor bedraggled bear that had been brought out for show.

The beast, obeying the commands of his keeper, stood up on its rear legs and hobbled around in circles. Suddenly, Lluava's view was rudely blocked. Looking up, she saw an average-sized man about thirty years of age. The expression on his face was almost a scowl.

"Ah, Thrane," said Yamir's father. "I am glad you chose to honor us with your presence. Thrane this is…what did you say your name was?" he asked the young prince.

"Varren," was the calm reply.

"Yes, Varren," said the walrus. "Varren, this is my eldest son, Thrane."

Thrane's dark eyes inspected Varren. "You look familiar. Have we met before?"

"It is possible," acknowledged the prince. "I have traveled the country thoroughly over the years."

"A soldier of the king," noted their host.

"It's odd for a human to be given a Theriomorph name," observed Thrane, continuing to stare down at Varren.

"My father named me thus in honor of your people," Varren explained.

Lluava could feel the tension mount between the two men. When it was almost too much for her to bear, Thrane turned toward her.

"And who is this?" he asked dryly.

Lluava could almost feel him staring through her, into her core. The feeling was more than unpleasant and made her squirm in her seat.

Varren began, "This is…"

"Lluava," she said. "My name is Lluava." Regardless of the discomfort she felt, she would not allow herself to turn away.

"Pleasure to meet you." Thrane's response was stark. He seated himself to the left of his father who had resumed his conversation with Varren.

Thrane chose to keep his thoughts to himself during this time as did Lluava. Preferring to take in the sights, sounds, and characteristics of these new people, she cared little for their discussion of the realm's policies. For instance, Thrane's short, angular beard was greased until it glistened, yet his father's face, with the exception of a few choice strands above the lip which had been allowed to grow long, was almost hairless. She found these oddities as interesting as the performance around the fire.

In a burst of sound and movement, Lluava was shoved aside as the panicked valley bear suddenly charged the seated guests. Varren pushed his partner aside, but then had no time to escape the rapidly approaching juggernaut. The bear lurched toward the prince— only to fall dead at his feet. Thrane's quick thinking and sharp dagger had ended it.

The animal's keeper wrung his hands and apologized profusely to Yamir's father and his honored guests. After scolding the man severely, Yamir's father dismissed him and gave orders for the bear to be removed.

As the sorry-looking carcass was dragged away, Lluava asked, "What could have frightened the bear so much?"

Varren answered but was careful to not look at her. "Some things are not meant to be tamed."

Yamir's father responded joyfully, "I'll drink to that!" Although the banquet resumed. Lluava remained uneasy.

Yamir seated himself next to Lluava after the third course. By then, the girl was fit to burst. She had not eaten so well in countless days. Lluava noticed that her friend's hair was not only spiked but also shone with the same gloss that Thrane used. He had also exchanged the wooden piercings in his ears with flashier studs of silver and gold.

"You look nice," Lluava said. She nodded toward the big older man. "Your father should be proud."

"Oh, he's not my father." Yamir chewed on a turkey leg. In response to Lluava's confused expression, he explained, "He's not my biological father. You see, Father is one of two people who govern our clan. It is a title, nothing more. Whatever Father says, goes. The only person that can overrule him is Grandmother. In time, Thrane will become the next Father."

"So if he isn't your father, who is?" inquired Lluava.

"I don't know," sighed Yamir, as he replaced the bare bone with a thick and dripping leg. "I was an orphan as far back as I can remember. Father took me under his wing, but I'm no more part of his family than any other person in the clan."

"What about Grandmother?"

"As I said, she has the final word about everything, though she usually prefers the solitude of her wagon. Actually, she rarely intervenes at all." Yamir took a large bite of the leg. Its juices dripped down his face, and he wiped them off with his sleeve. "She is the oldest person in the clan. Even the other elders claim that she was just as old when they were young."

"And what of her fortune-telling?"

"Oh, that." Yamir paused to remove a piece of meat stuck between his teeth. "People like to go to her to have their fortunes told. She makes a decent amount of money that way. I think she likes all the attention."

"But it isn't true, is it?" Lluava broke in. "I mean, she can't really predict the future. Can she?"

The silence that followed was the only answer she received. Yamir turned to the approaching food bearer. "Oh! Honey cakes! My favorite!" He reached over and grabbed several off the platter. "You should try one, Lluava. They're really good."

Still too full to consider the succulent morsels, Lluava passed them on, though not before she had seen the insignia pressed into the border of the tableware. The circular impression of two rearing stallions facing each other glinted in the firelight. Varren noticed it, too; his gaze lifted solemnly from the platter to their host.

As the fire burned down and the music ended, the clan members started to disperse. Talos escorted Rosalyn to her tent, while Yamir carried Chat's birdcage and steadied the rather tipsy boy. As Lluava and Varren prepared to follow them, the old crone, wearing a patchwork dress, made her appearance. She smiled a gummy grin as she hobbled past Lluava and bowed slightly to Varren.

"How does our lordship like our humble hospitality?" Grandmother asked.

Father wrinkled his brow. "I 'pologize," he said to them. "Sometimes Grandmother is too old to even know what's goin' on 'round her."

"Hush," hissed the crone. "Let our sovereign speak."

"I knew it," snapped Thrane. "You see, Father. We have led the fox to the rabbit hole. Now we will have to move again, thanks to Yamir."

"Calm yourself, Thrane," said Father. Turning to his guest, he asked, "Is this true? Are you grandson to the king?"

Varren curtly answered, "Yes."

"Then you lied to us," stated Father sternly.

"Tell me, sir, exactly when I lied to you," Varren responded. "You asked me my name, and I told it to you. I have answered all your questions truthfully."

"You said you were a soldier," sneered Thrane.

"No," noted Varren. "You said that, not I. And I *am* serving as a soldier for the time being."

Father grunted. "As ya say. But tomorrow ya and the rest of your party will leave this place as soon as the sun touches the sky."

"No!" croaked Grandmother. Everyone turned to her. "Father, ya will select a party to escort them as far as Elderdale. After that," her unseeing eyes were directed at the prince, "it is up to you."

"That is ridiculous," blubbered Father. His fat layers undulated like a turbulent sea.

Grandmother turned her sightless eyes upon him until he cast his own downward. "Ya will ride with them, too. An' ya will do as I say."

"As ya wish," Father acquiesced. He turned toward Varren and Lluava. "I will be escorting ya northward so ya will not have any trouble from other clansmen. At least until we reach the Elderdale split." Thrane at his heels, he hefted himself to his feet and waddled off.

With the mood of the evening tarnished, Varren and Lluava headed to their camp. Varren's own mood was as dark as the night air around them.

"I do not like this. Riding with bandits and thieves is not the way I prefer to travel, and, depending on their numbers, we could actually be slowed down at a time when every moment counts."

"I'm sure they're not as bad as you think. Look at Yamir, for instance," Lluava said, although she did not truly believe her own words.

"Yamir left them," said Varren. "And did you see their serving pieces? They are all stolen from raids on noblemen's caravans. That last one was Lord Bartlet's platter—his insignia was bright as day. I'll wager that was taken during the raid last spring when Bartlet was traveling home after a visit to the castle. He was injured in the attack although, fortunately, it was only a minor wound. I wish I could say the same for his guards."

Lluava, not knowing how to respond, walked the rest of the way in silence. Fortunately, the scene back at their camp lifted their spirits. Although Rosalyn had retired to her tent, Chat was still enjoying the results of the limitless supply of mead. He would not stop talking, although he slurred his words and could not stand up straight. Eventually Yamir and Talos persuaded him to lie down, and he promptly fell into a deep sleep. In hushed whispers, Varren filled in Talos and Yamir on recent events and warned them to be on their guard.

When the group resumed their journey in the morning, their numbers had more than doubled. The Cloven-Hoofed Clan had sent eight riders north with them, including Father and Thrane. Lluava suspected that Grandmother had had something to do with that choice.

The distrust between the two groups was evident. Chat kept close to Yamir. Talos did not let Rosalyn stray far from his sight, but if she knew the reason for his sudden attention, she did not let on. His thoughts went unspoken; however, Varren did not appreciate the unwanted aid and was unusually quiet. At night, the two groups, each within sight of the other, struck separate camps. Yamir was most affected by the tension as each group expected him to camp with them. Chat, however, was pleased with his trading, although his bird was less than thrilled about its new cage. Tied to the saddle, the raven perched in its new home that swung in steady rhythm with the pony's tread. The bird would mutter to itself until Chat dropped a morsel of bread into its cell.

At least the increase in numbers did not slow them down. The oppressive heat was abating, as well. Lluava did not know whether this was because they were pushing farther north or because autumn was almost upon them. Lazy afternoon showers popped up without warning and then dispersed just as suddenly. Although some complained, Lluava welcomed the swollen drops that splattered down on her head and body; she loved the feel of them sliding down her neck and chest. In the mornings, foggy mists, distorting vision, arose from the ground; yet, by the time they had eaten and saddled up, most of it had dissipated.

Only one thing prevented their travels from being ideal and put both groups on edge. Several scouts, including Chat, saw signs that they were being followed: a broken branch off the trail here, scraps of abandoned food there. Yamir verified that their unknown follower was alone. Whoever he was, he kept pace with them, making camp when they did and riding out as soon as their group moved forward.

The identity of their living shadow was finally revealed one morning when Lluava's heightened sense of smell detected a hint of smokeweed in the air. Although the clan members loved to smoke, they were not permitted to do so when on a mission.

"Jormund," declared Talos, scowling, when Lluava brought them the news. "Why would he be careless enough not only to follow us but to do so alone? I do not like this."

"Maybe he wants to kiss and make up," mocked Yamir.

"I don't think that's the case," Chat replied innocently. His bird cawed in agreement. Chat stroked its head, careful not to aggravate the scar that ran down one side of the bird's face. Its one dead eye always seemed to watch its owner. "See, he agrees."

Yamir smiled until Varren spoke up. "Unfortunately, I agree with Chat. A man as well-trained in the art of combat as Jormund would not make such a move without good reason. And now that he has been made an outlaw, with nothing to worry about but his own skin, he is one of the most dangerous people in the kingdom."

"Well, what does *Your Lordship* suggest?" asked Thrane sarcastically.

Father gave Thrane a dark look, but Varren ignored the jab and commanded, "Jormund is quite dangerous, so we must not let our guard down. We will double our night watch: two per shift. Furthermore, every night, after we make camp, I want a three-person team to scour the surrounding area for any signs of our dear friend. It would be nice to bring the traitor to the fort so that justice might be served."

"I'll serve 'em justice right 'ere," said one particularly swarthy clansman as he played with the tip of his throwing dagger.

"No," contradicted Varren sternly. "If we find him, we capture him alive and bring him to the fort."

The clansman dipped his head and whispered, "As ya wish."

When the groups reached the fork in the road for Elderdale and Fort Brinsdale, they set up camp at an adjacent abandoned farm. The clansmen argued that it was unlucky to camp so near a fork in the road and tried to urge them onward. Saying that he was not superstitious and that their mounts had done enough work for that day, Varren silenced them.

There was no house in which to seek refuge; the charred remains stood out starkly. A closer look revealed that the fire that had destroyed the house was caused by lightning, not by unnatural means, which eased everyone's minds.

They pitched their tents in the fallow field. Knowing that Jormund was following them, Varren would not allow the two groups to make camp separately. He had only to mention Grandmother's edict, and the clansmen silently complied. Several clansmen went in search of firewood and discovered a small abandoned barn beyond a stand of trees. There they bedded down their horses for a much-needed rest. Several of the animals were near exhaustion, and all had lost weight. A pair of clansmen were stationed at the barn to keep watch.

The horses were not the only ones weary of the journey; their travels had clearly taken a toll on Rosalyn. She had never in her eighteen years been on horseback so long in her life. She was accustomed to riding for pleasure, and her short jaunts through the woods at home were nothing like this. Her pale complexion seemed even whiter, and dark circles stained the skin under her eyes. She, too, had lost weight. But as far as Lluava could recall, the young woman had not once complained.

Through gaps in the closed flap of her tent, Lluava watched the stars turn. The cool air made her drowsy, yet she could not sleep. An unexplained agitation boiled inside her.

She rose well before morning's light as did Rosalyn. Lluava hauled water from the abandoned well and then stoked the fire and put water on to boil. Rosalyn dipped their stale bread in the water to soften it. Hacking and stumbling sleepily toward the flames, the men arose and then ate their meals and prepared for the day's ride.

As Lluava and Rosalyn scrubbed the pans they had used to reheat fatback and salted pork, Talos asked Rosalyn to accompany him to the barn to relieve the men and start saddling the horses. Varren approached with his own mount and Lluava's.

Moments later, a commotion was heard at the far side of the camp. They raced over to see what had happened and met several clansmen, their clothes bloody, hurrying back. Father frowned, worried; his son was not among them.

"Where's Thrane?" he demanded.

"Thane's dead," said one man, grimacing; it was the short one with the bulging eyes. "It happened too quickly. We weren't prepared."

"Thrane. Dead." The words resounded, cold as ice, as Father melted to the ground.

"How did it happen?" asked Varren, wasting no time in remorse.

The swarthy clansmen spoke up. "We were washing by the brook. Out of nowhere, the giant arose. Thrane led the attack but was cut down before our eyes. By the time we reached his body, the monster had vanished into the shadows."

Varren tersely commanded, "I want everyone armed and ready to fight. We have an elephant to hunt."

As they dispersed, Lluava spotted Chat by the forest's edge. "Chat! Warn Rosalyn and Talos."

"Right," came the faint reply as the boy disappeared into the forest.

She should go with him, thought Lluava. She started to run but stopped when she realized she was unarmed. Her partner was elsewhere. She hurried to her mount, reached into her unpacked satchel, and pulled out Issaura's Claws. Lluava had found it not only easier to travel with the Claws off her hands but also safer without the threat of accidentally slicing the lead or her steed.

Everyone was in motion. One person threw dirt to stifle their little fire; several others had mounted and now headed into the forest. Varren steadied his horse, which had become excited by all the commotion. Lluava hoisted herself onto her steed.

"We will scout the eastern edge of the clearing," Varren told her, pointing in that direction. He spurred his mount forward; Lluava dug her heels into her horse's sides and raced after him.

Only when they had thoroughly scoured the woods did they return to camp. The men were slow to return, since many had run off on foot rather than waste time saddling their mounts. As they neared camp, an all-too-familiar sound shook them to their cores.

Lluava slid to the ground and began to scour the area, yet all seemed calm. Leading her horse toward her still-pitched tent, she heard Chat's terrified voice shouting their names.

"What's wrong, Chat?" she asked as the boy, tripping over his own feet in his haste, ran up to them. Chat did not even pause to catch his breath. "The barn—an explosion—they're trapped inside!"

Chapter 34
Hunting for Ivory

The cool air chilled the sweat on her brow as Lluava rode wildly toward the barn. Her black coat snapped in the wind as did Chat's deep-brown one. Alongside them, Varren spurred his mount. In the sky, Chat's raven cried its ominous warning. Trees flashed past as they approached the clearing around the barn. Debris was scattered all around the surrounding pasture. Like giant lances, large wooden shards pierced the ground at awkward angles.

Dismounting, Lluava ran toward the collapsed wreckage. The explosion was responsible for more than one fire and smoke began to seep through crevices and openings. Fortunately, the flames were slow to take hold.

"Rosalyn!" she called. "Talos! Can you hear me?"

At first, there was silence. Then from somewhere under the chaos of broken posts and fractured wall, there came a response.

"We are all right," Talos's voice reassured them. "A beam is holding the rubble up, but the weight is causing it to bend. I do not know how much longer it will hold."

"Okay," huffed Lluava, as she peeled back one of the roof beams. "We are hurrying." Lifting another beam, she saw congealing blood oozing on its underside. She peered beneath a slab of wall and then quickly dropped the piece. There was no need for Chat, who stood nearby, to see the fleshy ruination that remained of his pony.

Lluava moved to another area where, with help from Varren and Chat, she lifted section after section of wall until finally a dusty arm shot up through a small opening and waved. Ever so carefully, the three of them lifted a large rafter off the wreckage, allowing some of the smaller pieces to slide free. As their work continued, several clansmen who had spotted the fingers of smoke came to help rescue their friends. Yamir, who was among them, worked to remove the gate of a stall.

Finally, the gap was large enough for Rosalyn to be hoisted out; Talos soon followed. Both of them were bedraggled, with dirt, soot, and blood coating their bodies and clothes. One of Rosalyn's ankles had swollen to the size of a large apple. She was helped over the debris so not to aggravate her sprain. Other than a mass of crusting blood at the base of his head, Talos was fine.

"Thank the gods," one of the clansmen said. The others nodded in agreement. Varren, too, bowed his head and whispered under his breath, "Thanks be to God."

"What happened?" Yamir asked.

"We were in the barn, saddling the rest of the horses," Rosalyn began as she sat down. Talos lifted her swollen foot and placed it on one of the shattered beams. "I was trying to coax a horse from its stall when I found a strange pile of what looked like black powder in the back corner. I scooped up a handful and brought it to Talos to ask him if he knew what it was." Rosalyn looked at Talos and signaled him to continue.

"When she showed me the powder, I knew what it was instantly." Talos's tone explained everything; there was no need for him to say the next word, though he did. "Flashbang. At that moment, I saw Chat running to the barn door. I shouted to him to run away. Everything went white, then dark. A sound followed, but for the next few moments, I could not see or hear anything. Honestly, I thought I had died." Rosalyn nodded in agreement. "When I realized I was lying on the ground and tried to stand, I found Rosalyn lying next to me. As I stood, I could feel the wooden encasement around me. Thank the gods my sense of hearing was restored, and I could hear Chat calling our names." He turned to his young friend. "Thank you so much for getting help. You saved our lives, Chat."

The boy blushed. "It was nothing," he murmured.

"No, really," insisted Talos, "if you had not been there, we might have been trapped until the beam collapsed or the fires consumed us. You have our greatest thanks."

Rosalyn added, "You are our hero."

"Haha!" Yamir exclaimed, mussing Chat's rusty hair and slapping him on the back. "Hats off to the hero!"

Chat smiled faintly. Behind him, Yamir blanched and quickly jerked Chat's coat aside.

"You're bleeding," he gasped. The hand that had patted his friend on the back had a crimson hue. Chat's brown shirt bore a large, dark stain.

"Why didn't you tell us?" Yamir demanded.

Looking down at himself, Chat weakly replied, "I didn't know."

"How couldn't you know?" Yamir asked Chat. Turning to Rosalyn, who was struggling to stand, he demanded, "How couldn't he know?"

Chat began to sink down. Yamir caught him and laid him on the ground. "Chat? Chat?" Yamir desperately cried out, "Rosalyn, do something!"

As everyone crowded around their injured comrade, Rosalyn ordered them to stand back so the boy could have some air. She peeled back the saturated shirt to reveal the wound. A thin, razor-sharp shard of wood was embedded deep in Chat's side, between two ribs.

"Pull it out," someone said.

Rosalyn shook her head. "If I do that, the wound will bleed freely. That is almost certain to..." She would not say the last words.

"Well, it can't stay in him," pointed out Talos, as he laid a hand on the shoulder of his betrothed.

Rosalyn's jaw tensed at the truth of the words. "I need strips of cloth and something with which to bind them."

Without a second thought, Yamir tore off his shirt and tossed it to Rosalyn. With her small knife, she ripped it into sections. As she did, she asked Lluava to bring something on which Chat could bite down. After placing the small stick in Chat's mouth, Lluava sat down and carefully took Chat's head in her lap. The raven, perched on a nearby beam, gazed worriedly at Chat with its good eye.

Rosalyn observed her young friend and warned, "This will hurt. Are you ready?"

Chat gave a little nod and reached over to grab Yamir's hand. Lluava placed her hands on Chat's shoulders to hold him down. With a precise tug, Rosalyn wrenched the piece of shrapnel from his side. Chat's body jerked forward, and Lluava had to use her full force to prevent him from moving the wrong way. She heard the wood crack in Chat's mouth as he bit down on it. Throwing the shard on the ground, Rosalyn immediately started bandaging the wound.

Lluava could see the pain in Chat's face. His eyes were closed tight, and his every muscle seemed so taut that it might tear. Brushing his long, rusty hair off his brow, Lluava began to gently stroke the boy's forehead and his body began to relax. His skin was warm and sticky with sweat, yet he was so very pale. She wanted to pull him close and tell him how proud she was of him and how much she cared for him, reassure him everything would be all right. But she could not bring herself to lie to her friend.

When Rosalyn was done, she removed the bit from Chat's mouth. He took a big, shaky breath and then reached inside his coat pocket. "Varren...."

The prince stepped forward. Chat extended his hand and dropped something small into Varren's hand. "Take this," the boy said. "It's yours."

Varren looked at the object in his hand. "Where did you get this?" He slipped the ring on his finger.

"I saw what you did back in Therial. The ring belongs to you, you should have it." Looking up at Lluava, Chat told her, "It's okay. I left my hat in its place. I know that doesn't cover much, but it's all I had."

"Oh, Chat…" The words got lost in Lluava's throat.

The boy took her hand and held it reassuringly. "It's okay." He took another shallow breath. "Can I talk to Yamir alone for a moment?"

Lluava nodded and carefully stood up. Talos and a clansman carried Rosalyn toward the campsite.

Chat clutched his coat tightly around himself. "It's awfully cold, isn't it?"

Lluava's stomach turned somersaults inside her. As she moved away, she heard Yamir solemnly reply, "Yes, Chat. It is."

Lluava walked to the edge of the woods; Varren stood at her side. She watched Yamir kneel down next to Chat. They were deep in conversation. What were they talking about? If only she could be there with them. Lluava knew they needed this moment together, a moment so tender and private that she turned away and cast her eyes toward the ground.

That was when she saw it. Leaning down, she picked up a blackened stub no longer than a caterpillar. When she showed it to Varren, he gave her a look of instant understanding. Then, with all her might, Lluava hurled the cigar butt into the dewy undergrowth.

When she turned to look back at Chat, she knew by the way Yamir bent over him that it was over.

"It is time," Varren said as he moved toward his horse. Lluava seized the reins of her own animal and mounted. Without a look at each other, they galloped off.

At first, Lluava did not know where to begin. The underbrush was thick, the trees densely packed. Yet she found it surprisingly easy to pick up the scent—the stagnant, sour smell of smokeweed mixed with the musk of the beast's hide. She forced all her senses to home in on him. As the distance between herself and her prey began to narrow, Lluava wondered if maybe this wasn't a little too easy. The thought made her more cautious.

Why would one so well versed in military tactics allow himself to be tracked so easily? Why would Jormund have left the safety of the Raiders' ranks unless he had a plan? Could he have gone mad? No, he must have a plan—some intention of which they were unaware. He wanted them to find him—that was the only answer. And when they did, Lluava had several questions of her own she wanted answered.

Soon the undergrowth was so unforgiving that they had to make their way on foot. Lluava shifted and was able to claw her way through the thicket. Varren hacked a path for himself with his sword. The scent grew stronger. Even without the capability to sense it, Varren seemed to understand that they were nearing their target. He motioned her to move right, while he circled left.

Acutely attentive to her surroundings, Lluava crept toward her prey. She glanced up each time a bird fluttered, a squirrel leapt, or a leaf wavered, as wary of the wildlife as she was of her target. If even one jay screeched or one squirrel chattered to give her position away, she would be in great danger.

Finally, she was there. Somewhere in the dappled shadows of the forest bottom, Jormund, the traitor, lay in wait. The smell of smokeweed was everywhere; in the still air, there was no way to know its source. Lluava would have to use senses other than smell to locate her target. Slinking from shadow to shadow, she searched but found no sign of Jormund.

He's here, she assured herself. He has to be.

Lluava inched toward another patch of shadows. A swishing sound forewarned her, and she crouched low. Missing her neck, the blade of a battle-ax embedded itself in the tree next to her; the fur on her back stood on end at the nearness of the miss. A low growl left her throat as she turned in the direction from which the projectile had come.

No sign— just underbrush and shadow.

The tigress moved quickly, without pausing, so as not to become a target for her invisible enemy. The quiet of the woods was more frightening than the sound of an approaching foe. Silence was friend to no one. Silence should never be trusted.

There! The breaking of a branch— a giveaway?

No— a trap. As she headed toward the sound, a great shape appeared at her side, and she was forced to skirt sideways to avoid the slashing ivory tusks. The need for subtlety vanished. The elephant trumpeted and charged. Lluava bounded up the nearest tree and vaulted off it as if it were a springboard. Slicing the air, Lluava missed the face, but her gilded claws left their mark etched along the left tusk. She dug her claws into the soft undergrowth and spun around to face her enemy.

Ears spread wide like wings, the elephant shook his head and stamped the ground until it trembled beneath Lluava's paws. She bared her teeth. Another thunderous stomp, then another. The vibrations made the tiger's insides tremble.

They began to circle one another. Lluava tried to position herself in front of the densest patch of forest. She needed to divert his attention from her plan.

"I have questions for you," she growled.

"Oh?" thundered Jormund, as he swung his tusks low to the ground, catching fallen leaves and tossing them in the air.

"How could a man like you kill your closest friend in cold blood? And not only that, but his love as well?" The questions came hissing from Lluava's mouth.

The massive animal snorted and closed the gap between them as Lluava slowly backed away. "Because I know how to play the game."

"Game? Game!" roared Lluava. "We are not mere pawns to be

manipulated by some higher power!"

"Aren't you? What is happening now is something far greater than you will ever comprehend." The elephant tossed more leaves in the air. Stale reds and bruised yellows fluttered down before once again finding rest.

"I have a riddle for you," the creature told her.

Lluava eyed him suspiciously.

"Less than two years ago, two men who died by my blade were traveling north of here." Jormund tossed more leaves, temporarily soiling the air with muted browns and sickly oranges.

"One human. The other Theriomorph." As the leaves fluttered down, the elephant charged through them. Hoping the close trees would protect her, Lluava leapt back into the thicket. In midcharge, the elephant reared, smashing down the saplings in his way.

"The two were partners on the border patrol."

Lluava slunk backward as Jormund shifted. The muscular figure reached down and snapped up a vine covered by undergrowth. Lluava tripped.

"The Theriomorph was in his dual form, and his human was beside him."

As Lluava regained her footing, she saw him lift an enormous broadsword from beneath a pile of leaves. Jormund, one step ahead of her, had wanted her to head into the thicket.

"The human was Teckner Larson."

Lluava's stomach knotted up at the name. Her thoughts jumped quickly to his living son, Byron.

Jormund encroached on Lluava. "The Theriomorph was a timber wolf."

Lluava tasted bile in the back of her mouth. She backed up as far as she could.

"What was the Theriomorph's name?" Jormund's voice mocked her.

As the question rang in her ears, Lluava tried to control her blind rage. Simultaneously she and the burly man charged each other. The thick blade sliced right past Lluava's head, but his elbow caught her jaw, forcing her off course. She had just enough time to tumble away from another deadly swing. Jormund thrust his blade deep into the earth where she had just lain.

Taking a moment to crack the joints of his thick neck, Jormund waved Lluava forward. She hissed her contempt in reply. With a swiftness that belied his bulk, the former general lunged at her.

Thereafter, he kept her at bay with combination after combination of offensive maneuvers. She struggled to maintain distance between herself and the sword; it was all she could do to stay away from the hungry blade. If she could not change the situation, she would soon be a meal for the cold iron.

As Jormund prepared to deliver his fatal swing, he suddenly turned; a figure had emerged from the underbrush, forcing him to parry an oncoming strike. Sparks flicked off the two blades as they collided. Varren's sword seemed small compared to Jormund's, yet it held. Jormund heaved, and Varren slid backward. Lluava swiped at Jormund's back. He turned around to whack Lluava's face with a thick, backhanded slap.

Even with Varren's help, they could not harm Jormund. When Varren sliced with his sword, Jormund counterstruck. When Lluava leapt to attack, Jormund kicked her in the chest, sending her flying backward. After slamming Lluava to the ground and sending Varren reeling into the brush, Jormund swung his sword, a blade made for double-handed combat, effortlessly around with one flick of a wrist. He smiled the entire time.

Then, as Lluava shifted into her human form, the giant brute drove his blade deep into a nearby tree. Now intentionally weaponless, Jormund changed into his dual form.

Trumpeting, the beast attempted to trample Lluava. She zigzagged, narrowly missing a crushing demise. At one point, she found herself underneath the belly of the beast. She regretted that she had not time to slice open the tender flesh and spill his entrails, but it was all she could do to stay alive.

As Varren struggled to right himself, his full concentration was on the two ivory lances that kept jabbing at him. Lluava, now forced to the rear of the animal, took her chance and jumped up, shifting into tigress form. Landing on the elephant's rump, she sank her claws deep into his thick hide. The beast screeched and tried to pin her against a tree. As Varren sliced at Jormund's face, his sword became embedded in the nearest tusk. The elephant flicked his head and ripped the blade from Varren's grasp. Defenseless, Varren was forced to retreat.

Jormund was more concerned about killing the prince than crushing the air out of Lluava's lungs. The elephant lumbered after her partner, and the tiger, gasping, dropped to the ground. She gave no thought to her possibly shattered ribs as she charged to protect her partner. Shifting back to human form, Lluava jumped up and grabbed the hilt of Varren's sword, still embedded in the elephant's left tusk. Violently Jormund shook his massive head and succeeded in flinging off not only Lluava but also the blade she still grasped.

There was no time for her to swing the sword before the elephant was on top of her again. Once more, she shifted into her dual form. Leaping up, she groped with her claws at the oncoming tusk, forcing herself to hang onto it while the enraged animal slammed her repeatedly to the ground. There was a loud crack. To Lluava's relief, the sound was not her ribs but the fractured tusk, which had split off.

The loss of the tusk served only to further enrage the brute. Lluava ran for her life as the beast, tearing through underbrush and shattering small trees, charged after her. She dodged this way and that, finally making her way back to the grove where she had left her partner. Jormund was close behind her, and Varren was waiting. As the elephant thundered past, Varren thrust his sword into the elephant's rear leg. It screamed and halted, facing Varren, who had no time to flee.

In that instant, Lluava saw an opening. Shifting back to human form, she hurtled toward Jormund and sliced his shoulder open with Issaura's Claws. As the elephant turned toward her, she slid into the underbrush under his head. Grabbing the broken tusk that lay half hidden in the leaves, she thrust it up into the beast's throat.

In her mind flashed the images of people Jormund had killed: Illena Zethra with her burgundy hair; General Argon Promethian, powerful yet just; Chat, innocent and brave; and her father, Haliden Kargen. With each face, Lluava forced the ivory weapon deeper into Jormund's neck. His blood spurted over her like crimson rain. With one final heave, Lluava leaped back as the enormous beast stumbled. Jormund emitted a gurgling sound as he tried to cry out. Then the animal, as if bowing to his future king, sank to his knees before Varren. Finally, with a long sigh, the elephant slumped onto its side and died.

As Lluava watched Varren draw his sword from the dead beast's leg, she realized that she was shaking. The discovery of an age-old truth had nearly cost her life: no joy is ever gained through revenge. Something inside her cracked; something dark was born.

As they left to find their horses, Lluava did not need to look back to know that Jormund had shifted for the final time into his human form. She knew that somewhere, embedded in the hole in his neck, was the broken tooth that had killed him.

***

Lluava made her way to her tent and peeled off her clothes. Using a water basin and a rag, she attempted to scrub off the blood. She did not want one bit of Jormund stuck to her.

As she left to meet Varren, she clearly saw the effects of mourning on everyone's faces, many still tear-stained. Rosalyn's eyes were red and puffy from crying, and Talos was no better. Heads close, they were talking quietly to one another, when they spotted Lluava and Varren approaching. Talos stood up and helped Rosalyn do the same. Her ankle still painful, she leaned on him for support. Yamir was nowhere to be found.

Before they could speak, Varren told them somberly, "Jormund is dead."

Nothing more was said. Nearby, two stretchers had been constructed from the debris. The smaller one held a body wrapped in an unburned saddle blanket; the longer stretcher held the body of Thrane. He had been sliced through from neck to navel. Organs crudely stuffed back inside him still poked out from the grisly gash. Lluava wished they would cover him, too, but clansmen believed that when one was dead, there was no need to hide it.

Kneeling beside Chat's wrapped body, Lluava wept silently. After several minutes of soundless sobbing, she reached over and grabbed the end of the blanket. She wanted to look upon her friend one last time, yet she wanted to keep him covered. Did she want her last image of Chat to be of him dead and stiffening? Finally, pulling together what courage she could, Lluava peeled back the blanket and looked down at the face she knew so well.

It looked like Chat, yet there was something different, something missing. There were his closed eyes, his large ears, and his buckteeth edging out between his thin lips. It was Chat; there was no mistake. Yet it was not her friend. No, her friend was gone. This was not he, but merely his impression left on the world. Lluava pulled the blanket back over his pale features. After a few more minutes lost in her own thoughts, she moved away so that Varren could pay his respects alone.

Talos and Rosalyn were discussing funeral arrangements as Lluava approached. They questioned whether it would be better to bury Chat here or take him with them. In Rosalyn's lap was the bloody shard. It was the size of Chat's dagger in both length and width. Hearing them talk about something so finite made Lluava's stomach turn. An inner darkness was growing within her. She could feel it. Somehow, she wanted to let the darkness take over, to kill the pain, forget the horror, and lose herself within its depths. She could not stay here with her friends and listen to them discuss the burial details.

Lluava began to slip back into the forest. The faces of her friends would only solidify what had just occurred. She did not want to look at them any longer. She had just lost Chat. Nothing seemed to matter. If they continued, who else would be lost? Talos? Rosalyn? Yamir? Varren?

Shaking her head violently as if to fling all those dark thoughts out, she let loose a tremendous roar. The echo reverberated off the countless wooden surfaces, fierce enough to challenge the dead.

"Are you going to run away once again to mourn by yourself?"

Violent emotions overwhelmed her as she recalled the loss of the grand master chief. What Varren said next only intensified her pain.

"However your inner beast might feel right now, you do not have to grieve alone. You never have to be alone."

Tears flowed against her will. "He was too young," Lluava cried.

"Death lays claim to any age." Varren moved nearer to the weeping girl; seeing no great resistance, he gently pulled her close to him.

"Why did it have to be him?" she sobbed into her partner's chest.

"I do not know." His voice had grown quiet. Lluava could sense the strain behind it.

"Some things, we mortals are not meant to understand."

Lluava begrudgingly thought about higher powers. If the gods were in control of life, they were truly vile and cruel. Gradually she became aware of the shakiness in Varren's breath; realized how upset he also must be. She turned to look into her partner's tear-filled eyes.

"We are going to be okay." It was more a question than a statement. Yet Lluava needed to say something to him. Didn't he deserve to be reassured as well?

With a slight nod, Varren released her. "With time…"

When they finally emerged from the forest, they saw that Yamir had returned as well. He looked as if he had aged several years. His childhood naiveté had been swept away. What remained was the stark impression of one who has seen too much of the horrors of the world. There was no joy in his features, just a sullen remorse. He sat next to his dead friend. As Lluava and Varren passed by, they shared a look with their solemn friend.

As Talos approached them, Varren said, "We need to talk."

Lluava could tell that some decision had been made, but about what? She had no idea.

As Varren ushered the other two away from everyone nearby, he explained, "Lluava and I have to make the rest of the trip alone. There is no other choice."

"What?" exclaimed Lluava. This was news she had not expected. Talos furrowed his brow.

"Rosalyn and you must take Chat's body to Elderdale. The town is a day's trek away." Varren pointed to the road that veered off to the right. "Yamir will go with you."

"Varren, I don't want us to split up," said Lluava, trying not to sound afraid.

"I know," he replied. "But you must realize that you and I are the only ones who have horses; the explosion killed the others. Two of us would have to walk, and with Rosalyn's hurt leg.…" He glanced over at Talos's betrothed. She was talking to one of the clansmen, but needed a staff to support herself.

Talos agreed, "We would only slow you down." It was obvious he did not like the situation any better than they did. He sighed, "When we reach Elderdale, I'll deliver Chat to the mortuary. They have ways of preserving a body for several days. That may give you a chance to return for Chat's funeral rites."

Lluava appreciated her friend's intentions, but the chances were slim.

"Do you know what the Cloven-Hoofed Clan intends to do now?" inquired Varren as he watched Father gathering his men together.

"I do not," admitted Talos. "Having brought us this far, they have no further obligation. I expect that they will return home."

"I see," said Varren. "I will ask Father, to be sure." Turning to his partner, he inquired, "Would you like to join me?"

Consenting, Lluava followed Varren to the small group of clansmen. Father beckoned them to his side. "I'm glad ya returned when ya did."

"It looks as if you are leaving," stated Varren, gesturing toward Father's comrades, who were packing what was left of their supplies.

"Yes." Father's nodding head sent reverberations through his obscene amounts of excess fat. "I am taking my son home so that he may be given the appropriate last rites." The man's acceptance of his situation caught Lluava off guard; she had expected more visible grief from a father who had just lost his son. She had not expected the clansman to be so stoical.

"I will say this, princeling," Father continued, "Yamir was right. This is our war, too. I wish I had realized sooner." He looked over at Thrane's body. "I will call the other clans together. Ya will not be fightin' alone."

"Thank you," Varren replied sincerely and he clasped the man's large hand. "We are continuing to Fort Brinsdale. We could find use for your assistance there." He paused. "I was wrong about you and your people. You are trustworthy and honorable."

Father nodded silently. He had not talked much since Thrane's death. He motioned for the others to head out, and Lluava watched the small band trek away. The stretcher with Thrane's body was in the midst of them— the father leading his son home one last time.

Soon after, Talos was ready to head to Elderdale; the seaside village was not very far from the split in the road. "We will meet you at the fort as soon as we can," he told them. He looked miserable. In his hand, he held the cage with the now ownerless raven; the bird had not uttered a sound since Chat's death. "I really wish I could go with you."

"I know," acknowledged Varren. "But they need you more." The friends gave each other a firm hug. Lluava also hugged each one in turn. Talos, with Yamir's help, carried the small stretcher; Rosalyn limped by its side. Lluava looked longingly one last time at the covered figure before her friends, a sorry band of mourners heading off to bury a friend, began the long walk down the road.

After the little group had disappeared around a stand of trees, Varren and Lluava mounted their horses. "To Fort Brinsdale," Varren said; and Lluava echoed, "To Fort Brinsdale." Then they were off.

Chapter 35
Fort Brinsdale

The day's journey had been tiring for Varren as well as for Lluava. They were more than ready for sleep when they finally stopped for the night. As she lay on her blanket, Lluava gazed at the needle-thin moon high in the deep, satin sky. Countless pinholes of light flickered through scrawny branches of pine. To save time, they had not pitched their tents, and the cool air made Lluava wish for heavier clothing. Excited by the knowledge that they were close to the fort, she slept restlessly.

Morning's glow awoke her. She must have fallen asleep, although she did not know when or how long she had rested. Turning on her side, Lluava observed Varren beginning to stir. His dark curls draped his face, shielding his eyes from the early light. She gave him a playful shove, and then rose to check on the horses.

They had picketed their mounts not far from the road on the only patch of grass they had found. The forest was not a natural habitat for grazing animals, so the horses had to make do with the measly scrub. Neither horse lifted its head to acknowledge Lluava's presence. They continued to nibble the dew-covered leaves of some unidentifiable hedge-bush.

"Good morning to you, too," she muttered, returning to the campsite. Varren had packed his blanket and was quenching his thirst from his water bag. Lluava sipped from hers before asking, "What do we do after reaching Fort Brinsdale? I mean, after we send word about the war to the other camps and the king."

"We do what is needed of us until the war is over," Varren replied. He brought out a package containing the last slivers of jerky.

"I meant after that. What are *you* going to do then?" Pretending to be more interested in the jerky than in the answer, Lluava took the packet that

Varren offered.

"We will be expected to aid in rebuilding areas damaged on the war front. After that, I will return to the castle to help my grandfather—if he needs me." After a hesitation, he added, "And take care of some personal business."

"I see."

Varren responded to Lluava's sullen response. "We are partners in the military, you and I, and will be so even after this war is over. Nothing changes that. When it is our turn to conduct border patrols, I will be at your side. You can count on it. When I have to be at the capital, I would like you to be there with me." He looked at her as if awaiting her response.

Lluava remembered their conversation several days ago— about what they had hoped to do with their lives before the war. Varren had not needed to explain what he was expected to do, but Lluava had spoken of her future for the first time.

She had admitted that she had not thought much about life after schooling. Her father had always encouraged her to become as knowledgeable as she could, so she remained committed to her studies far longer than many other farming children did. Though she did not have a plan for what might come next, Lluava knew she did not care for housework, nor did she want to nurse or teach, or be a storekeeper. Working on her father's farm was not an exciting prospect, but it was a good life, and she had admitted it, assuming that that was the choice she had left.

Lluava wondered if that conversation had caused Varren to offer an alternate opportunity. "You mean stay by your side until you are crowned and married...?" she asked.

"When I am king, you, as my rightful partner, will have the privilege of living at court; you will become my head counselor if you so choose. I will not force this upon you if your only desire is to return to a simpler life." Lluava could not tell if he was kidding her or being sincere. He watched her curiously, as if trying to read her thoughts. Then, after a moment, he continued, "As for marriage, there is no immediate concern about that."

"What does your betrothed think?" Lluava asked, trying to hold back the venom in her voice.

Varren did not notice. "Illia? When I do return to court, the first thing I will do is release her from her obligation to marry me."

Lluava was shocked and barely found her tongue to ask why.

"Illia Alcazar and I have been bound to one another since we were young as is the custom among nobility. She lives in the northern sector, so we have met only a few times. Last year, during the harvest banquet, her family visited the castle. During her stay, she found me one night in the gardens and implored me to release her from our bonds to each other. She is in love with another. I suspect a nobleman in the north. She said that if I cared for her at all, I would relieve her of her duties toward me."

Lluava felt giddy. Quietly suppressing signs of her joy, she listened patiently as Varren continued.

"At that time, I had not the courage to break a centuries-old custom. Children of nobility have been betrothed to one another for generations. The fact that one did not love the other was not sufficient reason for abandoning an ancient tradition.

"I have come to realize that as the heir to the throne, I will one day have the power to make changes to my kingdom. A custom is not justified merely because it has persisted for years and years. So the first thing I will do when I return home is to release Illia from her vows to me and allow her to live a happier life with someone she loves."

A light seemed to shine on Varren. Smiling, Lluava said, "You will be a good king."

"A good king needs a trusted counselor. So, what of my offer?"

"What of my family? Since my father's death, my mother has struggled to survive."

"You could move them to court if you like. Or, with the income you will receive based on your rank, you could hire several farmhands."

"Hmm." Lluava thought for a moment. "Would I be able to travel?"

"Yes. Actually, you would be expected to travel the kingdom as part of your service."

Lluava asked many questions and finally agreed to accept the position as Head Councilman when the time came.

A rustling of leaves brought them back to the present. Varren motioned Lluava to be silent, although there was no need. The muscles in her back tensed as she focused on the sounds. She gripped the Claws tightly as Varren slowly unsheathed his sword.

The noise was indeed the sound of footsteps. There were at least two people, and they were moving closer. Lluava listened to the rhythm of their approaching gait. She could tell by the heavy thuds that they were big men. Their tread was steady, careful; one shuffled as he walked. As if they knew where they were going, they headed straight toward the partners' camp.

Lluava mentally prepared for a fight. She counted down the moments until the intruders would appear. But when the strangers came into sight, she quickly stifled her attack. The two men in their pressed, moss-green uniforms were one of the most welcome sights she had seen in a long time.

"Hello!" she called out to the soldiers as they continued to approach. The two men were broad of shoulder and thick of neck. Although neither was particularly tall, both were extremely hairy. The shorter one had a pleasant face; his taller counterpart had a cleft palate, which displayed uncared-for teeth.

"Oye," the smaller one said to the other. "It's the prince. An' 'e 'as the li'l girl with 'im." His accent was thick and husky; his friend's was even worse. The other one looked at them and grunted.

The shorter one smiled at Varren and then at Lluava. "You're to come with us. You've been expected."

"By whom?" Varren asked.

"Why, by General Kentril, o' course."

Unable to contain her excitement, Lluava gave a hoot while her relieved partner praised his god.

The soldiers quickly escorted them through the forest. As the trees thinned out, they glimpsed Fort Brinsdale for the first time. Their escorts stopped to allow them to take in it all.

The fortress stood like a granite oasis in a desert of trees. Stone once carefully carved had been altered by the thumbprint of time. Cool, crisp sunlight, along with moss and lichen, dappled the walls. From the stone precipice, a cowbird peered down at its new audience and chimed its watery call. The heavy wooden gates, ribbed with iron, opened like an embrace. It was all so perfect in its aged beauty.

Once inside, the sound and smells of morning wafted around them. Soldiers coughed as they sluggishly moved about their business. A thick-browed man sharpened a blade in his open-walled smithy, while his apprentice tended to the furnace. Two large pigs, already spitted, rotated over large fires not far from the cook's lodge.

After dismounting, their taller escort took their horses to be brushed down and bedded in the stables. The other one led the way to the general's barracks. This building was similar in design to those of the southern camps but far older. The warped wood had grayed with time, yet it still appeared strong, even a bit forbidding.

Inside, a small hall led to three doors, two on the right and one centrally placed on the wall to the left. Ushered through the doorway on the left, they found Kentril seated at the far end of a long, narrow table. The yellow maps and diagrams scattered before him demanded his full concentration. Taking captive any resistant strands of black, gray had now conquered his scalp.

"General," the soldier prompted.

Kentril, finally realizing he was not alone, looked up. Seeing the weary, familiar faces, he quickly stood up, almost knocking over his chair.

"Your Majesty! Lluava!" he exclaimed as he hurried to shake their hands.

Lluava could not help herself and gave her former commander a hug.

"Please sit down." Kentril gestured to the empty chairs as he returned to his own. "Wilfreid," he called to their escort. "Bring our guests food and drink, and be quick about it." Turning to Varren, he inquired, "How are you? Did you two come alone? Where are the officers?"

Varren answered, "We are tired but will survive. We are alone. We rode ahead of the troops to warn you that a band of Raiders is making its way here.

General Argon is dead. He was killed by General Jormund, who was acting in concert with the Raiders."

"Argon dead?" Shock was clear in Kentril's voice. "And General Jormund?"

"Dead," Lluava said dryly. "Killed two days ago."

Before going into detail about their wretched journey, Varren started asking questions. "Have you sent word to the camps and the castle about the war?"

"Yes," Kentril assured them. "As soon as we arrived, the fastest messengers were sent to warn about the attacks and to ask for assistance. It's been a week and a half, but I have yet to hear a reply."

"If word has not arrived, then it must do so soon."

"I hope so," sighed Kentril.

"Did the privates, Thadius Sihia and Horus Ethril, arrive?" Varren asked.

"No. You two are the first," said Kentril in a matter-of-fact tone. "I'm sorry, Your Majesty." He rubbed his hand over the stubble on his chin. "Tell me more about your journey."

Varren somberly relayed what had occurred. As he spoke, Lluava realized that she had left the Claws in her saddlebag. She excused herself and walked quickly to the stables.

Her mount had been brushed and her saddle hung over the stall gate. As she retrieved the Claws from the dark interior of the satchel, Lluava heard a nickering from within the stable's gloom. Despite the warning signals in her head, she decided to take a look.

In the back stall was the dark and gallant Ulder. Seeing Lluava's friendly face only seemed to unsettle the stallion more. The girl attempted to soothe the horse with kind words.

"Varren will be happy to see y—"

Abruptly her stomach turned, and she retreated outside. Breathing deeply to steady her heartbeat, she forced herself to walk at a normal pace, trying not to draw attention to herself. Observing the men in the fort, she noticed what she had missed earlier. Most were clean-shaven, of a bulkier build, and looked up at her with dark eyes. A thick fur coat hung over the small railing of one of the barracks. On the back wall of the blacksmith's shed, a pair of fierce battle-axes and a long, thin sword hung alongside traditional weapons. The smith gave her an emotionless stare as he sharpened the edge of a short sword with a whetstone.

Reentering the general's barracks, she encountered several grim-faced guards. Inside the meeting room, Varren sat alone. Lluava quietly asked, "Where is General Kentril?"

"He stepped outside with one of his men. Why are you talking so softly?"

"I think we are in danger. We have to leave now."

Varren looked at her questioningly.

"In the stable...your horse...he is there." Lluava kept glancing at the door, waiting for someone to enter.

"That is impossible. That would mean Thad and Horus had arrived and... General Kentril lied to us." Lost in thought, Varren stopped.

The door swung open.

Kentril returned with Wilfreid, who bore platters of food. The general smiled at them.

"I'm truly sorry about the delay. The cooks here aren't known for speed."

Wilfreid set the plates before them. Despite the danger, the smell of roasted pork and honey biscuits tempted their noses.

Varren stood up. "Thank you for your hospitality, but Lluava and I must depart. We are expected at court in less than a fortnight."

The ends of Kentril's lips curled. "Leaving so soon? Can't you find a bit of time to break bread with me? We have not had the time to truly catch up since I left your service."

Feigning a look of regret, Varren replied, "Alas, we cannot stay. Perhaps at a later time."

"That is too bad." Kentril shook his head, as Varren started for the door. "Unfortunately, I can't allow you to leave just now." Kentril snapped his fingers, and four hulking guards pushed through the doors. Lluava gripped the Claws tightly as two men grabbed her arms. The other two seized Varren.

"I had hoped you wouldn't force me to do this," Kentril sneered. Varren's sword clattered on the floor as the two men forced his arms behind him. "I really hate to seem to be an inhospitable host."

Lluava twisted, breaking free long enough to give one of her handlers a nasty gash on his chest. Varren shouted angrily at the general as he was dragged out the door. Lluava continued to struggle until more guards entered and pointed their sharp weapons at her throat. Her inner heat was rising fast; soon she would release the tigress. At least, that was her plan, until she heard Kentril's cold voice.

"I wouldn't do that if I were you. If one whisker sprouts from your pretty, little face, I will have Varren killed in an instant. I cannot risk losing my men to your hot temper."

Lluava retorted, "You wouldn't do that. Varren is too valuable." She desperately hoped she was right.

"Will you take that chance?"

Kentril's question hung in the air. Lluava stopped resisting. The men forced her to drop the Claws. As she was pulled into the hallway, Lluava shouted at her once-trusted confidant.

"Why?"

His reply echoed down the hallway.

"For posterity, my chickadee."

They tossed her onto the floor of a cell, the stone tearing at her knees and elbows. The murky glow through the grate in the door gave her just enough light for her felid eyes to make sense of her surroundings. Oppressive granite walls had served as canvases for long-ago captives and were now filled with maddened scribbles and illegible words in other languages. A lumpy bed of rotting straw lay in one corner, while a rusting pisspot tainted the air in the other. Dirt and dust and rat feces coated the floor and left a film on the patches of her skin that contacted the ground.

Scrambling to the door, Lluava stood on the tips of her toes to peer through the grate. She could barely make out the dim hall lined with rows of cells. "Varren!" she called. "Varren!"

A hairy man shoved his piggy face up to the grate. He reeked of garlic. "Shet up," he grunted. Then he slid the cover over the grate, leaving her in darkness.

***

Time became irrelevant. Lluava soon found that she preferred to remain asleep; when she was awake, a total and utter fear, leaving her to sweat in terror of what might be occurring beyond these walls, consumed her thoughts. Her guard refused to speak to her. The only contact she had with him was when he shoved a small plate of moldy cheese and stale bread into the confined space. By the hunger pangs in her stomach, Lluava guessed that even that was not very often.

Kentril made his first appearance during the second day of her captivity. Dismissing the guards at the door, he strode into the cell. A fresh, crisp scent played with Lluava's nose, and she looked longingly at the ripe apple in the man's hand. In the dim light, Kentril surveyed his captive.

"Oh, Lluava, how have we come to this?"

Her stomach grumbling a pitiful complaint, she did not respond. She sat still on the mildewed bed. Making it shine even in the dull light, Kentril gently wiped the succulent skin of the fruit with a handkerchief.

"You were the best recruit I have ever trained. So bright and strong and willful. I had such high hopes for you." He lifted the apple to inspect it.

"I still do," he went on as he lowered the fruit. He moved closer and squatted down on his haunches, looking at her dirty face, her angled cheekbones, her smoldering emerald eyes. Reaching out, he tucked a wayward strand of hair behind her ear, and she forced herself not to cringe at his touch. He was so near that she could smell his minty breath.

"I thought of you as I would a daughter. You made me so proud." Lluava shifted uncomfortably when Kentril smiled at her. "This is why I want to offer you the chance to work with us."

"They're murderers," hissed Lluava.

"They're the future," Kentril coolly replied.

"A future of enslavement or worse."

"No." Kentril was suddenly all too serious. "With their advancements, technology, forward thinking, they could help us move into a new, more prosperous era. Try to understand, Lluava, the things that they could do for this kingdom would create peace and happiness for all."

"We were at peace, and we were happy before all of this," Lluava spat.

"The differences they could make…"

Lluava wanted to swipe at him, but all too aware of her current predicament, she held back.

"Replacing one king with another does not make everything better."

"No. Not a king. A ruler far greater than you can imagine. We would become a part of a great empire, larger and more powerful than has ever existed."

Lluava could not help but give Kentril her full attention.

He continued, "I am giving you one chance and one alone. Join me, Lluava. I will protect your family and provide you status in the new government. I might even be able to spare your friends' lives if they cooperate. This is a generous offer, Lluava, and the only one you will receive."

Memories of her loved ones overwhelmed her. Little Lamb soiling her dress as she played in the yard pounding out mud pies and handing them to Mouse to chew on. Her mother chastising them for dirtying their garments. She wondered if Lamb was preparing for the upcoming school year. Was school even in session anymore? And how big had Mouse grown? Lluava longed to see them again and wanted above all else for them to be safe. Kentril was guaranteeing her family safety. Isn't that what she had wanted since the beginning?

"Can I think about this for a bit?" Lluava inquired, astonished at how meek her voice sounded.

Kentril stood up and walked to the door. Knocking on the thick wood, he turned back to her as the door swung open. As if preparing to bite down on that tender fruit, he brought the apple to his lips and then stopped and tossed it to her. She caught it in midair and cradled the gift close to her bosom, as one would a newborn child.

"I'll need an answer when I return."

With that, Kentril stepped into the light and left Lluava to ponder her options. How had she not known of Kentril's treachery? Had she been so blinded by her faith in him that she had missed some small yet telling sign that he was aiding the Raiders? She thought about her family and the life she used to lead, reflected on all the pain and struggle she and her friends had endured since being drafted, and mourned the loss of her comrades.

The passage of time was defined only by her daily feeding. At intervals, the grate slid open, and the guard barked out, "Dinner!" Then he stepped into the doorway and, using the tip of his sword, pushed a crude tray of food and water toward her; most of the water sloshed out as it slid across the floor. Lluava learned to back up against the far wall to avoid dealing with the threat of his sword. She had considered grabbing the hilt, pulling the guard inside in order to catch him off guard and disarm him. However, not only were the odds of success against her, but also the likelihood of injury to her hands dissuaded her. The utter fear of what they might do to Varren halted all her dreams of escape.

Lluava noticed, to her dismay, that her ration of food had become significantly smaller after her conversation with Kentril. She suspected it was a tactic of some kind, perhaps to make her more compliant.

Except for the guard, her only other interaction was with a furry cellmate. As if on cue, the little rat scurried across the room to gather what it could of Lluava's scanty meal. She allowed it a few moments of uninterrupted gorging before her own desire for nourishment forced her to chase it away. Despite the gloom, she could always sense its presence, and the quiet tapping of its claws created a steady rhythm during her dreams.

On the third day after her conversation with Kentril, he returned. This time, he did not bear the gift of a piece of fruit. His voice was kind yet slightly hurried. "Have you an answer?"

"My family will be safe, as will my friends?" she inquired.

"Yes."

Lluava's stomach gave a low groan.

"And I will have security?"

"Oh, yes."

The rat scurried across the floor and veered into the shadows.

"And what happens to my partner? Can you promise his safety?"

Kentril hesitated.

"He is a political captive. I cannot guarantee anything with regard to him. That exceeds my authority. So, will you join me?"

Lluava sadly shook her head. "I can't." Hoping that this choice would not cost the lives of those she cared for most, she gave a silent prayer to an unknown god.

Kentril looked disappointed. "Then I must say goodbye to you."

"Goodbye?" Lluava replied questioningly.

"Yes. Goodbye."

"Wait!" Lluava called out as the door heaved open for the general. "It was you who sabotaged the obstacle course. And… and… and…" Lluava was struggling to think aloud when, suddenly, it all came to her. "That journal with the secret tunnel was yours. You used it to enter Durog, and you stole the flashbang and set it off in the woods. It was you, wasn't it?"

Kentril paused. He stood silhouetted by light in a way that prevented

Lluava from discerning his face.

"Do you want to know why?" His voice sounded off. Slowly the man turned toward her, and she saw his face. This was not the man she had known in Thowcelemine. His features were the same, but something about him was very different—something she could not identify. Whatever it was, it set her senses buzzing.

"It was you," Kentril grimly stated.

"What?"

As if he had been waiting for this question, he seemed relieved to divulge the information. "You are the cause of it all. You forced my hand and compelled me to do those things. You have been a thorn in my side from the very beginning."

"What?" she asked again. Lluava could not grasp the meaning behind his words. Her mind raced as fast as her heart.

"Don't play naive with me, chickadee," snapped Kentril.

He began to pace the small space before her. He seemed to take pleasure in telling her about his past trials and tribulations.

"Don't tell me you aren't aware of your striking resemblance to the ancient goddess, Theri."

What had that to do with anything?

"People of every race are impressionable in times of distress. Originally, I hoped the similarity could be kept a secret. And it was working." His train of thought seemed to switch abruptly. "Yet you surprised even me. You not only look like the goddess, but also you are spirited like her. You were far more talented than any other girl in the camp. I actually hoped that I could convince you to work with me. Unfortunately, your stark sense of right and wrong prevents you from ever being able to accept the big picture. With this realization, I saw the threat you could become, so I tried to stop you. Unfortunately, I underestimated your skills."

Once begun, Kentril could not stop. "I rigged the course so that when you ran across the bridge, it would break, and you would have—should have—fallen to your death. It was intended to look like an accident. You would have soon been forgotten. But you not only lived, you saved that other girl. Then you became an overnight hero. What a backfire! What a mess!

"Now a young woman who possessed the traits of the prophesied goddess had rescued a girl during an accident in the camps. People began to ask questions. They started referring to you as Theri and Issaura. Your growing popularity meant there was no way for me to put an end to you quietly." Kentril glared at her as if everything were her fault.

"With Ojewa breathing down my neck to transfer you to Durog so your skills could be utilized, I had to oblige them to avoid suspicion. I had hoped that Argon, with his hatred of females in his camp, would force you to return to Thowcelemine, where I could have rid myself of you quietly. Once more,

I underestimated your will.

"Not only did you endure the training, you excelled at it. Rumors and gossip swirled around you. Old legends were stirred to life. You kept me awake at night—one stupid little girl ruining the hopes and dreams of an empire. She—you—could have united the people and caused huge problems for my…." He paused. By the glint in his eye, Lluava could only envision the steely men across the sea who had been able to turn Kentril into a traitor.

"Obviously, I could not allow that to happen. You are right. I did use my knowledge of the forgotten underground entryway and stole the flashbang. To my great good fortune, I found you running in Durog's forest. When my attempts to kill you failed, I tried to cast doubts upon your loyalty. I persuaded some of the generals and council members that you were a possible threat, an enemy spy, and argued that you should be sent to Tarturus, the capital's prison. There you would at least be out of the sight and hopefully forgotten. Yet Argon, eternally hardheaded, had grown fond of you. He defended you so well that they released you into his care. I had no chance to lay a finger on you without risking an investigation. That was the last thing I needed when we were so close to accomplishing our goal.

"It boggled my mind—the biggest problem I had to deal with was one young girl. No matter what I did, you couldn't be touched. And now look at you, my captive in a war that is all but over.

"Do not mistake me. I do respect you. In a way, you are my greatest triumph. What drill sergeant doesn't dream of having the privilege of working with a recruit as strong, as smart, and as eager to learn as you? That is why I extended the opportunity to work together. There was only a small hope that you would accept, but I had to try. You had such promise; but now, what a waste of talent."

Lluava felt the hairs on the back of her neck bristle as Kentril talked. Her hands curled into tight fists. In a low tone, she growled, "You're just like Jormund."

Lurching forward right at her face, Kentril snarled, "I am *nothing* like Jormund! He was an ignorant, gullible pawn. The only thing he valued more than money was his reputation." His posture rigid, Kentril stepped back. "He worked for me! Do not think otherwise."

"How did you convince him to do that?" Lluava hoped Kentril would cool down if she could keep him talking.

"The accident," Kentril responded thoughtfully. "We were on a mission to deal with a large band of raiding Outlanders. Jormund tried to flush out the nomads during a sandstorm. There was a sound. He attacked blindly and delivered a mortal wound to Corporal Illena Zethra. She was the lover of Argon, Jormund's closest friend. How ironic. Fearing the High Councilors would discover his rash judgment—not to mention his best friend— he covered up the mistake and made it look like an attack by one of the nomads.

"Fortunately, I stumbled upon him during this act of deceit. I promised that if he worked for me, I would keep his little secret. Over time, I gained his trust and discovered that his greatest weakness was his own greed. We made a pact: his help in return for a title in the new order along with all the wealth commensurate with that rank.

"Jormund was motivated by his greed, by his thirst for power. I am not. I want what is best for the future. Do not confuse the two." Kentril moved to the door. He glanced back and shook his head.

Lluava could almost read his thoughts: How could one such as herself cause so much trouble?

"What a waste," he said as the door closed behind him.

Chapter 36
Plan Hatching

So this was fear.

Lluava lay on her rough, straw filled bed and stared blankly. No food had been brought since Kentril's departure, so there was no way to tell how long she had been trapped in the tiny cell. Her hunger pangs continued to worsen. Trying to get the attention of the guard outside her door, she beat against the thick wood until her hands bled. Buckling over in pain, she realized that she had been abandoned to die in this cold, damp, dark place.

Trying to find a weak point in the stone and wood, she shifted and clawed at every available surface, raking deep grooves in places where she attempted to break free. Though the mortar was old, it still held, and the door was reinforced by a sheet of metal in its center. Eventually she shifted back and screamed and screamed for someone to hear her. Desperate to evade a long, drawn-out death, she begged for someone to kill her quickly. She prayed to the gods to help her. She was starving. But nobody came. The grate remained shut. She was alone.

Lluava grew accustomed to the unholy stench of mildew and the vile odor that arose from her overfull pisspot. Other than her breathing, the only sounds were the occasional pitter-patter of rat feet on stone and the incessant grumbling of her stomach. As her body began to tire and her strength ebbed, Lluava tried to conserve her energy by lying on the rotting bed.

So this was fear.

Dreaming of rescue and release from pain, she slept more often to escape reality. Each time, the dream was the same: the door swung open, and someone stepped through— sometimes Varren or Talos or Yamir, other times Argon or someone else who had died. Once Chat sat down by her and talked and talked. Lluava lay there and listened to him. Although their conversation seemed to last for hours, she could only remember that he told her, "Your time has not yet arrived."

Although Lluava longed for the dreams, for they kept her pain and fear away, she soon struggled to tell them apart from reality. Once she was rudely awakened by a small, sharp pain at her ankle. Expending the least amount of energy, Lluava kicked the rat away. As long as she was still breathing, she would not become some rodent's meal.

So this was fear.

Slipping in and out of consciousness, nothing made sense. Fragments of thoughts, if they were thoughts, came and went. Bloody paws, maroon-smeared stone, guttural moans, a furless tail stuck in teeth. The murky, ceiling-to-floor darkness seemed to permeate her soul.

Lluava stared at the far wall without actually focusing on it. Her mind was elsewhere. She did not stir at the grating sound of the door. She could not fight; she could barely move.

Someone gagged. Footsteps moved quickly toward her. She forced herself to focus on the new arrival. It took several moments to recognize the dark features of the man looking intensely back at her. She struggled to pull a name from memory.

"Derrick," she whispered, her voice sounding like a raw canyon's wind. Her throat ached, and her lips cracked at their forced movement.

Seeing her move, Derrick stood up and shouted out the door, "This one's alive! I know her! Water! I need water!"

She tried to speak again, but the pain in her throat was intense.

"It's going to be okay," Derrick said as someone else stumbled into the room, water pouch in hand, and gagged. The newcomer quickly covered his face against the stench. Derrick took the pouch and gently lifted Lluava's head so that she could sip. The cool liquid dribbled down her throat. As soon as she tasted it, she wanted more. She groped for the pouch, but Derrick held it tightly.

"Whoa! Slow down. A little at a time, Lluava."

She nearly choked, and Derrick slowed the meager flow further. After she had lapped up every last drop of water that Derrick allowed her, the two men hoisted her in their arms and carried her from the prison. As they passed the other cells, she tried to croak out, "Varren," but no one heard her.

Outside, the light from the moon was unbearably bright; she buried her head in Derrick's chest until they entered another building. They laid her down on a cot, and she could not remember feeling anything so soft. After telling her to rest, Derrick left to deal with other business. As he moved away, Lluava thought she heard him say, "We have to stabilize her first." Within minutes, she was fast asleep. For the first time in a long while, she had no dreams.

When she awoke much later, she was given a bit more water. She spent the better part of the day sleeping, waking only for a sip of weak broth. Finally, she regained enough energy to make a fuss about leaving the bed.

Lluava was uncomfortably aware that she had been washed and the rags she had worn replaced with new black training attire. The soldiers watching over her refused to let her stand up; she was to rest and recuperate. However, she soon caused so much commotion that someone sent for Derrick. By the time he arrived, she had hobbled halfway to the door.

Her dark-haired friend was not in the mood to deal with such behavior. "Sit down!" he commanded.

Lluava continued to stumble toward the door.

"I want to see Varren. Where is Varren?" She was frustrated at her body's resistance to movement and distressed at having been separated from her partner for so long. What had they done with him? Was he alive?

Derrick moved in front of her and rather forcefully pushed her onto the edge of another cot.

"Sit."

"But..." she stammered. Why wasn't he letting her do what she needed to do? Suddenly her legs gave way. Derrick helped her onto the cot.

"Varren is gone, Lluava," stated Derrick. His face was like stone.

She was aghast. "What? Where?"

He hesitated before answering. "He was not left at the fort."

Lluava still did not understand.

"Do you know what happened here?" he asked.

She shook her head.

"I feared as much." With a gesture, Derrick sent the soldiers away. Then he continued.

"When we arrived here last night, the fort was deserted. It looks as if the Raiders left several days ago; however, it seems that you had been left to rot much longer than that. You should not have lived." His words were filled with amazement.

"That's why Kentril said goodbye," thought Lluava aloud.

"Wait—what?" Derrick put his hands on her shoulders and turned her toward him. "The general was here? Was he a prisoner, too?"

Lluava realized Derrick did not know.

"*You* might want to sit down for this," she said and proceeded to relate what had happened since their groups had split up. Derrick's face changed from shock to horror to anger and back to shock again, yet he stayed silent until Lluava had finished.

"So the general is one of them," he said, as though trying to make the idea real. "We were betrayed from the beginning."

"The question is what to do now," said Lluava. "You said Varren was gone?"

"If he was here with you, then, yes, he is gone. We searched all over the camp for signs of life. The Raiders abandoned several captives, including high-ranking officers from the fort, in cells like yours. Like you, they were left to die, and that's just what happened. It is a wonder that you survived so long. But Varren was not among them."

"Then he must be their prisoner," Lluava said, trying to reassure herself. "They wouldn't kill him. He is too valuable a bargaining chip."

"He is certainly more valuable alive than dead," agreed Derrick.

"We have to go after him."

Derrick scratched at his bristly chin. "Well, we do need to put an end to those vagabonds. First, though, I want to show you something." He helped Lluava stand and then walked her to the door. From that vantage point, Lluava looked out at Fort Brinsdale. It was not empty, as she had expected, but teeming with people of all ages and both races. Mothers comforted crying infants in their arms; youths helped the elderly unpack traveling bundles; children kept close to watchful parents.

"What is all this?" Lluava asked.

"They are the people of Elysia. They have come from all over and have traveled many days to be here."

"Why? For what?"

"For you," was Derrick's reply. "They have heard about you and have come to see you; they believe that you are their savior. Many refer to you as Theri or Issaura."

"They are mistaken. I can't...I'm not..." She felt panicky. "Send them away. Please send them away."

Derrick laughed. "I've tried. They refuse to leave. They're here for you and only you."

"How many are there?" There seemed to be too many to count.

"Several thousand at last check and more are arriving by the hour."

Her heart began to race. How could so many people be so desperate as to place all their hope in a young farmer's daughter?

"Lluava, you need an army. Here it is." Derrick gestured at the growing crowd, and the two watched as people drifted in. When she had seen enough, Derrick helped her back into the barracks.

"Do you think any of them are able to fight?" inquired Lluava, easing onto a cot.

"I've already sent a few soldiers to begin screening the refugees; they will determine who is fit and who is not."

"Refugees." The word felt strange on Lluava's tongue. "Such an uncomfortable thought."

Derrick grunted in acknowledgment. "Well, I have work to do. You stay and *rest*. I will need you to be at your best once we decide on our course of action."

Lluava found it surprisingly hard to rest, to do nothing. She could hear the clamor outside and wished she were doing something useful. After a bit, her solitude was broken when a little girl came in carrying a bowl of steaming broth. Her braids swayed as she walked, and when she came near, Lluava realized she was no older than Chat had been. Sorrow awakened within her.

"Don't you want the soup?" the girl asked shyly. "It's really good."

"Oh, yes, I do." Lluava reached for the bowl. Bringing it up to her face, she breathed in its aroma. She was incredibly hungry. Lluava blew on the top to cool it faster, then drank deeply.

Looking over the rim of the bowl, Lluava realized the girl was still standing there with her hands fumbling behind her back.

Swallowing, Lluava asked, "Is there something else?"

"Um...." The girl scuffed her feet on the floor. "Lady Issaura, you'd believe me, wouldn't you?"

"About what? And my name's Lluava."

"There are monsters in the ocean now." The girl recognized Lluava's skepticism. "I saw them myself. There were two of them in the water, and they were snarling and ugly. It was dark, and they scared me. I told Mama an' she gave me a thrashing for lyin'."

Sitting up, Lluava asked, "When and where did this happen?"

"Well..." The girl scrunched up her brow trying to remember. "It was several days before Mama told us that we were to travel here. We live in Brog. Or did." She moved nearer to Lluava. "You do believe me, don't you?"

"Actually, I do."

"I knew you would, Issaura. I told them you would!" The girl's eyes sparkled, and she hurried to the door. "My name is…. Oh, never mind." The girl had already vanished.

That afternoon, Lluava considered many things. Eventually a plan began to form.

***

As evening approached, Lluava received another visitor.

"Talos!" she exclaimed as her friend stepped through the door. "You made it!"

"Of course I did." They shared an embrace.

"You don't know how good you look," Lluava said. She smiled; not so long ago, she had thought she would never see a friendly face again.

"You look horrible," answered Talos bluntly.

"Where is Rosalyn? And the others?"

"Rosalyn is already tending to those in need. I think she has taken over the old medical ward."

"And Yamir?" she asked, elation clear in her voice.

"He is greeting the clans as they arrive."

"The clans are here?" She had almost forgotten Father's promise to summon the clans.

"Yes. The Silver Tongue and Razor Back clans are here already, and word is that the others are soon to arrive."

"I'm so happy you're here." Lluava held back her emotions; yet, in a whisper, she added, "I was so scared."

"I know." Talos gave her another strong hug. "But Derrick is developing our new strategy. I've come to fetch you and to give you these." Talos handed her Issaura's Claws. Before she could ask, he stated, "It looks like they tried to melt them in the smithy but failed." The Claws were thankfully unblemished.

With Talos's support, Lluava slowly made her way through the camp, back to the officers' barracks and the room she had once so violently departed. Along the way, she could not avoid noticing how people looked at her and whispered among themselves. Mothers lifted infants above the heads of the crowd to have a better look at her. Lluava wanted to hide from all the staring eyes and was relieved when they reached the other building.

Derrick stood in the same spot in which Kentril had stood. Also like the general, Derrick was sifting through a pile of yellowed maps. Talos cleared his throat, and Derrick motioned for them to come near.

"If we hurry and take the main road to the capital," Derrick said, sliding his finger down one of the lines on the map, "we could either overtake the Raiders or arrive before them and help defend the castle."

"The capital has yet to be notified?" Lluava was aghast at this turn of events.

"From what we know, the Raiders have been able to prevent all attempts to communicate with Cronus. Based on your information, I suspect Kentril has played a major role in this. So, for now, as far as the capital is concerned, we are still at peace," Derrick grimly explained. "They will be taken unawares."

Lluava thought of the loss of Thad and Horus. Kentril must be stopped.

Talos peered over Derrick's shoulder. "How will you deploy the troops?"

"I was hoping you would have a suggestion," replied Derrick. "It's not the skill at which I excel."

"I see." Talos thought for a moment and then said, "I would—"

Lluava interrupted, her voice still hoarse. "They aren't headed to the capital."

"What?" Both men looked at her.

"Where are they going, then?" Talos demanded.

"To the sea."

"Do you know this for certain?"

"No. But I have good reason to believe—"

"You want us to travel away from the capital on a hunch?" Derrick was clearly skeptical.

Talos turned to him. "At least hear her out."

At Talos's nod, Lluava explained, "The little girl who brought me my food said that she saw a pair of sea monsters swimming close to her town, north of here. I think she actually saw some of the Raiders' ships. Remember the snarling heads carved on their bows?"

"Yes, I do," acquiesced Derrick. "In that event, they could be bringing reinforcements to help them in the attack."

Talos considered this news. "That means we would have to use some of the commoners to fight with us."

"I'm not done." Lluava was a bit testy at being interrupted. Talos and Derrick exchanged looks. "I don't think the ships are harboring reinforcements. The girl only saw two; they would have needed more for that."

Derrick scowled, but Lluava would not be interrupted.

"Let me finish, please."

He nodded, and she continued, "I think those boats are going to take the Raiders home."

Now even Talos could not remain quiet. "I'm sorry, Lluava, but that's ridiculous. No commander would just give up without a good reason. I know the Raiders' numbers are low, but so are ours at the moment. I'm sure Kentril and the Raiders' leader realize this. More important, as the capital has no knowledge of the coastal attacks, they will easily be caught by surprise. Derrick is right. The Raiders are marching for Cronus."

Derrick agreed, but Lluava was still not finished. "Have you had your say? Can I continue?"

Talos nodded.

"Hear me out. Those ships will carry them home. Think about it. They have Varren, the sole heir to the throne. He is their leverage. What would you do? Risk keeping the prince here? Or take him far away, somewhere beyond the reach of rescue, and hold him hostage to use to your advantage?"

"Thor loves his grandson, but he is a good king, and his kingdom comes first," said Talos. "He would never risk the kingdom for one man, even one of his own blood."

"That may be true," acknowledged Lluava. "But His Majesty is old and does not have many years left. Let's say the Raiders can't persuade King Thor to bargain. They could kill Varren and leave the kingdom without an heir. There are no close relatives who have direct claim to that title, and more than one noble family might desire the crown. Talos, can you tell me that you can't think of any families that would lay claim to the throne after Thor dies?"

Talos's look was grave. "Offhand, I can think of half a dozen."

"Derrick, don't you think that the Raiders, especially with Kentril's inside knowledge, have the sense and patience to wait to strike until we are tearing the kingdom apart from the inside?"

Derrick clenched his jaw and curled his hands into tight fists, and Lluava knew she had convinced them.

"I believe the Raiders will rendezvous with their ships and then head back to their homeland taking Varren with them," Lluava said.

After a moment of silence, Derrick asked Lluava, "So where do we head tomorrow?"

"Brog."

***

Lluava was awake next morning well before sunup. It had taken all her motivation to sleep last night. As she observed the nearly five thousand people crammed into Brinsdale, she wondered were these refugees, or were they recruits? Word was spreading rapidly in this part of the kingdom; the coastal cities were already on the move, and now inland ones were following suit. Lluava's heart began to thrum. Somehow, she knew this day would mark a change in the course of the war.

Sentinels had called everyone to a sunken amphitheater at the back of the fort. Rows of seats had been chiseled from the earth, wrapping themselves around a grassy center that functioned as a stage. As the people gathered, Lluava thought the amphitheater resembled the coliseums of Durog.

Derrick and Talos attempted to organize the crowd, but their attempts were ignored. Talos pushed his way through the noisy, jabbering onlookers and beckoned to Lluava.

"I need you to get their attention. They are not listening to us. Please, speak to them."

"What?" Lluava looked terrified. Why would they listen to her? "I don't know what to say."

"Say anything," replied Talos. He grabbed her wrist and, weaving among the rows of seats until she was standing in the center of the stage, pulled her through the crowd. No one paid attention to them, and the noise level continued to escalate.

"It was all we could do to round them up and direct them here," Derrick shouted, clearly exasperated. He had not slept well and was irritable.

Sighing, Lluava turned to face the crowd. "I'll do my best," she said.

"Hello, everyone," she began. No one took notice, so she shouted out more loudly. "Hello! Can I have you attention, please!" A few people standing nearby glanced at her and then turned back to their conversations.

Lluava was becoming annoyed. "PLEASE, CAN YOU LISTEN TO ME?" she bellowed. However, even this achieved nothing. They had to be able to communicate with the massive crowd, to convince them to work together, to harness their power. But how?

Suddenly Lluava shifted, releasing a guttural roar, ending in an earsplitting screech that escalated higher and higher.

Silence.

All eyes were on her now whether she wanted them to be or not. Many of the humans looked horrified at the ferocious beast that had appeared before them, and the Theriomorphs gazed in awe. A baby cried. But at least she had their attention.

Lluava paused to steady the beating of her heart and cleared her throat.

"I am not good at giving speeches," she began. "I am Lluava Kargen, daughter of Haliden Kargen, and I am Theriomorph." Her audience was quiet as she struggled to compose something to say.

"Um…stand up if you are Theriomorph." A little over half the crowd rose to their feet. They were clustered in groups of their own race. Lluava remembered how the races had segregated themselves at Durog, and an idea came to her.

"Please stay standing for a moment. Thank you. I would like you to look around at each other, at your neighbors, and at those you do not know. Everyone you see is loyal to the same king, is a citizen of the same kingdom, and calls himself Elysian. Yes, half of us are human and half of us are Theriomorph—but we serve the same king and love the same land."

"Look around you. You have chosen to separate into two different groups. How can we be one kingdom when we continue to split ourselves from each other? How can we defend our country if we only work with half of its people?"

Lluava felt herself gaining confidence as she spoke. "Right now, we are two peoples fighting for one cause. This makes us weak, and the Raiders are not merciful. They will take advantage of the fact that we consider each other separate entities." She turned to face those at her back.

"Listen to me. The Raiders are strong, and their weaponry is more advanced than ours. How can we hope to keep a force like that at bay if we continue on this path we have chosen for ourselves? We must stop thinking about ourselves in terms of race and instead think of ourselves as Elysians. That is what we are: one kingdom, one people, united under one crown. I want each of you to find someone of the other race, sit next to him or her, exchange names, and tell one another from where you came."

For a moment, nobody moved. Then the little girl who had brought Lluava the broth shrugged free of her mother's grasp and walked up to a tall, red-haired human.

"Can I sit here?" she asked sweetly. Surprised, the man slowly nodded; then another person moved and then another. Soon the entire amphitheater was alive with moving people. After they had settled into new seats and made brief introductions, Lluava spoke up once again.

"Think about your reasons for traveling here. Was it for your personal safety? The safety of your loved ones? Are you seeking protection, or do you want to defend the way of life you love?"

"In a few hours, we will gather an army to travel north. The Raiders hold our prince captive." There was an audible gasp. "I believe they are trying to reach their ships, to transport him to their country across the sea. They will use him as leverage to destroy us. I am not asking all of you to come, and if you wish to stay here within the safety of Fort Brinsdale, you may do so. But if you wish to aid in this fight, Derrick and Talos,"—she motioned to the two behind her—"will tell you what you need to do."

Several men cheered. Lluava hoped that meant that they would be willing to help.

"I will be honest with you," she continued. "Of those who come, not all will return." Lluava spotted Yamir in the crowd, and she knew they shared the same thought.

"But all will be heroes."

There were more cheers. Lluava felt the excitement growing.

"We will travel as one people, one army. We will move quickly, attack hard, and free our crown prince. We will force the Raiders to crawl back to their country in defeat, and we will show the world that Elysia is a force with which to be reckoned."

Jumping to their feet, the Elysians cheered and cried out. Not a single person was left untouched by her speech.

"I can't believe you did it," exclaimed Derrick, and Talos replied, "I knew she could."

All around them, the crowd began to chant, "Theri! Theri! Theri!"

Chapter 37
The Osmund Survivor

Against Talos's better judgment, Lluava chose to travel in the first wave. He had futilely tried to dissuade her from traveling until she had recuperated. She almost gave in to her friend's plea and her body's cry for rest, but Derrick stood firm and argued that she must go. Their ragtag army would follow only their living goddess; without Lluava, they had no army.

Talos and Derrick screened those willing to fight and divided them into several regiments. Derrick, with several well-trained humans, would lead the volunteers who were less physically prepared. They would arrive after the fighting began and, with three times the number in the first wave, would serve as reinforcements.

The fittest, including Talos, other soldiers, and some of the people Talos had trained at Elderdale, marched under Lluava's leadership. They kept moving day and night, pausing only long enough to eat and, if they were lucky, to grab a quick rest. Lluava pushed them all to their physical limits. They were days behind the Raiders, and she had to make up for the lost time.

Daytime and nighttime became irrelevant; Lluava was immersed in her thoughts. She barely acknowledged Yamir's presence or Talos's, nor did she pay attention to Rosalyn's warnings about the strain on her own health. An embryo of fear was growing inside of her, clawing at her organs, trying to kick its way out. There were no signs that the Raiders were making their way to Brog. Could she have been wrong? Could she be leading the army in the opposite direction? Could she be dooming her country and all its people? If that were the case, the Raiders might not need the prince. Could her partner be…? No! Lluava willed the enemy to be traveling ahead of them. She had to catch up. She had to save Varren.

The regiment moved almost as fast as the scouts Lluava had sent ahead.

Their information had not proved useful until the evening when one returned with news that they had spotted the Raiders' camp.

"They are likely holding Varren captive in the center of the camp so they can guard him on all sides." Talos's words were not pleasant to hear, but they rang true.

"Well, we can't just charge in," Yamir said, as he studied the rough diagram of the camp scratched into the dirt. "Maybe we can surround them and force the brutes to return Varren."

Talos squatted next to Yamir and calculated various scenarios in his head. Talos counted again. "We do not have enough troops to surround them unless we wait for Derrick's reinforcements to arrive."

"That'll take too long," Lluava answered as she nervously paced around them. "By then, the Raiders will have either discovered us or arrived at Brog."

Yamir scooted to the other side of the drawing. "Well, we could—"

Lluava cut him off. "I'm going in."

"Lluava, you are not doing anything so rash," rebuked Talos. "Please do not try my patience with this."

She knew she had been too aggressive lately due to her exhaustion. Everyone around her seemed to be feeding on her agitation. She knew—but none of it mattered.

"I'm going in," Lluava repeated, and Talos stood up to face her. She refused to shy away from his glare. "I don't care what you do, but I'm going to rescue Varren."

They stared at each other. The intensity between them was enough to make Yamir step away. Finally, Talos broke eye contact.

"Curse the gods!" he cried. "If only they had given you one morsel of sense!" He sat down on his haunches and drew new lines in the dirt with his stick. "Here is the plan."

***

Breaking through the lines of the opposition's forested camp proved far simpler than Lluava had anticipated. Talos had ordered the entire army to attack one small section of the perimeter's forces. They outnumbered the Raiders five to one at their invasion point and were now wreaking havoc on the stunned enemy. Confusion reigned as the Raiders were caught unaware in the surprise assault. As the Raiders struggled to marshal their forces against the Elysian soldiers, Lluava and Yamir broke away and now led a small band through the camp in search of their captured prince.

Crouching behind a tree, Yamir whispered to Lluava, "He has to be nearby."

"Why do you say that?" Lluava questioned as she peered from behind the scabby trunk.

"Look at the Raiders standing guard over there. They aren't taking the bait and leaving to fight Talos."

He was right. Several men maintained their positions; they must be guarding something.

"It's going to be hard for us to break through," she said, pulling her head behind the safety of the tree.

"I've got that covered," said Yamir. Opening his satchel full of quills, he grabbed a handful. Signaling others to follow his lead, he turned back to Lluava for a moment. "Go for Varren. I'll see you soon."

With that, he charged out into the open, flinging his quills. One pierced the jugular of the nearest Raider, who, gagging on his own blood, sank down. The Raiders charged after Yamir and his followers.

With the path now clear, Lluava quickly crept deeper into the Raiders' camp. Moving from trunk to trunk, she spotted a prisoner bound to a tree. She approached him from the back. The man's hands were bound to the base of the trunk by a thick metal chain. As she crept closer, she recognized the tattered white uniform.

In the next moment, Lluava had reached the chain and started to pry it apart with Issaura's Claws. The screech of metal on metal caused Varren to stir.

"Who—?"

"Shhh." Lluava quieted her friend. She could see where Varren's skin was peeled raw around his wrists from his struggle to free himself. As he moved, scabs cracked and oozed.

"I'm going to get you out of here," she told him.

"Lluava?" he asked.

"Yeah," Lluava replied as she hacked at the heavy chain.

"Go," Varren commanded.

His voice sounded weak, and Lluava feared the treatment he had received. She continued to work the chain. "Not without you."

A sharp prick in the middle of her back caused Lluava to stop what she was doing. She slowly raised her arms, released her grips, and allowed her weapons to hang loosely on her hands. The girl paused for a second and then, in a flash, spun around, slashing the sword away from her. As Lluava sprang behind away from the tree, she recognized her opponent as none other than Thowcelemine's former commanding general.

Kentril looked pleased. "Alive and well, it seems," he said, studying her. "And quick as ever."

"No thanks to you," hissed Lluava as she continued to back up, leaving plenty of room between them. Kentril did not make a move.

"Did you know that this is not the first time the Raiders, as you call them, have arrived on Elysian shores? They have come several times, usually in small vessels so not to draw attention to themselves." He kept his eyes on Lluava as if trying to read her.

She was confused at this spontaneous information. As though he still headed Thowcelemine, Kentril seemed to want to educate his disobedient pupil. "Several years ago, I met them not too far away from where we are now standing."

Was he toying with her? Distracting her with this idle talk? Waiting for an attack, Lluava tensed.

"Niflhel is the future, Lluava. The great empire across the sea. Remember what I told you. Every decision I have made is to better Elysia."

Kentril took a step toward her. "We were making our plans for this very war. Unfortunately, a pair of Elysian soldiers on patrol stumbled upon our camp. I couldn't let them leave and warn the king, so I commanded Jormund to dispose of them quickly, and he did."

Lluava's eyes widened as she made the connection. "You killed my father!" she cried.

As she rushed forward, Lluava remembered Ojewa's warning: never make the first move. She had fallen yet again into Kentril's trap. She tried to sidestep, but it was too late. Kentril avoided her thirsty claws and sliced at her ribs. She heard the fabric rip and felt the blade brush her skin.

"Watch out!" shouted Varren.

Lluava whipped around and countered another blow. The thin, cutting edge caught the curve of the Claws. Still weak from her imprisonment at Fort Brinsdale, she struggled to keep Kentril's blade at bay. She could not risk letting Kentril see how weak she really was.

"We are both Theriomorphs," she said. "Why don't we fight with honor and battle in our dual forms? Unless you have no honor left."

"No weapons?" he inquired, seeming to like the thought.

"No weapons."

"You first."

They simultaneously stepped back. Lluava slid off the Claws, dropping them to the ground and kicking them away.

"What are you doing?" exclaimed Varren. Lluava heard the chains clank together as he struggled to free himself. She did not take her eyes from the silverback gorilla that appeared before her. She shifted and briefly took joy in her second form.

Varren was forced to watch as the two magnificent beasts attacked each other. Teeth and claws collided. Tufts of fur flew in the air. As the animals rolled around on the ground, it was hard to tell which one was where. At first, it seemed that Lluava was gaining the upper hand. The tigress, with her teeth, claws, and size, seemed to be a fierce opponent for an ape fighting with only four deadly incisors. But the gorilla's true nature surfaced quickly. Grabbing one of Lluava's forelegs, the monster gave a rough jerk and twisted it unnaturally behind her.

The tigress screamed, and Varren did the same. He forced himself to stand, shimmying the chain up the back of the tree. Looking around, he tried to find something, anything, that could help her.

Pain dulled Lluava's senses. It was sharp and raced up and down her foreleg. Had Kentril broken her leg? No. She could still move her toes. She had to fight through the pain. Clawing wildly, she lurched away from the beast's grasp.

The gorilla snarled. Behind it, Lluava saw Varren. His lip, red and swollen, seemed an odd compliment to the purple-green mark on his cheek. She wanted to run up to him and wipe the dried blood off his chin.

It was only a glance. Why had she risked it? The gorilla, beating her spine with its clublike hands, was on top of her. Lluava yowled. Desperately trying to shake the creature off, she sprang to her feet, but it clung to her fur like a hook in a fish. She sprinted toward Varren as fast as she could and then abruptly stopped—sending the grey missile flying forward, along with clumps of her fur.

The gorilla landed in a heap next to Varren's feet. As the beast stood up, Varren kicked dirt into its face. Digging at its eyes, it roared. The tigress took advantage and leapt at the ape. Sensing her attack, it swiveled and grabbed her, slamming her into the ground; then it turned back to Varren. There was not a shred of humanity in its eyes, just blatant rage. The stink of its breath permeated the air. With its thick arm, the ape crashed a fist down on Varren's head.

Pain seared Lluava's forearm as she tried to raise herself. She saw Varren slump down after Kentril's crushing blow.

"No!" she cried.

The great silverback gorilla turned to the tigress. He roared and pounded upon his chest before growling out, "You lose." He shifted into his human form and went in search of his sword.

Lluava crawled to Varren's still body. "Oh, gods, don't let him be dead," she cried, as she pulled herself toward her partner with her one good forelimb. She transformed and placed her head against his chest. She could feel his breath rise and fall and hear his faint heartbeat pulsing faster and faster.

"Varren," she called as she gently lifted his head. His eyelids flickered. "Varren!"

A strong grip on her neck pulled her up and shoved her away. Varren stirred as Kentril pulled out his sword.

"No! Please, no!" Tears welled up in her eyes.

"You're more trouble than you're worth," muttered Kentril as he pointed the blade at Varren's neck.

"No, no, no," cried Lluava. Kentril needed Varren for leverage. He would not kill him. He wouldn't. Kentril's expression said otherwise. Varren looked over at Lluava.

"I'm so sorry," she said.

"Do not cry." Varren spoke gently. Something in his eyes gave him away. The man who epitomized duty could not hide his secret any longer.

Kentril gave a thin smile.

"You love her." It was a statement, not a question. Kentril laughed; it was all too perfect. "And you love him. How cliché. "

Lowering his blade, Kentril moved toward Lluava. He now pointed his weapon at the woman. "Well, sometimes you lose what you love."

Varren pleaded, "Kentril, I am the one you want, not her. Let her go."

"And let her have another chance to smite me? I think not," snapped the ex-general. "You would have to say much more than that, young lover." He kicked Lluava in the side hard enough to force her into a fetal position. He then moved back to Varren. Sliding the edge of his blade over the chains, he said, "You are not in a position to bargain."

Lluava knew time was running out. She had to stall him. Someone had to be looking for them. "Please, Kentril, at least let me know how they swayed you."

The man snorted. "Why?"

"If I was truly your best student, can you not respect me enough to give me an answer?" Lluava did not really care about the reason; she needed time to formulate a plan. There had to be a way to escape this seeming disaster. Cradling her injured arm, she waited for his response.

He looked down at her. Lluava made sure she seemed too wounded to escape.

"As you wish," he consented. His voice even seemed to soften.

"I grew up in a farming village, yet I always dreamed of bigger things. As soon as I was old enough, I enlisted and trained in Durog. For the first time, I felt important, empowered. I never wanted to leave."

Lluava gave him her full attention, and he continued.

"This was a time of change in the military. Durog's grand master chief would retire in a few years, and we heard that the choice of replacement would be based not on seniority but on the best candidate, regardless of age. I knew I had to be the one they chose. For two years, taking every spare moment to better myself, I worked as hard as I could. Yet it was all for nothing."

Lluava lowered her eyes for a moment and risked a glance. The Claws glimmered on the far side of Kentril. "Why is that?" she asked, looking up at him.

"A new boy. Young, brash, arrogant, as are most of his highbred kind. An unproven officer transferred there from the north. I had to work so incredibly hard, while everything always came easily to him. He moved quickly through the ranks and graduated with my class. Argon Promethian was awarded the honor of commanding Durog. And I—" Kentril's words had a sour tinge. "I was sent to serve on the waters.

"A year later, I was our military's eyes on a sailing venture. A human and self-proclaimed scientist, Herald Salworth, lead the king's mission to explore the waters beyond our maps. We were given the *Osmund*, the fastest ship of all the king's fleet."

That name sounded familiar to Lluava. She tried to split her concentration.

"We had been on the waters for several months when a mighty sea storm, swept us up. When I awoke, I was stranded on a small island. There were no signs of any of my shipmates. Yet before the fear of death overtook me, I spied another vessel and signaled to them by smoke and fire. The men were large, thick-bearded. I had never seen the likes of them before."

Kentril began to pace as he talked. There was a look of pleasure on his face as he told his life story. "They brought me back with them—more like a prize than a captive. I was treated with courtesy, something one would not expect. When we landed, I was brought before their ruler in his palace. I had never seen such splendors. I was treated as their honored guest. Every afternoon, I would go to the throne room and speak with their king for hours. I learned about their culture, their technology. They are far more advanced than we are. Although their climate is considerably colder, they maintain lush gardens in grand buildings of crystal all year round. It does not matter what class one is born into; one's individual skills and intelligence allow one to be great. I began to realize how inferior my old way of life had been. When I was approached to join them in conquering Elysia, I accepted—happily. They will make this land great," he affirmed.

When Kentril moved to Lluava's opposite side, she cautiously inched herself toward her weapons. "There has to be more of a reason than that," she argued. She needed to keep him talking for just a bit longer.

"Perhaps there is," Kentril agreed.

Was he taking the bait? Lluava wondered.

"They brought me back within visual distance of Elysia. From there, I returned home on a makeshift raft. As I was the only survivor, people believed my fabricated tale of being stranded for months on a deserted island. I was awarded honors by King Thor and granted permission to live at court. I worked my way up the ladder of power, eventually becoming confidant to Prince Damian."

"My father," interjected Varren. He, too, had been listening intently to the traitorous general.

Kentril continued, "Everything was unfolding as planned. The king was old, and the heir trusted me more than anyone else. Then Isabelle, the queen-to be, conceived and had a son." He glowered at Varren. "Our plans were modified. One night a fire started in the prince's tower. Prince Damian and his sweet wife were killed. What a tragedy."

"My father trusted you!" shouted Varren. With arms, still bound, he struggled to shimmy to his feet.

Kentril disregarded him. "Unfortunately, the prince's spawn was not in his bed that night but in his grandfather's chambers. With King Thor dealing with the loss of his son, I offered to help raise the young heir. Logically, I should have been the one to raise you. But Thor—the stubborn, grizzly old fool—refused my offer." Kentril scowled at Varren. "I should have killed you then. It would have been just another accident."

For a moment, Lluava thought Kentril was going to strike Varren again, but the general moved away and resumed his account.

"Instead, I was awarded one last *honor*. I was named the commanding officer of Thowcelemine. Honor, hah!"

Lluava was tantalizingly close to the Claws. Suddenly Kentril turned back to her, and she froze.

"From there I worked in secret, meeting, preparing, and planning for this day." He squatted next to Lluava, his face inches from hers. When he moved away, the Claws were in his hand.

"When this is over, *they* will need someone to be their eyes and ears in their new colony. I will be given the chance to help them move this kingdom into a new, more prosperous era."

Kentril slipped the Claws onto his hands and tested the grips. "A bit tight," he noted. Looking at Lluava one last time, he said, "You should have joined me."

Lluava prayed that death would be quick. She closed her eyes as Kentril strode toward her. Slain with her own weapons, she thought; what a dishonorable death. She prayed that Varren would not mourn her.

There was an abrupt, ripping sound as metal tore through flesh, and a fatal wound dripped blood in a victim not prepared to die. Lluava opened her eyes. Kentril knelt before her, mouth agape, eyes wide. An arrow the length of his arm protruded from his massive chest.

Beyond him, the leader of the Raiders lowered his crossbow. The lifeless body of Kentril slumped into her lap. Lluava pushed him off. When she looked up, the man had vanished.

Chapter 38
The Forgotten Realm

Lluava, still stunned, struggled to her feet and stumbled over to Varren. Half his face was covered in blood from the wound on his brow. He looked fierce in this self-made war paint.

"We have to free you from those chains," she said, inspecting his bonds.

"Your arm—how is it?" Varren inquired, as he watched her trying not to use it.

"I'm not sure." Lluava tested her hand again. She could still move her fingers through the pain.

"I don't think it's broken," she told him. With her good hand, she gently manipulated her shoulder. The pain almost made her knees buckle. "It's dislocated."

Suddenly, there was movement in the shadows. Lluava snarled as several Raiders ran past. Without stopping, they moved northward, away from the fighting. Moments later, Yamir appeared. Looking at his comrades, he said, "Ya both look like chicken manure."

Lluava ignored his comment. "Help me with these chains," she said.

As Yamir strode past the body of Kentril, he asked, "Is that...?"

Lluava nodded. Pushing her aside, Yamir produced a quill and began to pick the lock.

Varren said to Lluava, "You should have someone look at your arm."

At that moment, Lluava was sizing up a tree. "No time," she said as she slammed her injured shoulder against the trunk, snapping the bone back into its socket. Some bark flew off at the impact. She muffled a scream, and tears rolled down her face as she waited for the throbbing to subside. By the time Yamir had freed Varren from the chains, Lluava could use her arm with extreme care. For the time being, she would have to sacrifice full range of motion, but it was worth that to have some use of her arm. She pulled Issaura's Claws from the grip of the dead general. Suddenly his voice rang in her mind: 'what a waste.'

Varren, using Yamir as support, could walk slowly. It was clear that he was too weak to fight. Lluava glanced again at the spot where the leader had stood. Then, accepting her responsibility, she moved to her partner's side to help him to safety.

"What are you doing?" Varren asked, as she slipped her arm under his.

"What does it look like?" she asked. He felt very thin.

"You have to go." Varren looked serious and refused to move forward. "Someone has to stop *him*."

This was foolishness; at any moment, other Raiders might discover them. "Partners are never supposed to leave each other's side," she told him. "I'm never going to do that again."

"And you never have to after you capture their leader. If you don't go now, we might lose our only chance."

"I'm not going to lose you again," she countered. She turned to scan the area, but no one was near.

"Lluava, I'll be here when you return," he reassured her. She could feel him pull her close.

Yamir, who had been looking from one to the other, chimed in. "I'll help him out of here. No worries."

"Go," Varren said.

Lluava turned, shifted into her dual form, and tested her weight on her injured limb. She ignored the pain and raced after the leader.

The complex overlay of scents, numerous footprints, and distant sounds of battle made it difficult for Lluava to track her prey. It appeared that the leader had retreated some distance before mounting a horse, possibly one tethered to the small tree now leaning at an unnatural angle, and riding off in a northeasterly direction. As Lluava sprinted, she could smell the salty tang in the air mingling with pine and decaying leaves. The ocean was not far away. She had to hurry to catch him before he reached his ships.

Loping after the horse and rider, she soon began to gain ground. The leader was not galloping at full speed; rather, he was moving at a steady trot. At that rate, it would not be long before she overtook her quarry. She ground her canines together as the pain in her shoulder intensified.

Lluava slowed down: she must be almost on top of him. Trotting now, she came across a riderless horse. Where was the rider? Moving carefully, she slowed to a walk. Suddenly, there he was; the leader stood before her with the ocean and shore clearly visible behind him. A small boat with oars had been pulled onto the beach. He could have easily run to it, yet he stood there as if waiting for her.

Shifting to her human form, Lluava took a second to test the Claws in her hands. Flexing, she thought how strange it was that, only a little while ago, she had had to pry them off the dead hands of her former commanding officer.

The leader watched her silently. He was a handsome man despite the beard, which he maintained fairly well. He wore no helmet, and his dark hair, like darkening blood, gleamed red in the light. The patches of gray above his ears matched the color of his wolf-headed cloak; the dead beasts seemed to snarl at Lluava as she stood looking at him. Standing tall, the man was awe-inspiring. In a different situation, she might have thought him attractive.

"Who are you?" she called out to him.

With one hand, the leader carefully pulled the leather riding glove off his fighting arm. Folding the glove over his belt, he answered, "I am Hadrian Alcove, Ambassador of Einherjar, true emperor of Niflhel, Nemorosus, Mictla, Aaru, and the territory Elysia."

Eyeing Hadrian's sheathed sword, Lluava stated, "We already have a king."

"You have a coward," he replied.

Brushing off the slight, Lluava demanded, "Why did you kill Kentril? He was loyal to you. And why didn't you kill me? You had the chance."

"So many questions," he commented in his thick accent. Had he always spoken this well? "Do you really need the answers?"

"Yes."

"Answers are not always what one truly needs," responded the Raider, adjusting his fur-trimmed cape. "If you are to fully comprehend them, however, you must first understand the actual origin of these humans. Centuries ago, the ancestor of King Einherjar sent his best fleet to explore the far waters. They went in search of new land to colonize, for our country was becoming overpopulated; we were exhausting our resources. The fleet was commanded by the chief naval officer, Landon Mandrun." Hadrian observed Lluava's reaction to his words.

"When Landon arrived on these shores, he proclaimed himself king. He never sent back word of the mission's success. For centuries, we believed the fleet had been lost in an ocean storm. That is, until the man-beast, Kentril, was discovered. This was how King Einherjar discovered the treachery of Landon."

The ambassador unbuttoned the top of his lapel to make it easier to move. "As for your questions, with that knowledge and Kentril's inside information, our country prepared to take back the land that is rightly ours.

"Kentril claimed he would be able to destroy the Mandrun line, but he failed. This was highly disappointing; yet, he proved useful in the end." Hadrian pushed up the sleeves of his coat. "You see, he did what he needed to do; he lured Elysia's heir into the trap we set. After that, his usefulness was over."

"So you killed him?" Lluava's voice was disbelieving.

"Yes. There is no place for a monster in our society. How could he believe that we would let a creature such as himself wield power?" Hadrian laughed. "He was a pawn, nothing more. It is unfortunate that I had to abandon the illegitimate prince. Your soldiers were moving in too fast; there was too much at risk. As for you," he said, briefly smiling at Lluava, "You are special. There is no need to kill you yet."

"Special?" echoed Lluava, but her question seemed to go unnoticed as Hadrian unsheathed his sword.

"Have you ever seen a rapier as fine as this?" he asked her.

Lluava gripped the Claws tightly as the Raider fondled his weapon. Feeling its wicked presence, Hadrian ran a finger down the edge of the blade ever so carefully so as not to cut himself. "Well?"

"Well, what?"

"You have come to fight, have you not?"

So he had been waiting for her, she thought. She growled her response.

"When you are ready," he said politely, like an instructor waiting on his pupil.

This irritated Lluava. "After you," she said.

"As you wish."

With that, the Raider darted toward her. He was fast—faster than she had anticipated. She barely blocked his attack and then parried another. As she attacked, then blocked, attacked and blocked again, Hadrian offered commentary.

"Swiftly, now," he said.

"Keep your arm straight."

"Duck and strike."

Why was he doing this? Was it all a game for him? Lluava forced herself to move faster, strike harder, think ahead; yet, nothing was working. Hadrian deflected her attacks as if he were swatting off a pesky mosquito. Lluava began to tire. Her body could not withstand the physical strain she had forced upon it. Between the lack of any real rest in weeks along with the numerous physical injuries and mental abuse she had sustained, Lluava was floundering.

Just as she thought she would not survive, the man stepped back, "Enough."

Hadrian did not look tired; on the contrary, he seemed quite refreshed. "In all regards, you are far more able than your fellows, yet not as skilled as I had hoped."

As he laid down his sword at his feet, Lluava wondered what his intentions were. Hadrian backed away from his weapon. Now unarmed, he spoke to Lluava.

"I will not be taken alive, so you have two choices. You can either kill an unarmed man, or you can watch as I return to my ship and sail away." He gestured at the boat behind him.

This was her chance. She could end it right now. Yet the idea of murdering a defenseless man knotted her stomach. But hadn't he done worse to others? Remember the bodies hanging from the Therial Oak? The people whose lives were taken because of him? What of Calitron? Every last soldier was slain. How could she allow a man capable of that to walk away? The darkness that had been incubating in her belly stirred restlessly.

Hadrian watched her inner struggle. This seemed less like a test and more of an affirmation. How could he be so sure of her decision?

Finally, Lluava lowered her eyes. "Go," she said.

She clenched her fists as she stood and watched the man escape, the man who had caused so much pain, so much death. Yet, if she were to kill him, wouldn't she become the same kind of monster?

Hadrian walked slowly toward the little boat. There was no show of fear as he turned his back to his enemy. Lluava could smell his confidence on the air. A rumble left her throat.

Hadrian pushed the boat into the ocean. Water lapped at its side, making it bounce, and he steadied it before stepping in. Then, shoving off with one of the oars, he waved.

"Until we meet again," he called.

"I hope for your sake it is not too soon," Lluava warned as he paddled away. "Tell your king," she snarled, "that the war is over. He has lost."

Hadrian's thick laugh resounded to the edge of the forest. He shouted back, "This is only the beginning. There is more to come. You cannot imagine what is about to occur. You keep calling this the war. It was only a way for us to test your strengths and your *many* weaknesses." Behind him, a falcon soared in front of the sun as it sank into the sea. Hadrian was illuminated by an aura of sick light. "The war isn't over. It hasn't even begun."

Lluava watched the man row toward one of the larger sea vessels anchored in the distance. Up and down the long stretch of beach, small boats thrust into the water. As they reached the pair of sleeping dragons, they were hoisted aboard for their homeward journey.

***

Several days later, Lluava stood at the top of a hill and watched the ocean in its relentless churning. The sky was almost clear of its milky imperfections. A few gulls cried as they scanned the throngs of people that headed down the slope to the village at the foot of the hill. A rickety gate slammed shut behind the last stragglers. The fence, tired and grey, shook with the impact.

It had been a fitting ceremony, she thought. Although they were under no obligation to do so, many townspeople had come to honor the one laid to rest, one who had unknowingly saved their lives.

He would have liked this place, Lluava mused. The little cemetery, though old, was visited often and was well cared for, its grass kept short and its tombstones swept. She had been told that when flowers bloomed, they were placed at the head of each grave.

Lluava looked down at the mounded soil at her feet. It had been a difficult decision whether to scatter his ashes to the winds or to bury them where others could visit. In the end, they did a bit of both. Buried somewhere under all that dirt was a humble jar, holding for all eternity its cherished contents.

Testing the direction of the wind with a moist finger, Lluava pulled the small pouch from her pocket. Opening it, she let the dark ashes fly. The breeze picked the fragments up and took them out to sea, where they would find new worlds to discover.

She watched until they disappeared from sight; then, squatting down by the gravestone, Lluava traced the words with her fingers.

Chattern Ryalls
Died in his 11th year
Scout in the King's Army
Loving Friend
Greatly Missed

If I had written this, thought Lluava, I would have said something like, "Chat, whose unending curiosity always kept his mouth open." She laughed as a tear slid down her cheek. It was time to attend the wake. Varren and the others would be waiting for her.

Rising to her feet, she scanned the ocean one last time. She breathed the crisp fall air into her lungs and then out again. A feeling of change, which she attributed to the season, had overtaken her; yet something stirred inside her, something that had begun of late and had not gone away. The words of Hadrian returned like a haunting memory of some forgotten horror. Their fight was over, thought Lluava. Or had it just begun? The young woman shivered from the chill in the air. She pulled her jacket tightly around her. Whatever came, she would be ready.

Epilogue

It had been a long day, and she had yet to find a moment for herself. After sweeping the floor with a battered broom, she was sure that the children were now asleep. She took one of the lit candles from the table and blew out the others. Following the wavering light, she made her way into the dark room. Methodically, she changed out of her patched dress and into a cream-colored nightgown. Before laying her tired dress over the small rocker tucked in the corner, she slipped the folded paper from its pocket. She gazed into the cradle to look lovingly at her sleeping son then headed to her place of rest. Pulling back the quilt, she placed the candle on the nightstand and slid into bed.

The dull light danced over the small golden wax seal, and she ran her finger over the raven-and-lion insignia. Long live the king, she thought as she broke the seal. She had become very fond of the flowing penmanship and was grateful that the correspondence over the past several months had helped her become quite literate. The letter read:

Dear Mother,

I miss you so and hope you are doing well. How is Lamb? And Mouse, how much has he grown? I hope he is not as much of a problem as I was at that age.

I'm doing quite well. As you know, since the end of the war, I've helped rebuild villages devastated by the attacks. I can finally say we are making progress. It's glorious to see human and Theriomorph working side by side as true equals. It seems it doesn't matter what race we are anymore. Today when we were laying down a sod roof, Yamir mentioned that when he finishes here, he wants to care for Chat's parents. I suspect that has something to do with Chat's last conversation with him, but I don't want to dwell on that. Regardless, I think that's a wonderful idea, don't you? Also, Varren has asked if I'd like to return with him to the castle when we are through mending these shattered towns. There are murmurs and whispers that there is a romance between us, but I assure you, at this moment, don't take those rumors seriously.

There are so many changes occurring all at once. The High Council has promoted Ojewa to colonel and named him the head officer at Thowcelemine. I think that's one of the best choices they could have made. He'll do great things there. As for Durog, both Colonel Skype and Admiral Merrow are co-commanding it. They are looking for someone who will specialize in land animals. There are rumors that Talos might be considered because of his outstanding courage and good judgment on the battlefield. At the moment, this is not of importance to him. Did you know he and Rosalyn are to be married soon? They are a match made in the stars. Even Byron has found peace. You wouldn't believe how many young women flock to someone who's a war veteran.

The villages treat us like some sort of mythic heroes, but it still makes me uneasy when people refer to me as Issaura or Theri, and that must happen several times a day. I can't understand why so many people believe I've come from the heavens. How can I be a goddess? I certainly don't act like one, that's for sure. I mean, if I were Issaura, wouldn't I know it? Wouldn't I have some memory of my previous life? Then again, does it really matter?

Ambassador Alcove's last words still ring in my head: "This is only the beginning. There is more to come. You cannot even imagine what is about to occur." If this was only a battle in a much larger war, so be it. King Thor's finest engineers are studying the weapons left by the Raiders. We will learn how to build their crossbows and wield battle-axes. If the Raiders return, we'll be ready. We'll show them a force so strong, they could never conceive of it!

I intend to visit before the full moon passes a second time. Until then, take care, my sweet mother. I love you so.

> *Your devoted daughter,*
>
> *Lluava*

Maessa gently placed the letter on the bed where the moonlight shining through the window illuminated it. Your grandfather would be so proud of you, she thought. She turned her head to look up at the silver plate nearing its zenith high in the night sky. As she stared at the glistening orb, miles and miles away her daughter was gazing at it, too…

That young woman, with her own special grace and beauty, stepped out into the milky light on her balcony. The stone walls and towers stretched up to the heavens behind her as if to caress the shining sphere. A young man moves behind her, enfolding her in his arms, strong and secure. As their forms are illuminated by the soft glow, their lips meet.

Lluava's adventures will continue in

Ullr's Fangs

Tome Two of The Incarn Saga

Ullr's Fangs
Prologue

A dark shadow glides across the moon, briefly interrupting her continuous gaze on the drowsing city below. Masked faces turn up to the slit-like window high overhead, pausing to watch the unaware owl glide ever onward. Reassured of their safety in the doorless tower, they cautiously breathe a sigh of relief.

Turning back to their circle, obsidian masks eternally grimace from under heavy-hooded cloaks like dismal effigies of their creators centuries ago. Hearts pound quickly, though muffled by the thick weave of their encasing garments. Time is running out. Soon they will be forced to disperse back into the shadows of the kingdom.

Almost inaudibly the youngest of them, still past his prime, alters the course of the conversation with three words.

"What of her?"

Silence coils around them like a snake squeezing the life's essence out of its prey. Slowly, several of the Ancients turn to one another and nod before the eldest speaks. "Her destiny has been sealed since the time before her inception. She is on the correct course and should not be interfered with. Her fame is only pushing her forward on her predestined path, which will soon lead her to the others. When that happens, the day we have been waiting for since our initial formation will have finally arrived."

The fear in the mind of the youngest does not abate at these words. He asks anew. "And what of her prince? There are rumors…"

He is quieted by the appearance of the elder's knobby age-tarnished hand. The dusty voice speaks again, "She is destined for another. That we all know. Her fate is etched in the stars. Fear not her partner, their paths will diverge soon enough."

"And if they don't?"

Something moist glints behind the two slits of the Ancient's mask. "Then we intervene."

NOTE FROM THE AUTHOR

As an author, writing the story is just the beginning. Next come revising, editing, formatting, proofreading, and marketing. Surprisingly, marketing requires a huge amount of time. If you enjoy an author's work and want her or him to publish more in a shorter time span, you can help! Spread the word on social media and by word of mouth. Post reviews on Amazon, Goodreads and other websites. Believe me, I would much rather write a new book than spend time promoting the one I have just finished. So go ahead—pin, tweet, post, review, and like. Thank you!

LEARN MORE AT

WWW.KATHARINEWIBELLBOOKS.COM

OR FIND ME ON:

Facebook   @KatharineEWibell   Pinterest   @KatharineWibell
Twitter   @KatharineWibell   YouTube   @KatharineWibell
Instagram   @KatharineEWibell   TikTok   @KatharineEWibell

MONTHLY NEWSLETTER SIGN UP!
Receive sneak peaks, giveaways, select deals, and my free Story Starter Collection!

ABOUT THE AUTHOR

Katharine Wibell's lifelong interest in mythology includes epic poetry like the Odyssey, Ramayana, Beowulf, and the Nibelungenlied. In addition, she is interested in all things animal whether training dogs, apprenticing at a children's zoo, or caring for injured animals as a licensed wildlife rehabilitator. After receiving degrees from Mercer University in both art and psychology with an emphasis in animal behavior, Wibell currently lives in Roswell, Georgia, with her dog, Alli, as she furthers her career as an artist and an author. Her literary works blend her knowledge of the animal world with the world of high fantasy.

APPENDIX I

Diagram of the Theriomorph Pantheon

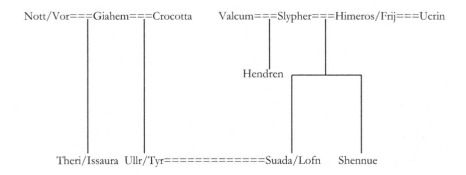

APPENDIX II

The Theriomorph Pantheon

Name	Sex	Divine Realm	Dual Form
Giahem	♂	King/Husbands/Fathers/Heavens/Males/ Sky	Gold Eagle
Crocotta	♀	Queen/Wives/Mothers/Prophecy/Mating Rights	Silver Hyena
Ullr/Tyr	♂	Young Men/ Inception of War/ Sun/ Courage	Bronze Wolverine
Nott/Vor	♀	Night/ Sleep/ Dreams/ Death/ Underworld	Black Raven
Theri/Issaura	♀	Young Women/ Cessation of War/ Moon/ Wisdom	White Tigress
Ucrin	♂	Ocean/ Water/ Wind	Blue Whale
Valcum	♂	Fire/ Volcanos/ Blacksmiths	Orange Orangutan
Slypher	♀	Earth/ Seasons/ Song, Dance	Pink Parakeet
Frij/Himeros	♂♀	Love/ Beauty/ Hermaphrodites	Purple Peacock
Hendren	♂	Knowledge/ Virtue/ Health	Scarlet Panda
Suada/Lofn	♀	Lust/ Seduction/ Desire	Emerald Anaconda
Shennue	♂	Mischief/ Mayhem / Illusions	Black Jackal

347

APPENDIX III

Pronunciation Guide

Aaru	A-roo
Acrian	ACK-re-an
Burok Dûr	ber-AWK DURE
Cherin	CHEER-in
Einherjar	ine-HAIR-ree-har
Elysia	ee-LAY-szuh
Ethril	EE-thrill
Giahem	GUY-a-hem
Giam	GUY-am
Illena	i-YEN-a
Illia	ill-YA
Issaura	i-SAR-a
Lluava	you-AA-va
Maessa	MAY-es-sa
Maruny	MAR-ou-ne
Mictla	MICKT-la
Nemorosus	NE-mo'ro-sus
Niflhel	NEEF-flell
Ojewa	OH-jay-wa
Raien	RAIN
Rosalyn	ROZ-za-lin
Shennu	SHEN-new
Sihad	SEE-had
Sihia	SI-high-a
Slypher	SLY-fer
Sonty	SAWN-tea
Talos	TAL-ows
Theri	TH'AIR-ee (rhymes with Carrie)
Theriomorph(s)	TH'AIR'EO-morf
Thowcelemine	TH'OW-cell-e-mean
Tucala	two-CAL-a
Tomius	TOE-my-us
Truden	TRUE-den
Ullr	OU-yer
Yamir	YA-mear
Ymen	YEM-en
Zepher	ZEF-er
Zethra	ZEE-thra

APPENDIX IV

Elysian Military Ranks

Terra Divisions	Private
	Corporal
	Sergeant
	Warrant Officer
	Lieutenant
	Captain
	Major
	Colonel
	General
	Chief General
	Master Chief (General)
	Grand Master Chief (General)

Aerial Divisions	Private
	Airman
	Sergeant
	Lieutenant
	Captain
	Major
	Colonel
	General
	Chief General
	Master Chief (General)
	Grand Master Chief (General)

Marine Divisions	Private
	Seaman
	Petty Officer
	Warrant Officer
	Ensign
	Lieutenant
	Commander
	Captain
	Admiral
	Chief Admiral
	Master Chief (Admiral)
	Grand Master Chief (Admiral)

Made in the USA
Monee, IL
28 April 2023

32638820R00208